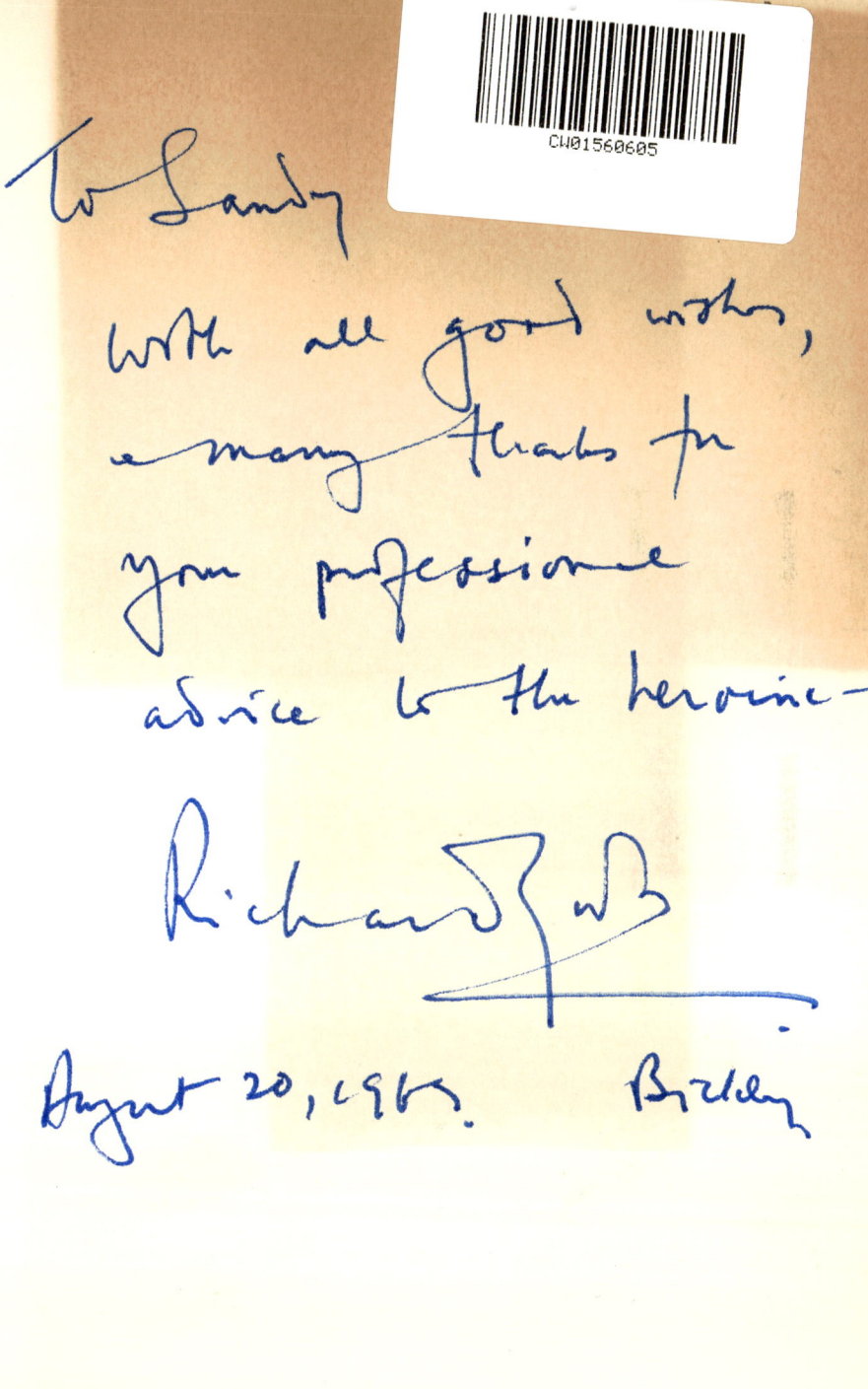

To Sandy

With all good wishes,
& many thanks for
your professional
advice to the heroine —

Richard Zwilley

August 20, 1965.   Berkeley

The Facts of Life

Richard Gordon

THE FACTS OF LIFE

HEINEMANN : LONDON

William Heinemann Ltd
LONDON MELBOURNE TORONTO
JOHANNESBURG AUCKLAND

First published 1969
© Gordon Ostlere 1969
434 30236 8

Printed in Great Britain by
Cox and Wyman Limited,
London, Fakenham and Reading

I hate a learned woman

EURIPIDES

THE FIGHT STARTED on a fine Thursday afternoon in the middle of April, when the latest batch of blood-samples came up from the clinic. I settled down on the high swivel chair, took a drop from each test-tube, spread it across an oblong glass slide, dried it, stained it to render visible the magnified blood cells, and examined it under the microscope. I knew my decision must be reached that very afternoon. I had already delayed overlong, to be sure of my ground. But women are always more cautious protagonists than men.

My laboratory was a long attic with sloping ceilings in a block of Princess Victoria's Hospital, ripe for demolition. It was far too small and far too full of books, files, specimens, and scientific paraphernalia, but I always dismissed my surroundings as unimportant. After all, Galileo saw the mechanism of the universe while locked up in a dungeon, and had Fleming's laboratory been air-conditioned he would never have discovered the secret of penicillin mould at all. The bench where I worked was hardly big enough for orderly arrangement of its test-tube racks, bottles of reagents, slide-boxes, open textbooks, pencilled notes, and coloured report forms (and I had an irritating obsession about neatness). Its woodwork and its small, deep sink were coloured with tissue dyes spilt by the carelessness of three generations – haematoxylin and eosin, gentian violet, methylene blue, Romanowsky's and Leishman's stains, Ehrlich's triacid, a spectrum of gleams from the lamp of science. That afternoon I was using a tissue-stain invented by myself. If this later became the rickety foundation of my case, I never knew whether to be proud or exasperated about it.

But that afternoon I wanted to go home. I was suffering an attack of migraine, with a headache and elusive brightly-lit battlements flickering across my vision, the 'fortification spectra' of medical textbooks. I searched my handbag for some ergotamine tartrate tablets, and swore when I found the vial was empty. I tried to push up the window, but in four years' battle it had yielded only eight or nine inches. The migraine was connected with my period, which was due, with my usual intolerable pre-menstrual tension. It is peculiar how women always seem to menstruate at the crises of their lives. Even Mrs Pankhurst and all her suffragettes couldn't do much about that.

'Sheriff —'

I spun round my chair. Professor McRobb was at the door. She never used Christian names. Had she married – an event we thought as immediately improbable as the melting of the polar ice-cap – she would have been one of those disconcerting British women who refer to their husbands by their surname.

'I thought I'd climb up to see what you've found in my specimens, Sheriff.'

'I'm about two-thirds the way through. But I've checked the suspect one.'

'And what's the score?'

'I don't really think there's two ways about it.' I changed the slide under the microscope lens. 'Have a look for yourself.'

I both admired and pitied McRobb. Now that any woman whatever can make herself reasonably attractive and even has a social obligation to, as a man to wear a clean shirt, McRobb paraded her frumpishness. She was sharp-faced, with a red tip to her nose winter and summer, her greasy brown hair drawn into an old-fashioned bun from which a number of metal devices always seemed in danger of exploding. She seldom wore make-up and her stockings were generally wrinkled. I sometimes wondered if this caricature were deliberate. A clever woman is often a sensitive one, with a secret terror of sexual rebuff which grows a protective skin of ugliness. And the single-minded

2

woman whose life cannot afford the luxury of a man assumes the same clumsy armour. I had felt both emotions when starting as an over-ambitious medical student. As McRobb now looked down the microscope's twin eye-pieces I watched her fingers gently twisting the fine-adjustment screw. They were white, soft, and delicate, lost from a Leonardo, who always flattered his women with such intelligent hands.

'That certainly looks like an immature myelocyte to me.' McRobb's voice had an unchanging flatness. 'Though, of course, I'm not a haematologist.'

'It's an immature white cell all right. And it shouldn't be there. That's the long and short of it.'

McRobb twisted round the chair, drawing her white coat tightly round her skinny body, displaying her absence of breasts. Some women doctors strip their white coats whenever possible. Others seem to live in them. It's a division probably with deep psychological significance. I sometimes suspected McRobb wore hers for a nightdress.

She felt in the pocket and offered me a cigarette, complaining resignedly, 'My second packet today. If I'm in for a carcinoma of the bronchus, I suppose it's a privilege choosing the way you're going to die.'

She closed her gas-lighter with a masculine snap, and sat silent and thoughtful.

'Nobody else has discovered immature myelocytes in the blood of women taking this drug?'

I shook my head. 'Not that I've heard of. Though they wouldn't show with the standard laboratory stains, of course.'

'Not even the newer fluorescent ones?'

'No. I've checked that. They show only with the modified fluorescent stain which I've been using.'

'The stain you concocted yourself?'

'That's right.'

She blew twin jets of smoke through her thin nostrils. 'You're sure of your facts, Sheriff?'

'Completely. Look at the slide.' McRobb turned to the microscope. 'Those myelocytes each have a large, unlobulated nucleus. And each nucleus has a powerful attraction for the stain.

3

There's no sign of the nucleus breaking up, as in the normal mature cell. They're great big blobs in the middle.'

'Thus they're immature,' murmured McRobb.

'Exactly. Thus they're abnormal cells to be found in the blood of a healthy woman.'

'I agree.' McRobb raised her eyes from the lenses. 'Let's square up the situation. For six months my gynaecology department's been trying out a new oral contraceptive – what's it called? I can never remember drug makers' fancy names.'

This was one of her affectations. 'Cyclova.'

'Sounds like a bloody ballet dancer. And from sixty-odd women who volunteered to take cyclova, an abnormal blood-picture has appeared in one. So what's the significance?'

I put out my cigarette in the saucer serving for an ash-tray. The smoke was making my migraine worse.

'It's not entirely easy to say. But abnormal white cells circulating in the blood are always horribly sinister.'

'We should stop the trial?'

'Yes, without question.'

'And on withdrawing the drug, these changes will regress to normal?'

'My God, I hope so!' This was an alarming doubt. 'Deliberately to have caused some blood disease – a leukaemia, for instance – certainly isn't a matter I'd like to carry on my conscience.'

'It wouldn't look too good in the newspapers, either,' agreed McRobb dryly.

'But I don't honestly think that's likely. The changes strike me as a straightforward toxic effect of cyclova on the blood-producing tissues. The same principle as lead poisoning. Remove the drug, and things should revert to normal. But if the woman went on taking it, as she'd have to as her contraceptive, then I suspect some condition like leukaemia might be induced. Of course, we can never be sure. But even the risk of finding out isn't worth taking.'

'I agree with that, too,' said McRobb briefly. 'Exactly how much did you know about this cyclova stuff in the first place?'

'Not enough. Perhaps it was wrong or even immoral of me to

4

suggest we tested it. But you remember I once did some half-baked work on a long-acting oral contraceptive of my own? I heard cyclova was long-acting, so I asked for some samples out of interest. The drug people assured me it had been tested in the States. They're a perfectly reputable firm. I took them at their word.'

'So what are you going to tell them?'

'It shouldn't be put on the market.'

'And how do you suppose they'll react?'

'They'll hardly be overjoyed. Though they may not be serious about releasing it. They try out hundreds of products for each one which eventually reaches the public.'

McRobb stood up. 'This loss doesn't strike me as a grievous blow for the world. We already seem to have more brands of oral contraceptives than cigarettes. Same power of advertising, too – soon they'll be giving gift coupons with each packet.' She added, 'I suppose the blood of that woman was normal otherwise?'

'Absolutely.'

'Shouldn't we do a sternal puncture?'

'I don't think she'd take kindly to our boring into her breast-bone. Who knows? In a couple of years topless swimsuits might be the fashion.'

McRobb glanced at her man's wrist-watch with its sweep second-hand. 'I must leave you to sort it out. My new house-man's trying her luck with a D. and C., the remains of a back-street abortion. I gather she isn't a Catholic or anything fancy like that.'

I sat at the microscope and rearranged the slides. 'One of Mrs Ramsay's abortion efforts?'

'I should imagine so, though the patient won't admit it. Soapy water in a syringe. These professionals don't progress much in their methods.' She stubbed out her cigarette. 'But Mrs Ramsay knows her job. And she tells the women to come here at the first sign of trouble, or of success, whichever way you look at it. If the police locked her up, there'd be bloody murder done on the local pregnant girls.'

'Won't she be out of business under the new abortion laws?' That spring they were first introduced.

5

'On the contrary, she looks like being busier than ever. If I admitted half the women who wanted me to terminate them, I'd have no beds for the ones who wanted to have babies in the old-fashioned way. Our clever gentlemen in Parliament never thought of that.'

'I'd hate to lose an institution like Mrs Ramsay.'

My first case at Princess Victoria's, eight years before, had been clearing out a criminal abortion induced by the renowned Mrs Ramsay. Though McRobb was only three or four years older than me, she was then awesome as my registrar. All we students had been scared of her, and few finished unetched by the acid of her tongue.

I always remembered the patient. She was married (most aborted women are), eighteen, with two babies already, her breasts warm and tender with her third pregnancy. I sat gowned and masked between the anaesthetized woman's legs in the theatre, while McRobb leant watchfully over my shoulder, sniffing frequently, which I found extremely irritating.

I fumbled as I clipped the needle-pronged volsellum forceps into the uterine cervix, the portion of the womb jutting into the vagina like the tied neck of a balloon. McRobb swore as I took my first Hegar's dilator from the sterilized row on the instrument tray. 'Start with a number nine, work your way up to number sixteen,' she commanded. 'You bloody girls always want to split the cervix.' But after I had cleared out the rudimentary placenta and foetal membranes with ovum forceps, McRobb said brusquely, 'Good, Sheriff,' ripping off her gloves, throwing them into the corner, and stalking from the theatre with no apparent further interest in me or the patient. That remark gave me greater satisfaction than I ever drew from my later glories.

Afterwards, McRobb let me operate on such cases alone, until they became commonplace. I wondered if seeing so many criminal abortions led me later to research on contraception. Perhaps so. That and the disability which stopped my operating for good.

When McRobb quit my laboratory that April afternoon, I sat again at the microscope to finish the blood-samples. My specialized knowledge of the blood had come more or less by accident. When I had to abandon practical surgery, I worked for a year or so in the hospital's haematology laboratory, performing routine investigations on the patients' blood specimens. I had started the work confident that blood was a straightforward material, and ended it depressed that we knew little about it.

In the fluid part of the blood – the plasma – circulate red corpuscles carrying oxygen to the remotest cells of the body by the chemical, haemoglobin. These red corpuscles show as thick-rimmed circles under the microscope, rather like doughnuts, five million of them to each millilitre. The other blood cells, the white cells, are the body's scavengers. They are fewer than the red ones, larger and more complicated, each an irregular round granular cell with a dark, knobbly nucleus. Like all cells they die, to be replaced by young but mature ones from the efficient blood-factory in the marrow of the bones.

But sometimes the mechanism goes wrong. Immature white cells appear, and far too many of them. So 'leukaemia' has become another dreaded word in the common speech of the twentieth century.

After finishing the samples, I went down to the secretaries' room on the ground floor and dictated a letter.

Department of Experimental Physiology,
The Medical School,
Princess Victoria's Hospital,
Holborn,
W.C.1.

G. D. H. Lloyd, Esq.,
Managing Director,
General Drugs (Great Britain) Ltd.,
484, Piccadilly,
W.1.

Dear Mr Lloyd,

'Cyclova'

We have now completed six months' clinical trial of the above drug in the gynaecology and family planning units of Princess Victoria's, under the direction of Professor Sandra McRobb and myself.

7

I was not intending to make a report for a further three months, but I must draw your attention without delay to a disturbing feature among the sixty-four women volunteering to take the drug for us. In brief, an abnormality has been discovered in the blood-picture of one of these volunteers. We have observed the presence of abnormal circulating immature white cells (myelocytes), which in my view indicate that cyclova is in some way interfering with the normal blood-producing function of the bone-marrow.

The woman was free from any other abnormality, haematological or otherwise.

The possibility of cyclova inducing some disorder of haemopoietic function (e.g., the leukaemias) has decided us to discontinue the trial. Professor McRobb and I had no reservations about taking this step.

In my view, there can be no question of the drug appearing on the market until considerable further investigation and modification of it has been undertaken.

While grateful to you for supplying me with samples of cyclova for a limited trial, I cannot hide my disappointment that your assurances of its proved non-toxicity are apparently without foundation.

Yours sincerely,
Ann Sheriff
M.D.
Reader in Experimental Physiology.

I cannot hide my disappointment . . . I felt the raspberry well put. I signed the letter, went back to the lab., collected my belongings and made off home. My migraine had vanished.

8

2

I HAD OFTEN enough passed the offices of General Drugs –
'Great Britain' – at the Knightsbridge end of Piccadilly, one of
the traditional grey-faced buildings erected in imitation of the
Duke of Wellington's nearby Apsley House at Hyde Park
Corner. The following afternoon for the first time I went inside.

I was shown into a waiting-room downstairs, which was self-
consciously modern, with hidden lighting, stagy furniture, and
a long low steel and teak table. This displayed their bright,
shiny, expertly produced advertising booklets, which dropped
through family doctors' letterboxes by the hundredweight, often
unread and always uninvited. General Drugs were pressingly
generous to the profession. Their smart desk diaries kept doctors'
appointments, their long-playing records provided clinical information on one side and Mozart on the other, their soap and
brushes scrubbed surgical hands, and golf-balls with their name
sped on Sundays down countless fairways.

After only a few seconds I was collected by a young redheaded
secretary in a dress which, after the fashion, reached barely to
her pubis. I wondered if she ever felt cold.

The managing director's office upstairs was quite different
from the waiting-room. It was plain, with white panelled walls
and heavy lemon curtains matching the two easy chairs and
sofa. There was no desk, just a table I took to be Harrods
Hepplewhite. There was a Munnings on the wall, on a pedestal
in the corner a solid sculpture which might have been a Hep-
worth. Opposite the door stood a grandfather clock. There was
only one telephone, no files nor papers at all. The whirr of

9

computers seemed far away, as indeed they were, at the company's headquarters in the Middle West of America.

Lloyd was waiting in the centre of the room. 'Dr Sheriff, how kind of you to come at such short notice.'

'Honestly, it's no inconvenience. I'm on my way home.'

He stood looking at me for a moment, seeming puzzled. Perhaps he had expected someone like McRobb. I am just thirty, and lucky to have one of those faces which will safeguard a woman's looks as long as she safeguards her figure. My cheekbones stand out, my chin is pointed, and if I am pale that only started with my illness. I am short, less than five feet six. My hair is dark, and I am careful to keep it stylish. And I had in fact already been home, to change into my new mustard-coloured suit and the pair of shoes I couldn't really afford.

'Won't you sit down, Doctor?'

The armchairs were by a double-glazed window overlooking Green Park. I noticed the grandfather clock didn't tick.

'I don't know whether you smoke, Doctor?'

I took a long cigarette from the box Lloyd offered. I too was trying to sum the stranger up. I had suspected that like many Englishmen working for large American companies he might have adopted and overdone the airs of his employers, like some *babu* squatting on a Bombay office stool once aped the affectations of the British raj. But he seemed quiet, almost shy, too austere for easy transatlantic cordiality. He was a tall man, thin, with a greying edge to his thick dark hair, beautifully served by his tailor. 'Distinguished' was the label to be stuck casually on his looks. Both Lloyd and his room I found somehow encouraging. Perhaps they were two parts of a plan to reassure the medical profession, who tend to regard commerce of any sort as an extension of piracy.

'I took the liberty of telephoning you at the hospital, Doctor, because I felt we must meet as soon as possible.' He had a solemn voice, and was calling me 'Doctor' too often. 'Your letter this morning was something of a thunderbolt.'

'Should I have softened the blow? On reflection, perhaps I did sound rather prissy.'

'Let's hope it's not really a thunderbolt. Rather a firecracker, to wake us up.'

'I'm afraid I'm causing you a lot of trouble.'

'On the contrary, Doctor, we at General Drugs are grateful you took an interest in our product at all, and so brought this new information to our notice. Naturally, I shall have your findings examined by our scientific staff.'

All this sounded reasonable enough. 'It's never pleasant to face an unexpected set-back in any research. No more for a company, I should imagine, than for an individual. The misfortune's happened to me before now.'

'No, it isn't pleasant.'

He seemed undecided what to say next. I saw him looking at my hands and wondered if he thought the joints abnormally thick – I was sensitive about that. Or perhaps it was my weddin g ring. I had noticed on his table a red-and-gold volume of the *Medical Directory*, the doctors' *Who's Who*. He had been looking me up. And as in *Who's Who*, it's what you read between the lines which counts. My entry had no former surname proudly discarded between parentheses, so he would assume that I was unmarried. He would know that I won the gold medal with my M.D. and had published scientific papers on the blood, contraception, and reproductive physiology – restricted to three by the *Directory*'s publishers, in this age when the output of a thrustful young professor can match that of a popular novelist.

'I'm interested how you first heard of cyclova, Doctor?'

'By chance, from a reference in the *Boston Journal of Physiology*. I didn't know if you'd consider me sufficiently distinguished to carry out a limited trial for you.'

For the first time he smiled. 'That's a refreshing modesty I seldom run across in research people.'

'Thank you.'

'But do I understand, Doctor, you found this abnormality in the blood of only one volunteer?'

'That's correct.'

'From a total of sixty-four?'

'That's one point five six per cent. A perfectly significant figure. Of course, we should have preferred to investigate a far larger sample. But testing an entirely new oral contraceptive based on an entirely new principle, we didn't want to put too many women at risk. And it looks as if we were right, doesn't it?'

'I accept the rebuke.'

He began to sound less stiff. Perhaps he had suffered unhappy times with women doctors. Even the most charming of us, holding down a man's job in a man's world, are liable to conceal a tensed spring of aggressiveness, to be triggered by some casual ill-thought remark.

'I can only offer you my personal apologies,' he added, 'and assure you that everything we wrote to you about the drug – six months ago, when I released the samples – was in perfectly good faith.'

'I'm sure it was.'

'Though I'm a little curious why these blood changes haven't been noticed by others before.'

'Surely that depends on the volume of research done on the drug? And by whom?'

'General Drugs employ only first-class people, you know,' he said a little shyly. 'Research conducted by our own staff or by independent clinicians is performed to the highest standards of skill and responsibility. The same principles apply to our whole sphere of operations.' He paused. 'Surely I've no need to emphasize to you, Doctor, that we are a well-established firm, highly regarded by medical men and women all over the world? We have won the praise of hospitals, of universities, even of governments and of international organizations. We are naturally proud of our reputation. And equally aware of its being at stake with every new drug we issue. Perhaps you will agree that some recent products have brought great benefit all over the world. To give one example, our new anti-malarial drugs have been found most valuable where the normal malarial suppressants are starting to fail. To give another, our latest broad-spectrum antibiotics have done much for that troublesome business of cross-infection in hospitals.'

I had the feeling he had said all this many times before, and he saw I was not impressed.

'Besides, there is common humanity,' he continued. 'That alone would surely hold us from issuing any product before we were certain of its freedom from untoward effects. Or as certain as it is possible to be. This is something quite separate from our obligations to the Dunlop Committee in this country, or the Food and Drug Administration in the United States. We have our own standards of safety which are even higher than the official ones.'

'I've no quarrel with you about that.'

'I'm glad of the encouragement, Doctor. The saddest part of my job is the repeated discovery that so many professional people imagine pharmaceutical companies to be heartless. The bigger the company, the lower is assumed its morals. It's just not true, you know. How could it be? Humanity is our business.'

That was his company's slogan. It was the moment I first became suspicious. The man was trying to head me off with charm, to brush me aside with ill-selected platitudes. It wouldn't work. Not with me.

'I'm sure you conduct your business with the greatest integrity, Mr Lloyd,' I told him. 'But I'm concerned only with the particular case of cyclova. I must repeat my opinion of this drug being unsuitable for sale to the public.'

'I appreciate your opinion, Doctor. But perhaps you will appreciate my own surprise? Cyclova has been given a perfectly clean bill of health after a – well, a full programme of research in the United States.'

'I should be very interested to read the reports.'

'I think they would put your doubts at rest. But of course they must remain confidential until the drug is put on the market – if it is.'

'Confidential for business reasons?'

'Every successful business has active and envious competitors.'

'Even a business making its money from humanity?'

My temper was rising. I mustn't fly off the handle, I told myself, I *mustn't*. My quick temper had lost me too much in life already. Luckily, Lloyd said blandly, 'I accept your point. But we *are* a business, so we have to make money. Even Pasteur and Lister had to make money to live. I wish we could operate with the open-handedness of the Rockefeller Foundation, but unhappily we have no Rockefeller to give us the means.'

I stubbed out my cigarette. I certainly knew that General Drugs was big business. They or the firms they controlled supplied about half the hospital's drug stocks, everything from aspirin for headaches to immunizing agents against the rejection of surgical transplants.

'Perhaps you can share my disappointment at your unexpectedly discovering this effect of cyclova on the blood,' he persisted gently. 'The blood of women taking it in the United States would have been examined most carefully, as a matter of routine. I can assure you of that.'

Was he inferring I had made a mistake? I hated performing anything badly, to be thought in the slightest incompetent. Like so many women doctors, I was a perfectionist. We become impossibly severe with ourselves, liable to emotional – even psychological – breakdown if falling short of our self-set criteria. Perhaps this is feminine vanity. Perhaps it is fear of being taken for a feckless and impractical woman. But any woman's achievements are more personal and deeper rooted in her feelings than a man's. She can write novels because the characters clash by usurping her own emotions. She can't paint or compose symphonies because these stir only the emotions of others.

'Your own research workers probably weren't using the best stain for the blood-samples,' I told him tartly.

'I know little of the technical side – my function is to administer. But I'm certain they'd employ the most reliable techniques.'

'Might I doubt that? The stain I used isn't in general use. It's a modification of a fluorescent stain invented by myself.'

I saw his face light up. He suspected that my methods were possibly faulty, or possibly might be faulted. Like many research people, he had decided, I was so dazzled by my own inventions as to be blind to their defects. Perhaps it was the weakness he had been probing throughout the interview.

'That's very interesting,' he said.

'The stain's nothing secret,' I told him hastily. 'It's been published in the medical press.'

'Then our laboratory people will look it up.'

'I'll send a reprint with my full report on cyclova on Monday morning.'

'Monday morning?' He pressed a bell in the wall beside him. 'You're not going to let us spoil your week-end writing reports?'

'Honestly, I set aside this week-end to write it.'

He was now anxious to dismiss the business of our meeting as quickly as possible. The pubic-skirted secretary reappeared and disclosed the secret of the silent grandfather clock, which was full of bottles.

'A glass of sherry, Doctor?' he invited.

Why do people always offer professional women sherry? I should much have preferred gin. To save bother I accepted, and the girl brought the glasses with a cloying winsomeness I suppose she imagined was charm. But I am always too hard on the harmless little affectations of the young.

'What exactly are you going to do about cyclova?' I persisted. I wanted to pin him down before leaving.

'I can do nothing before seeing your full report.'

'And then?'

'It will go at once to our head office in America. We have excellent communications, you know, by telex. Distance means nothing in the business world of today. It will be up to them to decide our next step.'

'They might well scrap the drug?'

He nodded. 'They might well.'

'Or ignore my findings?'

'Perhaps we can cross that bridge when we come to it, Doctor?'

He looked slightly pathetic. I suppose I must have been a wearisome visitor. To relieve him, I turned to ordinary chat. 'I suppose you meet a vast number of medical people?'

'It's almost my whole job. Mutual confidence between ourselves and the profession is essential.'

'Don't you get tired of them?'

'No, not really. All doctors differ – much more than lawyers or teachers or businessmen. You are a profession of individualists.'

'"Kittle cattle", Nye Bevan once called us.'

15

'And he should have known. I don't find it easy to handle *any* people,' he confessed unexpectedly. 'I haven't the natural flair I envy in so many others.'

'That doesn't strike me as so,' I complimented him.

He smiled faintly. 'I work hard at it.'

I wondered idly if that meant he worked on the doctors' everlurking weaknesses – professional pride and jealousy, frustration over indifference by colleagues or the world, a softness for honours and status, or (what could be more valuable to a businessman like Lloyd) a true high-mindedness and devotion to humanity. Plus, of course, money, drink, and the other sex, like everybody else.

As I got up to leave, he said, 'The weather's wonderful for April, isn't it?'

'I hope I haven't kept you from your garden?'

He glanced quickly at his watch and told his secretary, spreading a folder of unsigned letters across his table, to send for his car. 'Indeed, I must rush straight home. On Friday my wife has people to dinner.' He smiled again. 'What people, I don't know. But it is Friday, and so people will come.'

'I'm glad we had this talk, Mr Lloyd. It's cleared the air a little.'

'Your letter was too disturbing for me to leave until Monday.'

'It must have been disturbing,' I agreed. 'The world doesn't want another thalidomide, does it?'

This was perhaps an unfair thought to leave him with over the week-end.

3

I GENERALLY WENT into the hospital on Saturdays. It was a day without teaching or administrative chores, giving me three or four uninterrupted hours in the laboratory during the morning to assess my progress for the week. Often there was none. Sometimes the week's work simply disproved that of the week before, or of the month before, or even the year before. Medical research is never a steady progress towards the final unveiling of the panacea. It goes in spurts, disappearing up blind alleys, knocking itself breathless against unexpected obstacles, shooting ahead from the inspiration which comes in the middle of the night. It is more a creative process than a scientific one. Its workers suffer more the turmoils of the poet than the hard-headed puzzlements of the engineer. Perhaps that is why we are all a little peculiar.

My department at Princess Victoria's was small, an offshoot of the main physiology faculty which taught the students the workings of the human body they were later to apply to patients in the wards. It really consisted only of myself. I had a part-time technician, and whatever professional help I could cadge from the physiology staff. When I was appointed Reader four years before, the post was new, I could choose any line of research I fancied, and I decided to investigate the workings of human reproduction. Consciously, I had no particular reason, except that it was a subject of increasing practical importance. Subconsciously, my reasons were doubtless more powerful, and even made up my mind for me.

I started by studying the preservation of frozen human semen, largely because there was a low-temperature research unit in the hospital investigating the survival of viruses at sub-zero. This 'cryobiology' was then the fashion, and scientists are as susceptible to fashion as couturiers or playwrights. I knew that the semen of bulls could be refrigerated for a decade, to father prize calves long after their fathers had been cut up for dog-meat. So why not the seminal fluid of men?

I discovered that human semen could be kept alive in a solution of glycerol at minus eighty degrees Centigrade. I allowed myself to imagine some national genetic refrigerator, guarded in the Bank of England like the country's gold reserves, containing the semen of great men for later reproduction by women with infertile husbands and a co-operative turn of mind. If England had need of some Milton living at this hour, there would be a fair chance of some Milton being produced. It was an open field of research on which little had grown, though perhaps the enthusiasm with which the human race reproduces itself naturally had made the quest as unnecessary as the reinvention of the wheel.

In the early sixties I first had read Gregory Pincus's trial of an oral contraceptive on the women of Puerto Rico, as the 'pill' dawned in the lightening skies of sexual freedom. I applied myself to testing the later products which dropped so steadily on to the market. All contraception is horribly unnatural. Technology and passion never mix. The 'pill' like the mechanical contraceptives had to be used in the cool-headed spirit of a pilot strapping on his parachute. What of the woman who forgot her dose, I wondered? Or the girl starting her evening with the best of intentions and succumbing to scrambled love in the back of a car? What of rape? What of the awful situation when each partner believes the other to be taking the precautions? Afterwards, there was only Mrs Ramsay. I saw the need of a retrospective contraceptive, a 'morning-after pill', and had gone a good way towards perfecting one when I was forestalled by other research workers in Scandinavia. That was the disappointment I had mentioned to Lloyd.

Then I became fascinated under the microscope with the merging of the male sperm and the female ovum. I would

18

demonstrate this to my class with the germ-cells of the sea-urchin, a creature whose sex-life is sadly deficient in drama or titillation. The vastly magnified photograph showed the tadpole-like sperm drawn with the most mysterious of embraces inside the globular egg. This microscopical fusion was to me the fundamental movement of all life, more awesome than the circuits of the stars and planets. Where there were two cells, male and female, now there was one, different from either. The process was the essence of human joys and savageries, I thought, the visible substance of love, the plainest indication we had of the working of the mind of God.

I saw that once the sperm has entered a bright ring appeared between the two transparent envelopes of the egg. This seemed to prevent the entry of other sperms. Only one pierces each ovum, the remaining millions in the male's emission left outside to wither and die like rejected suitors. Supposing this space were to be artificially provoked by a drug? I asked myself. We should have a simpler form of contraception less meddlesome to the body than the 'pill'. I was busy with this when the storm about cyclova brewed up and soon blew everything else from my mind.

I had two other reasons for crossing London from my home that Saturday morning. The first was a small ceremony at Princess Victoria's which I felt morally obliged to attend.

At eleven o'clock the new housemen were to be officially invested with their jobs. This was always performed with a certain pomp, perhaps to give not only the newly-qualified doctors but the rest of us reassurance over our hospital's importance. Once the occasion had brought a fine biannual flowering of the consultant staff, but Saturday was a busy time for private patients, interest dwindles in hollow ceremonies, and now it was conducted only by McRobb, Ma Saintsbury, and myself. We entered the committee-room together, Ma Saintsbury in academic robes with the cerise hood of a Fellow of the Royal College of Surgeons, I in my mustard suit, and McRobb in her white coat.

There were six new resident doctors, three men and three girls, standing at the far end as self-consciously as I myself eight years before. Ma Saintsbury addressed them down the length of the massive table, overloudly because she was becoming a little deaf. The room itself was dark-panelled and oppressive and you seemed to smell the gun-smoke of savage little vendettas fought between the lines of forgotten agendas. Its only decorations were the crests of Oxford, Cambridge, and London Universities, and the three portraits which hung there longer than anyone could remember. Elizabeth Blackwell, cropped, boyish, tunicked like a modern Chinese, the first British woman doctor. Sophia Jex-Blake, Edinburgh's Joan of Arc, puddingy, large-eyed, and anxious. And sweet-looking Elizabeth Garrett Anderson, with the lovely mouth and a hospital named after her in north London. Our goddesses. I wondered what they were really like.

'Now I must ask the indulgence of you three gentlemen while I address myself specially to the ladies,' I heard Ma Saintsbury continuing. I knew her speech by heart.

'You, ladies, represent a triumph.' She looked more motherly than ever. 'A triumph of reason over prejudice, of determination over wilful obstruction, of humanitarianism over resentment, of self-sacrifice in the face of humiliation and even physical aggression.'

The three girls looked suitably pleased with themselves.

'It may be difficult for you in these thankfully enlightened days to realize that the middle of the last century was the battleground of women in medicine. We could be accepted as nurses – Miss Nightingale made that point plain enough. But the men of this world assumed that God had given them some wonderful exclusiveness in curing rather than merely comforting human sickness. All sorts of arguments were produced against female doctors, a magnificent catalogue of ingenuity and stupidity. The men even maintained that we were incapable of the necessary intellectual effort, the female brain having been found by anatomists as somewhat lighter in weight than the male.'

She gave a contemptuous laugh, dutifully echoed.

'Sir William Jenner, Fellow of the Royal Society and physician to Queen Victoria, once declared, "I have but one dear daughter, and I would rather follow her bier to the grave than allow her to go through with such a course of study." I am glad to reassure you that the daughter survived, and grew into a lively champion of women's rights.'

Another laugh. The responses always came as reliably as those in church. Each audience must have known from their predecessors exactly what Ma Saintsbury would say, and were on their best behaviour. Winning a house job in your own hospital was still a privilege. Or rather, failing to was a black mark, they said like being expelled from school. Though of course I didn't go to that sort of school.

'Women have a long and useful tradition in medical work,' Ma Saintsbury continued. 'As long ago as the eleventh century, the University of Salerno numbered many women among its medical teachers, including the professor Trotula, the first true gynaecologist.'

I wondered if she had looked at all like McRobb.

'Trotula's books on gynaecology were widely read, and mentioned in Chaucer. And as we are mentioning literary matters, you may recall that Shakespeare in *All's Well That Ends Well* makes Helena act the King's physician – and act it very well she does.'

I doubted if they had read either. Few intelligent adults are worse educated than newly-qualified doctors. I had forced myself to read, to take an interest in the arts, telling myself the usual excuse of overwhelming professional work was sheer laziness.

'But the battle is too long over, the victory too firmly won, the satisfaction too deep for recrimination. Women doctors are today accepted almost everywhere. In the Soviet Union, they even form the greater part of the profession. During the last war, the medical women in our Armed Forces were truly officers, holding His Majesty's commission – *not* members of the women's Services, but with the same ranks and duties as their male counterparts.'

Ma Saintsbury had been a major. It was an experience she treasured as other women their honeymoons.

'Now I ask you, ladies, to gaze on the three portraits hanging in this room,' she ended. 'I ask you to reflect for a moment that

21

without those determined and very brave women you would not be standing here this morning.'

But it was all a sham. Feminism is the most unnatural feminine activity. In the medical school, the married girls were concerned firstly with the man they had got, the others with the one they hoped for. I wasn't married when I qualified, but I longed for the mastery of a man. Alone in bed, when I fondled my labia and pressed my clitoris against my symphysis pubis, like all women since Eve, I felt it a cheerless garden with no serpent. Yet I had forced myself away from men. I pretended that my career came before my emotional life. And I ended up by wrecking both.

The performance finished with the housemen receiving 'Charges', legal-looking documents specifying their somewhat idealized duties. Another puff to our self-inflation. We were really a second-rate London hospital. To look at we were awful, an ugly marriage between Gilbert Scott's St Pancras Station and Butterfield's Keble. We were less than a century old, and London hospitals flaunt their antiquity like the Livery Companies, or the public-houses catering for tourists. We had enjoyed one distinction, and that had died with the dawn of the National Health Service.

Princess Victoria's medical school had once been exclusively for women, but now, thank God, they admitted men as well. I often wondered at the atmosphere in the old days. A group of males can always rub along together, but a group of women has the incipient deadliness of a shoal of basking piranhas. Through half the consultant staff being women a feminine atmosphere lingered, leading to an urge, sometimes despairing and sometimes frantic, to establish ourselves among our peers. To understand this was to understand much of the psychology of women doctors. Or perhaps to understand much of the psychology of women.

4

'THAT'S THAT FOR another six months,' said Ma Saintsbury with satisfaction. 'Now let us take some refreshment.'

McRobb and myself followed into her Dean's office next door. It would be sherry again.

'I *am* finding it difficult hearing everything people say these days,' she confessed. 'I really must get the otologists to equip me with a hearing-aid. Though that seems such an awful move, so irreversible, another step nearer the grave.'

Ma Saintsbury stripped off her robes. Rather than one of the country's leading surgeons, she resembled a prosperous, bridge-playing suburban housewife. She had recently grown not only deaf but fat, looking like an eiderdown trapped in a dress. She was in her year of retirement, and we kept re-electing her Dean of the medical school because she enjoyed it. She was well-liked, jovial, honest, and firm on committees – particularly with the men. She had no children, and I often wondered what had happened to her husband, a little man with a smudge of moustache who must have got lost in her.

'Do pour the sherry, Ann. That's a pretty suit you're wearing today.'

'Thank you, Dame Christina.'

'It's such a shame nobody comes on parade when I present the housemen's charges,' she complained without rancour. 'Except for you two faithfuls. I expect the next Dean will drop the whole idea. Which is a pity. Hospitals are becoming far too businesslike.'

I handed her a glass of sherry. The office was overcrowded

with the three of us. It was a dim, old-fashioned little place, with an ancient roll-topped desk, a swivel chair for Ma Saintsbury, and a hard one for me. McRobb sat on the edge of a table, swinging her legs. I noticed her stockings were wrinkled again. She took a packet of cigarettes from the pocket of her white coat, and said, 'Hospitals are becoming far too much places where you have to earn your living. Those three young men this morning have women and children to support, God help them.'

'When *I* qualified, a teenage bride was an outright freak.' Ma Saintsbury sipped her sherry. 'Even after the war, women somehow remained girls until the age of twenty-three or so, like those lively ripe heroines of Jane Austen's.'

'Don't you think the modern young mature earlier?' I asked.

'No, they get more money,' said McRobb.

'I suppose you can buy married bliss like any other commodity,' I observed.

'It's all those advertisements for wall-to-wall carpets.' McRobb snapped her lighter. 'The contemporary urge for gas-cookers, washing-machines, babies, and similar consumer durables. That's what drives them into marriage, not sex-mania.'

'That's true, Sandra,' agreed Ma Saintsbury sadly. 'For years after the war we had to do without. We used to make dresses from curtain-material, which was off the ration, and cadge nylons from the Americans. I'll always remember when I came back to the hospital. Half of it was rubble, and black-out curtains were still up in the committee-room, hanging there like nuns' habits.'

Ma Saintsbury was reminiscing more frequently about the war, the great adventure specially organized for her benefit.

'God sent such a glorious summer that year, to warm our ruins and wounds in Europe. And we really didn't think twice about using atom bombs on the Japs. I know things changed for ever in a radioactive flash, but I can't honestly think what all the present-day fuss is about. We remembered Singapore, you see, and those two fine battleships lost the same December day, and there were pictures of Japanese prison-camps in all the newspapers.'

To head her off, McRobb asked me, 'How did you get on with those cyclova people yesterday?'

'What's this?' Ma Saintsbury disliked being left out of anything.

'You remember, the Professor and I were testing a new ora contraceptive on volunteers.'

'Do speak up, Ann. The traffic outside gets worse every day.'

Ma Saintsbury knew about the trial, but I had to explain my findings in the blood, and ended by recounting my inconclusive meeting with Lloyd.

'What do they want another oral contraceptive *for*?' demanded Ma Saintsbury. 'The market's flooded as it is.'

'A woman need take cyclova only once a month,' McRobb explained.

'So when she menstruates it would remind her?'

'You don't menstruate on cyclova. Menstruation's artificial with the other ones, anyway, just to cheer the girl up. Though some women,' McRobb added dourly, 'would forget even to menstruate if they could.'

'And with cyclova,' I pointed out, 'even if they miss a dose, it isn't disastrous.'

'How odd that a wanted pregnancy is such a joy, and an unwanted one such a tragedy,' observed Ma Saintsbury.

'The opposite applies to money,' said McRobb. 'Nobody likes working for it, but they love winning it by accident on the pools.'

'You must let me know what happens, Ann,' said Ma Saintsbury firmly. 'Don't let those drug people get away with a thing. They'll only try to take advantage of your being a woman.' She put down her glass. 'And now I have something to say. A little proposition for Ann. Don't go, Sandra, stay and hear. She may find your advice useful. How would you like to leave Princess Victoria's?' she asked me.

I looked surprised, fancying she meant some sort of temporary exchange job. 'I haven't thought of it.'

'Wouldn't you like to spread your wings, Ann?'

I felt a nervous flicker of excitement. 'That might depend a lot on the perch, Dame Christina.'

25

'That item should hold no misgivings. You know Longfield University? The new one in Kent. Opened with a tremendous flourish a couple of years back. Science-based for national advancement, the apple of the Government's eye, so they've got plenty of money to splash about.'

I nodded. This was more exciting still.

'My dear old friend Tilly Dawes is a big noise down there. She wrote saying they have at last made the decision to set up a Department of Reproductive Physiology. She asked if I could recommend anyone suitable as its first head. It isn't a large field, of course, few people are specializing in it. Naturally, I should like to recommend you, Ann.'

'But that's the sort of job I've dreamt of!' I exclaimed. 'Though it was a dream I couldn't expect to come true for at least another ten years.'

'It would come true next October, to be precise. The appointment's to be made in June.'

This was a wonderful chance. My career in a laboratory had been thrust on me rather than chosen, but the urge to make the best of my capabilities burned in me as fiercely as ever, as it had since I was at school.

'You would be a Reader to start with, just as you are here,' Ma Saintsbury explained. 'But Tilly says in time the post would certainly be upgraded to a professorship.'

McRobb smiled. 'Welcome to the club.'

'But could I make a success of it?' I asked doubtfully.

'Don't be stupid, Ann,' said Ma Saintsbury briefly. 'I'm doing a kindness to Tilly, sending her someone so able. I expect you'd like to think it over?'

'I suppose that I should. But it won't make any difference to my final decision. I want the job.'

'It's *so* nice to see my girls doing well.' She gave another of her motherly glances. 'Your year was awfully good – quite vintage. Look at Iris Quiply. A Member of Parliament.'

'I'm having lunch today with Liz Kilson – Liz Monkhood that was,' I told them. It was the third reason for my being in central London that Saturday.

'Our bouncy Liz?' asked Ma Saintsbury fondly. 'What's she

doing now? I understood she'd retired to become a lady of leisure.'

'I don't know. The invitation came out of the blue.'

'It's getting on for twelve.' McRobb put out her cigarette. 'I must go and lecture. It's an unpopular time, if I'm a minute late the class will scatter like frightened birds.'

'And I've lots of dreary things to do.' Ma Saintsbury turned to her desk. 'I'll write to Tilly, though of course you'll have to send a formal application later.'

Outside the office, McRobb said, 'You were right to snap that job up, Sheriff. Particularly as it was handed you on a plate.'

'But I might not get it?'

'With Ma Saintsbury and Tilly Dawes behind you, you will. You know how the system works.'

'It was all so unexpected,' I told her. 'The more I think of it, the more I realize it's exactly what I want.'

'I'll miss you,' said McRobb.

I was touched as I realized that she meant it.

5

I STOOD IN the Gothic archway leading from Princess Victoria's into Holborn. The weather was still lovely, the sun glinted on the red buses and across the road on the half-timbered face of Staple Inn, where Dr Johnson wrote *Rasselas* in a week to pay for his mother's funeral. I was a Londoner, and I loved London. Though admittedly I hadn't seen much of anywhere else. I couldn't afford it.

It was too late to catch a bus for my appointment with Liz, and too early to warrant a taxi. I looked round indecisively, until my problem was solved by a large black car appearing from the hospital.

'Ann, you look lost. Do you want a lift anywhere?'

'Oh, hello, Charles. I'm going to the West End.'

'Fine. I'm off to a meeting at the Royal Society of Medicine. It's more or less the same way.'

He opened the door, and I slipped into the front passenger seat. 'You can drop me somewhere round Oxford Circus. I've a lunch date in Curzon Street.'

'I'll do no such thing! Am I the type to tip a lady on to the pavement? Which restaurant?'

'The Crécy.' Charles looked impressed. 'Liz Monkhood is paying.'

'*She* can afford it.' We edged gently into the traffic. 'How do you like the car? It's new.'

'Most comfortable.' I stroked the leather. 'But I'm poor material to impress with cars. We haven't got one, remember. I can't even drive.'

'That's a blissful ignorance in London. This model has got electric windows. Look.' He demonstrated. 'And electric seats. They go backwards and forwards automatically. Wonderful engine – fuel injection.'

'Is it a Rolls?'

'A Merc. I thought of buying a Rolls, but it seemed nice to keep a treat in store. Who wants all their birthdays at once?'

Dr Charles Crawless had a refreshingly unabashed pride in his personal possessions. He was fat, pink, and boyish, with a narrow black moustache and chestnut hair plastered across his broad forehead. He was one of the new-generation consultant physicians, who was informal with his patients, materialistic in his outlook, enthusiastic over his pleasures, and dressed with a smartness more appropriate to Park Lane than Harley Street. He specialized in cardiology. He was on the senior staff of Princess Victoria's and the Canonbury, a lesser hospital in Islington, one of our satellites, where I had once been surgical registrar.

Charles was an old friend. He was the only male one in the profession I really had. In early middle-age, he was doing well. I believed he had a good income from advising life-insurance companies in the City, his private practice in Weymouth Street was large and growing, and he was starting to handle those patients who lead to professional contact with the powerful, the noble, and even the royal, bringing knighthoods and similar things so much desired by males. Charles was ambitious, but an ambitious doctor is the best to choose. Though he cannot afford the risk of spectacular cures, neither can he afford the risk of his patients unduly dying.

'I've just had a wonderful piece of news,' I told him. 'Ma Saintsbury's offered me a job at Longfield University – the new department of reproductive physiology. A Readership, later to be a Chair.'

'Professor Ann? I say, that's splendid! Congratulations. But it means we'll lose you. Which is sad.'

'You'll have to suffer that, Charles,' I told him cheerfully. 'I'm determined to take it.'

'I hope all goes well.' He accelerated expertly between a pair of buses. 'I'm glad I bumped into you just now. I was intending to give you a ring, as a matter of fact.'

'What about?'

'I was talking to George Lloyd last night. You know, the fellow who runs General Drugs.'

This was a surprise. 'I wasn't aware you even knew him.'

'Fairly well, as it happens. We're both members of the club.'

Charles was proud of his club. It was originally founded for actors, he explained, but as they thought it desirable to mix with gentlemen the membership over the century had widened. He claimed it was the only one in London where the members conversed rather than glowered at each other from behind newspapers. But I knew nothing of such institutions. My husband was never a member of one.

'I ran into George yesterday by the merest chance. I'd looked in for a drink about seven, and he happened to be in the bar. He mentioned he'd just seen you.'

'How did I strike him?'

Charles laughed. 'I don't think he expected a good-looking girl to have such command of her facts. Or of herself.'

'That sounds *dreadful*!'

'You did him a lot of good. Put him in his place. He's not a bad chap. I've rather taken to him, in fact. He has a difficult time of it, those Americans are tough taskmasters, expecting him to show a religious dedication to his job. None of our free-and-easy English ways. He's sold his soul to General Drugs, I suppose, though he got a damn good price for it.'

'It seems a selfish way of life. Nothing but making money.'

'Our yardstick of success is the survival of our patients. Theirs is money. It becomes quite impersonal once you have enough.'

'I wouldn't know anything about that.'

We wafted away from a traffic-light. 'Automatic gears,' murmured Charles. 'Admittedly,' he went on, 'these pharmaceutical companies do occupy a grey sort of area between business ethics and professional ones. But what of it? Without drug manufacturers we should have no drugs. There wasn't much point seeing penicillin in the pharmacopea until the Americans started making the stuff by the ton. On the whole, I suppose they do a pretty good and pretty responsible job. Technically, anyway.'

'I've never had much to do with them. I often wish I'd been more successful with that long-term contraceptive of my own – you remember, three years ago I let you see my work on it.'

'Yes, I do remember. And you asked me very firmly to keep my trap shut.'

'I was ashamed of my incompetence. I didn't see why everyone should know about my failures. Though I never expected to grow fat on it.'

'Yes, it's a pity Britain doesn't permit the patenting of drugs, we'd make fortunes,' said Charles. He added, 'Do you appreciate, Ann, you've casually strangled one of General Drugs' prize babies?'

'What? Cyclova?'

'So George Lloyd told me.'

'Surely it isn't so important to such a huge concern? Anyway, it was a highly suitable case for euthanasia.'

'But my dear sweet Ann!'

We had almost reached Oxford Circus, and Charles was edging left across the traffic looking anxiously at the glittering edges of his machine.

'Do you realize the size and expense of the apple-cart you are upsetting? Golden apples! Diamond-studded cart! No wonder I found the costermonger last night looking somewhat wan. Tell me, Ann, as the expert, what would you put as the qualities of the ideal oral contraceptive?'

I took a cigarette from my bag. Charles quickly leant across to produce a glowing lighter from the dashboard.

'It should be easy to take, a small pill,' I told him. 'Long-acting, so the woman wouldn't have to remember too many doses. Remaining effective if she missed one dose, or even two. With some retrospective effect, possibly – though I've a bee in my bonnet about that. With no long- or short-term side-effects. And cheap to make.'

'Exactly. Do you see that apart from the retrospective effect you have described cyclova?'

31

'You mean, they're really serious about manufacturing it?'

'I might tell you that General Drugs intend to turn the pills from the Middle West like the grains of wheat from the prairies. Using the very latest mass-production methods, to keep their costs right down. In fact, they've already started. I got as much from George Lloyd last night. The "R. and D." – that's what they call the research and development – on this drug has been enormous.'

'No wonder Lloyd sent for me in such a hurry,' I observed with satisfaction.

'No wonder, indeed. Even that's only the half of it. George also let on – you won't let this go further? I had it in secrecy – they're mounting one of the biggest and swishiest marketing campaigns ever known in the drug business. They've taken on special advertising people who usually handle Detroit. And I needn't tell you how Detroit pushes its wares.'

'I don't see what cars have to do with contraceptives,' I said tartly. 'Except to increase their sales naturally.'

'I suppose it's the same principle,' said Charles airily. 'After all, we treat an infection in the lung or the brain basically the same way.'

'This is all rather alarming, Charles,' I admitted. 'I seem to have stirred up a hornets' nest.'

'That's about it.'

'Well,' I decided, 'I shall stand my ground and swat some of the hornets.'

'Which is exactly what I'm afraid of. I'd hate you to get into a tussle with General Drugs, Ann. They're tough nuts. Really tough. Do you know, they've millions of dollars tied up in this project? George told me they're launching it on a global scale, interesting the governments of "underdeveloped" countries, as the saying goes. Where copulation must be the poor devils' only enjoyment, and they're too poor or too ignorant to do anything about it. The Indians are definitely biting. They've even hopes of the Chinese. Who knows? Our own hospitals already use communist-made antibiotics.'

'But why are you left to tell me all this?' I demanded. 'Why didn't Lloyd put it frankly to me yesterday?'

32

'I'll explain.' We were caught in a traffic-jam at the corner of Berkeley Square, Charles looking apprehensively again at his endangered coachwork. 'These drug companies are neurotically secretive. They're scared of their competitors so much as smelling a whiff of steam from their factories. Only when I told him that I knew you, and had done for some years, did he open up about the awful headache you'd given him. And quite frankly I encouraged him to talk. I thought I might be able to iron things out between you. In the end, George agreed I approached you – reluctantly, but he agreed.'

'But there's nothing to iron out. The drug can't be used. It's unsafe. The least the company can do is perform another series of trials and modify it.'

Immobile in the traffic, Charles rested his elbow on the steering-wheel and stroked his moustache with his forefinger. 'Perhaps General Drugs wouldn't see it that way. Putting it off now would be like rebuilding the ship instead of launching it. Scrapping it altogether would cause less expense and trouble.'

'Knowing these new facts doesn't change my case a jot, Charles. How can it? If a drug's dangerous, all the advertising men in Madison Avenue and Mayfair combined can't alter the truth. I'm sorry if they're going to lose their money. But they should have investigated cyclova properly in the first place,' I ended primly.

'I suppose you did know they'd done trials in the States, Puerto Rico, Brazil, and Canada? That's a pretty good cross-section.'

'I knew it had been tested, but not how extensively.'

'And they found nothing ominous at all. Nothing. Of course oral contraceptives have been blamed for about every disease that woman is heir to. Obesity, fibroids, baldness, everything from cancer to frigidity. It's the same as putting our ills down to the H-bomb or the weather. You know how the patients love to blame something or someone for their complaints?'

'I suppose you did read Doll's report on intravascular thrombosis?'

'Yes, I did. But what were the figures? Only four per hundred thousand women. Only a third of the mortality rate in pregnancy. The pill's safer.'

'But I've found something much more serious than thrombosis,' I pointed out.

We started to move again. 'I'm interested why, exactly.'

'Because I used a different stain for the blood. One I made myself.'

'That was clever of you.'

'Not really. Like a lot of these things, it turned up more or less by accident. One of the bottles of fluorescent stain in the haematology lab. had been contaminated with alcohol of the wrong strength. I found it had the edge in showing up immature cells. They look normal with the standard stains. Didn't I send you a reprint?'

'I don't think we were particular friends in those days.' He smiled, relieved at the conversation becoming personal. 'Guilt by association. That's never so strong as in sexual cases.'

I laughed, glad myself of a break in the tension. 'Women tend to see things in black and white. The goodies and the badies.'

'I'm glad my badness wasn't permanent.'

I asked from curiosity, 'How is Henry these days?'

'I see him often, of course, at the Canonbury. I'd like to tell you he was going to the dogs, but of course he's flourishing. He doesn't change. He's damned infuriating most of the time. Still, he's a bloody good surgeon.'

'Oh, I'd no complaint about the standard of his surgery.'

'Here's the Crécy.' We drew up. 'I hope I haven't made you cross with me, Ann?'

'Why should you?'

'Some of your remarks about cyclova sounded a little vinegary. I'm only trying to help you.'

'I'm cross with the drug people.' A man in dove-grey sprang from the restaurant to open the car door. 'They're treating me like a child.'

'I suggest you have another chat with Lloyd in the light of what I've said.'

I wrinkled my nose. 'Not a particularly attractive prospect.'

34

'I'm sure you'll handle him all right. Remember this – they don't want to market a dangerous product any more than you don't want them to. Understand?' He paused. 'And, Ann – don't be hot-headed.'

I laughed again. 'Don't you know me too well?'

'That's a privilege I prize,' said Charles. 'I hope you have a nice lunch.'

6

CHARACTERISTICALLY, LIZ HAD asked me to lunch at the most expensive restaurant in London. And characteristically she was late.

There was a crowded cocktail bar inside the main entrance, where a waiter found me a small round table and took my order for a gin and tonic. I was sitting against one of the faintly tinted mirrors lining the wall, and settled down to the depressing exercise of wondering how much Liz would think I had aged. I wasn't doing badly, I decided. My hair now called for tinting, but not much. I was still slim. My looks depended on the state of my health, which at the moment, thank God, seemed sound. I glanced down at my hands, wondering if they appeared too concave between the bones, opening and closing my fingers with an ease I found sensuous. When I was ill, everything seemed to go. Even my eyes became ugly, black-rimmed and sunken. And once I was told my eyes had the dark serenity of a Renaissance Madonna – by Liz's brother Trevor, of all people. He must have been feeling steamily romantic that summer's afternoon.

I lit a cigarette, inspecting the smart-looking people, noisy over their drinks. I supposed Liz expected me to be impressed, but I had been to the Crécy before, with my husband. I wondered if it would be friendly not to tell her. Liz and I had come together more or less through the chance of taking the same bus each morning to Princess Victoria's from Barnet in north London, where Liz had lodgings and where I lived. We were third-year students, just starting in the wards. I'd done my preclinical anatomy and physiology at Princess Victoria's itself,

36

which was cheaper, but Liz had been to Cambridge. She seemed from the start genuinely fond of me. I suppose it is pleasant for anyone to take a crony agreeably worse off than themselves.

In that summer eight years before when we both qualified, I had the whole of August between passing my finals and starting work as a doctor in hospital. The other girls in our year dashed abroad, but I hadn't the money. I could have made some by doing locums round the country, but the final examinations had exhausted me, because I had my eye fixed so sharply on winning honours. Liz invited me home for a month, not entirely a warm-hearted invitation, because she expected me to be rather overwhelmed.

Liz lived not in a house but a Hall, square, white, and Georgian, part of a pattern of chequered fields, sedate trees, and water-meadows between the Berkshire and Hampshire Downs in the Kennet valley, countryside with the exquisitely subdued beauty you find only in England and Englishwomen. The only eyesores were concrete pill-boxes built in Ma Saintsbury's war when the Germans were expected (very reasonably) to come marching down the river any morning on London, but even these were abandoned, overgrown, and encrusted with lichen, mellowing into the country like memorials to all our other enemies since the Romans.

We both behaved pretty badly that month. We were very much professional women. We scattered medical advice, all uninvited and mostly unwanted, armed with twenty centuries of Hippocratic authority. Fond little misconceptions and comforting old-wives' tales we shrivelled with the bright eye of science. Liz's mother had died – slowly and too young, five years before from a carcinoma of the cervix – and helplessly watching her eaten by cancer, Liz claimed, decided her on studying medicine. Liz's father, who had made a lot of money from shipping, didn't know what to make of us. It must cause confusion in a good many households to discover they have no longer a daughter but a doctor.

Then the portentous afternoon arrived. At the end of August the house appointments were to be announced at Princess Victoria's, and we had arranged with a former fellow-student called Carol to telephone from London with our luck. I was desperate to win the job of house-surgeon to the Professor of Gynaecology, where McRobb was then the registrar. It was the essential first step in a career I hankered after, planned in over-confident detail, and then locked away in my heart. Girls with flighty ambitions weren't popular in the medical school, which had something of the schoolgirls' mass antipathy to 'swanking'.

Before the telephone call was due, I strolled down to the river with Liz's brother Trevor. He was some two or three years older than her, pale, fastidious, and shy, tolerably good-looking with a lock of fair hair which fell over his forehead when he was agitated, and he walked with a limp. He had read law at Queen's and worked in London, but was unmarried and spent a good deal of his time at Monkhood Hall. He had taken to me in a cagey sort of way. I wondered if he thought me unworthy of him or if he were simply frightened about making love to such an aggressively professional person. In those newly-qualified days I prided myself on a level-headedness about men. It took two or three years before I saw in myself as big a fool as the rest of us.

'You know, I adore those clothes you're wearing,' he said unexpectedly. We were leaning on the parapet of a stone bridge talking of nothing in particular.

'They're not very smart.' I had a plain white blouse and a black skirt which an unkind eye could notice as threadbare.

'But they suit you. I always notice a woman's clothes. It's remarkable the number who ... well, don't dress *badly*, but with a little imagination could make themselves so much better.'

I laughed. 'You should have been a dress-designer instead of a solicitor.'

'I thought of it,' he told me seriously. 'But like painting or acting, it's too risky as a practical proposition. And it's the *movement* of a girl in her clothes which I always admire.'

'Didn't that go out with flowing skirts and cartwheel hats? Nobody even notices how a woman moves any more.'

'You're wonderfully graceful, Dr Ann.' He always used my title, not entirely playfully. 'You're like a ballet dancer. I ad-mire serene movement, like the surface of this river here, unbroken, steadily progressing, eddying and whirling so gently.' He pushed back his lock of hair. 'And I myself am condemned to stump my way through life.'

'Liz told me you'd had osteomyelitis.' I was matter-of-fact, still the professional woman.

'It was a tragedy,' he said with sudden bitterness. 'Or a stupidity, which is worse.'

He abruptly pulled the right leg of his trousers over his shin. I saw a deep irregular furrow biting into the bone of his tibia.

'Everything about it was stupid and ridiculous. It was no horrible accident. I was a kid of seven, just jumping off a table. Nobody noticed I'd broken it for a week. Then it went septic. I lay on my back for a year, while the doctors packed it with long strips of gauze soaked in . . . what's that stuff with the pungent smell, like chlorine?'

'Dakin's solution. We never use it these days.'

'And every so often they picked out little spicules of bone with their forceps. Most unpleasant. Memories of childhood! They couldn't give me penicillin, because there wasn't any. Or not enough. It was during the war, when they were keeping it for the casualties. I don't think my doctors had even heard of it. They tried that other stuff . . . what did you call it? "M. and B.". But the bug inside me was a staphylococcus, so it didn't touch it.' He dropped his trouser leg. 'Now it's an extinct volcano, but I grew up with one leg shorter than the other. So people can describe me as, "That fellow with the limp".' He brushed back his lock of hair again. 'Sorry to inflict this on you. I certainly wouldn't have done had you been an ordinary girl, not a doctor. I'm ashamed of that leg.'

'But what is there to be ashamed of, Trevor? How can anyone be ashamed of illness? You wouldn't be ashamed of catching cold.'

'I've even asked the doctors to cut it off, and give me a nice clean tin one.'

'Oh, no!' I was possibly less horrified at his distress than the prospect of such blatant malpractice. 'It's nothing to stop you leading a perfectly normal life.'

39

'People look down on me,' he said decisively. 'Everyone does. The family. Liz. Particularly Liz.'

'I don't.'

'Don't you?' He sounded sceptical. As if undecided whether to be acrimonious or pathetic, he asked, 'What girl wants to interest herself in a cripple?'

'Aren't you too hard on yourself? You sound as if you were half-paralysed from polio. And even *that* wouldn't make the slightest difference to a girl who loved you. Surely you must see that's the truth?'

He looked me in the eyes. 'Would *you* interest yourself in me?'

I wondered if all this was some highly novel approach. 'Of course I would.'

He paid me stumblingly the compliment about my eyes. 'Your hair's lovely, too. Can I touch it?'

'If you like.'

He reached out his hand gingerly. Then suddenly he grabbed me, pressing himself hard against me, biting at my mouth, his hand under my skirt, digging his fingers between my tightly-closed thighs. This onslaught – on a professional woman, too – was so unexpectedly savage I wondered if I was to be raped in broad daylight within shouting distance of his home. But the tussle ended as suddenly as it started, with Trevor pulling away, turning his back, and saying half to himself, 'I'm no good at this sort of thing, you know.'

I said nothing. Continuing our conversation seemed to present some difficulties. Then I glanced at my watch. The telephone call from London was due.

'I must go,' I said hastily.

'Ann —!'

He tried to grab my hand, but the news I wanted was worth more than any man in the world. 'It's from the hospital – about our jobs.'

'Ann, can't I see you in London? Surely I can? Can I find you at the hospital?'

I don't remember what I replied. I broke away and ran up the long winding narrow path towards the house. I arrived breathless to find fair-haired, plumpish Liz, looking worried, on a terrace outside the dining-room.

'Heard anything?' I demanded.

She shook her head. 'Perhaps Carol's forgotten. She's got a terrible memory.'

As I felt in the pocket of my skirt for cigarettes she added, 'Ann, there's something I've simply got to tell you.'

I wondered for a second if it was about Trevor's oddities.

'I should have done before,' she went on quickly. 'But it's got to come out now. I know you put in for the Prof's gynae. job. Well, I did, too.'

'You bugger!' I shouted, inaccurately but feelingly. Women doctors have a fine line in bad language, which we claim to pick up from the patients. 'You sod! What did you do that for? You know I want that job more than anything in the world.'

Liz looked nervous. My temper was well known. 'I only put in for it on an impulse, as we were leaving to come down here. I meant to tell you, Ann, honestly. I suppose I found it too horrible a thing to confess.'

'Don't you mean,' I said angrily, 'you left it till the last moment so you couldn't be shamed into changing your mind?'

Liz said nothing.

'*Why* did you do this to me?'

'You'll probably get the job, anyway, Ann,' she said faintly.

'Do you imagine so? You with your Newnham airs and graces? With all your money and all your arse-licking? God! You know they're snobs at Princess Vikki's, like everyone else. Can't you even afford to give me a chance?'

Liz started to become irritated herself. 'Oh, you're always pleading poverty.'

'Can I help it if I can't afford decent clothes, or sometimes even a decent meal?'

'Why should you always expect *me* to share your discomforts?'

'You impose enough on me. You make me sick! Borrowing my notes when you're too lazy to attend lectures, pinching my diagnosis on ward-rounds and passing it off as your own —'

'What's wrong with that?' she asked crossly. 'Everyone does it. You've got plenty from me, haven't you? Look at your nails.

You only varnished them because you're imitating mine. You were a scarecrow before I bothered to take an interest in you.'

'That's a bloody lie.'

I knew she was right. I had been at my most dowdy, but I had grown to imitate her in clothes and ways, quickly gaining confidence in myself. If Liz, who was neither particularly intelligent, interesting, nor even pretty, could have all the men she cared to lay hands on, so surely could I? My fear of humiliatingly failing to attract a man began to evaporate. I started to feel that I could dominate them, as I dominated the facts in my textbooks. She was the unknowing author of many future pains and ecstasies.

'I don't know why you descend to making a living at all,' I told her sullenly but more calmly.

'Taking up medicine wasn't easy for me.'

'You don't imagine it was easy for me, do you?'

This undignified encounter between two professional women was ended by the telephone ringing in the house.

'You go,' said Liz agitatedly.

When I came back, I said, 'I got the Prof's job.'

Liz bit her lip. 'Congratulations.'

I deliberately said nothing. She asked, 'Did I make my second choice, on the medical unit?'

'You got the anaesthetic job.'

'Oh. I see.' This was the wooden spoon. 'Well,' she declared, 'I'd better go up to London and buy a book about it.'

It was the first time in her life she hadn't got exactly what she wanted.

Afterwards, we were as close as ever. The friendships of women are unbelievably more complicated than those of men.

7

WHEN LIZ APPEARED in the bar of the Crécy that Saturday
lunchtime she didn't notice how I looked at all. She was as usual
far too preoccupied with herself. She sat on the edge of her chair,
clutching her handbag, a little fatter, her hair well-kept, her
make-up expertly done, her short plain bronze dress with a
diamond clip far smarter than my mustard suit. I was glad to
notice she seemed excited to see me.

'But it's over five years, Ann! How time slips by. Isn't it
frightening? We're jet-propelled to the hereafter. What will you
have to drink?'

'I've just finished a gin and tonic.'

'We'll have two more,' she told the waiter. 'I read that article
you wrote in the *B.M.J.* Or was it the *Lancet*?' In hospital she
had been perilously vague. 'Wasn't it comparing the different
methods of contraception? Though I forget which you said was
the best buy.'

'Oh, that! A rehash of other people's work, mostly.'

'I was most impressed, seeing your name in print. Though we
all knew you'd go a long way. How are the others at Princess
Vikki's? I've been meaning to go back, honestly, but those
invitations to reunions simply slide past until it's too late to
accept. Life seems to have become so hectic.'

It always was for Liz.

'Most of the hospital's been rebuilt, with glass and plastic
flooring and gay notices. It looks like a supermarket. They keep
slapping coats of paint on the old building to brighten it up, and
I think that's what holds it together.'

'Do you see anything of the girls?'

I shook my head. 'Not much. Carol flushed herself down the brain-drain to America. Jane runs a family practice with her husband in Somerset in the brief intervals between her pregnancies.'

'What a shame! She was one of the brainiest.'

'Perhaps now she's one of the happiest?'

Our drinks appeared.

'So you're a back-room girl?' asked Liz. 'Isn't it dull?'

'No, it has its excitements.'

I decided to tell Liz nothing of cyclova, which had been pressing on my mind since leaving Charles Crawless. It would take a lot of explaining, and even then she probably wouldn't grasp it.

'But weren't you going to do gynae.? I always thought gynae. such a sensible thing to specialize in. Only three operations – hysterectomies, slinging up prolapses, and scrapes. Though the midder in the middle of the night would be a bore.'

'I had to give up those ideas when I developed rheumatoid arthritis.'

'I heard about that. I *was* sorry.'

'It could have been worse. A carcinoma, for instance. That's the only way of looking at it. I'm pretty free from symptoms at the moment.'

'Are you getting good treatment?'

'I went to a top rheumatologist. He put me on aspirin, but he's thinking of changing me to small doses of corticosteroids.'

'Doesn't that make you grow a beard, or something?'

'Not really. Though all drugs have their unlooked-for side effects,' I told her feelingly. 'Mother Nature's a mean old thing. What she gives with one hand she snatches away with the other.'

'Poor Ann! I suppose neither you nor anyone else knows what causes it?'

'I only know that it came on after a period of emotional stress. I suppose you heard about my divorce?'

'I was amazed at the time.'

44

'Our marriage was a non-starter, really. Henry and I didn't mix.'

'Wasn't he awfully clever, too?'

'He's certainly got a first-class brain. A wonderful ability for withering irrelevant facts like arsenic on weeds. Anyway, a lot of the blame was mine.'

'Now you're being kind.'

'I wouldn't waste kind words on Henry,' I said thoughtfully. 'They're a foreign language to him. When you reach thirty you begin to develop a little reliable self-knowledge, and I'm starting to blame myself. But I blame Henry for my arthritis. Not so much for the pain, but because it stopped me operating.'

'Perhaps you're better off not doing gynae.,' said Liz consolingly. 'All the female gynaecologists I ever heard of were Lesbians. McRobb!' She shuddered. As students, we always shuddered at the mention of McRobb. 'Do you suppose she's queer?'

'You could never tell. She's the most efficiently insulated woman I've come across. She may just be neuter, her ovaries shrivelled like a couple of dried peas. She's a great friend of mine these days.'

'How remarkable,' said Liz.

We both sipped our drinks, and Liz announced, 'I'm intending to go back to practice.'

This struck me as alarming.

'To be absolutely candid, Ann, that's one reason I asked you out today. It shouldn't be too difficult, surely? I keep getting these things sent to me.'

She felt in her bag and produced a folded paper. I recognized it as one of the circulars hopefully put out by the Medical Women's Federation to entice married practitioners from kitchen and crib to the clinic.

'They *must* be getting hard up for spare hands in the Health Service,' Liz observed. 'I could do something part-time, surely? Jeremy's seven now and started at school, and of course there's always nannie.'

'But what's your husband think of the idea?'

Liz hesitated. 'That's the point. He's left me.'

45

'Oh,' I said mildly.

'That's the other reason I wanted to see you, Ann. You've been through all this. Is it so horrible?'

'It isn't exactly a joyous process.'

It would be worse at Liz's age. In your early twenties you can throw off a husband almost as easily as breaking a date. Later it becomes crueller, because by then love is a settled way of life.

'I don't see how I could bring myself to get a divorce,' she explained hopelessly. 'It always looks so simple when you just see a paragraph in the evening papers. But it must be awfully unpleasant, collecting evidence and that sort of thing. We might have a legal separation, or something. I went to see Trevor this morning to find out my rights.'

'And how is Trevor?'

'He's getting awfully important.'

'I bet he's not married.'

'How did you guess?' She was impatient with the irrelevance. 'My Derek went off, just like that. With a woman from his office. He called her a "personal assistant" or something grand, but she was only a secretary trained to bash a typewriter. I really can't understand it, Ann.' She was genuinely baffled. 'We were always perfectly happy. We had lots in common – though I suppose Derek would never have taken an interest outside his business if I hadn't stimulated him. But I'm an educated woman. What does he expect to talk to this secretary about?'

Liz was a lazy woman and a lazy doctor, and doubtless a lazy lover. You love as you live. Derek must have found his secretary's pelvis livelier. And the uneasiest of advice for a woman to hear is that of Louis the Fifteenth's doctor – 'Ah, sire! Change is the greatest aphrodisiac of all.'

To encourage her, I said, 'Perhaps he'll get bored and come back?'

'I wouldn't have him! There's no question of that.'

She's new to the game, I thought.

'And think of the career I gave up for him.'

With the mysterious magnetism of precious metals, money had attracted money. Young Derek had been rich – insurance, I believed. But Liz had romantic ideals, and announced it a toss-

46

up between Derek and practice in an inhospitable and much under-developed corner of Central Africa. But I for one never saw a serious chance of her dossing down in some remote and stifling hut, rather than sharing a comfortable Sussex bedroom with her insurance man.

'Don't you think you might be a little rusty after all these years?' I asked guardedly. I didn't see why our patients should suffer for Liz's personal ill fortune. 'It isn't that easy for women to find good part-time jobs, especially in hospital. There's twenty-eight per cent of women doctors not practising – they can't all be raising young families, a lot of them would like to work if they had the chance.'

'You're always quoting figures at people,' said Liz impatiently.

'Forget the figures and remember that hospitals are run by men. They're prejudiced against us, however deafening the thunder of beaten breasts when they deny it.'

'Couldn't I help in your family planning clinic?'

This struck me as a possibility, a higher degree of sympathy than skill being required. I said evasively, 'We couldn't pay you anything.'

'That doesn't matter. I'm going to soak Derek for every penny he has.'

She was indeed new to the game.

'I can only ask McRobb,' I promised.

'Ann, you're splendid. Isn't it satisfying, having something like medicine to fall back upon?'

'But what do you know about contraception, Liz?'

'Not much. I tried the pill once, and it made me feel so bloody I wouldn't let Derek near me.' She gave an unexpected school-girlish giggle. 'Perhaps that's how it works?'

The headwaiter approached, and as Liz studied the menu I ran my eyes over the dozen or so women in the bar. They were young, all attractive, one even pretty. I wondered how many were on the pill, and thus – in a roundabout, negative, entirely feminine sort of way – allying themselves to the terrifying age-old scourges of famine, pestilence, and war in keeping the population of the world at a manageable level.

47

The pill was so different from other forms of contraception. It was the woman who made the choice, who swallowed the medicament, who voluntarily called on herself the curse of barrenness. Unlike any mechanical device outside or inside her womb, the pill changed the chemistry of her blood. And so it changed the woman. A shining example of good sense and self-sacrifice, the twin weapons of females who want to get things done, in the best tradition of Lysistrata.

'Would you like oysters?' asked Liz.

'That would be fun.'

But I doubted if those in the room appreciated their contribution to solving the world's worst biological problem. They just wanted a regular man inside them without the inconvenience of a regular baby to follow. And who was I to cavil?

'Some wine?' suggested Liz.

'It's Saturday. I've no work to do.'

In the end we had two bottles, and forgot all about General Drugs, George Lloyd, Charles Crawless, the pill, and even Derek.

8

ON SUNDAY MORNING the soul of time flies from the body of the clock. You get up late, yawn more than usual, spill cornflakes down your dressing-gown, smoke too much, and drop ash over last night's washing-up in the sink. It's a morning which makes slatterns of us all. When you put your hair in rollers, contemplate a hundred pressing tasks and fiddle with one useless one, wind the eight-day alarm-clock, cut your toenails, and copulate on top of the bed in the sunlight.

'Sunday isn't a day,' said Kit. 'Scott Fitzgerald was right when he called it a gap between two other days.'

'I hate hot week-ends in London,' I told him. 'It seems so incongruous, somehow.'

'Like having a lovely day for a funeral,' he agreed.

The sun was already defeating the curtains when I woke, and now through the open bedroom window I could hear traffic stampeding past the end of our road into the country. I was still in bed, but Kit had collected our papers from the front door three storeys below. We didn't live in Chelsea, as I usually claimed, but in Fulham, in a flat on the top of a Victorian house off the wrong end of the King's Road. The floodlight pylons of the Chelsea football team towered outside our windows, and on winter Saturdays our pavements ran twice with a strange scarved and beribboned human torrent. Once our area had been like the Boltons, one of nannies, smart delivery-vans, well-caged gardens, and sadly inhibited dogs. But now it seemed infected with some blight which peeled the paint and split the brickwork, broke the windows and loosened the tiles, and here and there consumed whole buildings down to their flat foundations.

'Perhaps we should make an effort to get out at week-ends?' Kit suggested, without really meaning it.

'I prefer the contemplation of the country in solitude,' I said firmly, 'rather than the experience with a million others.'

'Do you think we should buy a car?'

'No. I was talking to Charles yesterday, and he said anyone with a car in London was crazy.'

'Charles who?'

'Charles Crawless. You remember, darling, the cardiologist from Princess Vikki's. He came to dinner with us.'

'The velvet hand in the velvet glove?'

'That's the one.'

'With the tall blonde wife. One of those couples it's so difficult to correlate to each other. She was extremely opinionated.'

I laughed. 'I heard that's what Charles used to say about me when I was married to Henry. He was an enormous friend of Henry's.'

'Why do I always feel painfully jealous whenever you mention Henry?'

'Don't we always get more jealous over the past than the present?'

'Perhaps you're right.' He looked thoughtful. 'The past has all happened, we can't do anything about it. Though you're not jealous of Myra?'

'Not for a moment.'

'But unhappily my wife is very much in the present.' He stretched. 'Some tea?'

'Lovely.' Sunday morning, a day without rails.

I watched Kit shuffle from the bedroom, in his slippers and old red-and-yellow Paisley dressing-gown, with the split down the back which I kept telling myself I must mend sometime. He was forty-four, stocky, with blue eyes and brown hair going grey, square-faced, resembling a good-tempered mastiff. I suppose he was what Victorian novelists would have named a 'ne'er-do-well'. He was the most intelligent man I had ever known, though I admit that intelligence, like beauty, can often be in the eye of the beholder. He was kind, gentle, and considerate, except when he was drunk, which was when we had our rows. He was by profession a writer. His acquaintance with books was expectedly more intimate than my own, but I was continually surprised at his assessment of people, and his feeling for the strange paradoxes which grapple in the human heart, which were quicker and sharper than my professionally trained senses. His knowledge of the world was so much deeper than mine, because he had wandered down so many unexplored lanes off the dull main roads of life. Much of his taste and worldliness rubbed off on to me. All I had learned from my husband was surgery.

Kit came back with a tray of tea-things, his pyjamas sagging open at his breast, showing his spikes of hair. He poured two cups. We started the ritual of reading the press.

'The Sunday papers are too vast and empty,' he complained. 'Echoing with over-familiar cultured voices mixed with screams of sexual anguish.'

'There's always the business sections,' I pointed out.

'I suppose it's pleasant to feel that the world's now rich enough for the serene contemplation of money on Sundays, as the righteous once contemplated God.'

I looked down the front page. 'I have a sickening feeling that the news is always the same. It just seems to advance and recede in importance, like the tides. Would that be a sign of age?'

'Undoubtedly.'

'There's adjacent advertisements for Fortnum's and Oxfam. Pregnancy diagnosis two guineas, results same day. Lots of societies to join. Anti-bomb, anti-hunting, anti-vivisection – that's muddled – and anti-fluorine in the water, which is simply stupid.'

'Surely one of the charming lunacies of England is one half of the population continually forming societies to stop the other half doing something?'

I read on, 'Coronaries can kill in the prime of life, fight cancer with a will, help against multiple sclerosis, give to conquer arterial disease. Charity is never cheerful.'

'A wonder people still bother with the trouble of committing

51

murder and suicide,' Kit observed. 'It seems you need only sit and wait.' He impatiently bundled up the pages. 'I've been putting off having my bath. It's the horror of that awful first look of yourself in the mirror in the morning. One of the most appalling experiences of life.'

'What's the time?'

'Getting on for ten.'

'God, I must get up. I've got that report to write.'

But I stayed in bed lazily as he went through the other door into the bathroom. I heard him micturate, as usual loudly, right into the middle of the water in the lavatory. Then he passed flatus. The symphony of marriage. The young unwed, as Mc-Robb pointed out, expect sex, romance, and homemaking fun, all glossy and odour-free. They don't appreciate the frightening power of the sounds of intimacy. Even when you're married you don't, until suddenly they've gone. I'd stopped Kit noisily gargling in the morning, telling him it was medically useless. He could never argue with me on a professional point. I heard the bathwater running, and Kit tunelessly starting to sing. Sunday morning, which distils the essence of marriage. But of course we weren't married.

I was still in bed when Kit came out of the bathroom, naked and drying himself.

'It's no good looking at me like that,' I told him. 'You know I've got the rags on.'

'At least you make no bones about it. Myra used to be horribly coy, using all sorts of devious expressions – having a headache, feeling depressed. I don't think the woman wanted anyone to imagine that she ever menstruated at all.'

'What did you used to say to Myra when you wanted to get into her?'

'Something about playing bears.'

I laughed.

'Yes, it was terribly common. The lower the social status, the more intimate the euphemisms. Lady Chatterley would have talked gaily about fucking. Poor working-class Mellors would have mouthed some awful gentility, like, "How about a bit of passion, my love."'

He sat facing me on the bed. I reached out for his flaccid penis.

'*Lady Chatterley* is only another *Alice in Wonderland*,' I said. 'Lawrence had tuberculosis, and the tubercular are liable to fantasies.'

'But you can't properly depict men and women in books unless you paint them sexual antics and all.'

'That's valid psychology. And some people's antics are oddly ingenious.'

'What's it like, walking about with a chunk of cotton-wool inside you?'

'You don't notice it. Behind the Iron Curtain,' I told him, 'they have no internal sanitary towels. Nor Sellotape. It's true. A Polish woman doctor visiting Princess Vikki's told us. It's a wonderful reflex, darling,' I said fondly. 'Aren't you ever afraid it isn't going to work?'

'With Myra it often didn't.'

'Perhaps she didn't try hard enough. Do you know, when I was a student one of the boys asked me if I was a fellatrice. In my innocence, I'd no idea what he meant. I imagined it was a female secret society.'

'But, my darling, it is! Of enormous membership.'

'Lawrence didn't know the right words. That was his trouble.'

'If I confessed to being an occasional cunnilinguist, do you suppose I'd be taken as some sort of interpreter?'

I continued stroking him. It was thrilling to have such power. 'Did you know that the average American male has an erection of six point three inches, at a position slightly above horizontal? I'm quoting Kinsey.'

'That's even more fascinating information than about the Sellotape.'

'And at the age of twenty the average couple copulate two point four times a week. At forty it's one point three.'

'I suppose this is the point three?'

I leant forward over him. He ejaculated almost immediately and I looked up at him. He was lying back on his elbows, his eyes half-closed. He was subjugated to me. To have successfully stimulated him, to have achieved his reflex, gave me a sensual

53

pleasure almost equalling a material sensation of him in my vagina.

I got out of bed, throwing off my nightie, preparing to dress in slacks. 'When I move to Longfield,' I told Kit, 'on Sundays we'll do the gardening. With hoes and rakes and pruning shears, and a trug. I know exactly the sort of place I want. A nice little house set in the Downs, with brilliant flower-beds and neat young trees. Perhaps a paddock. Even a horse.'

I had a secret ambition to ride. It might have been a lingering imitation of Liz.

Kit started to dress. 'If you get the job,' he said dampingly.

'Ma Saintsbury's promised.'

'I wish I'd half the jobs I'd been promised.'

'My profession's different,' I told him.

'Are you coming to the Feathers?'

'Not this morning, darling. I've got that report to do.'

'I'll face it alone, then. Andrew promised to be there. I want to talk to him about my novel.'

That meant Kit would boozily be asleep all afternoon in the chair.

'Where are you taking me to dinner?'

Like going to the pub at midday, this was another of our Sunday habits. A working woman deserved her treats.

'But, my darling, I told you – this evening I've got to meet Veronica off the boat-train.'

'Why can't her mother meet her?' I asked shortly. His daughter Veronica had been working for a year in France.

'Well, you know how it is with Myra.'

I decided this an unrewarding argument to press. 'How old's Veronica now? Sixteen?'

'Seventeen.'

'A year's a long time at that age. You won't recognize her.'

'I know. It frightens me a little.' Suddenly he laughed.

'What's the joke?'

'I was just thinking of all the Americans I know, with erections six point three inches long in a position slightly above the horizontal.'

I gathered my brief-case and files on cyclova and went

54

through to the little dining-room where we worked. With the fair-sized living-room and cupboard-like kitchen it made up our flat. We shared the same typewriter, and I saw I would first have to file away the typed and much scribbled-over sheets of Kit's novel. He was awfully untidy. But he complained sometimes that I kept him in a well-swept and garnished cage.

When Kit had gone to Oxford from the Navy after the war, he had taken a bad enough degree in English, as he explained, to raise hopes of earning a living by writing. Accepting warmly the advice that the best novels are written in cheap hotel bedrooms in the South of France, he had set off at once, with little money and a one-way ticket. But the bedroom was finally neither cheap nor conducive to work, being in the luxurious villa of an American woman, the mangled psychological remains of four husbands. I could understand this arrangement. Kit was splendid enough between my thighs now. At twenty-three he must have been terrific.

The novel was still being written. The pages I tidied away that Sunday morning was the same book in yet another disguise, and it had never been published in any. When the American woman had gone home Kit found a job on Fleet Street, but the jobs on Fleet Street are as impermanent as its products. He turned to the B.B.C. as a rock which sustained a good many limpets, but after a year or two even the B.B.C. shook him off. He claimed they didn't appreciate his originality. But by then he was saddled firmly with his prime interests in life, drinking, betting, and women.

Kit certainly *had* seen his books published. Half a dozen of them, valuable works a hundred pages long, giving simple information on English literature, philosophy, religions, architecture, beekeeping (the most difficult), and the working of the human body. He had a friend in publishing who commissioned them and found them profitable. Kit got a hundred guineas advance, and his facts from the public library.

The book on the human body came my way through our hospital journal. It was so shot with errors I wrote shrilly to the publisher. A few weeks later, Kit replied. He had known nothing of his subject, he artlessly confessed, but accuracy of

55

information was surely immaterial to a reader improving his mind by such abysmal means. I repented my first letter and wrote more kindly. It must have touched Kit, because he wrote asking to meet me. Or perhaps he just thought I might be an interesting prospect for bed.

During the three years we had been living together Kit abandoned his handbooks to concentrate again on the novel. He had a few articles accepted by the newspapers, the *New Statesman*, or *Punch*. He no longer backed horses, because I insisted he didn't. I didn't know if he still had other women, but I doubted it. When the fire glows comfortably into the lengthening evening, you don't risk killing it with fresh coals. He still drank. I knew I couldn't stop that. We lived on my pay from the hospital, and I loved him.

I put a sheet of paper in the machine and typed at the top,

CYCLOVA

Underneath I wrote,

REPORT ON A CLINICAL TRIAL
AT PRINCESS VICTORIA'S HOSPITAL, LONDON
By
A. Sheriff, M.D.
and
Professor S. N. McRobb, M.D., F.R.C.O.G.

It was going to take me a while, because I can type with only two fingers.

9

ON THE LAST Sunday of every month I called on my parents for supper. Three weeks later it was a cold, wet April evening, the usual sequel to a burst of hot weather which lures us to mistake the last bite of winter for the first breath of spring. I took the Piccadilly Tube to Cockfosters, the last station on its northern end, and walked a mile along streaming pavements with the rain glistening on my shiny red raincoat. In the right mood, I enjoy walking in the rain. It has the stimulus of combat against the elements with the security of dryness and warmth under one's impervious husk. The significance is probably psychological, and doubtless sexual.

I turned the corner towards the house where I was born. It was indistinguishable from any other house in the street. It had a pompous mullioned bow window downstairs, a door with a coloured glass panel, two front rooms upstairs, and a steep slate roof with earthenware chimney-pots, slightly askew. It was always too cold in winter, in summer too stuffy, and too dark all the year round.

In front was a tiny neat garden behind a low brick wall and an invariable privet. Behind was a larger garden with a feather-board fence, a tumbledown shed, an ever-mown lawn, and washing-line which flapped on Mondays. It was organically clasped like a Siamese twin to the house next door (within my memory we never spoke to the neighbours). It was the house you keep seeing all over London, as regularly as the red tin bus stops. It was conceived by Victorian speculative builders for the new Pooters, who becoming aware of enjoying the fruits of the

57

greatest Empire the world had known, set off every morning importantly dressed to labour long hours behind high desks as clerks in city offices. Like the Empire, the house had survived the Zeppelins and the Luftwaffe and was now looking painfully seedy.

'Dad's still having a nap,' said my mother at the door.

'How is he, Mum?'

'He gets tired easily.'

I took off my raincoat, dripping on to the coloured cracked tiles of the narrow hall. 'Shall I hang it in the kitchen?'

'Give it me. You shouldn't be out in this weather at all. You'll catch your death.'

I no longer bothered to correct my parents' medical misconceptions. If my mother believed that wet feet gave you a cold, so did millions of other mothers. She looked at the cardigan over my dress. 'Aren't you going to take it off? You'll miss the benefit when you go out again.'

She was a firm believer in 'the benefit'. 'I'll keep it on, Mum.'

'How's your rheumatism, dear?'

'Not too bad.'

'I can't understand you getting *rheumatism*. Not at your age. Surely it's old people who get rheumatism?'

'There's a lot of different forms of it,' I said. But I knew that I hadn't convinced her.

I went into the bow-windowed parlour, where the new gas-fire glowed. When I lived at home, we had prudently looked on its pink and fringed three-piece suite as more decorative than serviceable, our life proceeding in a room beside the kitchen, always untidy with familiar old furniture in which you got to know the feel of every spring. Only within the past year or two had I been entertained in the parlour, a change marking a distinct one in my status. I was a consequential visitor, not one of the family.

As a student, my physical presence in the house had been more burdensome for my parents than my financial barrenness. I had my student's grant, they certainly couldn't afford to supplement it, and I was obliged to pay what I could for my keep. But the scholar who worked furiously each evening in one

58

of the bedrooms commanded their lives with a severity they found baffling. I couldn't recall how often I stormed down to complain about the television, which even distantly clashed horribly with such matters as the structure of the brachial plexus or the pathology of cerebral tumours. But they bore it meekly. As a doctor, I should be a decoration dazzling everyone in sight. In fact, I did my best bookwork when they were quiet and in bed, between ten and four in the morning. Women always study more intently than the men, lavishing on their books a more steadfast feminine passion which a man can never achieve.

The house had been patchily improved by my brother and myself since we started making money. The brassbound geyser in the bathroom which roared like a volcano had been replaced with something less fearsome, in the parlour was the gas-fire and some furniture from Heal's. The room was a curious mixture of old and new. There was a bright plastic cloth on the table, with cups, plates, a jar of jam, and a bottle of ketchup for the meal, on the modern sideboard an old-fashioned family Bible and a transistor radio. Over the mantelpiece a reproduction of a Dufy regatta, which I had given them, backed their wedding photograph, one of my brother during his National Service, and a third in a silver frame of my mother's father, cheerful in high-necked khaki a few weeks before he was killed at Ypres. This melancholy reminder somehow gave my mother a comforting feeling of the continuance of things. To her, Death was not the Reaper, rather some long-distance runner forever lapping a circular track. She believed we had all lived before, several times, often in circumstances of magnificent and Oriental splendour. She claimed to be 'Psychic', in the right circumstances the dead showing little reticence towards her and the future hiding few secrets. She would sit in her bedroom for hours with packs of cards and strange charts I had never been allowed to glimpse. All unscientific rubbish. She was a peculiar woman. I suppose I inherited much of my personality from her.

I lit a cigarette and looked round again, warming myself on the fire, taking command of the room. My parents – and I – were lower middle-class. The class which sparks off revolutions, hangs its tyrants, smashes up its capitals, impoverishes its task-masters, and throws up the most ferocious of dictators.

'Ronnie and Paula are coming today, a bit later,' said my mother, returning from the kitchen.

A depressing prospect. Some time ago I realized that I really disliked my brother, and I was just starting to realize that I really disliked his wife. As my mother started fussing with the table, small, grey, and skinny, in a chain-store dress and a flowered apron, she asked, 'How's your new flat, dear?'

'It's hardly new. I've been there three years.'

'How time flies.'

My parents had never visited me, nor even fished for an invitation. Perhaps they sensed something about Kit. Like a lot of people, they would cling to ignorance to save themselves the trouble of outraged delicacy or even shame.

'I shan't be there much longer. I'm getting another job.'

'Oh?'

'At Longfield. The new university in Kent.'

'Won't that be nice?' she said comfortably. 'Where's Long-field now? Isn't it on the way to Hastings?'

'More or less.'

She sighed and said dreamily, 'I haven't been to Hastings for donkey's years.'

'Why don't you get Dad to take you this summer?'

'Perhaps I would. But we're thinking of moving, too.'

'Moving?'

This was shattering. They were as much part of the house as the mice behind the wainscoting.

'You see, dear, dad's retiring this year, and we thought it would be nice to find a little place somewhere down by the sea. Nothing big, just a bungalow would do, where he could get on with his gardening. There's lots of estates going up on the coast, you know.'

'Isn't that a bit daring, Mum?'

I saw their vision of a red shingled roof and roses climbing against the white clapboard in the sun. I knew the reality of uprooting yourself at sixty-five, to face only loneliness, frustration, and death.

'I *know* it's just the right thing for us.' She had been probing the future. 'That's why I'm glad both you and Ronnie could come today. You see, it'll need a bit of capital.'

This is a bloody nuisance, I thought.

'You're ever so good to us.' She was reassuring herself.

'I get nothing from Henry, you know. They said I could always earn my own living. I didn't argue the toss.'

'You should have struck a better bargain, my dear.'

'I'd have paid to be rid of him.'

'It's a pity you didn't stay together. You had such a lovely wedding.'

My father appeared. He was wearing his Sunday suit, another sign of my changed status.

'And how's the doctor?' he asked cheerfully.

'Not so bad, Dad, thanks for asking.' It was frightening in that house how I slipped back to the speech of my youth.

My father stood looking at me proudly, filling his pipe. He was short and bald, with bright eyes and a thick grey moustache. He made harmlessly feeble little jokes, through nervous habit rather than an urge to lighten human existence with humour. Or perhaps they were compensatory for a lifetime spent tramping hopefully and admiringly through damp and empty houses. He was a clerk in an estate agent's, with an office which I remembered from childhood had half-frosted windows like a public house's, tall handsome wicker wastepaper baskets, ink-stains on the brown lino, and dark-suited solemn gentlemen. My first excursion into pride had been seeing the name of my father's firm exhibited on little wooden flags outside abandoned dwellings all round the district. I thought he was wonderful to be associated with such civic exhibitionism. By now, I fancied that he had grown quite frightened of me.

'What are you giving us for supper, Sal? Not more of that Russian crabmeat, I hope? They could shoot it to the moon, as far as I'm concerned.'

She told him that we were having cold ham.

'What, on a freezing cold night like this?' He then gave an imitation of some outspoken, weirdly-accented character in a television series. As I had never time to watch the programmes this was lost on me, like much of my parents' conversation. But I laughed, and he seemed pleased enough. Then I saw through the bow window a car drawing up in the rain. It was white and American, a huge cocoon of metal to move only two people about. My brother Ronnie had arrived, with his wife.

10

RONNIE CAME INTO the house waving a bottle of whisky (undoubtedly my father made some joke). My brother was a far less dutiful visitor than me. Like father, he was short, fat, and balding. He was eight years older than myself. I gathered I had been something of a surprise to my parents, and should have loved knowing the failure of exactly what form of contraception I owed my existence to. Probably *coitus interruptus*, so devastatingly misleading in its apparent efficiency. Or perhaps my father had thought of some particularly tickling joke just at the crucial moment.

Ronnie was prosperous. Though precisely how prosperous, and precisely why, he refused even to hint. I must still have had some sisterly concern for him because I found the mystery worrying, particularly when I recalled how his commercial career had started at the age of sixteen. In the grey years after the war he had been fined and elaborately lectured by the local magistrates for selling in the streets orange squash, made from juice intended by the newly-benevolent Government to provide vitamins for babies. After his National Service he had gone into my father's office, but declaring the pace too slow had started dabbling in property on his own. The boom which had lined so many unworthy pockets and littered so many of our cities with hunks of concrete was on the wane, so he reverted to his original line by entering the liquor business. Though where his shops or warehouses were, he would never tell. I wondered if the bottle displayed proudly on the mantelpiece had originally been hi-jacked.

63

'Hello, Paula, you're looking well,' I said.

'Oh, thanks, so are you.'

She was small and silent, and adored Ronnie, or at least the things which Ronnie bought her. I noticed her nervously twisting a large diamond ring I hadn't seen before. This strengthened my resolution. It would be Ronnie paying for the seaside bungalow.

When the others cleared the dishes into the kitchen after the meal, Ronnie and I found ourselves alone.

'Ron, you'll have to put up the money for this house they're on about,' I told him. 'I'm skint, honestly.'

'Go on?' He gave a mocking grin, the prerogative of all brothers towards their younger sisters. I hated it. 'Who's ever heard of a skint doctor?'

'I don't get much in my sort of work.'

'Why don't you switch to a more profitable line? That's sense to me.'

'You don't understand these things,' I told him impatiently. 'My salary's a secondary consideration. It has to be.'

'Then get a man to keep you, like any other woman.'

'You know what happened when I did.'

'Plenty have a second try. You're young enough, and still got your looks.'

I knew I should have to tell him about Kit. I was resigned to it, and though it was the last thing I wanted him to know it was the only way of escaping my moral obligations towards my parents.

'It's rather the other way round. I've a man to keep. More or less. He doesn't earn much.'

'Have you, now?' Ronnie looked highly interested. 'That doesn't sound a very nice arrangement to me.'

'You wouldn't even begin to understand it,' I told him shortly. 'You're not sensitive enough. I love this man very much.'

He pulled out a packet of small cigars. He was much wiser about cancer than I was. 'So Ann's in love?'

'Can't you at least be human about it?'

'I saw Cliff the other afternoon.'

'Why do you want to tell me that?' I asked angrily.

64

'I thought you might be interested.' He lit the cigar. 'He's doing well. A nice little garage business out Hounslow way. Half a dozen branches. If you'd stayed along with him, my dear, you'd have been all right.'

'You're being ridiculous.'

'Am I?' said Ronnie. 'I thought it was a distinct possibility at the time.'

I was eighteen, learning anatomy in the bright, cold, stone-floored, phenol-smelling, dissecting-room at Princess Victoria's. I had not then met Liz. I was at my most drearily unattractive, my clothes old, my hair unkempt, even dirty. I was scared of men – or rather, I was scared of myself. But no one in my class could imagine how I yearned for one, more ardently than the few girls famous for flitting round our supply of males. And my work didn't help to dampen desire. Dead shrivelled penises set you thinking of warm live ones. I studied the structures of masculine erection and ejaculation in admiration not only of their anatomical ingenuity. Then there were the boys' jokes, delivered slyly or heartily according to temperament. 'Did you hear of the woman student, Ann, who thought Alcock's canal was the vagina ... she couldn't remember the name of the glans, Ann, but she had it on the tip of her tongue last night ...' They were probably being made in the days of Burke and Hare.

Cliff was a friend of Ronnie's from the R.A.F. He was a large man in his mid-twenties, red-headed and red-faced, with big hands, and he sweated easily. He sold cars in a garage in Barnet. Both he and Ronnie being unmarried, over three or four years he was regularly in our house recalling the horrors of Service life, loudly and cheerfully, while drinking beer. Then one evening Cliff suddenly realized that I was a mature woman, an exciting discovery for a man after years of blameless childish familiarity. He asked me out, to a dance, or the cinema, I forget. That same evening, in the back of his car somewhere off the Barnet by-pass, a spot I noticed he reached with practised ease, his penis burst into my unsullied vagina. He never expected to have me that first outing, and anyway felt some sort of responsibility over me towards Ronnie. But I gave him no room for excuse or restraint,

65

I was co-operative to the point of leaving him breathless. When we got home Ronnie knew immediately, and was affronted.

I suppose I had Cliff in me a dozen times, in his car, on the grass, once very comfortably on the spun-rubber mattress of a brand-new caravan in his darkened motor showroom. Then he went to another job up north. I had no regrets at his leaving. My curiosity was stayed, my mind clear, as a badly aching tooth once filled can be comfortably forgotten. As for my virginity, I regarded that as an overvalued fragment of medieval property law. And Cliff never realized that I was a virgin. I was sure of that. It was a flattering distinction which I found afterwards I shared with Sally Bowles.

I certainly never loved Cliff. I have never loved anyone but Kit. I used him as a practical means to a practical end, an animated dildo. I was glad the experiment brought itself to a finish, because the disturbance was upsetting my concentration on my work. And my work came before everything.

But Cliff wrote to me. Long rambling pages filled with the sad, stereotyped, passionate outpourings of the inarticulate. The letters disgusted me. They nailed me in my place. They were savage accusations of my deliberate blindness to his mental inferiority, and the guilt stung horribly. I tried to stifle the correspondence, but he wrote of how much he admired me. That infuriated me. He had *no right to*, I was someone a person like Cliff could never understand. I forget how I got rid of him. Perhaps he found another girl. I was sensitive about the affair, even so long after, and detested Ronnie knowing so many of the details. Perhaps that was the only reason I disliked by brother at all.

Ronnie delicately dropped his spent match into a small white china ash-tray on the mantelpiece, inscribed in blue and gold CHEDDAR GORGE. 'Poor old Cliff. Now you don't want to know about him.'

I said nothing.

'I suppose it's understandable.' He gave his mocking grin again. 'You ought to invent some drug to give people loss of memory.'

'Then you could take it and forget you were ever up in court.'

'A youthful prank.' He broke a little ash from his cigar on the edge of the china dish. 'The kids get up to a hundred things worse these days. It started me on my business career.'

'Your business!'

'It's quite legal, don't worry. I don't like the old folk knowing too much about my private life, that's all.'

'Or me knowing?'

'I suppose so. Still, what have we to complain of, either of us? We've come a long way.'

'I'm going further. Before much longer I'm likely to be a professor.'

But he was unimpressed. The degrees of academic standing mean humiliatingly little to the public – doctors, professors, schoolmasters, are all learned, possibly odd, and vaguely bogymen.

'What do Mum and Dad want this bungalow for?' Ronnie complained. 'I've only just got her a washing-machine. Automatic, best there is. She's already after a tumble-dryer.'

'They seem to have set their mind on it. I suppose we ought to help if we can.'

'They're not worth it. No, they're not. You despise them, don't you? I do. Come on, Ann, admit it. You despise them both.'

I looked at him uncertainly. 'Why should I?'

'Because they're ignorant. You despise anyone who's less clever than you are. And the less clever they are the harder you spit on them. Look at Cliff. Look at me. I don't mind. I don't need to be clever in your way. Do you know why *I* despise Mum and Dad? Because they're common. You see, I'm a snob.'

He gave me a hard look. He seemed to be challenging me to argue with him, perhaps to convince him that he was wrong. Of course, I did scorn my parents, more honestly than he did. My brother's attitude towards them, like his attitude towards so much, was a grisly mixture of bravado and fright. I had come to look down on them, gradually but steadily, during my medical course at Princess Victoria's. Only then I began to see what had urged me to study medicine. I had brains, and with brains I

67

could rise above my family, above my mean circumstances, and above my dull acquaintances. As a medical woman I should become important, admired, and strikingly independent. It was the same force which directed women with other attributes into becoming famous actresses or famous courtesans.

Then a curious incident occurred the night before I was to leave for my first resident job at Princess Victoria's. My parents had given a party in the room where I now stood arguing with Ronnie. It was an overwhelmingly grand occasion for them, showing me off, newly-qualified, to their friends. There were some twenty people there, an official from the local Council, the partners from my father's firm. My mother had made an enormous cake with CONGRATULATIONS ANN in pink icing. It was like a wedding-breakfast, but better – a girl could get herself married any day, with no wits nor particular effort at all.

Afterwards, amid the crusts of sandwiches, the crushed cigarette ends, and the dirty glasses, I found myself alone with my father. He sat in his chair half-asleep, though he never drank much. Perhaps it was the strain of a whole evening's jokes.

He pulled out the old-fashioned pocket watch which he kept for ceremonial occasions. 'It's well past eleven.'

'I must go to bed.' Standing by the empty fireplace, I stubbed out my cigarette. 'I've a busy day tomorrow.'

'Won't you stay awhile, Ann?' he had asked shyly. 'We could have a little talk. We never seemed to have much chance, you and me.' As I said nothing, he continued, 'We're proud of you, Ann.'

'I'm proud of you, too.' I was lying. 'You had to put up with a lot while I was a student.'

He dismissed this with a faint gesture. 'It was worth it, to see you going out into the world on your own.'

'I've been at home far too long. But I'll miss it.'

'It isn't exactly Buckingham Palace.' He hesitated. 'You're twenty-two, and I never had a fatherly talk with you. Perhaps I should have, years ago, when you were a girl.' I began to feel horribly uneasy. 'You know – "Always say no and keep your legs crossed".' He gave a sharp laugh at this observation, which was remarkable for him, an intensely prudish man. I supposed it showed how embarrassed he felt. Then he added, 'What's the point of me giving you advice about anything? God knows, you're far more learned than me in those sort of things.'

I felt sorry for him. Not only had the poor man been denied the pleasures of a father's duty, but our positions had become reversed – I was the dominant one, to be respected, listened to, and sought for advice. I wondered if he felt he had bred a monster, whose values he was totally unable to grasp.

'I'll only say this,' he continued. 'Know yourself, girl. You're a strange mixture of the lion and the lamb. But I know you'll always respect the honour of the family.'

I thought he was joking. The honour of our family must have been a tawdry thing indeed. Then I saw he was serious, and I found myself crying. Next I was sitting in his lap kissing him, while he patted and comforted me as when I was a child. It was the only natural and spontaneous action I had taken in the house for five years.

After a minute or two we both became aware of our foolishness. I sprang up abruptly, without speaking or looking at him, and left the room.

The next morning I took a taxi to Princess Victoria's, with my pair of cheap suitcases, my cardboard carton of books, and my microscope in its varnished wooden box. I had been allotted the worst room in the residents' quarters, at the end of a long corridor over out-patients', one of a pair next to Iris Quiply, the future Member of Parliament. It was hardly big enough to contain the white-painted iron hospital bed, the deal dressing-table with cracked mirror, the bookcase and lopsided wardrobe. Continuity in the hospital's work being essential, my predecessor had moved out within the hour, leaving her hair-slides, spent tubes of make-up, old medical journals, laddered stockings, and other bits of personal rubbish everywhere. I busily arranged my books, my three dresses, my cheap toilet things, my stethoscope and rubber percussion hammer. I felt an incredible burst of elation. I had my own room, I was my own mistress, I had left home irrevocably, for ever. My face flushed with excitement, I sat on the edge of the bed covering it with my hands, starting to giggle and laugh out loud. Everything which mattered lay ahead. At twenty-two I had at last severed the umbilical cord.

On the wet evening of that supper in Barnet, Ronnie managed to leave the seaside bungalow still vague, but he promised Mum her tumble-dryer.

11

A GOOD MOMENT to catch Ma Saintsbury was one-thirty on a Monday afternoon, when she had her meal sent on a tray from the staff dining-room to the dean's office, and sat alone working through a week's accumulated business. In clinical surgery, forgoing your lunch-hours is a sign of established success.

'Why, it's Ann.' She was sitting at her old-fashioned desk, finishing her coffee and glancing at *The Times*. 'Any more news from the cyclova front?'

'Not a thing.' Automatically, I addressed her more loudly than normal. 'A formal acknowledgement of my report, that's all.'

'How long now since you sent it?'

'Three weeks today.'

'I'd chase the blighters up. Make a nuisance of yourself. Don't let them think it's all been some nasty dream.' She folded the newspaper with a sigh. 'Do you imagine there's going to be another war?'

It was a frequent question of hers, as though inquiring about the weather prospects.

'People seem to have forgotten the last one so quickly,' she observed sombrely.

You poor dear woman! I thought. Thank God we have already had longer to forget our war in peace than our parents to forget theirs.

'The blitz was *so* so terrible. I was here you know, in the hospital, before I joined the Army. They came every night in the winter of 1940. I used to operate among sandbags, down in the basement under the casualty department. I don't think it was really very safe if we'd had a direct hit. The ordinary people went down the Tube. The Government wouldn't let them in at first. I suppose they were afraid of panic, or mass-drowning, or perhaps damage to railway property. We made several silly mistakes with civilian morale in the early days. We didn't even fire the guns. We were afraid of hitting our own night-fighters, who unfortunately hit nothing. Then we let the guns and the searchlights blaze away, and though they still didn't hit very much the *son et lumière* cheered us all up underneath. It was really quite pretty, watching the beams fingering the clouds.'

I listened patiently. I had two favours to ask her. 'I was only a baby. I was evacuated with my mother to Essex.'

'Enjoying your extra milk, cod-liver oil, vitamins, and fresh air? How strange that those Dorniers, Heinkels, and Junkers were the unwitting harbingers of the welfare state. That's how it began, you know. It was the first time the Government took any real responsibility for its children. The idea would have stuck, socialism or not. I remember that terrible fire-raid on the night of the full hunter's moon.' Her voice took quite a fond ring. 'The Huns were awfully clever. They waited till the Thames was at lowest ebb, then sent down land-mines first to smash the water-mains and drive the fire-fighters to cover. We thought it was going on every night till the end of the war. They certainly had no apparent reason to stop. By then the people had started breaking into the Tube stations, or simply bought tickets and wisely stayed below the ground as long as the Germans were above it. They flopped everywhere. I saw it. Even on the stopped escalators, with all those girls advertising stockings and undies staring at them.'

'I've seen the drawings by Henry Moore in the Tate,' I told her. 'They're very touching.'

Kit had shown them to me. It was strange to think of his fighting in a war in which I had been an infant and a liability.

'Later we got everything properly organized with bunks, canteens, playrooms, and so on. I used to go down to check the first-aid posts. The stations got quite cheerful, with sing-songs, funny men from the B.B.C., lots of clergymen, and American senators getting themselves photographed in tin hats. There was a tremendous mateyness. Such a pity it didn't last after the war. But I suppose for the very first time in our history, the bombs were something which fell with equal generosity on all classes.'

I smiled. '"The Dunkirk Spirit"?'

Ma Saintsbury snorted. '*That's* been devalued like everything else. It makes me mad, hearing it invoked by any threadbare politician inviting us to suffer for his mistakes.' She paused, and added pensively, 'Do you suppose the blitz was the sunset of the British Empire? At least it was a blazingly glorious one.'

'I only think there's an enormous revulsion against war of any sort,' I remarked. 'Among the young people, at least. Which is reasonable enough, as they're the ones who'd have to do the fighting.'

'I do hope you're right. I'd be too old now to do anything. I should hate that.'

'I wonder if I might ask you to look at my draft application for Longfield, Dame Christina?' This was my first favour.

'Of course you may, Ann.'

I opened a cardboard file on her desk. During the past week my application had pushed even cyclova down the ladder of my mind. Ma Saintsbury read carefully through my two sheets of typed foolscap.

'This seems splendid, Ann. It's so nice writing about yourself for a job, isn't it? You can throw modesty to the winds.'

'I also wondered if you could advise me on my choice of referees?'

'Who had you in mind?'

'I need three. First, Sir John Osgood.'

She nodded. 'Chairman of the Society for Contraceptive Knowledge. And of course of practically everything else. Very useful. You know him well?'

'His daughter happened to be a patient of mine when I was registrar at the Canonbury. I've seen a lot of him since – been to lecture his Society, that sort of thing. He's interested in my "morning after" pill.'

'And the second one?'

73

'Andrew Bramlington.'

'A wise choice. Bound to be next President of the Royal College of Obstetricians. And an admirer of yours – professionally speaking, of course.'

'I wondered if you would consent to being the third, Dame Christina?'

'I should be honoured to find myself in such company.' She drew a sheet of paper towards her, and continued in a business-like way, 'Let's think who's likely to be on the selection committee. The vice-chancellor, of course, Lord Wrotham. He's a dreadful ass. A life peer, who made such a mess of running a nationalized industry, I suppose the Government felt he could do less damage in a university.'

Ma Saintsbury had a valuable store of pointed gossip.

'My Pal Tilly Dawes, naturally.' She jotted down the names. 'There's a vote in your pocket. I had another letter from her yesterday. With her United Nations hat on, she wants someone to run the population bureau in Geneva.'

'That could be a wonderful job – the population troubles of the whole world on your desk.'

She smiled. '"Megamedicine."'

'At its most effective,' I said firmly. 'Birth now sets a bigger problem to us than death.'

'These international jobs are very much what you make them,' said Ma Saintsbury knowingly. 'There're some awful idlers, neurotics, and drunkards sponging on the U.N. They're all installed to suit some subtlety or other of international diplomacy. Personally, I think Tilly should send an old chicken like me, to baffle the South American delegates. The Swiss air does terrible things to their passions.' She wrote down another name. 'Janet Bickens is a headmistress and a Catholic, so you may be in trouble there. But she's broad-minded, or as broad as they're allowed to get. And Jim Samways. A local man, county councillor, pillar of the establishment, sound as a bell, pathetically flattered by his association with the founts of learning. The founts *do* spurt from the most surprising places these days, don't they? Who would have imagined Longfield as a *university*?'

'There was a first-class technical college there, surely?'

'My dear, at a technical college you merely do things. At a university you are supposed to think. There'll be a few other odd-bods, but they'll take their cue from the vice-chancellor, and he'll take his from Tilly. Heard of any other applicants?' I shook my head. 'Then you should be home and dry.'

'I do hope so,' I said fervently. 'I do hope so.'

'I like to hear that, Ann. Enthusiasm always helps.'

But I knew in my heart that excitement over the job was outshone by my excitement over the things it would bring. I already saw the house, the paddock, and the horse. We could start saving at the bank. Perhaps in the country Kit would stop drinking so much.

'There's just another thing.' This was my second favour. 'I'm giving Liz Kilson – Liz Monkhood – a clinical assistant's job in the family planning clinic. I suppose that's all right with the hospital committee? She doesn't want any money, though we might cover her expenses, I suppose.'

'Liz working again? Her husband's far too rich to permit such foolishness.'

'They've had a domestic crisis.'

'Oh, I see. Yes, of course, Ann, get her along. What the aisle leads away from us the divorce court so often returns, a rustier but humbler and more understanding doctor.'

She forgot for the moment that I had undergone the same process, and looked flustered. I gathered up my folder without comment. 'I'll telephone Lloyd at General Drugs this afternoon.'

'Turn the screw, Ann, turn the screw.' As I reached the door, she added, 'At Longfield, you'll have the trial of settling into a new community.'

'That's one of the things I'm looking forward to.'

'Don't you get lonely on your own?'

'I've plenty of friends.'

Ma Saintsbury turned towards her own papers. 'I always hoped your exile from the lush pastures of marriage wouldn't be permanent. I've no cause for despondency, surely?'

I smiled. 'Not despondency, perhaps. Only patience.'

I wondered if she had somehow got to know about Kit. Ma Saintsbury somehow got to know about everything.

75

12

I WENT HOME that evening resolved to type out my final application for Longfield, and I wish that I had.

But Kit wanted to visit the pub. He seemed in a vaguely surly mood, which I knew would bring a resentful snap if I tried dissuading him. As I finished washing up our meal I nearly decided to pack him off by himself. I didn't really believe he would pick up a woman, or telephone one of his old girl-friends. He certainly wouldn't seek out his wife, however drunk he got. But sometimes, beside him in a bar, as he talked away to his circle, I saw the women's glances tinted with desire. Or I probably imagined I did. It was a fleeting suspicion which crept upon me like a mood. But fundamentally I was frightened of losing Kit. It wasn't the titillating, baseless torture which many women inflict on themselves. He had casually deserted a dozen or so women already, and if I felt that I alone had the qualities to hold him, I never dared to tell myself too loudly. I neatly folded my apron, hung it in its precise place behind the kitchen door, and told him I was coming.

'Ten minutes,' I said. 'All I need to make myself beautiful.'

He seemed genuinely glad, and I was pleased.

We went to the Hat and Feathers, about half a mile up the King's Road in the fashionable direction. It was a nondescript pub, with neither the preserved charm of the past nor the pressing comfort of the present. There was one U-shaped counter, from which partitions stalled off the three bars, public, saloon, and private. I often wondered who patronized the little private bar. Introverts, shamefaced maidenly tipplers, shaky alcoholics? It raised Victorian visions of children sent with jugs for father's supper-beer. But now father drank it from self-opening cans, the acme of our civilization.

At the door of the saloon bar, Kit turned. 'Money.'

I felt in my bag for the five-pound note which I had meant to push into his pocket. He gave no acknowledgement. He never made any sign of noticing I gave him money, and I should have been appalled, ashamed for a week, if he had. I suspected I was wrong in the way I handled these affairs. Kit had a little money of his own. He claimed that his handbooks brought in more than the mean rewards of most modern novels, there were small irregular sums from a one-man literary agency in Fleet Street, run by a friend in whom Kit invested long ago after some large but sadly exceptional win at the races. I paid the bills and gave him cash whenever he asked for it. I should have made him a set allowance every month, or simply handed over my salary to him, had I been properly sensitive to his self-respect. But I preferred our system as it was, and I stuck to it.

It was Monday, so the pub was almost empty. But two couples we knew were there already. One consisted of a middle-aged actor doing mostly radio, and therefore unimportant – I had learnt such shades of distinction from Kit – with a middle-aged blonde wife who drank rum in cider. The other was Andrew the publisher and his young wife with protuberant eyes and a nervous manner, whom I suspected was suffering from over-activity of the thyroid gland. They all seemed pleased to see Kit. I was pleased myself, sitting on a stool, watching him talking and joking, holding the floor, a lord for a while in his fuzzy-edged kingdom. To the pair of women laughing with him I said in my mind, 'Not you, tonight, but me, in an hour or so shall have him with me and in me.' Unless, of course, he got so drunk as to be incapable.

Perhaps because he was basically depressed and disturbed, Kit that night did drink more than usual. I never tried to keep up with him, though I had a strong head. So have many women doctors – I had watched McRobb finish half a bottle of whisky and still talk lucidly about her perinatal mortality statistics. If people bored me I drank, and then I suppose I bored them. I liked the comfort of alcohol, and excused myself that it might have been drugs instead, knowing for certain of two women from Princess Victoria's who had fallen into the soft embrace of morphine, and suspecting there were more. It was easy to lay hands on, and I could understand how a hypodermic caress tempted a woman whom the caresses of men had passed by.

When the pub closed, Kit suggested, 'Let's call on Roland and Jane.'

'Yes, they're fun.' They were two friends in Chelsea Square. I must have been half-drunk myself to agree.

I at least could sense after a few minutes that Roland and Jane were unpleased with their involuntary hospitality. They must have been going to bed. They gave us a couple more drinks. Kit repeated a lot he had said in the pub, rather less coherently. We went home in a taxi, Kit spilling coins all over the road as he paid the driver.

As I pulled off my dress and threw it over the bedroom chair I said, 'I should have stayed at home to write that thing for Longfield.'

'You're not going to Longfield,' said Kit.

I glared at him. I sat on the edge of the bed and stripped off my stockings. He started undressing in silence. After some moments I asked, 'What do you mean?'

Kit threw his trousers on top of his jacket on the floor. 'What do you want to bury yourself in some half-baked pseudo-university for?'

'I'm an academic.' I had the grotesque tottering dignity of alcohol. 'An academic's proper place is in a university.'

'They're building them everywhere these days, like petrol-stations.'

'That's not fair. Longfield offers a lot from being new.'

'Yes, prefabricated buildings and prefabricated ideas.'

'Longfield represents my ambition. I'm sticking to my ambition.'

'Why, for God's sake? You baffle me. You could do as well for yourself in London.'

'I'm sick of London. I want calm, the quiet calm of university life. You know, that's something I never had? I never went to

Oxford like you. And I resent it.' In my bra and girdle I reached for a cigarette from the dressing-table, and used three matches to light it. 'I've achieved all my other ambitions. At least, the ones I had left after that bugger Henry messed up my life for me. But I couldn't do anything about going to a proper university. Now I can. See?'

'You always had a rather Disneyland view of Oxford.'

'And I want a house. A house with a lawn where I can swing on one of those canopied chair things in the summer. With a rack under the sunniest window for indoor plants. Long and green and trailing on to the carpet. I'll water them with a special little can. Do you know, I've never lived in a house detached from another house? I've never lived in a house of my own where you go upstairs to bed. Henry was mad on flats. He seemed to think they were smarter. That's another thing which shows how stupid he was.'

'But Christ, Ann! If that's all you want we can get it in Ealing.'

Cigarette drooping, I fumbled to undo my bra. 'I want to mix with academic people. They're considerate and gentle.'

He gave a loud laugh. 'They're as spiteful as Glasgow razor-gangs. Clever and conceited, a horrible mixture. And generally dull, which is worse. Remember I showed you north Oxford? There's your little dream-villa for you. Rows and rows of them, red-brick and seething with malevolence and frustration. You can smell it, like bad drains.'

'You're warped.'

'You're getting above yourself, aren't you?' He was naked now, and sat on the bed beside me. 'I know what it is.' He looked at me mockingly. He was sobering up. He always did before me, a dangerous imbalance. 'I've made a discovery. You imagine you're what the television masses call an "intellectual". Brilliant woman don, witty and charming, stuffed with apt quotations like a Périgord goose, vomiting them up prettily at little sherry parties, trading second-hand epigrams with second-rate minds, and a fine line in profound rubbish to reassure yourself you're worth your job. That's how you see yourself, isn't it? Well, it's beyond you. Everything worthwhile inside

79

your head, every original thought, I put there. You're really a dull little woman.'

'That's a conceited bloody lie!'

'It isn't. And you know it. At least you're clever enough not to deceive yourself quite that easily.'

'How can you call me a dull little woman?' I demanded furiously. However muzzy I was, I had a frightening suspicion that he might be right. It was unlike Kit to fight me seriously unless he was sure of himself. Searching for something wounding to say, I told him, 'I'll get more money at Longfield. That will please you, won't it?'

'I admit that I'm rapidly ageing, but I agree my services are worth more.'

'That's the most horrible thing you've ever said to me.' I wondered how long it had been in the back of his mind. 'It's horrible, horrible! If you don't enjoy making love to me, I'd rather you cleared out at once.'

'But I do enjoy it. You've a great talent and appreciation for the bed. As Hemingway put it of another woman who used her money to glue her man.'

I tried to hit him, but the alcohol had made me ataxic and he easily grabbed my wrist.

'Let me go, let me go!' I cried, struggling.

'You're oversexed, that's your trouble.'

'I'm *not* oversexed.'

'Yes you are. I've never known a woman so fond of it.'

'That's biologically normal, isn't it?'

'Biologically! Perhaps you're right. There aren't any under-sexed women, only scared ones.'

'I've only been fucked by two men, apart from you. That's the truth. And one of those was Henry.'

'Henry of the ice-cold prick.'

'Henry could be all right sometimes,' I said, trying to be insulting. 'Better than you.'

'You once told me a long day's operating always made him randy. That's disgusting.'

'You're jealous of him.'

'Not when I've got you like this.'

80

He twisted my arm and I screamed.

'You're a nymphomaniac.' I tried to bite him, but he pulled away easily. He was becoming practised with my antics. Still holding my arm tight he continued tauntingly, 'The case of nymphomania, Doctor? Does it exist? Is it a male fantasy? The solitary lustful woman in the room next door, in every crummy hotel you stay in. The farmer's tarty daughter you're going to meet on a country walk. The sexed-up typist who keeps bending down to pick up paper-clips while you try to look up her skirt.'

Most rows start with the general and end with the personal, but with Kit it was the other way round. I began to feel tired. I was crying, tears running down my face and dripping on to my bare breasts.

'I want you to go. To get out now, in the middle of the night.'

'I won't. If I did, you'd pick up someone even worse for you.'

'You make me sound like a whore.'

'Isn't there something of a whore in most women? After all, it's an overwhelmingly feminine occupation.'

'You don't give a damn about me, you sod.' He dropped my arm. We started to calm down. 'Can't you understand how much I love you?'

'I do, perfectly. What you don't understand is the *way* I love *you*.'

'There aren't ways.'

'I'm more organized about it than you are.'

'You've had enough women to try your hand on.'

'It isn't so coarse as you care to put it. My idea is to catch a train, enjoy a pleasant journey, and have it carry me somewhere. You'd just throw yourself underneath it.'

'Where's this particular train going? Nowhere.' My cigarette had dropped on to the floor. I looked for it, saw it had gone out, and kicked it somewhere. 'Time goes on and on. Myra isn't any more amenable.'

'I'm working on her.'

'She still hopes to get you back. Or she wants to get you back, at any rate.'

Kit yawned. The scene was starting to exhaust him, or to bore him. 'She'll find another man. It always happens.'

81

'At her age?'

He smiled. 'That's a nice slice of healthy bitchiness. It reassures me that you're normal.'

'You can hardly expect me to look upon her as an elder sister.'

'Yes, you do love me,' he said thoughtfully. 'So constantly it's easy to take it as a matter of course.'

I decided surlily to ignore this call for a truce. He had called me a dull little woman. That to my mind was worse than being a nymphomaniac or a whore.

I went into the bathroom, wondering if he was right about the sex business, if I was dominated by it. But I could control myself, I decided. When Henry left me, I could have cut loose with a dozen men. But perhaps it was my disease which did the controlling. I caught sight of my aspirin bottle on the glass shelf over the basin. I was pretty ill after Henry's departure, and arthritis would put off even the most eager searcher for a spare cunt. I tried to remember if I even felt like it. Any illness knocks the sex out of you, though with T.B., they say, you get more lecherous. Hence Lawrence again. I decided against my nightly dose of aspirin. After the alcohol, it would irritate my stomach.

When I got back, Kit was lying across the bed, snoring. I managed to cajole him under the covers, still asleep, and got in myself. That was the time when usually anxieties and perplexities started buzzing in my brain, but that night my head was an empty hive. I could think only about Kit, snoring beside me. Not with any particular feelings of worry or hate, but just a shuffled pack of visions flipping before my eyes of Kit moving about our flat or our London haunts. It had been our worst row for a long time. It left me in an emotional vacuum, quite tranquil, as though I'd been taking drugs. Perhaps that was subconsciously what we quarrelled for.

I had no idea of the time, but it was still dark when Kit woke me by fondling between my legs. I lay on my back motionless, excitedly realizing that he was making love to me. I snatched at his body, pulling him on to me, kicking off the bedclothes, flinging my legs wide, heaving up my pelvis for his penis to plunge into me. I held him tight, tight, tight, with arms and legs, head back, breathless with the pressure of his chest, feeling him stirring faster and faster among my lower viscera, biting his neck, crying, 'Sex, sex, sex!' and, as I felt my orgasm coming, shouting at him to twist my arm.

Masochism. Sado-masochism. Always running together, needing each other, male and female, gold and grey threads gloriously intertwined in the most wonderfully breathtaking of tapestries.

I always enjoyed being woken and copulating quickly, half-dreaming and half-awake. When I first married Henry I bought an alarm-clock, but he never cared much for the idea.

13

KIT AND I woke shamefaced, and ate our cornflakes in a mood of oversweet reasonableness.

'Of course I'll shelve my application, darling, if that's what you really want,' I told him.

'No, no, I wouldn't hear of it. I could never forgive myself if you made such a sacrifice.' He grinned. 'Just think how you could throw it in my face for years.'

'I know you don't like the idea of leaving London.'

'I'm rather an old dog to change his kennel. And I must say I'm not particularly attracted by the intellectually *nouveaux riches* who are bound to infect such places. Am I being vain? But I do get so bored with pretentiousness.'

'Of course you're not vain. Though we could be choosy, make our friends at leisure. After all, I'll be in the job for the next thirty years.'

'I'd another reason for wanting to stay in town.' He looked proud. 'I've decided to take a job myself.'

'But, darling, what about the novel?'

'That's almost finished. I was going to see Jim at the agency. He could find something for me. He's millions of contacts. Perhaps a job in television? Everyone seems to work in television these days. Research, synopses, that sort of thing. Later they might let me try a script or two. I'd make a lot of money. It's exciting, isn't it?'

'It's thrilling.'

After the storm we papered the splits in the sails with good resolutions. And we always thought them weatherproof at the time.

'You'd be a famous scriptwriter,' I said cosily. 'I'd be a professor.'

'Why do you *want* to be a professor?'

I considered this, holding my steaming coffee-cup in both hands. 'For a platform. Who listens to me now, reader in a small department of an insignificant medical school? My ideas only rustle a few dry pages in the back of scientific journals. As a professor, people would have to sit up and take notice. Yes, I'll have influence. I might even stir an important tongue or two in my favour.'

'Or a mind or two, which would be much more difficult.'

'But neither of us need wallow in our sacrifices,' I pointed out. 'Why can't we stay on here? I can commute every day to Longfield. Thousands of people do it the other way round.'

'You'll get bored with the journey.'

'When I do, we can think about that house again. Is that a bargain?' He nodded. 'Or perhaps we should really buy a car and take driving-lessons?'

This notion for some reason struck us as hilarious, and did much to dissipate any lingering clouds. Then I caught sight of the clock. 'My God, I must dress. I've an appointment with that man Lloyd at ten.'

'You only rang him yesterday afternoon? That shows they think you're important.'

'Maybe so. But with this hangover, I'm afraid Ann is not at her best.'

At ten o'clock I sat again in the contemporary waiting-room in Piccadilly. The pubic-skirted secretary appeared, asking me up to Lloyd's office with such pressing charm she turned the invitation almost into a seduction. My mind still glowing from physical love, in the way a woman's does but never a man's, I wondered in the lift if Lloyd ever slept with her. I decided the secretaries of powerful organizations with ambitious executives must enjoy the strange workday modern nunhood of air hostesses and bunny girls. But it was unnatural, I thought sympathetically, for a man to be shut up eight hours a day with a pretty girl he couldn't lay hands on.

'I have Dr Sheriff, Mr Lloyd.'

85

'How very pleasant to see you again, Doctor.' The same creaking charm. 'I'm afraid we're adding a lot of bother to your busy life.'

'It isn't so busy. I've no patients in the accepted sense. I more or less make my own hours.'

'But you have a home to run as well?'

'No, I'm divorced. That's why I use my maiden name.' He invited me to the armchair. 'Possibly you know my former husband? He's Mr Tambling, a surgeon on at Aldersgate.'

Lloyd offered me the cigarette-box. 'I may have met him at one of our parties. You must come to the next one, Doctor. We try to get a few interesting people along, from abroad or outside the profession. Otherwise at these medical affairs one gets rather tired of always seeing the same faces. But that goes for all parties, I suppose.'

'You know another friend of mine – Charles Crawless.'

'Yes, we meet at the club frequently. A very likeable man. You must forgive me for not putting you completely in the picture about cyclova at our earlier meeting, Doctor,' he went on quickly. 'I was far too secretive. But, of course, I must be always aware of those above me.' He looked heavenwards. 'When Charles very trenchantly made the point that it was only right for you to know the facts, I saw that my reticence was an error. Will you accept my apologies?'

So far so good, I thought. 'I'd like to get this cyclova business cleared up in the next week or two, Mr Lloyd. I'm leaving Princess Victoria's and London altogether for a post at Longfield University. Where in due time,' I added to impress him, 'I shall become a professor, no less.'

'I congratulate you, Doctor.' He inclined his head gravely. 'That must be a very exciting prospect. Might I add, you'll do much to dispel the public image of a professor as an eccentric old man probably up to no good?'

I smiled. 'As far as you're concerned, I *am* up to no good.'

'Well, now you know exactly how big a project the cyclova operation is. I wouldn't suggest you were so naïve as to under-estimate the shock of your findings in our headquarters.' He rose from his chair and took a sheet of typed foolscap from the

86

table. 'As I promised, within an hour of receiving your report, every word was sent by telex to the States. Of course, I had photostats made for all our top people here.'

'And that's the reply?'

He nodded, sitting down with the paper on his knee. 'In America they called a board meeting – a special board meeting.' He seemed to think that I should be impressed by this. 'Advice was taken urgently from the leading experts in both endocrinology and haematology in the United States.'

'Who?'

He looked awkward. 'I know it's stupid, but again I am bound by secrecy. It is quite ridiculous, sometimes, how we are muzzled. But there it is. I know if I gave the names you would recognize them as people of the highest standing. They may be professional acquaintances of yours, or even personal friends.'

I began to have a sinking feeling. This elaborate speech would have no point had they accepted my findings. 'Yes, but what did you decide?' I asked briefly.

'Our board decided, after the most careful consideration, that the risk must be faced.'

'But that's criminal!'

He raised his eyebrows, but continued steadily, 'Let me point out one or two things, Doctor. I think they might put your mind at rest. In the first place, no responsibility for cyclova can possibly attach itself to you. Not a scrap. You have prepared your report, we have read it, and we have independently made up our minds. I have already dictated a letter to you plainly making this point.'

'Thank you,' I said ironically.

'You have done your professional duty, and if any untoward effects of cyclova *should* appear, nothing will disturb your conscience.'

'Isn't it rather presumptuous of you, claiming to understand my conscience?'

'Will you be patient with me? And understanding of me? I will tell you frankly our line of thought.' He leant forward, a man about to embark on a distasteful and worrying task.

87

'Surely you could not really imagine a concern like General Drugs taking chances with human health and life?'

'No. Humanity is your business.'

Ignoring this, he continued, 'We at General Drugs simply cannot believe that any untoward side-effects *will* appear. This product has been most thoroughly tested. Nothing whatever sinister was discovered. Nothing! It seemed to us the perfect contraceptive for world-wide distribution. Then came your report. Of course, I can understand how you feel about this work. It was a large part of your year's research, and naturally over-shadows anything that I or anyone else can tell you about cyclova. But try to see our view. General Drugs can take the picture as a whole, we are able to look at your findings coldly and without emotion. There is no discourtesy implied, Doctor. It is simply a matter of scientific assessment of the entire facts. Surely you must be with me there?'

'So your faceless men, huddled round a table somewhere in the middle of America, decided to put the whole world at risk to leukaemia?'

'We don't think there *is* a risk, Doctor.' His voice had a new note of firmness and finality.

'You thought me wrong in my methods? That I made a mistake?'

'Mistake?' He looked surprised. 'That's far too strong a word. Aberrant findings can creep into any form of research. Surely you'll agree with that, too?'

'You must all be mad.'

I was really angry now, and the hangover didn't help. I saw him glance quickly at the door, in the hope that his secretary might interrupt us. I thought fleetingly that he could hardly ring the bell and offer me another sherry.

'Very well, I've made one of the biggest errors in a laboratory since Max Pettenkofer swallowed live cholera organisms just to prove they were harmless. I'll accept that. What I *won't* accept is your failure to check my findings. Your failure to make *absolutely sure* that I'm wrong.'

'I'm afraid that's counsel of perfection. It's a matter of time. Marketing campaigns these days must be mounted with the

88

precision of military ones. The marketing people sometimes seem to have the rest of us by the scruff of our necks, and I deplore it. But there it is. The most modern methods are ours, and we must use them.'

'Or your competitors would outsell you?' He gave a faint shrug. 'But how long would you need? Six months? Two would do.'

'Even two months is a long time. But aren't we escaping from the point? We at General Drugs think cyclova is safe. If we didn't, we wouldn't market it at all. If we feel confident of going ahead, then we must go ahead to the utmost of our ability.'

'It's my stain, isn't it?' I was furious now, clenching and un-clenching my fists, digging my short nails into my palms. 'Your experts decided it was some cockeyed stuff invented by a crank. Didn't they? They said, "Don't panic, boys, the silly woman's used something she made up in the kitchen." That's why you won't take me seriously.'

Lloyd looked hard at me. 'The fact of your stain not being in general use did, I believe, have some influence with our board.'

I stood up, 'Right, Mr Lloyd. You flood the world with cyclova, I can't do anything about that. But I'll tell you what I *am* going to do. I'm going to make a fuss. I'm going to stir up trouble. Not only here and now, but at Longfield. I'm going to bombard everyone in earshot so stridently the public will over-hear and take some notice.'

'I should be the last to expect, or to wish, that you stifle your opinions, Doctor.'

'That's a pretty sentiment, when you've got the laws of libel behind you. But you wait,' I threatened angrily, 'you just wait.'

He bowed. 'Everyone at General Drugs will wait with the greatest interest.' It was the first time he had been openly rude. 'Meanwhile, I must offer you my personal good wishes for your new appointment.'

I disregarded the lift, hurried down the stairs, and almost ran out of the building. I hailed a taxi and sat biting my lip, shaking with anger. I was appalled at General Drugs unleashing a possible killer on the world. But the personal slight stood in my mind just as large and as darkly. They had ignored me, brushed me aside. They thought I was a silly little woman. That was worse than being a dull one.

As the taxi reached Princess Victoria's I began to calm down. Perhaps Lloyd was right. Perhaps I did see my work on cyclova out of proportion. The layman looks at the sun with wonder, the astronomer sees it as a pin-point among uncountable bigger suns. And I was always so dogmatic. Once I made up my mind, nothing would budge me. And if I were wrong, I should be doing almost as much damage keeping cyclova from the world as General Drugs by selling it if I were right. Perhaps I really was silly.

I paid off the cab and hurried up to my laboratory, deciding to be as good as my word. To make a fuss – but how? Letters to the newspapers? Chasing after Members of Parliament? I could hardly chain myself to the railings outside Lloyd's Piccadilly office. Then I said, 'Damn!' Lights had started flashing in the corner of my eye. Bloody migraine. I hoped I'd remembered some ergotamine tartrate in my bag. I was feeling unbearably tense. I counted in my head. It was almost twenty-eight days since I wrote that first letter about cyclova. Another crisis, and I had to be menstrual again.

14

ONCE EVERY THREE months I gave a short lecture to the junior nurses on contraception. It fell that time on a Tuesday, exactly a week after my stormy interview with Lloyd. I invited Liz to come along. It was the first morning of her return to the profession which for six of its busy years had the distraction of training her.

We met in the staff dining-room for a cup of coffee before-hand. 'I'm never quite certain,' I told her, 'if I'm supposed to arm the girls with a little professional knowledge the better to handle the female patients, or with a little private knowledge the better to handle the male students.'

'What's Matron think?' asked Liz. She had her elbows on one of the plastic-topped tables, looking strange in a shining new white coat.

'My dear, we're terribly progressive now and call her the Director of Nursing Services. As she's married and a realist, I suspect which idea's in the back of her mind. Though of course such notions must never come to the ears of the hospital com-mittee. They'd be horrified. Those worthy non-medical ladies and gentlemen still believe women climb into bed on their honeymoons in a state of imperforate expectancy.'

'They ought to read the papers.'

'Or talk to McRobb. She's got figures to prove the hymen has generally vanished by fifteen. She claims that shortly it'll be shed with the milk-teeth.'

'Or perhaps they've just got short memories?' suggested Liz. As I looked at my watch she asked, 'What are the nurses like these days?'

'They don't change. Thank God a lab. job relieves me of the touchy diplomatic warfare. Though I suppose I'm too senior now to be a combatant.'

'They can be bloody when you're a houseman,' said Liz feelingly.

'The junior nurses were all right. They were dead scared of the hospital and everyone in it, and regarded women doctors as treading wonderful heights impossibly beyond reach.'

Liz finished her coffee. 'But I remember the staff nurses were bitches.'

'They generally knew just enough medicine to convince themselves they could do the job better.'

'A bitchy ward sister was horrible. I think ours spent her life discovering new ways to show us up in front of the patients.'

'Though a nice sister was wonderful, always calling you "Doctor" at the bedside, covering up your mistakes, giving you coffee and biscuits just like the men.'

'I suppose there's sex in it,' observed Liz sombrely.

'I don't think they cared for our competition. Particularly as we could haul men into our bedrooms more or less as we fancied.'

'I always envied the men on the staff. They had all the nurses fawning on them and falling in love with them. Or at least feeling that they were supposed to.'

But it was time to end this licking of well-healed wounds.

My talk was in the small, bright, over-polished lecture-room of the nurses' home. Liz sat in the front row. About twenty girls were behind at schoolroom desks, shining-faced, spotless in their impossible Victorian uniforms, expectant that the talk would prove more entertaining than their usual discourses on such things as the bones and diet for peptic ulcers.

'There is only one absolutely reliable and completely non-toxic means of preventing conception,' I started. 'And that is the total avoidance of intercourse. However, this is not wildly popular, so science must do its best.'

I stood in front of the blackboard in my white coat. Ann Sheriff, the professional woman, doctor of medicine in the University of London, author of various scientific papers, descendant of Elizabeth Blackwell, Sophia Jex-Blake, and the rest, arbiter of life and death, born and unborn. They didn't laugh at my little joke. Perhaps they were shy. Or perhaps they thought I was serious.

'The periodic avoidance of intercourse is common enough among couples who for personal or religious reasons prefer to keep the scientist out of the bedroom,' I continued. 'As you already know, only one egg is shed by the woman during each menstrual cycle, about the middle of the month. Neither this egg nor the male spermatozoa can live for more than three days inside the female reproductive tract. So the couple must abstain between the seventh and nineteenth day, when the egg is dangerously at large. This is known as the "safe period", or the "rhythm method". But it's rather risky, particularly if the woman hasn't a menstrual cycle which runs like clockwork.'

I saw them all busily taking notes. I enjoyed lecturing. Perhaps there is something of an exhibitionist in all women.

'Another simple method is *coitus interruptus*, which is remarkably popular, particularly for what I might call casual copulation. It certainly *looks* a hundred per cent effective. The man withdraws on orgasm, and there are the sperms, harmlessly fired into the air. But alas, the temptation to prolong the fleeting moment is often too strong. The failure-rate is put about twenty-five per cent.'

McRobb had such strong views on this ineffective practice she wanted posters warning of its dangers stuck in public lavatories alongside those warning of V.D.

'The rubber condom is obtainable, and indeed seems disposable, almost anywhere.'

I took one from the pocket of my white coat, tearing the foil packet, unrolling it and holding it up like a toy balloon. They became more interested. From my other pocket I took a neat white case, opening it and explaining, 'This is the vaginal diaphragm, or Dutch cap. You see, it is just a circle of rubber with a coiled spring in the rim. It should be used with a spermicidal jelly, which it holds against the cervix of the uterus to destroy the sperms. The failure rate is some five per cent. It's a useful method, allowing contact between the two partners.'

Wasn't it a Frenchman who said love was the mutual friction

93

of skins? It certainly must have been an Englishman who said condoms were like washing your feet with your boots on.

'But the diaphragm has to be retained for eight hours, which can be uncomfortable for a woman inclined to have intercourse in the morning. And some women can't get it in. You'd be surprised at the widespread ignorance about such details.'

They had stopped note-taking and were leaning forward eagerly. I had come up to expectations. 'Exhibit three is an intrauterine contraceptive device.' I produced one. 'All manner of ingenious plastic coils, loops, hooks, and spirals have been designed for insertion inside the uterus, no anaesthetic being needed. These I.U.C.D.s, as they're known, could be most valuable if used on a world-wide scale to make some sort of start at solving our population problems. Once fitted they need no more attention nor even thought – though admittedly they have sometimes been found to cause abdominal discomfort and intermenstrual bleeding. This might be overcome by more thorough research and more careful design.'

I felt compelled to add, 'In the eyes of some people, these I.U.C.D.s are abortifacients, not contraceptives. This is because they act by preventing the normal implantation in the uterine lining of the already fertilized ovum. In my view, the distinction cannot be made at such an early stage of conception – the fertilization of the egg and its implantation are part of the same single process. And the I.U.C.D. is not new. Once there was something called the Gräfenburg ring, made of pure silver, to be inserted into the wombs of high-born ladies. Little really ever changes, you see, only appearances do. Somewhere in the world is probably some weed, chewed by a tribe long extinct, whose very extinction sprang from the plant's property of inhibiting female ovulation. Which brings me to my last item, the pill.'

They started taking notes again. My final specimen, a gaily wrapped pharmaceutical package, wasn't so exciting.

'Let me explain how the pill works.' I started drawing with coloured chalks on the blackboard. 'It's really a beautifully simple piece of biochemistry. The pituitary gland, which as you know is situated at the base of the brain, secretes hormones which act upon the female ovary. In women of childbearing age these hormones come in monthly tides, stimulating the ovary to develop and extrude one single egg. The ripening egg itself is also a temporary endocrine gland, secreting its own hormones called "oestrogens". These affect the lining of the uterus and make it ready for the pregnancy which normally may follow.'

It was all oversimplified, but the poor girls had at the time to learn with equal intensity the basic elements of medicine, surgery, anatomy, cooking, sociology, waitressing, and general skivvying.

'Once the egg has been extruded from the ovary, the empty follicle produces yet another hormone, named "progesterone". This is the hormone which, by and large, controls the changes of pregnancy. Now, during pregnancy there are large amounts of oestrogen and progesterone circulating in the woman's blood. And their effect on the pituitary gland is to prevent it putting out the hormone which stimulates ovulation. Hence, if we can administer to the unpregnant woman extra oestrogen and progesterone, made not in her own glands but in our laboratories, we can do the same trick and simply stop her producing eggs at all. Without an egg there is no possibility of conception. The famous "pill" is generally a mixture of oestrogen and a substance analogous to progesterone, which cannot itself be given by mouth. So you see all women on the pill spend their lives in a state of permanent endocrinological pregnancy. I hope their husbands don't mind too much.'

I held up my packet. 'The woman swallows her pill for twenty-one days, then if she stops the lining of her uterus will be shed, giving her the appearance of a normal period. A woman taking the pill every day of her life needn't even appear to menstruate. But she might find that rather depressing, and think of the sad effect on the profits of the sanitary-towel manufacturers.' I wondered vaguely if General Drugs had a subsidiary making them. Quite probably. 'The pill also exerts an important indirect effect on the plug of mucus normally blocking the uterine cervix, an item which is now attracting the attention of research workers as having a possible role in contraception.'

I went on more meaningfully, 'But even the most ingenious modern pharmaceuticals, like the most ingenious modern domestic appliances, can present unexpected snags. Several undesirable side-effects have been found or suspected in the pills in current use, the most serious of which is thrombosis in the veins. Any drug with the slightest doubt about its safety to life should be abandoned, however beneficial it may seem to humanity in general and the pocket of the pharmaceutical company in particular.'

I gathered my exhibits. It would never do leaving them about when the sister-tutor followed me at the blackboard.

'Our study of oral contraception has taught us much about the mechanisms of human conception as a whole,' I ended. 'But our knowledge is still of only a corner of the process. Why should some women conceive and others not? Why should the same woman conceive at some times and not at others? What urges the sperm in its wriggling race through the cervix into the uterus, into the Fallopian tube leading towards the ovary, in search of the female's egg? It is a feat comparable less with swimming the Channel than the Atlantic. What finally brings the sperm to merge with the egg? It may be a chemical attraction. It may be electrical. It may be a visitation of the Holy Ghost.' They suspected I was joking, but I wasn't. 'We now know that many factors play a part in human fertility, internal and external. Temperature, climate, even altitude have some effect. The town of Potosi in the Andes had no baby born among the first Spanish settlers for fifty years.' I ended with my other little joke. 'Rather far-off, but just the place, I should say, for a sly week-end.'

One gave a little giggle. Another clapped. I was a success. I was one of the girls, one of them. Well, I was more fun than listening to the sister-tutor on bandaging.

15

'THAT WAS IMPRESSIVE,' said Liz. She seemed genuinely awed. 'I never imagined that I should sit at your feet in the lecture-room, Ann. Or perhaps I did. You always seemed to grasp things so quickly and explain them so easily. Do you remember when you coached me on chromosomes before our finals? Turner's syndrome, Klinefelter's syndrome, sickle haemoglobin, all that sort of thing. I still don't think I really understand, and thank God they didn't come into a question. It's nice to feel I don't need to know about them now.'

'Are you at all worried about taking this clinic, Liz?'

'I'm assuming that sister will know all the answers, as usual.'

'Mrs Robinson's very good,' I reassured her. 'She's part-time, with three kids of her own. She regards contraception as something of a prize joke played on Nature, which is perhaps the best attitude.'

'Or non-attitude?'

'Attitudes are awful, aren't they? Once people feel they have to strike one about anything whatever, it takes them over, they become frozen in it. It's quite bizarre, like the patients with their arms stuck in the air for hours in catatonic schizophrenia.'

We were picking our way from the nurses' home towards the out-patients' department amid the jumble of structures old and new, temporary and permanent, building and built, into which Princess Victoria's had grown. Wherever you stepped at the time there appeared to be piles of contractors' materials. They seemed to have become an integral part of the hospital's fabric.

'I can't stand cranks,' said Liz.

'As you might imagine, in this job I'm much exposed to them. You can't believe the fuss and trouble McRobb and I encountered over getting the clinic started. In this day and age, and in a London teaching hospital. It's fantastic. All sorts of stupid objections were raised, not only by the hospital committee, but by some of the medical staff, who ought to know better. You know, I'm still not allowed – well, not supposed – to see unmarried women. That's exactly the same as saying you mustn't put a guard in front of the fire before the children grow up.'

'It's always the men who produce these arguments, isn't it? They don't have to bear the bastards.'

'They say if you teach a girl contraception she'll get screwed more often. But an unmarried girl might well be getting more sex than a married one. And anyway, it's generally the same man.'

Liz began to hum an old Noel Coward tune. *'Don't put your daughter on the pill, Mrs Worthington, don't put your daughter on the pill. . . .'*

'That's only worth while if they *are* getting regular sex – if they're biologically married, so to speak. And most girls can't afford it. God knows why they can't get it on the National Health, like their barbiturates and tranquillizers.'

I wondered if Kit would have liked his daughter taking the pill. I had met her fleetingly with him in the King's Road. She had come back from France long-haired, wide-eyed, and tight-trousered, a sitting duck. But she wasn't my responsibility.

We had skirted the new concrete slab of the medical block to reach the even newer steel-and-glass out-patients' department. 'How about the Catholics on the hospital staff?' asked Liz.

'They didn't make too much fuss about the clinic. They just got together and wore a collective pained expression. No, I don't mind the Catholics at all. They just say what they believe, there's no logic about it however hard they try to dress up their views with reason. So it's futile arguing with them. And some stretch a point. You know – "Contraception is sinful, Mrs Jones, but last door on the right as you go out you'll find Dr Sheriff." In fact, I admire our Catholics. They've got to struggle under two sets of ethics, medical and spiritual, not like the rest of us. They've got a conscience. Which I haven't.'

'Conscience? Surely a form of anxiety-neurosis?' declared Liz. 'A guilt-complex, or what have you.'

'Maybe you're right. I've always believed it's not inborn but synthetic, built from a million psychological influences since we left our mothers' wombs and even before.'

We entered the supermarket-like out-patients' hall. 'My very first day in the hospital as a student,' Liz confessed, 'I felt sick, physically sick. Now I feel surprisingly at home. Remarkable, isn't it? Once you've been through an institution like Princess Victoria's, I think you're part of it for the rest of your life.'

'Ma Saintsbury would like to hear that.'

'It's a wonderful stimulant for me. I was getting terribly depressed. God, that sod Derek! There's someone without a conscience for you. Do you know what he's trying to do now?'

Down the length of the hall Liz talked earnestly of the soddishness – hardly the sodomy – of Derek. I'd noticed how she revelled in the details of her cloven marriage, while I even then loathed mentioning the crack-up of my own. But I had really hated Henry. I suspected that she loved Derek as much as ever.

Once a week I occupied the last room on the right before the out-patients' exit. With yet another obscure concession to delicacy or prudery, the card slotted into the door read, FAMILY CLINIC – I was denied my PLANNING. Inside was a small bright compartment with the usual desk and screened examination couch. Mrs Robinson was waiting in her white overall. So to my surprise was McRobb.

'Sheriff, Ma Saintsbury wants to see you,' McRobb said at once.

I had intended to stay in the clinic, holding Liz's hand. Now I should have to push her into the deep end. But I felt I could safely leave her with Mrs Robinson, the experienced N.C.O. with the raw young officer – a view Ma Saintsbury would certainly appreciate. I told Liz I'd be back, but left her looking profoundly doubtful.

McRobb and I made our way to the dean's office. Ma Saintsbury had been away for a week in Scotland, acting as external examiner in the surgery finals. It had been a useful interval, forcing me to simmer down after seeing Lloyd. When I had discussed his intransigence with McRobb, she agreed we should do nothing before seeking Ma Saintsbury's advice. We were both determined that I should make the threatened fuss. But we were sensible enough to see that a fuss, to be effective and not to recoil, must be a well-organized one.

Ma Saintsbury greeted us by asking, 'How's bouncy Liz enjoying her return to the fold?'

'She's already the best-dressed woman on the staff.'

Ma Saintsbury chuckled. 'It's delightful how she sees life as some swift-moving revue, with herself in the star part. Well, now – I gather you've had more trouble from these tedious drug people?'

'They're simply ignoring Ann,' said McRobb shortly. 'They're going ahead, pushing their poison on the world.'

'Would you mind speaking up a bit, Sandra? Coming home in the aeroplane seems quite to have upset my ears.'

I took over the conversation, recounting to Ma Saintsbury my meeting with Lloyd. She made notes, now and then interrupting me with a question, then leaned back in her chair and said, 'I *told* you they'd take advantage of your being a woman. Quite disgraceful. An attitude that's not only insulting but a hundred years out of date.'

'They need another Sophia Jex-Blake after them,' said McRobb grimly.

Ma Saintsbury looked at me admiringly. 'Perhaps they have?'

'Dame Christiua! I hope I'm not a militant female?'

A horrible thought. Severe necklines, tight lips, high principles, aggressive outbursts, and frigidity. But perhaps she was right? I wondered anxiously. I was certainly carrying a most unwomanly fight to General Drugs. Something to my relief, she replied briefly, 'My dear Ann, you're far too clever to be simply militant. So they've made up their minds for good and all?'

I nodded.

'It could be a very dangerous decision on their part.'

'I left them in no doubt about that.'

'As I understand it, they wouldn't go ahead with cyclova if the slightest risk were involved. The blockheads have simply decided that the slightest risk doesn't exist.'

'I took that as their attitude.'

Ma Saintsbury fiddled with her ball-point. 'Ann, may I ask you something important? Are you sure you didn't make a mistake in interpreting those blood-smears?'

'Perfectly.'

'And have you yourself any doubt whatever about the efficacy of the stain you used?'

'None.'

'Right,' said Ma Saintsbury. 'Let battle commence.'

McRobb immediately suggested, most unoriginally, I sent a letter to *The Times*.

'Would they even publish it, Sandra?' I asked. 'There's a big risk of libel, whether we're in the right or not.'

'And coming from Ann it would hardly carry the firepower needed for this assault,' observed Ma Saintsbury thoughtfully. 'It would be different if she were already at Longfield. Everything from Longfield seems news, even the sordid little antics of the students. No, we must get someone important interested, some figurehead for our movement. Perhaps the president of one or other Royal College? Perhaps a Fellow of the Royal Society?'

'If they'd bite,' said McRobb.

'Yes, they may well regard Ann as unreliable, just as these nasty drug people do.' Ma Saintsbury had an affectionate candour. 'Things *are* so difficult these days. During the war you could simply order everyone about.'

'How about approaching a Member of Parliament?' I suggested.

'I should imagine a good many M.P.s would slaver at the chops with the prospect of hammering a big drug company. They'd queue up to play the combined part of St George and Lister. Such lovely publicity for them!'

'If they thought I had a good case,' I added warily.

'Oh, they wouldn't trouble themselves too much over that. If you're right, they'd be in clover. If you're wrong, the public will soon forget all about it, except for the fact that Mr Bighead, M.P., was a fine champion of good causes. But I think we'll keep that particular shot in our locker,' she said reflectively. 'It's ammunition which might well blow up in our faces. Isn't there someone in the profession you can turn to for help? Someone unlike Sandra and myself, who could be seen to be independent?'

'I've thought of turning to Charles Crawless.'

'Now, that's a good idea. Doesn't he know this man Lloyd?'

'A little. Socially.'

'Charles would certainly have faith in you, Ann. And he's very much the rising physician. Perhaps even a strong word from him to Lloyd might induce them to think again?'

'I don't think even the word of God could alter a boardroom decision at General Drugs.'

'Perhaps you're right. You tackle Charles Crawless, Ann. See if he can draw in one or two other young consultants. *Then* we can draft a letter for them to sign. Not to the newspapers, but to one of the medical journals, where the risk of a libel action would be much diminished. We can be confident that the newspapers will anyway lift the story from the journals, and print it with sensational discretion.'

'I think Charles's would be the only advice I could trust,' I told her.

'Though you'd better get on to him quickly. He's off on a trip to America in a week or so, I believe.' She rose, looking satisfied with her morning's work. 'Ann, would you like to pop down to Longfield for a look round?' she suggested kindly. 'I could easily fix it with Tilly Dawes.'

'I'd love to. But wouldn't that smack of canvassing?'

'I don't think that matters in the slightest. I've never known anyone get a decent job without canvassing like mad. Dear me, is that the time? I've a case waiting for me in the theatre. Quite extraordinary, a decent-looking middle-aged man with his penis stuck in a stone hot-water bottle. I didn't think such objects existed in these days of electric blankets. Perhaps he kept one especially. His story is of having a bath and looking in some sort of cupboard for the towel, when for reasons best known to himself he had an erection. Apparently, a hot-water bottle fell from a shelf and impaled itself. There's a tremendous amount of oedema and strangulation by now. I shall just have to chip the stonework off with a bone-chisel.'

'I suppose he thought it was a good idea at the time,' observed McRobb.

16

'NO, IT'S STEREO,' said Charles Crawless.
He had the pained tone of a man explaining some personal fact
like his nationality, his breeding, or his fortune, which would be
obvious to a less dim questioner.

'I'd never have mono. With stereo you really *hear* the orches-
tra. It's just as good as sitting in the concert hall.'

'Isn't that amazing?' said Kit.

'It's all Danish equipment. The Danes are awfully good at
this sort of thing.' Charles fondly stroked the long flat box of
grained plastic and dull metal. 'Transistorized, of course.'

It was the following Saturday evening, towards the middle of
May, and we had just finished dinner in Charles's new house at
Godalming. He was keen to show the place off, and when I had
telephoned flattering him with the need of his advice he had
invited us eagerly. It was newly built, and everything worked
by pressing buttons, even the loo. The ice in the drinks came
from a machine, the steak was cooked by microwave, and the
wine was opened explosively by compressed carbon dioxide.
Under the floor the heating for a chilly summer's evening
roasted your feet, upstairs the new baby was monitored by a
pea-sized microphone (Charles seriously talked of substituting
closed-circuit television), and even the blonde *au pair* girl from
Munich looked as if she were full of springs and driven by
electricity.

'You can't see the loud-speakers, you know.' His wife Nancy
sounded triumphant.

Kit elaborately peered round their stylish, huge-windowed

sitting-room. 'I really don't think I can. No, not a single speaker in sight.'

'Look more carefully, Kit,' she directed. 'They're built into the wall.'

'Why, so they are! How wonderful.'

I hoped desperately that Kit wouldn't give way and just get drunk. He had agreed to come easily enough, though he disliked the Crawlesses. He had been particularly considerate and loving to me since my row with Lloyd, calming me down, turning me into the cool winds of reason, and encouraging me the fight wasn't lost. Kit alone in the world knew how to handle me. He saw precisely how much my mental state was caused by true professional concern, and how much by anger and buckled pride. It was a distinction I found difficult to see myself, nor did I believe I was the only woman doctor with such blindness.

'Why don't you play something, Charles?' I suggested. 'We'd love to hear your machine in action.'

Charles's eyes lit up. 'What would you like?'

'Beethoven's Fifth,' said Kit promptly. 'Real classical music.'

'Have you got it?' I asked.

'We have three versions,' said Nancy.

Charles delicately dropped the record on the turntable. Kit sat forward with the look on his face of a teenager in the front row of the Proms. I wondered nervously if either Charles or Nancy saw how he was pulling their legs. I decided they took him seriously, but I knew that if Kit saw this too it would only encourage him to try harder. At least the music would stop his remarks for a while.

I settled back in a Swedish chair with my whisky. I drank only whisky after dinner. I heard somewhere it was a taste which indicated a woman had passed forty, and if I still had ten years to go there were plenty of other atypical things about me. But to my disappointment Charles tired of his toy after the opening phrases, and with a brisk click eliminated Beethoven from our company. 'As you've no car,' he remarked, 'we'd better look up the trains to Waterloo.'

'I've got them in my mind,' I told him.

'You memorize *trains*?'

'Why not? It's quite simple once you've looked them up.'

'You *are* clever,' said Nancy.

Charles stroked his little moustache. 'Then we'd better have our chat, hadn't we? Would you like to come to my study? Nancy, give Kit another drink.'

Kit winked at me, and Nancy saw it. 'Of course, Kit, give me your empty glass. It *is* sensible of you not to drive, isn't it?'

Charles's study was a small room off the hall, almost entirely filled with electronic equipment – dictating machines, a small electric typewriter, another record-player, and a transistor radio.

'This record-player's mono.' He sounded faintly ashamed. 'I use it for discs of lectures, refresher courses, and so on, in cardiology. It's common practice in the States. I'm hoping to pick up an interesting batch during my busy few weeks there. I sit and listen to them in the bath, you know.'

Lucky Nancy, I thought. If Charles hadn't been impelled by a thirst for new gadgets, it might have been women. As he arranged a couple of chairs amid the cables and microphones I noticed a photograph on the wall. Four people in the sunshine, wearing holiday clothes on the deck of a yacht, all holding glasses and grinning. Charles, Nancy, Henry, and my replacement.

'You look as though you had a good holiday.'

'Oh, that.' Charles gave an embarrassed laugh. 'It was taken last summer at St Tropez. The Tamblings and ourselves shared a boat.'

'What's she like?' I had never discussed her with him, or anyone. 'No, that's an automatic question,' I added quickly. 'And horribly unoriginal. Forget I asked it.'

'She's all right,' said Charles offhandedly. My excuse was too self-conscious to be taken seriously. 'A little dull.'

'Is she attractive? That's another unworthy question, isn't it?'

'Yes, she's very attractive.'

'He's happy with her?'

'I think so,' he said deliberately. 'Yes, very. Though of course, she isn't in your class at all.'

'You mean intellectually?'

'I mean all round. From the point of view of personality. You wouldn't expect her to have much brains.'

'Perhaps my personality was the trouble. I don't suppose Henry imagined married life to be one bed of roses. Though now I can reflect on the disaster, he might have found it like newly-laid asphalt under a steamroller.'

Charles smiled. 'Ann, you're doing yourself an injustice. You can be the sweetest and most loving girl in the world when you feel like it. Some marriages simply die, like people. Just as naturally and far more resistant to treatment.'

'Henry and myself were mismatched. That's the long and short of it.'

'You can make a mistake in choosing the wrong spouse as in choosing the wrong car.' The comparison was typical of Charles. 'The danger arises when the couple won't admit it. Or one of them won't. All sorts of psychological strains occur. I see cases every day in practice. You were very sensible letting Henry go.'

I opened and closed my hands. 'It was after we separated that my arthritis developed. I always blame him for it.'

'I know you do. I sometimes wonder if again you might be a little unfair on yourself. It's a physical disease, not a psychological one. It may have afflicted you in the long run anyway, you know, even if you'd never met Henry.'

'But it can be brought on by stress.'

'I'm not entirely convinced about this stress business. Illness is a stress in itself. And none of us knows exactly how long a disease starts before we find the first symptoms. Though in your case . . . well, doubtless you know yourself best.'

I decided to let it go at that.

'What are these problems you bring?' he asked.

'The cyclova business.'

Charles gave a slow, deep physician's nod. 'I rather thought that might still be worrying you. I haven't seen Lloyd for ages. He seems to have forsaken the club.'

'Perhaps I've been keeping him too busy. Anyway, he's ignoring my report. He thinks I've made a mistake.'

'That's somewhat discourteous of him.'

'I'm not concerned with the niceties of politeness. I'm only

107

concerned with stopping a world epidemic of leukaemia. That's why I want your help, Charles. I've got to give my findings some publicity. My idea was getting you to buttonhole one or two top people in the profession. If you can interest them enough, they might sign a letter protesting about the behaviour of General Drugs, for publication in one of the journals.'

Charles stroked his moustache. 'That might be a wee bit difficult. You know how cagey the big boys are about committing themselves to a cause.'

'Even a good cause? An essential cause?'

There was a silence. Charles played idly with a knob on one of his machines.

'Well, what else do you suggest?' I asked.

'You could put out your findings as they stand. No one could stop you doing that.'

'The medical journals would take ages to publish the paper,' I told him impatiently. 'By then, half the world might be taking cyclova.'

'Send it briefly, as a letter. The editors would print it in a week.'

'But, Charles, that's my point. It would be going off half-cock. I must have someone powerful and respected behind me. Someone the authorities will listen to.'

'If your results are correct, surely they'll stand up for themselves?'

'Of course my results are correct. But they've got to stand up against the extensive trials done in the States by General Drugs, however misleading those might be. I'm not deceiving myself on that score. It's criminal, their marketing this drug without taking every scrap of research into account.'

'Ann the perfectionist.' Charles smiled. 'When manna fell from Heaven, the people underneath didn't subject it to chemical analysis. They ate it. Do you know what I advise you to do, Ann?'

I shook my head.

'Drop the whole idea.'

I looked at him in astonishment. 'That's out of the question.'

Charles held up his hands, a gesture to calm me down. He

went on quietly, 'Listen to me, Ann, please. That wasn't a suggestion made on the spur of the moment. I've been thinking about this damned cyclova since I gave you a lift that morning. Will you let me tell you exactly *why* I advise you to forget about it?'

'Very well,' I said defiantly. 'Tell me.'

'Do you realize quite what you're taking on? General Drugs! They're big, rich, and powerful. My God, they are! Their influence can be found everywhere – though in some places you can unearth it only by digging very deeply and carefully indeed. When they set their minds to it, things happen. Grants fade away, research men lose their jobs, the pet schemes of health administrators, on a national or even international level, mysteriously run into the sand. Though perhaps that's an over-black picture I've painted,' he admitted. 'General Drugs *do* have considerable influence in the world, and they *do* exert it, but always for the best. I agree, for the best as they see it. But by and large, that has turned out as best for the progress of medicine. I am absolutely certain they wouldn't play politics at any level from purely commercial reasons. You see, that would not only be unethical, but in the long run bad for business.'

'What's all this got to do with the rights and wrongs of my quarrel?' I asked shortly.

He smiled again. 'Ann against Goliath? That's a wonderfully attractive notion. But I always had the impression of David being particularly lucky with his shot that afternoon, plumb in the middle of the frontal bone. I'm only drawing your attention to the strength of your enemy.' He leant forward and said in a fatherly manner, 'Ann, you don't really think they'd go ahead with cyclova if there was any danger, do you? Not in your heart of hearts? Though of course you're perfectly entitled to have a go at them. If you're determined, and if you really think you're in the right.'

He added the last words so casually it took me a moment to realize what his lecture was leading to. Charles thought that I had made a mistake with the blood-smears. But I didn't feel angry. Not with Charles. When Lloyd told me plainly that I had erred, he had some motive. But Charles was on my side. He was giving me a truly impartial opinion. The doubts I had suffered on my taxi-ride from Lloyd's office returned to pain me. For the first time I had a real suspicion that after all I was wrong.

'You said you were using an unusual stain for the blood-samples, Ann?'

Charles had read my thoughts, and was prompting me.

'That might have let me down, I suppose.' I fell into a silence he made no attempt to interrupt. 'I simply assumed it to be reliable.'

'Was it a bottle you'd had in the lab. for some time?'

He was showing me a way out.

'No, I made it up freshly for this particular trial.'

'But you didn't change it at all? Not during your work on this specific series of blood-smears?'

'No.'

I sat with my hands crossed in my lap, looking at him.

'Of course, you can get contaminants from an empty bottle,' he suggested. 'Sometimes the original reagents you use for the mixture are stale or defective. There's really quite a wide possibility of error, when you come to think of it.'

I gave a brief sigh. 'I suppose there *was* the chance of an artifact. When the first immature cells showed up, I should have repeated the examination after making up a fresh bottle of stain. It was foolish of me.'

'Don't be angry with yourself,' he said gently, 'it's something which could happen so easily in any laboratory. Often it works the other way round. They only discovered Ringer's solution because the lab-boy filled the flasks with tap-water instead of distilled.'

I noticed that Charles had simply assumed that his hypothesis of a faulty bottle of stain causing all the fuss was the right one. And the possibility of my making a mistake, now the responsibility had been transferred by him to a few ill-mixed chemicals, was easier to accept as a certainty. I suddenly felt weary of the whole cyclova business. He was right. I wasn't being noble. I was being pig-headed.

'You could always look at the woman's blood again,' he suggested.

'I looked at it yesterday. Naturally, we're following her up. It was normal, but by now she's been off cyclova for almost two months.'

Charles stood up. 'You asked my advice, Ann, and I've given it. If you don't take it . . . well, I'm used enough to that from my patients.' He gave a laugh. 'You really can't imagine how bloody-minded some of these fringe royals can be.'

That was the end of it. We got back to the sitting-room to find Beethoven's Fifth was in full blast. Kit was lying back in his chair with his eyes shut, Nancy was sitting opposite, very upright, with an expression of strained enjoyment. After a few minutes of politeness, we left.

'What did Charles say?' asked Kit, as soon as we quit the house.

'Don't ask me. I don't want to talk about it.'

Kit was aching to know, but he didn't inquire again. He alone in the world knew how to handle me.

I CAUGHT A train at Charing Cross the following Monday morning, and sat against the carriage window, too interested to read my paper. This was the journey that I was going to know intimately, click by click in the rail – at least, until I could persuade Kit to leave London.

First over the river, rippled and glittering in the sunshine, the colour of chocolate blancmange, busy with white pleasure-boats shipping tourists to Kew, a severe-looking police-launch, a string of barges downstream behind a tug doffing its funnel to Waterloo Bridge. Then the Festival Hall, with a glimpse of rehearsing musicians in shirt-sleeves drinking coffee behind the plate-glass window of their rest room. When I was thirteen, my father had taken me to see the Dome of Discovery and the Skylon at the Festival which seemed to celebrate nothing but the nation's bankruptcy. Southwark Cathedral, modish boutique of religious thought. A glimpse down the throat of Tower Bridge. Waves of peaked roofs, lines of crushed terraces, the slums of today south of Surrey docks, succeeded by concrete slabs and fingers, the slums of tomorrow. Miles of suburban villas, all identical. Then green. Green fields, trees and hedges, the overwhelming green of an English May-time, as still, dim-shadowed, and unworldly as the bottom of the sea.

The excitement of my first trip to Longfield had submerged my other troubles without succeeding in drowning them. Early on the Sunday I had gone to the hospital, climbed up to my laboratory, and examined the suspect blood-smears again under the microscope. I looked closely at my bottle of stain, pricked my finger with a needle, and used the stain to prepare a slide of my own blood. It looked normal enough. Then I went to the medical wards, found one of the house-physicians, and took specimens from two patients already diagnosed with leukaemia. But their disease was too advanced, and as I expected my stain showed nothing that would be concealed by others.

Sitting on the high chair at my laboratory bench, I brought myself finally to accept Charles Crawless's explanation. I had at last talked about it that morning to Kit, who agreed that I should drop the idea of being some scientific suffragette. I knew Kit had a reasonable grasp of the facts. Though he had no knowledge of medicine he quickly picked up any details I put to him, claiming a training in writing about beekeeping was invaluable.

It was something of a relief to throw up the sponge, particularly after Charles had impressed me with the callous strength of my adversary. I began to feel I had been stupid, becoming so agitated over the drug. There were so many stupid things about me, I thought. But at the age of thirty they had become too troublesome, or too humiliating, to face squarely and put right.

Tilly Dawes was waiting on Longfield platform. I had met her once before with Ma Saintsbury. She was an untidy, wispy-haired, short little woman with thick glasses, who could be taken for a char or a grandmother awaiting her old age pension. She was a professor of biochemistry, a Fellow of the Royal Society, and a Member of the Order of Merit.

'You're younger than I remembered,' she greeted me. 'And prettier.'

I felt that was a pleasant start.

Tilly Dawes had a red Mini outside the station, which she drove up the long hill into the town, unlawfully fast and extremely dangerously.

'You'll like it here,' she remarked. 'At least, *I* like it. It was a bit of a wrench, unseating myself from my chair at Newcastle. But I've never regretted it.'

'How long have you been here, Professor Dawes?'

'Five years. I'm one of the founding fathers and mothers. We've seen the worst of it, getting the place organized. Only now are we finding things reasonably shipshape. Though there are some terrifying whirlpools of chaos for the unwary to slip into.'

'It must have been awfully hard work.'

'Yes, but it was fun. You can't imagine the appeal of spending the Government's money in large quantities. Or should I say the money of my fellow-taxpayers? I've discovered that cash needn't be your own for the pure enjoyment of getting rid of it. It must be wonderful to be even a borough treasurer.'

'You're lucky the Government is so generous.'

'Oh, this place is the educational apple of its eye. The University Grants Committee has been left in no doubts about *that*.' She drove over a zebra crossing, shaving a pair of startled pedestrians. 'Longfield's a pretty little place. Though ruined, of course. Nowadays it seems to be all car parks.' We entered the busy main square. 'A hundred years ago it was a village, existing purely and simply to serve the needs of the big house for food, drink, and labour. You can still find one or two of the original shops tucked round the back. Now the High Street's just the same as everywhere else in the land, Boots', Smith's, Lyons', and Tesco. And, of course, Marks and Spencer's. I buy all my outfits there. They've done far more towards egalitarianism in the country than the socialists.'

I smoothed the skirt of my mustard suit. I hoped she wouldn't think me overdressed.

'What's your husband do, Dr Sheriff?'

'I'm divorced.'

'I see. Have you been left with a bunch of kids to bring up?'

'We hadn't any children. That's why I'm thinking of keeping my flat in Town and coming down here every day.'

'Several of the staff do. We're really only a limb of London. I've got a little place on the Downs, which my husband finds peaceful for messing about with his paints.' He was a Royal Academician. 'That monstrosity's the old technical college.' We passed a building resembling a chip of Princess Victoria's. 'Our nucleus, or embryo. Would that be the right term?'

We drove down a road of solid Victorian dwellings, the homes of the first commuters, then turned through a pair of elaborately decorated black iron gates set between twin brick lodges. We were on the main drive of Longfield House itself.

'Why, it's wonderful,' I cried.

'It *is* rather nice,' Tilly admitted. 'Haven't you seen it before?'

I shook my head. The tarmac drive wound steeply uphill between huge oaks, then you saw the house half a mile away across a shallow dip. Tilly Dawes considerately stopped the car. I sat staring at the long, low Elizabethan building, dull brick and stone with window, gable, and tall chimney spaced from the twin-turreted gate, six to a side, notes in the chord.

'I wonder how it struck the sixteenth-century visitor?' I speculated, fascinated with the scene.

'There would have been smoke pouring from the chimneys and horses,' she said thoughtfully. 'Though the oaks would have been insignificant. An Elizabethan would have been impressed even more than us. That was the object of the place, rather than to put a fitting roof over a nobleman's head.'

She started the car. 'There are three courts beyond, which give us ample space. The House is the centre of the university, but not much teaching goes on there. Only a few lectures on the arts side. It holds the offices, and the great hall makes us feel very pleased with ourselves when we gather in it on special occasions. I might add that the vice-chancellor's installed himself very comfortably in about a dozen rooms at the back. Now I'll show you the business end of the institution.'

She drove past the House and over the brow of another hill. The new half-finished university lay spread in the valley below us like a neatly-arranged collection of assorted white boxes.

I clasped my hands tight in my lap. 'It's an exciting prospect,' I admitted. 'For me, at any rate.'

'That's engineering, that's applied physics, and over there's low-temperature research, geology, and metallurgy,' Tilly pointed out. 'My little lot's the square affair on the right.' It was the biggest building of all. 'You'll be in the zoology building, that flashy place with all the glass. Though don't ask me where, they're already complaining they're short of space.'

'I'd be perfectly happy to work in a tent.'

'I expect we can do better than that. Expansion is our religion down here, however pointless. Everything's arranged on the best principles of social engineering, you know,' she explained airily. 'Which means we poor humans have to fit ourselves somehow into the architect's ideas. Do you drive a large car?'

'I don't drive one at all.'

'The prerequisite for mental peace at Longfield. Architects have a strange antipathy to cars. Perhaps they regard the motor age as strictly temporary.'

As she drove nearer the buildings I said enthusiastically, 'This seems just the perfect place to work. The best facilities in the loveliest countryside.'

'I suppose I should ask what you're proposing to work *on*, Dr Sheriff?'

'I'm intending to continue my research at Princess Victoria's on chemical contraceptives. Not the oestrogen-progesterone mixtures of "the pill", as they call it. Plenty of other people are working on that.'

'Yes, it's getting rather old hat,' Tilly agreed. 'Not so long ago you could hold the conversation at a dinner party with it.'

'I've got two main ideas.' I was eager to impart my plans. 'One is to stop the sperm impregnating the ovum at all. The other to stop the fertilized ovum being implanted in the lining of the womb. A "morning-after" pill, you know. I think I'm on to one which could be feasible.'

'That's an interesting concept. Though you might run into some strong moral objections.'

'Should I? You mean the retrospective aspect? But surely, "Repent and ye shall be forgiven" is the basis of Christian morality?'

'Doubtless,' said Tilly Dawes shortly. She drove along a circular road skirting the new buildings. 'I suppose you're the target for a good deal of moralizing?'

'Mostly misguided. At least, that's what I like to think.'

'But surely, Dr Sheriff, everyone now accepts the principle of birth control? Unless they have particular religious or aesthetic reasons not to. We talk about it quite openly. Though of course we talk about everything quite openly these days.'

'A lot of powerful people accept it in the same sense as they accept people want to amuse themselves on Sundays. Grudgingly, to say the least. You'd be surprised at their little stratagems to restrict the knowledge or practice of it. Anyway, these folk miss the point. Science isn't so concerned with old-fashioned "family planning" these days. We've invented effective methods, we have mass-communications to make them known, the walls of ignorance are slowly crumbling under our attack. How many children a couple want, and when they want them, is a matter for themselves. We've now moved on, in a rather frightened way, to population control. Trying to keep the inhabitants of the world at a faintly sane level.'

'Why do you say "frightened"?'

'Because we think the solution is already beyond us. Surely you must have heard of the "population explosion"?'

'Yes, I have.' She narrowly missed two students on bicycles. 'I do wish those girls would look where they're going. Or were they boys? You can never tell these days. It's a wonder the human race manages to reproduce at all. Yes, I have heard of the population explosion,' she resumed, 'but I dismissed the expression as too slick by half.'

'It has a ring of truth. After all, the people in the world have doubled in the past fifty years.'

She looked amazed. 'The baneful effect of medical and nutritional science? A hollow reward for our labours. I wonder what Hopkins would say, if he saw his discovery of the vitamins running to its uncomfortably logical conclusion?'

'And remember, half the population of the world's still undernourished and under-doctored.' These were pet themes of mine, and I was enjoying myself expounding them to an academic as eminent as Tilly. 'Nevertheless, we go on reproducing ourselves at two per cent a year.'

'A geometric progression, of course?'

I nodded. 'Exactly. In another six hundred years – which isn't all that distant, just as far ahead as the Black Death is behind us – the global population will have so increased that we shall be obliged to exist on one square yard apiece.'

'That will make the parking problem even more difficult,' observed Tilly.

We left the new buildings behind. Two or three miles farther along the road the ground flattened out, and we came to some rows of long, drab, military-looking huts.

'Our splendid new university boasts many ancient buildings apart from Longfield House,' Tilly remarked. 'This is an airfield abandoned by the R.A.F. We lecture in some of the huts, the students live in others, they're extremely inconvenient and the roofs leak. But we can't have everything at this stage. Our academic gowns are designed by a top-flight Mayfair couturier, and cost the earth. Our students enjoy their meals in a wonderful cafeteria, almost as good as a works' canteen. We ourselves dine with pomp, and the vice-chancellor has just engaged a butler, at a salary more substantial than a lecturer's.'

'What are your students like?'

'Not drug-fiends and sex-maniacs as you'd expect from the newspapers. A lot of them are rather dull. They like letting off steam occasionally, but students always did. Everyone seems to forget that Bertie Wooster repeatedly did battle with the police on Boat Race night. Do you read P. G. Wodehouse? I adore him. I read one of his books every week, over and over again. It takes well over a year to get through the lot. Unhappily, the young seem to have lost the art of good misbehaviour.'

'Now they run amok in the pursuit of high principles rather than policemen's helmets.'

'But perhaps the motive's the same.'

Tilly turned her Mini off the main road into a lane. 'Students are immature,' she reflected, 'but they don't know it. Or perhaps they know it too well, and resent it. Or they may be fired by the sad inescapability of two children and a semi-det. *That* prospect's worth trying to change the world to avoid, don't you think? Some are very earnest, but students were always earnest, too. It's only with age that you start to realize life isn't a magnificent saga, only a rather bad low comedy. I hope you can stay for lunch at the cottage?'

'I'd love to.'

'You can watch my husband messing about with his paints.'

The 'cottage' turned out a three-storeyed mansion. As she drove between the brilliant azaleas lining the drive, Tilly added,

'You'll enjoy starting your department from scratch, Dr Sheriff. Though the delights will be frequently tinged with exasperation, I'm warning you.'

'Of course, all this is assuming that I'm appointed?'

'I don't think there can be any doubt about that. Sir Robert Boatwright will be on the selection committee. I expect you've heard of him?'

'He gets in the financial pages of the papers, doesn't he?'

'He's an intelligent millionaire with a very pretty wife. I should imagine you'd be exactly his type.'

The car stopped at the front door. 'Mind those mongrels,' said Tilly, as a pair of splendidly bred Irish wolfhounds came bounding out at us.

18

'BUT THE IGNORANCE!' complained Liz. 'One girl yesterday asked whether it was true that you went mad if you took a bath while you were menstrual.'

'That's an old one,' I told her. 'Quite a chestnut.'

'And all these myths about getting pregnant if you do it at the full moon.'

'Who knows? There may be something in it. The ferret only breeds in the spring and summer. But if you keep them in the lab. and provide long June evenings by turning the lights on. they'll reproduce even in November.'

'I'm beginning to think I'd rather handle ferrets than people,' said Liz sourly.

'And we've been aware for years that birds who live among the bright lights of London have bigger sex organs than the ones who nest in the country. There's no knowing the influences on such a delicate business as reproduction.'

'But I thought everybody knew all about their sexual apparatus these enlightened days? Everyone seems obsessed with indulging them.'

'Everybody gets hungry,' I pointed out. 'But there are few knowledgeable cooks.'

'Some of the girls coming to the clinic ought to go about with an L-plate on it,' she declared. I fancied she had been talking to McRobb.

'But the ignorance is our fault, isn't it?' I admitted. 'We're supposed to be the teachers.'

'Can't they read books about it?'

'Oh, books. But reading a book about anything is an enormously ambitious project for a lot of people. And those books are awfully chilly. The dreadful line drawings of male and female anatomy. They always remind me of slices of cold brawn. Quite enough to put anyone off sex for good.'

'The men are no better.' Liz had been on her own for the second Tuesday clinic, as I had laboratory work to catch up after seeing Tilly Dawes. It was the following morning, and we were sitting in my laboratory in the attic, Liz in a short, flared-skirted, smart green suit. She said that she had come up from Sussex to shop, though I expected she just wanted to talk to somebody. 'I didn't know I'd have to deal with *men*,' she complained.

'Yes, we also advise sub-fertility couples,' I explained. 'Though, of course, McRobb does the clinical work on the women. Helping people who can't have children is as much part of family planning as helping the ones who have too many. I think it's important to realize that, to keep the whole subject in perspective,' I added firmly. 'I suppose you know that fifteen per cent of marriages are permanently childless?'

She smiled. 'Ann and her figures again. But it isn't often the man's fault, surely?'

'That's another popular misconception. It is in about a third of cases.'

Liz looked surprised. 'As much as that? No wonder the poor boys looked shattered when I handed over a test-tube and directed them to the loo to produce a specimen of semen. They asked *how*, of all things. I had to *tell* them, then they looked even worse. One of them even expected me to do the job for him.'

I laughed.

'I can't turn up next Tuesday morning,' Liz continued apologetically. 'I've got to see Trevor and the accountants. It's the only time they can manage.'

'How are things going?'

She wrinkled her nose. 'It's an awful bore. I thought I could just storm ahead, an outraged wife after her rights. But we get bogged down to things like income-tax returns and who pays the gas-bill. There's no romance these days even in divorce.'

'You're going to divorce him, are you?'

'That seems inescapable.' She sounded rather helpless.

'Have you heard anything more of Derek? What he's up to?'

'He's still living with this woman. They've got a flat near Regent's Park somewhere. I bet it's a mess. He was dreadfully untidy without me to keep an eye on him.'

'How old's this girl?'

'Twenty. Derek's thirty-eight.'

'Perhaps it's just temporary sexual aberration?' I suggested hopefully. 'Like the ferret with the light left on?'

'That's his look-out. *I'm* not having anything to do with him again.'

After a pause, I asked, 'Do you miss him?'

Liz hesitated. 'Yes, of course I do. There's not much joy in living your life alone.'

'You could marry again.'

'You haven't, Ann.'

'Yes, I have.' She looked startled. 'All but for the formal blessing of society in a registry office. I've been living with someone for three years now.'

'You *are* a dark horse.' Liz sounded admiring. 'Anyone I know?'

I shook my head. 'A man called Kit Stewart. He's a writer.'

'That sounds romantic.'

'Perhaps it is. But it's not very profitable. Even Kit wouldn't claim to be a success.'

'Is he nice?'

'Wonderful.'

'He's lucky to have you, Ann.'

'Occasionally I think so too. Mostly I don't.'

'You always had this hockey-team modesty,' she said reprovingly.

'I mean it. I must be dreadfully difficult to live with. I'm either a burning flame or a wet blanket, nothing in between.'

'But don't you want to marry him?'

'Of course I do. But there's the usual obstacle. He has a wife who's unwilling to let him go. You see, you've got more sense about Derek.'

'Or less.'

'But things are progressing,' I told her cheerfully. 'After three years, I suppose she reckons she's lost the tug-o'-war. Though it never was a struggle between us. Kit just fell into my arms. But now at last she's agreed to see me – this afternoon. I don't think she merely wants the pleasure of throwing sulphuric acid in my face.'

'I hope something comes of it,' Liz said sympathetically.

'So do I. Though whatever happens Kit and I are together, and we'll stay together for ever and ever.'

Liz took a taxi to Harrods, to lunch off fruit-juices in the health bar. Since Derek had left, she explained, she had been letting her figure go. What was the point in preserving it, she asked, with no one to look at it? I told her severely it was anxiety stimulating her appetite. She agreed that this was sound enough psychology, though adding it was possibly better to be driven to the refrigerator than to the bottle. We parted sensing that our intimacy had moved from its present shallows to the depths we enjoyed in our student days. There is nothing leading to quicker friendship between women than mutual commiseration on their sexual difficulties.

I finished my morning's work, checking the blood of women on ordinary oral contraceptives, each specimen prepared with my own fluorescent stain. I had the vague idea of proving myself wrong over cyclova, by finding immature cells when in reality there could be none. But even this inverted satisfaction was denied me, all the slides I examined appearing normal. I packed the thin glass oblongs away, took off my white coat, and went down to lunch in the staff-room. I was wearing the mustard suit and the expensive shoes again, because I wanted to make a good impression on Myra Stewart. It struck me that I had seemed in need of making a good impression on a large number of people over the last few weeks.

19

ON GETTING HOME from Longfield on the Monday evening I heard that Myra was willing to meet me. Kit had spent most of the afternoon with her in the lounge of a West End hotel. They were discussing the future of their daughter, which now appeared to be a pressing if unexciting topic.

'I think Myra's coming round,' Kit had told me excitedly. 'Yes, the old bitch is coming round. Work on her, Ann.'

'How far did you get today?'

'Only as far as her admitting that a divorce was on the cards. You know what Myra's like, darling – tough and secretive. It's like negotiating with the Chinese. She could drag it out for years.'

'Has she got another man?'

'I don't think so. But that may be behind it. Of course, I ought to handle the whole thing myself. After all, she's my bloody wife. But it's you she wants to see. Perhaps she's written me off as too unreliable even to manage my own divorce.'

'I'm not afraid to take it up with her,' I said determinedly. I was glad of the chance. I was certain I could manage her more ably than Kit could. 'Where's our confrontation to be?'

'Obviously, on neutral ground. She said she didn't want to sit in any more hotels. I suggested the Tate Gallery. You can meet her by that little circular affair where the girls sell postcards to the tourists.'

I arrived at the Tate that Wednesday afternoon promptly at two. There was Myra, by the postcard stall already. I had met her a few times when I first knew Kit, when I was introduced with formality – which proved unsuccessful – as a doctor-friend. We had suspected and disliked each other from the start. She was a slim woman of about forty, in a short, gay pink dress. She wore a wide-brimmed elaborate hat, as though on her way to Ascot. I wondered if this was to emphasize the formality of the occasion. I noticed with surprise that her daughter was with her, long-haired and short-skirted.

'I'm sorry I kept you waiting,' I apologized.

'Oh, it's Dr Sheriff.' She sounded as though it was a chance encounter. Perhaps that was what she wanted to believe. 'No, not at all. We've only been here a minute, we're early.'

We didn't shake hands. We stood facing each other, a good yard between us, which was doubtless of deep psychological significance. Looking at her carefully I saw that she was a pretty woman, rather peaky, with large green eyes. I knew nothing of her personality, apart from Kit's descriptions, which I had to admit were unreliable. Yet she had so dominated my thoughts for three years I felt that I knew her well. I recognized that this could be a dangerous stroke of self-delusion.

'Should we go down to the restaurant for a cup of coffee?' I suggested. 'It has some awfully nice murals by Rex Whistler.'

'No, I don't think I care for anything, thank you.' She had a detached and distant voice, as though always thinking of something else. This impression was deepened by her habit of never looking at your face but somewhere over your right shoulder. 'I thought Veronica could go and enjoy the pictures.'

'I'm sure she'd like that.'

'Veronica, amuse yourself for twenty minutes, darling.' Now Myra was looking over her daughter's shoulder. 'Have you some money? Buy yourself a catalogue.'

'The paintings are individually labelled,' I pointed out.

'Veronica would prefer a catalogue,' said Myra.

She used the same tone, but I saw that I had already made a mistake. I had assumed somehow that I would take charge of the meeting. I had to remind myself that I was not the thoughtful, respected, professional woman, but just another contestant for Kit's bed.

'I'll go and see some of the Impressionists,' said Veronica.

125

'Though I don't suppose they're so representative as the ones in the *Musée du Jeu de Paume*.'

Her French accent seemed splendid to me.

'Shall we find somewhere to sit down?' asked Myra.

We wandered into the first gallery, and found one of the leather-topped well-upholstered benches for wearying pursuers of culture. I didn't even notice the paintings.

'It must have done your daughter a lot of good, being in France,' I started politely.

'A lot of good?' asked Myra.

'I mean, learning French. And her general education.'

'Yes. Yes, that's so. She speaks French very well, don't you think? I can't speak any languages, none at all. They weren't in my own education, you see. I had a very poor one.'

Her voice took an almost dreamy sound.

'I'm sure that can't be the case, Mrs Stewart.'

'I'm not very clever. I'm not like you, Dr Sheriff. You're an educated woman.'

'That's not at all the same as being a clever one.'

'No,' she said vaguely, 'perhaps it isn't.' She paused. 'But I can't understand you, Dr Sheriff.'

'In what particular way?' I began to feel uneasy. It was bound to be a trying interview, but I persuaded myself I would end it with some sort of advantage.

'Oh, in every way. We don't think along the same lines, you see.'

'Do any two women think along the same lines?'

'Yes. Most women do, about the important things.' She sounded a little more sure about this. 'But not in the same way as you. Most women aren't educated, you see.'

'About what sort of things? You mean sex, men, and love?' I decided to bring her to the point – if she knew exactly what her point was. 'I assure you I think about such things just like any other woman. Or that I *feel* about them like any other woman. Thinking doesn't come much into it.'

'Do you?' She sounded doubtful.

'I know that I love Kit, and that he loves me.'

'Yes, I'm sure you do. Yes, that's obvious.'

'I'm sorry, it wasn't very considerate of me to put it like that. I didn't mean to hurt your feelings.'

'Oh, but you've done that. Long ago. When you took him from me.'

I could say nothing to this.

'And now you want me to give him his freedom?' She was still looking over my shoulder.

'Kit does.'

'You want me to give you *your* freedom. That's what it is, really, isn't it?'

She held the whip and the educated woman was going to suffer the lashes. An amiable form of sadism for a sensitive female with little formal learning. Perhaps it was some sub-conscious revenge on a bullying schoolmistress, I asked myself with rising irritation. But I must keep my temper, this afternoon of all times I must keep my temper.

'Kit and I have been living happily together for three years. We intend to go on the same way, whether you decide to divorce him or not. If you don't want to release him, we can't do anything about it. For practical purposes it won't make much difference.'

'But I suppose it would be tidier.'

'Of course it would. There are all sorts of disadvantages in our not being married.'

'What, exactly?'

I tried hard to think. 'Well, when we go abroad there's this business of passports. We have to leave them at the reception desks of hotels.'

'*Do* you? I don't remember leaving my passport with any receptionist.'

'They have to fill in the police forms.'

'Is that what happens abroad these days? I haven't been for so long. Why should the police want them to fill in a form about you?'

'It's a formality.' I was starting to feel quietly desperate. 'They do it for all travellers.'

'I'm sure they don't,' she contradicted me. 'You must be mistaken. What business is it of the police who you are?'

I was searching for some way to haul her back from this lunatic conversation when a fat man in a dark suit sat heavily beside me, puffing gently. He grinned. 'It's hard on the feet, and no mistake,' he announced with Yorkshire throatiness.

I just stared at him. I couldn't imagine what he was doing there.

'Mind, it's worth it,' he went on. I continued staring. 'A real treat for the mind, this. You don't often see such beauty under one roof these days, do you?'

The man caught my eye. His grin faded, then he looked deeply uneasy, rose abruptly, and made off. I supposed it was another black mark against Londoners when he got home.

'I was devoted to Kit,' Myra said suddenly. The feebleness of the utterance made it the more disconcerting. 'Despite his faults, which were many and often bad. But I've no need to tell you about those. You've had ample time to find out.'

'We're none of us perfect.'

'No. No, we aren't. And he was very good to me on the whole. We had a proper home together for several years. We married, you know, when Veronica was on the way.' I didn't know this. 'Though Kit went off several times, he always came back to me.'

'Will you think me cruel if I say there's no chance of his doing so again?'

'No, it's not cruel, if it's the truth. I don't think any truth can be as cruel as a deception, do you?'

'Perhaps not as cruel as a self-deception.'

'We had a lot of troubles, of course. Mostly about money. I don't suppose that bothers you.'

'I'm not particularly well paid.'

'I'm speaking comparatively. I work as a secretary.'

I found this continuing emphasis on our differing positions galling. Only the brain I was born with had made me one of a learned profession. Otherwise, with my personality I should have been lucky to hold a job in a shop.

'Do you really intend to divorce Kit or not?' I asked directly.

'Yes, I think I do. There's no point in doing otherwise, is there? They say they're going to change the law soon, so he'll just be able to get rid of me. But I haven't quite made up my mind. There's Veronica, you see.'

'She seems very grown-up.'

'I want her to have a career,' said Myra.

'What sort of career?'

'I'm not sure. Perhaps to be a doctor, like you.'

'The training's awfully long, and awfully tough.'

'But Veronica's very intelligent.'

'Has she got her A-levels? It's a mundane point, but these days even a child with the deepest sense of vocation can't start medicine without them.'

'No, she hasn't. But there are places one can go to pass the exams quickly.'

'Certainly, there are plenty of crammers in London. But even the exam wouldn't assure her a place in a medical school. It's awfully difficult for women.'

'Then perhaps she mightn't be a doctor. How about a lawyer? Do you think she might make a lawyer?'

'How can I say? I know nothing of her abilities.' I was exasperated. Myra seemed to have trapped me in the role of careers' mistress.

'I think she might be a good lawyer. Do you imagine you could help her to become a lawyer, Dr Sheriff? You must know lots of important people.'

'I'd certainly do all I could.' I couldn't believe the wild, dimly-perceived scheme was real in Myra's mind. 'The brother of a friend of mine is a solicitor. He might have some suggestions.'

'That would be very kind.' She sounded gracious. 'Of course, it would be expensive to become a lawyer. I couldn't afford it.'

'I expect there are grants available.'

'Otherwise, Kit would have to pay.'

'I'm sure he'd pay what he could.'

'Dr Sheriff, I could rely on you to see that. Please ask your friend to find how Veronica can become a lawyer.'

A straight deal, I thought. Make my daughter a lawyer and you can have my husband. But the whole thing was laughable, a fantasy. Then our conversation was closed by the prospective member of the Bar appearing at the door of the gallery.

'We must meet again, Dr Sheriff.' Myra stood up. 'I think we have conducted ourselves very sensibly, don't you? We have really made progress. No hysterics. It's so much better like that.'

She departed abruptly, hurrying Veronica out as though not wishing the girl to be contaminated by my glance. I was left sitting on the bench wondering exactly what had been achieved. I had come to face Myra with the imminent prospect of her husband's divorce, and had ended by taking responsibility for the education of his daughter.

20

KIT LAUGHED.

'Don't worry about that crackpot Myra. Veronica's the sweetest kid alive, but she hasn't the brains to become a police-woman, let alone a luminary of the law.'

'Wouldn't she like to be a nurse?' I suggested, a shade desperately. 'Or an air hostess? Her French would help.'

'That's the sort of thing she'll end up with. Receptionist at a hotel. Cashier in a bank. A secretary, like her mother. The world is an oyster which opens to any pretty girl with a nice smile.'

Kit was lying on the sofa in our flat. Those days he seemed always to be in a good mood, which was heavenly. It was after our evening meal, the same day that I had met Myra. I was sitting opposite, reading through some notes from the laboratory, both of us half-listening to a concert on the radio. Domestic bliss. The priceless unexcitement of settled intimacy.

'But why should Myra want to produce these high-flown notions?'

'She's having you on, my darling. They're a form of reaction, of over-compensation. She's had plenty of competition before, but not on such an elevated intellectual level.'

'Thank you,' I told him primly. 'I'm glad I've varied the sequence for her.'

He grinned. 'Well, I'm frank. Doesn't that make you feel safe?'

'I don't see why it should.'

'Beware of the man who makes a secret of his past. That only indicates his guilt over the likelihood of slipping again.'

'What an involved piece of reasoning!'

'It's as good an excuse as any for a boastful sexual exhibitionist like me.'

I reached out for our hands to touch, a gentle satisfaction. 'What do you suppose Myra's really after?'

'She wants you to crawl a little.'

'I don't mind how much I crawl for you, Kit.'

'Don't overdo it. She's playing a delaying game. She'll give in at the end.'

'I'm not so sure,' I said doubtfully. 'Though I suppose you know her best. She's a peculiar woman, isn't she?'

'Weird.'

'Why did you marry her? Apart from having her in the family way with Veronica.'

'Did she tell you? That's amazing. I always kept it dark. I'd the vague feeling it reflected on the child.'

'I suppose Myra assumed I'd know.'

'Anyway, that wasn't the reason. We'd already made up our minds. Well, more or less.' He yawned. 'I don't think anybody really knows why they married anybody in particular. Don't we just put up with our partners, and day by day feel either glad or sorry about it? Living hand-to-mouth emotionally is surely the basis of all successful marriages? The mind wilts at the prospect of a lifetime of unrelenting contented monogamy, even if that's what most people get.'

'That's a man's view.'

'I wonder how much love there is left in a burnt-out marriage,' he speculated. 'Like your parents', for example.'

'You've never met them.'

'But I can see them. I bet their marriage is just a habit, like everything else in their lives. Isn't that so?'

'What are you trying to say?' I objected. 'That marriage becomes a series of conditioned reflexes, like with Pavlov's dogs? Ring the dinner-bell enough and they salivate, even if there's no dinner. Produce the regular, empty little signs of affection and your spouse is happy enough, even if there's no love behind them. That's it, isn't it?'

'All this happens only to other people,' said Kit lightly. He never argued seriously unless he knew he would win. 'You're meeting your parents tomorrow, aren't you, with your brother?'

'Yes. Ronnie won't ask me to his own house. It's up in Cricklewood somewhere, but I haven't set eyes on it. He won't even tell me where his office is – if he's got one. It's all so stupid and unsatisfactory, and rather worrying. I only wish I knew what he was up to.'

'Preoccupation with secrecy is one of the lovable little failings of millionaires.'

'I'd forgive him instantly, if he *was* one,' I said feelingly.

Kit stretched. 'I met Andrew in the pub this evening. He's desperately keen to see the novel.'

'Oh, Kit, I'm so glad.'

'It's really coming on, you know. I'm getting it straight. At last I really believe I'm starting to see the end of it.'

My pleasure was false, perhaps by then transparently so. Kit had so often in the last three years started to see the end of his novel. And Andrew, with the practised enthusiasm of his trade, always expressed himself eager to read it with an equally practised lack of commitment. As for Kit's proposed job on television – well, the idea tided us over a difficult morning.

I had arranged to meet my family in Barnet the next afternoon at five-thirty, when my father got home from work. I felt that before becoming preoccupied with my new department at Longfield, I really should do something about the seaside bungalow. It was starting to assume enormous significance. My mother had gone into one of her psychic spells, and declared that she already saw it, nestling in isolation against rising green clifftops and emanating happiness. My father was using his estate-agent's skill in discovering the exact whereabouts of this unlikely vision, which he seemed to think might lie somewhere near Eastbourne. That struck me as an agreeable spot for them, though I knew property there would be pricy. If they assumed their two children would feel obliged to contribute towards the peace and contentment of their final years, I supposed they were right. But the time had come for me to have a serious word with my brother.

My mother provided tea, with chocolate swiss roll. It had been my favourite as a child, and she couldn't understand its allure might be lost. I found Ronnie was there already, his wife sitting at the corner of the table, nervously twisting the diamond ring on her finger. It occurred to me that I had hardly spoken more than a dozen sentences to Paula in my life, though I felt this a deprivation I could tolerate.

'If only my pools would come up,' sighed my father, stirring his mahogany-coloured tea. He had his own 'special' large cup, gold-rimmed and white, which I remembered for years. My mother took elaborate pains to avoid cracking it. 'Then I'd buy a villa somewhere glamorous, like Majorca.' He winked. 'I'd go and live there with one of them models.'

I said sharply, 'You'd get tired of her posturing and posing all over the place.'

My successor with Henry was a model.

'I never knew why you didn't do the pools, Ann.' My mother's tone had genuine mystification. 'With all your brains, you ought to work out the winning perms.'

'The pools are something I just can't understand, Mum. Like driving a car, or what cricket's all about.'

'You're better closing your eyes and using a pin.' Ronnie helped himself to sugar. He always put too much in his tea. I told him often he would become obese, reduce his expectation of life, develop diabetes, coronary thrombosis, chronic bronchitis, and osteoarthritis. But he never took any notice.

'I only wish we'd owned our own home all these years,' declared my mother tragically. The house where I was born was rented from my father's firm. 'Then we might have capital put by.'

Then the row blew up, with amazing suddenness.

'I'd like to help you, Mum, as much as I can,' Ronnie assured her. 'You know that. But business is going through a difficult time at the moment.'

I stared at him hard and asked, 'What business?'

'That's my business,' said Ronnie, looking pleased with the quip.

'I don't give a damn how you make your living,' I told him. 'But I think you should take responsibility for this bungalow.'

He nodded in the direction of Paula. 'I've got responsibilities already, haven't I?'

'Because I'm not married, that doesn't mean I've none,' I reminded him.

'I could never understand why you didn't marry again, Ann.' This was predictable. My mother brought out the remark on my every visit.

'She's got more sense,' observed my father.

'I've been ill, Mum, don't forget. No man wants to tie himself to an invalid.'

'But you *look* all right,' she said, quite aggressively.

'Well, perhaps I'll give you all a surprise one day.'

'I hope so.' My mother shook her head. 'You're getting on, you know.'

This was irritating enough, then Ronnie grinned and asked, 'Who's having secrets now?'

My mother looked interested. 'You mean, you've someone in mind?'

'Vaguely. Just vaguely.'

'Go on, Ann, there's nothing vague about it,' scoffed Ronnie.

I regretted bitterly telling him about Kit. I didn't think he was trying to pay me out for my suspicions about his business. It was just big brother teasing, a habit which I have seen persisting grotesquely into senility. Then I decided on an impulse to confess everything. They would have at least a chance to understand my inertia about their house.

'I've a boy-friend.' It sounded girlish and stupid. 'He writes books – technical books, you know, on various subjects. I'm afraid he hasn't much money. I'm hoping to marry him. Unfortunately, he's married already, so I must wait for his wife to divorce him.'

'Oh,' said my mother. She paused. 'Why couldn't you choose someone who wasn't married?' she asked accusingly.

'They're rather thin on the ground.'

'It doesn't sound very nice to me.'

I felt my face go red. It was incredible how my mother, of all people, could make me feel guilty.

'Ann knows her own mind,' my father supported me.

'I had a premonition something like this was going to happen to Ann,' she continued gloomily.

'You and your ridiculous premonitions!' I burst out. 'Good God, I'm not a sixteen-year-old. If you must know, I've already been living with this man for three years.'

'You're living in sin?' My mother was aghast.

'It isn't thought sinful any longer. Why do you have to go on pretending I'm a child? You're just being bloody stupid.'

'Easy, easy,' said my father.

'Dad's all right. He treats me like an ordinary person. But you're always fussing over me, still trying to dominate me, and I'm fed up with it.'

I saw two red blotches on her cheeks. 'I'm your mother, aren't I?'

'You're just bloody ignorant, that's your trouble. So are you, Ron. A criminal into the bargain, for all I know.'

'I told you so!' Paula's shrill voice came from the corner with alarming unexpectedness. 'If you don't give them the truth, they'll think the worst of us.'

'Shut up,' growled Ronnie.

'The way you carry on,' Paula persisted, 'they've every right to think you're bent.'

He shouted at her, 'Shut your trap!'

'I never thought I should live to be insulted by my own children,' declared my mother quiveringly.

'Ann didn't mean it, Sal,' my father put in nervously. 'She's a bit edgy. She's got a lot of worries in her profession.'

To assert herself, my mother went on, 'You'll come to a bad end, my girl. I know it – I've seen it. You can't argue with Fate. I shouldn't like to say what's in store for you.'

'What rubbish.' I stood up from the table. I loathed that parlour, with its plastic cloth and cheap cake and overstrong undrinkable tea. 'You disgust me. All of you. You grub about with your petty ambitions and squabbles and try to drag me back to your level. You'll never succeed, not if you live to be a hundred. Ever since I went to school, my life's been a struggle to get away from you. It was a terrible effort, my God it was an effort. But you wouldn't appreciate *that* for one moment, because you're too uneducated. I've nothing in common with you. I've had enough of you. I'm never coming to this house again.'

I made for the door, aware of my father imploring, 'Ann! Ann! Finish your tea.'

Nobody stopped me as I grabbed my coat and slammed the glass-panelled door behind me. I strode down the road uncertain whether to be ashamed or exhilarated. The relationship between parents and children became impossibly selfish, I decided. When the children grew up and the parents grew old then the elderly began to see how emotionally dependent on them they were, and resented it. Hence the occasional explosion. It was all very trying. For a second I even felt glad that it was impossible for me ever to have a child myself.

21

I WENT DOWN for my interview at Longfield in the middle of June. I was determined to look my best. I had my hair set and retinted early that morning. I had bought a cream silk suit with a short jacket and a flared skirt reaching just above my knee. It was French, cut with a skilful complexity to make it look starkly simple, and unnervingly expensive. I had new coffee-coloured grosgrain shoes, and I'd decided I had better buy a grosgrain handbag to match. I was dressing up for the most exciting day in my life – certainly far more exciting than the day that I married Henry.

The morning was bright and warm, I took the train again from Charing Cross, this time reading a book. I had to be at Longfield House by twelve. According to Tilly Dawes, everything would be over by one. She had invited me again to her 'cottage' for lunch.

The journey, like any once pioneered, seemed much shorter. At Longfield Station I took a taxi and at the House presented myself to a porter in his glass cubby-hole under the gate tower – just like an Oxford college. He led me across the sunny main court, through an archway to another court beyond, and finally into a large, light-panelled room with tables and easy chairs. It seemed some sort of staff common-room, for the moment used to gather the applicants.

I knew there were six of us short-listed, only one other of them a woman. There was one occupant of the room already, reading the *Guardian* on one of the seats set into the deep, leaded windows. He was a pleasant-looking, sandy-haired man about thirty-five, wearing a smart blue suit and a tie that from its affrontingly jarring colours must have represented some important institution indeed (our English tie-code was as much a mystery to me as cars, cricket, and the football pools).

The other candidate looked up. 'Hello,' he said in a friendly tone. 'I'm John Gresham.'

'I'm Ann Sheriff.'

'I heard you were to be one of my rivals. You're medically qualified, aren't you?'

'Yes.' None of the others were. They were specialist physiologists or biologists, essentially laboratory people. 'Not that it makes much difference. I've been doing lab. work almost all my career.'

'I should think it would impress the committee tremendously,' he said chivalrously. 'I expect they'd like a doctor about the place, in case one of the more elderly dons breaks a leg or collapses.'

'My clinical medicine's getting rather outdated.'

'I shouldn't think that matters. They'll appoint you on the off-chance of your giving them the kiss of life.'

We laughed. The tension was dented, though not broken.

I sat at the other end of the window-seat, picking up a magazine. I had no idea which one it was. I was starting to suffer the nervousness of an amateur actor faced with costume and grease-paint, in the final realization that the curtain will surely enough shortly rise.

'You're from Cambridge, aren't you?' I asked. Gresham nodded. 'I remember reading your paper on phosphorylating agents in primitive life.'

'How very flattering. Though the main work's been done in California.'

'I find the origins of terrestrial life a fascinating subject. Here we are, and nobody knows why.'

'I suppose we haven't really come an awfully long way from Genesis and all that.'

'At least we know now it must have been a chemical process.' It was soothing to talk of technical things.

139

'In the beginning,' he declaimed, 'there was some methane, and some ammonia, and some electricity. Hence a sludge of hydrogen cyanide. Hence amino acids. Hence adenosine monophosphate. Hence you and I, having this enjoyable if somewhat overshadowed conversation.'

'I suppose it does us no harm,' I reflected, 'to realize we evolved from the scum of the earth, generated in a primaeval thunderstorm.'

'But you're more concerned with the practical side of reproductive physiology, aren't you?'

'Yes. I suppose *that's* the effect of my clinical background. Being trained on people rather than guinea-pigs.'

'You're of more use to the world than me,' he remarked a shade ruefully. 'At the moment I'm engaged busily in growing three tadpoles from the egg instead of one.'

I looked at my watch. Gold, my best one. A present not from Kit, but from Henry. 'We're very early.'

'The others can't be much longer.'

'Do you know anything about them?'

'There's an Australian, an American, a Scotsman, and a lady from Keele.' He added more matily, 'Don't you hate this business, sitting about beforehand, being perfectly charming when we'd like to cut each other's throats?'

'I haven't had much experience of it. I had to apply formally for only one big job in my life – the one I hold now at Princess Victoria's. That wasn't too harrowing, because I was the only candidate.'

'I seem to spend all my time putting up for jobs. In the last six months I've been to Liverpool, Exeter, Oxford, and York. It's a way of seeing the country, I suppose. If I don't click this time, I'm going whoosh down the brain drain. Canada, here I come.'

'You should enjoy it in Canada,' I told him enthusiastically. 'I've an old girl-friend who settled there, and she'd never return.'

He gave me a look from the corner of his eye. 'You seem to have discounted my chances pretty heartlessly, haven't you?'

'Oh, no, I didn't mean that at all,' I said quickly.

I opened the magazine and started reading intently. I still didn't know which one it was.

The other candidates arrived. We sat about, talking nervously. The men wore more striped institutional ties. The woman was a mess, fat in a bright flowered dress. A youngish official of Longfield University appeared, in black jacket and striped trousers, like an old-fashioned physician or a modern restaurateur. He politely invited the fat woman to the committee-room. I looked at my watch again. It was exactly noon. I turned back to my magazine, seeing nothing.

The Australian and the American followed her before the selection committee. Each stayed away about ten minutes. They returned blank-faced, looking at the carpet, slumping into their chairs, reaching for a newspaper, non-committal to their fingertips. We had stopped talking to each other by now. It was like waiting for a viva in examinations, only worse, because in an examination a third of us would have gone home successful. The very pleasantness of our surroundings was somehow more racking than the befittingly sordid tiny little unswept rooms where they crammed examination candidates. I looked at my watch once more. Everything was going to be all right, I told myself. The job was fixed for me, Tilly Dawes had said so in as many words. But I had the nagging fear something might go wrong. I suddenly realized that I hadn't thought of Kit all morning.

'Dr Sheriff,' said the official quietly from the doorway.

We went down the corridor into the small committee-room, light-panelled like the one I had left. There was a round table with one vacant chair. I took it. My nerves had left me. I was self-confident again.

'Very kind of you to come down and see us, Dr Sheriff,' said the Chairman automatically.

I looked round the table. They had the humane practice of labelling the committee by strips of card set before each member. The Chairman opposite me, Lord Wrotham, was a tall, thin, wrinkled man with small pale blue eyes. I had seen his photograph now and then in the newspapers, generally pronouncing balefully on the national economy. On his right was Tilly. Then Councillor J. Samways, the local representative,

141

short, square, pink, and bald. On the Chairman's left sat Sir Robert Boatwright, a large bristle-haired man with an upturned moustache, reminding me of pictures of Field-Marshal Hindenburg. On his left I encountered a crisp-looking, fair, middle-aged woman, Miss Janet Bickens, the Catholic, my lost vote. Next to her was a pale, good-looking, dark, middle-aged man, J. R. K. Hollins, Esq. I had no idea who J. R. K. Hollins, Esq. was.

'You all have copies of Dr Sheriff's application?' asked the Chairman of the table in general. He looked at me and added, 'Dr Sheriff, why exactly do you want this post?'

'Because I have reached a stage in my career when I honestly feel I can do justice to my work only with wider scope and greater responsibility. When I heard of this post, I was excited at even the possibility of achieving these ends at such a university as Longfield.'

There was a satisfied grunt. It came from Councillor J. Samways.

'If you were appointed, Dr Sheriff,' continued the Chairman, 'what sort of research had you in mind to embark upon?'

'I should continue the work I am now doing at Princess Victoria's on the control of human fertility. This really falls into two parts. One is the investigation of the biological effects of existing and new oral contraceptives. The other is the investigation of other methods of biochemical contraception, as distinct from mechanical methods. I realize that this subject of research may not be encouraged, or may even be objectionable to, certain people.' I was careful not to look at Miss Bickens. 'But it is a well-established line of study, even an essential one in the eyes of some leading academic centres.' I had the sudden alarming feeling I might appear to be lecturing them. 'Of course, you may not think my abilities sufficient for such problems of worldwide significance,' I ended modestly.

'You've done some research on the blood, I believe, Dr Sheriff?' Sir Robert Boatwright held up a reprint of my paper on my blood-stain, which I had sent with my application. He had a loud aggressive voice, and seemed inclined to make an impression on the committee rather than me.

'Some years ago. These days I'm concerned only with the physiology of reproduction.'

'I see. And why did you make the change?'

'I found the second subject more interesting, and imagined the results might be more rewarding.'

'Rewarding financially, you mean?'

'Oh, no! I mean rewarding to mankind as a whole.'

'Perhaps the two subjects are not unrelated? I was brought up in the belief that one's blood was the essential matter passed on to the next generation. But I'm no scientist,' he added jocularly. Even his laugh was fierce.

'Are you intending to live in the area?' asked the Councillor. A genuine Kent voice. Rarely heard since the county was swamped with Londoners.

'I was going to travel every day from my flat in Chelsea.'

'I think Dr Sheriff means until she can find suitable accommodation locally,' said Tilly quickly. 'Don't you, Dr Sheriff?'

'Yes, of course. I'd love to live in such delightful surroundings.'

The Councillor looked satisfied, but didn't grunt.

'What about teaching?' asked the man called Hollins. He smiled at me. He seemed more friendly than the others. 'About how much lecturing would you be prepared to do each week?'

'As much as the university wished. Personally, I enjoy lecturing. I have never believed my research suffered from that particular duty. Uttering your thoughts before a roomful of critical students is a great help in organizing your mind.'

'The lecture does the speaker some good, if not the audience?' said Sir Robert.

Everyone laughed.

'I always remember,' declared Lord Wrotham, 'when I was at the university myself, hearing a lecture defined as, "The passage of material from the notebook of the lecturer to that of the student, without passing through the mind of either".'

Everyone laughed louder. Well, we were getting along.

'You are married, of course, Dr Sheriff?' inquired Sir Robert. He had noticed my ring.

'Divorced.'

'I see.' He glanced at my duplicated application, where I had mentioned this briefly. 'I notice you live not far from me. I've a feeling I've heard of you locally. You must be quite a personality in the area?'

I felt the sudden fear that he knew about Kit. My mind raced after possible ways that I might have crossed his path. The pub, perhaps. But that was unlikely. He must have lived in one of the most fashionable streets of the district. Anyway, if he knew of Kit, what of it? My private life was my own. I bet myself he probably had a mistress or two tucked away somewhere. He looked the sexy type.

'I'm not aware of it,' I told him. 'I don't live a particularly sociable life.'

'I wish I didn't. These City functions will be the death of me.'

'What specifically are these biochemical methods of contraception that you are investigating, Dr Sheriff?' I had almost forgotten Miss Bickens.

'I have two in mind. One is a method involving interference with the ovum after implantation. The other is a method of blocking the entry of the male cell into the ovum.'

No point in being evasive. A vote lost is a vote lost.

'I hope I'm not being too technical?' I added.

'Not at all, Dr Sheriff,' she said politely. 'Thank you.'

'I believe you also have plans – or at least ideas – for spreading the knowledge of birth control methods on a global scale?' asked Tilly.

'Surely that sort of crusading isn't necessary these days?' asked J. R. K. Hollins.

'I'm afraid it is,' I told him. 'There's dreadfully widespread ignorance in this country, and I hate to imagine the state of those nations with a largely illiterate population. Propaganda is just as important as pills. The most wonderful invention in the world is useless if nobody's heard of it.'

'You would associate the name of Longfield University with this propaganda?' asked Lord Wrotham.

'That would be almost inescapable. But as such propaganda is already associated with bodies like the World Health Organ-

144

ization and the United Nations, I would not think it in any way detrimental.'

'Any other questions?' he asked.

Silence.

'Thank you, Dr Sheriff. Would you mind waiting outside a few minutes longer?'

I passed the tadpole specialist in the doorway of the waiting-room, as he succeeded me. We said nothing. I don't think we looked at each other. I went back to my seat and picked up the magazine. I could feel my heart fluttering inside my ribs like a caged bird. The tadpole man seemed an age. Finally he came back, and we all sat looking at our reading-matter in thunderous silence.

Of course it was going to be all right. I made a good impression on the committee. That was obvious. I had handled the questions with more skill than I imagined I possessed. I didn't put a foot wrong. I had lavishly buttered Councillor Samway's local pride. Even the Catholic headmistress was amiable.

The door opened.

'Would you all mind waiting here just a few moments more?' said the official. 'Dr Sheriff, will you come with me, please?'

I followed him from the room, trying hard not to look gloating, smug, in the slightest pleased with myself. I'd got it. I'd won. What I wanted most in the whole world, even more than a divorce for Kit, was in my hands. I re-entered the committee-room, composing my face into an expression of gravity, fitting for receiving such a post in such a shining university.

'Dr Sheriff,' said the Chairman. 'There are a few more questions that we'd like to ask you.'

22

I SAT STARING at him, hardly believing him, the fingers of the Devil gripping my stomach.

'I shall do my best to answer them.'

'Sir Robert?' invited the Chairman.

Sir Robert Boatwright turned so that he faced me squarely. 'Might I ask you to amplify an answer you gave Miss Bickens? About these methods you're investigating, or preparing, yourself. Perhaps you could tell us, as simply as possible, how such agents are proposed to work?'

'Certainly, Sir Robert. My first method depends for its effect on preventing the implantation in the womb of the fertilized egg —'

'That's the one I'm interested in,' he interrupted. 'This medicament would not, in fact, act like the other "pill" we hear so much about?'

'Not at all. The principle is entirely different. The male and female sex cells unite, but the new combined cell does not become embedded in the lining of the womb, and so does not develop.'

'Isn't this what is commonly known – or as commonly as these things *are* known – as the "morning-after" pill?'

'Yes.'

Any hopes I had that the committee might simply be seeking further technical information were frozen by his next question. 'You mean it's an abortifacient?'

'No. It isn't. It's a contraceptive.'

'But, Dr Sheriff! Surely a contraceptive, by simple definition,

146

is a device or chemical which prevents conception? With this method conception has in fact occurred. The woman has become pregnant and you are interfering with it. So your drug is an abortifacient.'

I bit my lip. 'Will you permit me to disagree with you, Sir Robert? To my mind, conception is not simply the union of sperm with ovum, of male cell with female. For all we know, this may happen dozens of times in the life of every woman. It may proceed no further for any number of reasons.'

'That's a little hypothetical, isn't it?'

'It must be hypothetical. We are unable to demonstrate the process of human fertilization *in vivo* under the microscope. Our need to postulate so many theories about these early stages only strengthens my view. Which is that conception isn't completed until the fertilized ovum is embedded in its rightful habitat, and starts to divide and grow. It is all one and the same process. Only then could the woman be said to be pregnant.'

'In your view.' His voice now had an edge on it.

'It is the view of several other scientific workers.'

'Perhaps you will admit, Dr Sheriff, that this is not entirely a scientific question?'

'I cannot see it as anything else,' I said simply.

The Chairman was looking uneasy. Why, I asked myself, *why* had this man Boatwright decided to attack me? I knew nothing about him, apart from Tilly's casual aside. He was very rich, and much thought of in the sad, dehumanized world of City offices. I blamed myself now for not looking him up, trying to find out something about his life and views.

'All I can say, Dr Sheriff, is that I certainly should not like my own daughters to take this drug of yours.'

My heart sank further. It was a bad sign when men started talking in such contexts about their own daughters. I suddenly found myself thinking of Sir William Jenner, Queen Victoria's hyperpaternal physician. Under the table, I dug my nails into my hands. I must fight on doggedly, I must match his wits, above all I *must* keep my temper.

'May I be fair to myself by pointing out, Sir Robert, that this particular method has already been studied elsewhere? It is generally recognized as a useful one – the only possible one – for establishing contraception after intercourse has taken place?'

'What significance are we supposed to see in that?'

'We must face the reality that intercourse occurs in some circumstances casually, without the time or personal disposition for forethought.'

He raised his thick eyebrows. 'Must we? It's hardly the sort of fate which would overtake any decent girl.'

'You'd be surprised how often it does,' I told him sharply.

Lord Wrotham stirred in his chair. I shouldn't have said that.

'Dr Sheriff —' Miss Bickens's quiet voice. 'Would there not be the danger, if such an agent were used, of an ill-formed foetus? Supposing the egg were already fertilized, that life were already in existence. Might there be the possibility of your pill not *entirely* doing its work? For instance, the implantation you are aiming to prevent might be partially achieved. We take drugs for all manner of things, from easing our headaches to curing our major disabilities, but we know from common experience they are often enough not a hundred per cent effective.'

'Admittedly, the foetus might grow,' I explained. 'But if malformed the mother would lose it at an early period of pregnancy, quite naturally. Just as she would were the foetus damaged for other reasons.'

'But supposing she didn't?' Miss Bickens persisted gently. 'Might one envisage the baby growing in the womb, and then being born, and then living, yet with some severe malformation? An imperfect heart, for example? Or lack of limbs? Perhaps blindness?'

I sensed a slight, definite stirring round the table. Sir Robert might have turned on me his artillery, but her words were a quiet, deadlier stab.

'That, of course, is a possibility,' I admitted.

Why have we become caught in this technical argument? I wondered desperately. What has it remotely to do with my suitability or not for the post? I felt myself growing frustrated and angry, and told myself I must keep calm, calm, calm, not under *any* provocation lose my self-control.

Tilly Dawes, who had been staring intently at her square of white blotting-paper and scratching busily with her pencil, announced sharply, 'The drug Dr Sheriff mentions would not, of course, be used until this possibility had been thoroughly discounted.'

'Professor, I wonder if you would give the candidate the opportunity to answer her own questions?' asked the Chairman mildly.

'I should only have said exactly what Professor Dawes has told you,' I asserted.

'I don't like the sound of this pill.' Sir Robert looked at the others. 'I shouldn't like it to come out of *this* university.'

'I agree with Sir Robert,' nodded Councillor Samways.

'Dr Sheriff could simply drop the whole project, if that's all you want,' said Tilly, eyeing him crossly.

'Professor Dawes!' murmured the Chairman again.

I said quickly, 'I certainly shouldn't undertake any research not approved by the university.'

J. R. K. Hollins on my right smiled. 'There's academic independence for you.'

No, I shouldn't have said that. I was being too eager to please.

'Dr Sheriff, a word —' began Councillor Samways.

I saw the quarter of attack shift to the Councillor with the sickening feeling that he was encouraged by Boatwright's pugnacity. It was always the same on committees. Awkward opinions can lie comfortably unsaid through inertia, self-doubts, or moral cowardice, but once the first stone is cast the rest come in showers.

'We here were having something of a discussion before you came back,' revealed the Councillor, 'about the present work you're doing at Princess Victoria's Hospital in London. I see from your application that you're concerned in the running of a family planning clinic?'

'That's correct. In conjunction with Professor Sandra Mc-Robb.'

'An extremely eminent gynaecologist,' put in Tilly Dawes. That time the Chairman didn't bother to object.

149

'I've no doubt.' The Councillor tidied his papers into a neat pile. 'I take it, Dr Sheriff, at this clinic you prescribe pills and certain articles?'

'Yes.'

'Would I be right in assuming you would continue this sort of work if appointed here?'

This time I wouldn't fawn. I'd tell the truth. 'I should certainly like to. If one is studying human reproduction, it is all too easy to imagine that everything happens in a test-tube. The final result of one's work lies with human beings, and it is human beings who should be studied.' I added pointedly, 'That is where my medical qualification is valuable to me.'

'And who foots the bill?' asked the Councillor.

'I envisaged running such a clinic with the local health authority, so the National Health Service would pay for the drugs and appliances in certain circumstances. But in others, for example with unmarried women —'

'What!' exclaimed the Councillor.

I told him patiently, 'Under the recent Family Planning Act, the concept of "social need" —'

'I know all about that,' he interrupted.

'I don't see why advice should be lavished only on married women.' Now I felt my cheeks going hot. 'It's sheer blindness to imagine that single girls don't need it.'

'You mean sex on the rates?' muttered the Councillor.

'I mean that it costs fifty pounds for a maternity bed, and fifteen pounds a week for the institutional care of an unwanted child. We count the cost of contraceptives in shillings.'

'You don't appear to set much store on chastity, Dr Sheriff,' cut in Sir Robert.

'It is not I who am involved. Whether my patients set store on chastity or not is entirely their affair. It is my duty only to help them.'

'The very fact that you are there to help them increases their temptation to be unchaste.'

I suddenly felt exhausted. I couldn't battle any longer with them, or with myself. I heard Tilly Dawes complaining, 'This meeting is getting out of hand. We are supposed to be interviewing Dr Sheriff for a job, not engaging her in a debate on public morals.'

'Professor Dawes, will you kindly remember that *I* am the Chairman of this committee?' This time Lord Wrotham sounded annoyed.

'Well, keep your meeting in order, then.'

'I require encouragement neither from you nor from anyone else to do that.'

There was a silence. Everyone looked uneasy.

'If you would be so kind as to withdraw again, Dr Sheriff —' began the Chairman.

'*Must* you prolong the agony?' demanded Tilly.

'I hope you don't think we're being hard on you, Dr Sheriff.' The damage done, Sir Robert's voice became quite gentle. 'Naturally, we should have to think very carefully before allowing the name of this university to be associated with birth control, particularly in its more dubious forms. Personally, I should not like to see Longfield associated with the subject in *any* form. But as I said, I am not a scientist.'

'Stop lecturing the girl,' barked Tilly.

'I may be old-fashioned,' he went on, ignoring her, 'but I believe we have a duty to preserve certain standards of morality. God knows, we see all round us today the most frightening results of laxity and permissiveness. Drugs, sex, enjoyment – isn't that all the young people think about? We have the responsibility of making it less easy for them to destroy themselves.'

I said nothing.

'We have ten illegitimate babies a week in Longfield,' remarked Councillor Samways warningly.

'You wouldn't if I were working here,' I told him tartly.

'Dr Sheriff, if you will withdraw —' began the Chairman again.

'Take a vote, man, take a vote,' demanded Tilly.

'I shall, once Dr Sheriff has withdrawn.'

'You stay right there, Ann. After the way you've been treated, you've a right to see your opponents stand up and be counted.'

'Professor Dawes! You must realize that was most irregular—'

'Anyway, she knows well enough already,' Tilly went on savagely. 'It's as plain as a pikestaff that I'm on her side, and so is Mr Hollins. Miss Bickens, the Councillor, and Sir Robert are against. Under university regulations, you yourself have the two votes necessary for a decision. Well? Which way are they going?'

The Chairman looked sadly discomfited. Then, perhaps because she had goaded him too much, he gathered his papers, shuffled them briskly, and announced quickly, 'My votes award the post to Dr Gresham.'

'A very wise choice,' said Sir Robert Boatwright, in tones of great satisfaction.

'Listen —' I was on my feet. It was over, nothing mattered any more. 'I have never before been subjected, thank God, to the experience just suffered in this room —'

'We can understand your disappointment, Dr Sheriff,' said the Chairman weakly.

'That's nothing to do with it,' I blazed at him. 'Your antipathy isn't simply towards my work. That's a symptom, a by-product. And my God, a nasty one! You ought to look at your history-books. Your sort haven't changed in a hundred years. People with my ideas – men like Francis Place, Richard Carlile, and Dale Owen – were hounded and persecuted, all of them. Charles Bradlaugh and Annie Besant ended up in front of the Lord Chief Justice. Marie Stopes ended up as a sort of national joke, which was worse.'

'Dr Sheriff,' ordered the Chairman. 'Please leave this room at once.'

'I will *not* leave. You've all made it plain what you think of me, and I'm going to make it equally plain what I think of you.'

'Hear, hear,' said Tilly Dawes.

Lord Wrotham shouted at me, 'Leave the room!'

'Let her go on,' boomed Sir Robert. 'She has a nice line of talk. You're very slick, Dr Sheriff. Too slick, to my mind, by half.'

'I'm not faced with the comparatively narrow medical or social problem of getting people to use science to better their lives. To better the lives of all of us on this planet, in the long run. I'm faced with a battle against ignorance and prejudice. That's all it is. My work's only one of a million targets. When anaesthetics were invented, your sort of people hollered that it was sinful to give a woman chloroform in childbirth. You said God had declared she must suffer, there it was, written in the Bible. It needed a queen to take chloroform for the birth of a prince before it became respectable. I'm trying in my own small way to dispel ignorance and crumble prejudice, though it's a heartbreaking job. But I keep at it, because *that* is the essence of the advance of civilization.'

'The lady has taken on a great deal if such is her ambition,' said Sir Robert smugly.

I turned on him fiercely. 'Yes, I have taken on a great deal. How many isolated, single people have brought humanity more than a step or two along that path? Jesus and Mohammed, Darwin and Wilberforce, Plato and Freud. Precious few. I'm humble enough, or I'm sensible enough, to see that my battle's lost before it's started. But if I can enlighten just one mind in my life, I shall be happy.'

'You're on the scene a little too late for the suffragettes, aren't you?' asked Sir Robert rudely.

'That's a typical remark. A man's remark,' I snapped at him. 'Who makes the big decisions, whether about suffrage, about contraception, or the whole lives of women and children? You men. And you don't have to bear the babies or suffer the abortions, or struggle with a home and a husband and ten kids you don't want.'

'I don't really think we should sink to personal abuse, Dr Sheriff.'

'Oh, shut up, you loud-mouthed great oaf,' I said.

I turned and left.

I strode rapidly through the room where I had waited, then out of the building, without looking right or left. I walked on through the town, down the long hill to the station, my mind empty. I felt somehow surprised to find myself in the place. I stood in the ticket-hall as if unknowing what to do next. I saw there was a train to London in twenty minutes. I went down to the end of the platform, sat on a hard wooden bench, and cried.

The electric train clattered in. I quickly tried to make myself presentable. I found the last carriage empty, and took a corner seat. My mind was still paralysed. I opened my book automatically. It was a copy of Eliot's play *The Cocktail Party*, belonging to Kit. Two lines immediately struck my eye —

Half the harm which is done in this world
Is due to people who want to feel important.

So much for Sir Robert Boatwright. He had made his mark, and destroyed myself. Ann Sheriff, who had fought her way from a dingy nest of benighted superstition in Barnet to lift a corner of the world's blanket of ignorance, had reached her possibly inevitable check. My brain – my weapon – had been struck away useless by the prejudiced bombast of an insensitive money-maker.

Lights danced across the printed page. Dazzling, a string of jagged edges. Migraine. I felt in my new handbag, hoping desperately I might unthinkingly have slipped in some ergotamine tablets. But I hadn't. I remembered the date. I was just due to menstruate again.

23

NICE AIRPORT, A whiff of hot air hitting you at the plane door, the smell of flowers and burning paraffin. I stood on the tarmac as the other passengers ambled towards Customs, fascinated with the sage-green mountains falling into the still blue sea, a geological crescendo. There were palm trees, a heat-haze softening the angular white distant buildings of Nice. Traffic spurted along the flat coast road and small boats divided the water with twin white plumes. This was the famous Côte d'Azur, as different from Malaga – where I had been before with Kit – as Bond Street from the suburbs. It was the former playground of reigning kings and home of exiled ones. The shrine of chance, haunted with mathematical myths. The workshop of Picasso, Somerset Maugham, and Serge Voronoff, who tried to make old men young again by giving them the testicles of monkeys. I supposed it would now be overrun with tourists and strident with cars, but it was a curiosity as much to be visited in a lifetime as the ruins of Pompeii.

The bus took us to Antibes, twenty kilometres westwards along the coast. I had expected Antibes to be a bland-faced resort, with huge white hotels, flashy villas, and seedy pensions, a materialized picture-postcard. I was delighted to find as we finished our journey the crowded twisted streets with their workaday shops, which Kit struggled through with our suitcases as we walked away from the busy bus-station. We emerged from alleys between old stone houses on to the massive ramparts, built to withstand the sea and enemies, separated from the squat, grey, isolated square fort by the forest of yacht-masts in the harbour. And the flat was charming. Just two small rooms, plain, white-painted, with deal furniture, a cupboard kitchen and a shower, all up four steep flights of stone steps and facing the sea contemptuously over the jostling heads of the holiday-makers.

The journey was Kit's idea. He was wonderful when I got back from Longfield. He said I must get away at once, surely Princess Victoria's would give me a week or so's leave? The same afternoon he went to B.E.A. in Lower Regent Street and bought two tickets to Nice. Then he persuaded his friend Jim, who ran that Fleet Street literary agency, to lend us his holiday flat. On the Saturday after my interview we were off. I bought nothing new, made no preparations, just packed what I could lay hands on. The cream silk dress, the coffee-coloured gros-grain shoes, the matching grosgrain handbag, I left behind. I felt I could never bring myself to wear them again.

'The market's within a stone's throw, just beyond the church,' explained Kit. 'It's open every morning except Monday, but don't expect any bargains.'

We had already opened the tall windows over the sea. The suddenness of our departure was a delightful spice to our arrival, and we were unpacking as excitedly as a honeymoon couple.

'I didn't realize you knew Antibes so well, darling?'

'It's not far from Juan-les-Pins. Where I went after Oxford.'

'With your girl-friend?' I asked amiably.

'That's it.' Kit tossed his pyjamas on the bed. 'I had pen, paper, no money, and a copy of Connolly's *Rock Pool*. Which wasn't published in England till after the war, and everyone thought rather naughty. Incredible. It was the book's fault that I came here at all. It gave me romantic notions about the Riviera. I imagined when I was flat broke I could get a job as a barman, or something. But of course, the world's got so bureau-cratic. I needed a work-permit, and God knows what. Even our fantasies must bear an official rubber stamp.'

'So you picked up this woman instead?'

'I'd have starved picturesquely had she failed to take a fancy to me.'

'Weren't you supposed to throw your last francs on the table in the casino and win a fortune?'

'I hate casinos. They're far too solemn, like cathedrals. Same principle of single-minded devotion, I suppose. I must have a drink.' He looked round. 'Do you suppose Jim's left a bottle anywhere?'

In the minuscule kitchen he found a half-full bottle of Pernod and two glasses. He mixed the drink with water, and we leant close together on the rusty iron rail which ran waist-high across the window.

'Is this absinthe?' I had never tasted it before. 'Isn't it supposed to turn you blind?'

'Another fragment of lost romanticism. The Government insist they make it purer and weaker these days.'

I said contentedly, 'It's lovely here.'

'I've always wanted to come back. But Myra wouldn't go abroad.'

That explained her nonsense about passports and police forms.

'What was she like?' I persisted. 'This woman you had down here?'

'Really quite nice. The women who pick up young men always are. They're so grateful.'

Our two bare forearms pressed together on the rail.

'Didn't you feel ashamed of yourself at the time?'

'Who feels ashamed of a business deal, particularly one satisfactory to both partners? I never thought twice about our relationship, to tell the truth. We drifted into it pleasantly, and as pleasantly drifted out again. It was conducted in an atmosphere of great comfort and superb cooking. Emotionally, it was in a gratifyingly low key. You know how I hate bedroom dramatics.'

'Except when you're drunk.'

'True enough,' he admitted. 'But a man's a slave to his inhibitions, not his passions.'

I sipped more of the cloudy yellowish aniseed-water. 'I still can't understand why I didn't get that job at Longfield.'

'Now, my darling! You know our rule. Not a word about it. Not till we get home, at any rate.'

157

'Can you blame me for itching after a post-mortem?'

'There'll be other jobs,' Kit said encouragingly. 'And better ones.'

'At the moment, I never want to venture out of Princess Victoria's. It's cosy there. Too cosy, I suppose, which is why I've *got* to venture again one of these fine days.'

There was a roar as a power-boat started up, and a girl with streaming long hair in a tiny bikini came threading among the small craft, bouncing over the ripples, water-skiing. A sport beyond my abilities. Even swimming was difficult when my rheumatism was bad, and my joints had started to stiffen again after that morning in Longfield. There must be a psychological element in it, I decided, whatever Charles Crawless's opinion. I opened and closed my fist. I must see my rheumatologist as soon as we got home. He'd probably start me on corticosteroids.

'You know the main reason I wanted that job, Kit? Because I've become a teacher rather than a research worker. And that's your fault.'

He looked puzzled.

'Before I met you, I only wanted to sit in a back room with a microscope. After the dust-up with Henry, I simply embraced obscurity. I found real comfort in withdrawal from human contacts. But you stimulated me, you restored my confidence. You made me not only more sure of myself, but more articulate.'

He grinned. 'Flattery.'

'It's true. But I'm worried. I'm starting to ride hobby-horses, and ride them for a fall. I'm a woman of "progressive views", but I never bothered to question whether they were right before coming against that awful committee at Longfield. That's arrogance, a fault I've seen in too many scientists. In the end I'll get nowhere, simply because my pet ideas bore everyone Boredom is more deadly to a cause than any amount of arguing.'

'That's true,' Kit admitted. 'Jesus took great pains to avoid boring his audiences. The parables are terribly clever. And terribly cunning. Like good advertising copy.'

'Am I turning into a militant woman?' I was not wholly joking.

'God, no! A militant woman sticks to her one strident note.

You couldn't, you'd collapse and become normal. You're too much of a mixture, Ann. You can be tough, but you can also be very soft. Mostly – you're soft.'

'I'm lucky, having you to put me firmly in my proper place every night.'

'Which might have done your other female pioneers a lot of good.'

'Oh, I don't know. Marie Stopes had some notorious love affairs. Beatrice Webb was violently in love with Austen Chamberlain, though I don't suppose there was much actual sex in it. Had there been, the effect on her, the Fabians, and the Labour Party might have been interesting.' The girl on water-skis roared past again, in the opposite direction. 'Do you know that you can develop abscesses on your ovaries from that?' I pointed out.

Kit looked blank.

'There was a case reported in the Australian *Medical Journal*. You get a douche of sea-water with such force it runs up your vagina and uterus, right through your tubes, and out the far end.'

'How can you talk of the equality of women?' asked Kit.

We were to stay in Antibes only a week, but Kit's instincts were right. It had already begun to push Longfield from my mind. We soon fell into a routine which beguiled us that our normal way of life, with my daily scurrying from Chelsea to Princess Victoria's, was an existence as unreal as the previous incarnations of my mother. We stayed in bed late with the bright sunlight flooding through the unshuttered windows, cheerfully deaf to the racket of the motor-scooters. In the mornings, we wandered through the old town, down steep narrow streets somehow always lined with overflowing dustbins and much urinated in by cats and men, the walls chalked with political slogans which looked far more thrilling than ours at home. In the Place General de Gaulle, Kit bought yesterday's London papers and we sat drinking coffee or *bière à pression* amid the shopkeepers and bank-clerks, watching the merry-go-round of traffic. Then we made for the glass-roofed vibrant market, its trestled stalls piled carelessly with foods which were displayed in West End provision stores like jewellery. Our French was shaky, and we often ended with unwanted or unlikely purchases, but we ate them just the same. I was proud of my cooking, and enjoyed the strange ingredients – though affronted when Kit woke twice in the night with pangs of indigestion. We ate occasionally in the little pizzaria round the corner opposite the Hôtel de Ville, two rooms underground, always full and noisy, the pies coming with a hot breath from the fiery brick oven on to our plates. It was here that one evening I gave a gasp, and as Kit looked sharply across the table, I said, 'That man who's just come in – I could have sworn he was Sir Robert Boatwright.'

Kit twisted round. The man stood in the doorway, mopping his face with his handkerchief. He had the same brush-like hair and upturned moustache, but as I watched he turned to a fat woman beside him and chatted complainingly in French. The image faded, like a picture in the fire.

'You've got Boatwright on your mind,' said Kit.

'Can you blame me?'

I had gone straight to see Ma Saintsbury the morning after the interview and found that Tilly Dawes had telephoned her already. Tilly had nothing to reveal that I did not already know, except for one item. While I was out of the room, between my first and second bout with the committee, Boatwright had brought up something about my 'living with a man'. Tilly Dawes had informed him, and quite properly, that my private life was of no concern to the committee in general or him in particular. But the point had been made. It must have helped Miss Bickens and Samways to see me more easily as a corrupter of mankind in general.

'Now I've calmed down, I feel only how strange the whole business was. My qualifications were better than the others',' I told Kit assertively across the restaurant table. 'They were certainly better than Gresham's. Tilly Dawes was all for me, and she's a tremendous power down there, with her O.M. and all that lot. In the normal way, the committee would have followed her like lambs.'

'Perhaps you looked too sexy?'

I swirled the red wine round my glass. It was the first time I had mentioned Longfield since the day of our arrival, sticking conscientiously to Kit's prescription of silence. Though of course it remained a cloud which hazed the sunlight, and now and then blotted it out completely.

'Perhaps I shouldn't have appeared as if I practised what I preached,' I admitted half-heartedly. I paused. 'And you've never even heard of Boatwright?'

'Never. I'd cut my throat, Ann, if I thought that I was behind all you had to suffer.'

'How *could* it be any fault of yours, darling? I'm only mystified how he could have found out.'

'People talk. That's something you and I have to put up with. There's no knowing where gossip spreads to, any more than your own bad cold.'

'But it worries me. How could Boatwright get even an inkling about us? He surely knows nobody we do. We don't move in the same social areas. I can only suppose he hired a private detective.'

'I think that would have been taking his committee-work too seriously altogether,' said Kit, calling for the bill.

We performed an enormous amount of copulation in the flat. Once my period was over, we tried, several times a day, all the positions that we'd heard of or could imagine. Kit on top, me on top, forwards, backwards, sideways, on a chair, an involved business across the edge of the bed which pulled the adductor muscles inside my thigh and almost put us out of action. I even became a shade anxious, and asked him once, 'I suppose we're not just a couple of perverts?' We had decided to try it standing up, a method I'd heard from McRobb which enjoyed remarkable popularity among her middle-aged patients.

'Nonsense!' said Kit. 'That randy little man Apollinaire once wrote to his girl-friend, "Your body has nine doors and I have opened them all" – which gives us a fair run before we reach the limit of decent possibilities.'

'Nine . . . ?' I murmured wonderingly.

Kit said he regarded it as a form of therapy for my psychological injuries. He had suddenly taken an interest in psychology, bringing with us an armful of books on it, and pleasing me by asking for explanations of the exact differences between neurosis and psychosis, an Oedipus complex and a castration complex, claustrophobia and agoraphobia. He declared enthusiastically that he would write a handbook on psychology, to go with the ones on philosophy and beekeeping. On our last morning, as we lay in bed enjoying the sun and enduring the scooters, he was reading and suddenly gave a laugh.

'Listen to this – "Thus psycho-analytic theories suggest that man is essentially a battlefield, he is a dark cellar in which a maiden aunt and a sex-crazed monkey are locked in mortal combat, the affair being refereed by a rather nervous bank-clerk".'

'What's the book?'

'*New Horizons in Psychology.*'

'That's about the case,' I assured him.

'But surely it can't all be true? About the ego, the id, the censor, all the cerebral menagerie?'

'Freud's only been dead thirty years. Give a little longer for his ideas to acquire proper assessment – say, two or three centuries.'

'But is psychology any more use for solving our problems than astrology? Which at least comes with the blessing of antiquity.'

'You're unfair.' I sprang as usual to the defence of science. 'The very word "psychology" has done a lot already. When you study the antics of a man, a group, even a country, "psychologically" instead of "morally", what have you achieved? You look with your mind rather than your emotions. Surely that's a worthwhile advance?'

'The doctor has spoken,' said Kit submissively. The bell in the church began to toll, almost over our heads. 'It's not Sunday?'

'It's a funeral. Didn't you notice? They have two or three a week. Always early in the morning, before they set up the market or the tourists are about.'

'It seems so inappropriate to die down here.' Kit sighed. 'Like dying in one of those glittering blocks of luxury flats. Yet people do and often alone. The porters break down the doors weeks afterwards. The smell must be awful, particularly with the efficient central-heating.' He tossed the book aside. 'When I die, will you put a notice in *The Times*? Or perhaps one of those regular entries, once a year? "Kit Stewart, dear and affectionate husband." I should *be* a dear and affectionate husband, even if still of Myra's. "Sadly missed." Why are the dead always such nice people?'

'Don't say things like that, Kit.'

'You sound quite frightened?'

'I am frightened.'

'How would you bury me? I think I'd prefer Harrods. Certainly not the Co-op. What an awful indignity, to die in Littlewood's pyjamas in a Times Furnishing bed, and be buried by the Co-op.'

I got closer to him. 'I don't know what I'd do, Kit, if you were taken from me.'

'Find another man.'

'Don't!' I sounded angry. 'I shouldn't, never. I couldn't I know it. There couldn't be anyone like you, Kit. No one I'd tie myself to, look up to, pride myself in my devotion to.'

Sensing that he had really upset me, he said, 'I'm sorry. Perhaps I've been reading too much about the death-wish.'

I held him tight. 'Now, now, *now*,' I whispered urgently. 'Have me now.'

Kit kicked off the bedclothes. 'The French generally do it in the morning, I believe. I suppose that's why they never have a cooked breakfast.'

That afternoon we went home.

Arriving at the flat tugged the wound I had suffered in Longfield, but it was starting to knit into a scar. Like any other scar, it would in time contract, fade, and almost disappear. Kit was right when he said the best I could do was forget my application to the university had ever been made. Except for one comparatively insignificant point. I was determined at least to try and find how Boatwright had got to know about Kit.

163

24

WHEN I GOT back to Princess Victoria's I threw myself on my work with almost physical ferocity. In my week away, I found that Ma Saintsbury had with her usual sensitivity placed before the hospital committee, neither asked nor even prompted by me, a scheme for raising my status in the medical school. I was to have a larger and more convenient laboratory in the new part of the hospital, with air-conditioning, stainless steel sinks, and workbenches of easily cleaned plastic. I would have a qualified assistant and a full-time technician. Ma Saintsbury had even fought for a high salary. As the laboratory wasn't yet finished all this would take effect at the new academic year in the autumn, but I was grateful enough for the promise. As Ma Saintsbury knew, it would prevent my feeling unwanted – a terrible sensation for a woman. And perhaps she was feeling slighted herself. After all, it was she who had recommended me to Tilly Dawes in the first place.

But what work was I to do? My chances at Longfield had been sunk by the twin torpedoes of my 'morning-after' pill and my sperm-blocking agent – as far as my professional achievements had come into it at all. I felt a strong if illogical reluctance to work on both for a while. The bitterness over cyclova had left me disinclined to continue serious research on the oral contraceptives either, though I would carry out any routine blood-tests which McRobb wanted. I decided to turn my attention on the placenta. While on holiday I had half-made up my mind to explore the chemistry of this strange organ. It was still comparatively mysterious, and offered the possibility of my hitting on some function as yet unknown, or at least imperfectly grasped.

We were already aware enough that the placenta brought oxygen from the mother's blood to the developing foetus, and transferred the waste-product carbon dioxide back again. We knew that nutrition for the baby's growth and the products of its excretion passed by the same two-way system – though the transfer of proteins, fats, and antibodies of high molecular weight, I had noticed, was not fully understood and might be worth while investigating. But it was the function of the placenta as a transient endocrine gland, secreting its own hormones, which invited my curiosity. I decided to spend a preliminary six months examining the steroid hormones it created and stored, trying to confirm, or perhaps establish for the first time, their exact chemical structure.

In this work I would need a regular supply of human placentas. I asked McRobb. She herself brought up the first, warm and still steaming, from the delivery-room.

'We should have a good crop this week, Sheriff,' she announced.

I looked at the dark-red, granular tissue in the small enamelled bowl. With a pair of forceps I started to separate its tattered amniotic membrane and translucent umbilical cord, as thick as my little finger, with the two arteries twisted round its single, valveless vein.

'I always think it's hard,' observed McRobb, 'that such a personal organ as a placenta should be slopped ignominiously into a bucket by the midwife, to be quite callously and unceremoniously incinerated. Did you know what the ancient Egyptians did with their placentas, Sheriff? They preserved them lovingly in urns. When little Ptolemy went away to the wars, something of him was left behind for Mum to weep over. I forget if it was the Egyptians or some other lot who carried their placentas into battle on the tips of their spears. The forerunner of the gay lancer's pennant. It would be quite a sight, the Horse Guards clattering down the Mall outside Buckingham Palace with their placentas trailing over their brass helmets.'

'I'm afraid I haven't your erudition in the minutiae of reproduction,' I smiled.

McRobb lit one cigarette from another and leaned against the cluttered wooden bench of my attic laboratory. I reflected that we had chatted a good deal together over the past year, since I had first started work on cyclova, and she always seemed to find something surprising to say.

'I've been thinking again about that do of yours at Longfield,' she continued. 'It's fishy.'

'I don't want to talk about it. I'm just trying to forget the episode.'

'I don't think I'm *going* to let you forget it,' she said decisively. 'Something was up. To my nasty mind, at any rate. They didn't want you in the place. Why?'

'They seemed to imagine that I intended to run my department as a brothel, or something.'

'Which reminds me,' McRobb broke off with concern. 'Did you hear they'd arrested Mrs Ramsay?'

'No!' It was like hearing the arrest of some busy and useful functionary, like one's grocer or bank manager.

'She's up at Quarter Sessions next week. She's been as busy as ever, you know, despite the new laws. *I* haven't the beds for one in five of the abortions I'm now being implored to take on. And, of course, you can't simply put them on the waiting-list and ask them back a year hence. The back-street girls will continue to flourish until the Government complete the job and build shiny abortion palaces all over the country. Perhaps that's the idea. They could convert all those empty cinemas.'

McRobb perched on the edge of the bench and swung her legs. I noticed her stockings were wrinkled, as usual.

'Anyway, our back-street practitioners have the weight of tradition behind them, and nothing is quite so traditional as the pattern of an unwanted pregnancy. At first, you know, the girl just won't believe she's fallen. It's only when she's a fortnight overdue that panic sets in. Then it's off to the chemist's for castor-oil, aloes, jalap, colocynth, all the things mother told her about. A good purge – sound eighteenth-century medicine. "Female Pills", as advertised for "irregularity", become enormously popular. And ergot, if she can get her hands on any. Though lead's dropped in favour. Did you hear that the girls who used to work with lead in the Potteries had a marked tendency to abort?'

I shook my head.

'The next step,' McRobb went on, dropping her cigarette ash in the sink, 'is a shift in the attack from the chemical to the physical. Falling downstairs, beating their bellies, jumping off the kitchen table. Or getting their husbands to jump on *them*. The foetus continues to sit there, snug, warm, and well-nourished, unheeding the raging storms outside. But hope springs eternal in the human uterus. Amazing perseverance. The girl buys a Higginson's syringe and pumps cocktails of arsenic and potassium permanganate up her vagina. Some of the more progressive ones favour soft drinks. When she imagines her girl-friends or the boss eyeing her midriff suspiciously, she sticks in a knitting-needle and as likely as not perforates her vaginal vault.'

'And ends up in your wards, anyway?'

'Exactly. Another of my beds blocked. They never seem to use slippery elm these days,' McRobb reflected. 'Slippery elm used to be quite a favourite round these parts. If the husband or boy-friend's got money, of course, everything's easy, and always was. It's all a tragedy,' she ended, on an unexpected note of sadness. 'One of the worst in the world. I've always been lenient about performing abortions, as you're aware. I've too tender a conscience to act otherwise. If the girl doesn't want a child, but in the heat of the moment omits the precautions, I take the intention as good as the deed.'

'I don't think those ideas would go down very well at Long-field.'

'They *couldn't* have turned you down for your professional views, Sheriff.' McRobb frowned. 'Or for any views. They've all sorts of oddbods down there, Commies, mystics, pacifists, all-purpose protesters – you name it, we'll protest against it. The current fashion, like hair and pot. At Longfield they think it's progressive and all that, giving them the right image. No,' she decided. 'Someone was in for you.'

'I know someone was. Boatwright.'

'But *why*, for God's sake? He's sane. He wouldn't want you deprived of the job unless you appeared utterly incompetent. As a business type, he must know the importance of hiring the best talent on the market. That's plain common sense. What's he make his millions from, anyway?'

'Juggling with money. Those unit trusts they keep advertising in the papers to create your fortune.'

'Oh, nothing useful, like making things?' McRobb stubbed her cigarette out in the saucer. 'It doesn't add up, does it?'

'There're other matters.' As she looked at me inquiringly, I added, 'Personal matters. I try to keep them out of a gossip-ridden place like this. Perhaps you knew, or anyway suspected, that I live with a man?'

'I wish to God I did,' said McRobb.

She sat on the edge of the bench in silence for some moments. 'I'll have a nose round,' she decided.

'I wish you wouldn't, Sandra. Honestly. I'd much rather bury the incident.'

She grinned. 'You'd take on the world, wouldn't you, Sheriff? As long as it wasn't for your own good.'

25

I HAD ANOTHER appointment with Myra that very afternoon. She had written to Kit, a formal note which might have originated in the mind of a solicitor, and probably had. She suggested the pair of us meet because 'another development' had taken place. This filled both Kit and me with hope. 'We're getting on,' he had remarked warmly. 'The Chinese are weakening. Remember, we've nothing to lose, and she has nothing to offer but concessions.'

This time I suggested a rendezvous in the American bar at the Savoy. I had been there only once before, and knew that it would certainly be expensive, but I felt if the encounter turned out as dreary as our last one the surroundings might as well be agreeable.

I arrived promptly at five-thirty, when the bar opened. I took a table against the wall by the door, ordered a gin, and started nibbling Savoy crisps. A quarter of an hour passed. Myra was late. Perhaps she had forgotten the meeting-place, with her infuriating vagueness. I sat wondering how Kit had put up with this, on and off, for fourteen years. Possibly he relished it, as giving him a chance to get away with his own little deceptions.

At five to six the daughter Veronica appeared, alone.

'I'm sorry,' she apologized quietly. 'My mother couldn't come.'

She was wearing the same dress as before, but the hair which had been flopping over her shoulders was now drawn back, secured with something, and fell in a loose tail down her neck.

'Why couldn't she come?' I demanded at once.

'She's ill.'

'Then I'm sorry.' I was badly disappointed. My expectations from the meeting had grown steadily since getting the letter. 'I hope it's nothing serious?'

'It's not serious.' This was the first conversation that I had conducted with her. I noticed that she had the same wandering vagueness as her mother. 'She's got a cold.'

'A cold!'

'She didn't think she should go out.'

'She's extremely unfortunate to catch a cold at the beginning of July.' Why exactly, I wondered, had Myra made Veronica her envoy? 'Won't you sit down?'

'Thank you.' She timidly took the edge of a chair.

'Can I get you a drink?'

'Could I have a tomato-juice?'

I had somehow expected her to order a Martini or a bloody mary. It suddenly occurred to me that even the Savoy was 'licensed premises', and I might be breaking the law having her there at all. She was the same age as my most junior students, and I resolved to treat her in exactly the same way. But it was infuriating of Myra. Another stroke in her Chinese tactics.

'You must have enjoyed your year in France?' I asked, pleasantly enough.

'Yes, it was most enjoyable.' She fell silent, shy of me. Then she added quickly, 'I hope you're not annoyed that mother didn't come? She thought it would be useful if I met you, all the same. To talk about careers.'

Her tomato-juice appeared. 'Naturally, I'd be pleased to give you what advice I can. As I would to any girl of your age,' I added.

'I don't think I really want to be a doctor or a lawyer. It would be awful, to spend all my teenage life just learning.'

All her teenage life! Death begins at twenty. But I must be more tolerant of the little stupidities of the young, I told myself. And physiologically, as far as the perishability of our organs went, perhaps she was near the truth.

'What *do* you want to do, then?'

'I'd like to work in a bank.'

'For any particular reason?'

'They always look so quiet and calm. Everyone moves so slowly and talks so softly. You couldn't get pushed about, working in a bank.'

I decided her motives, however odd, weren't my affair. 'I don't know anything about banks, I'm afraid. But why don't you write to one? They're always putting advertisements in the papers for female staff. Very fetching advertisements, too.'

'Perhaps I might.'

She sat pushing round the paper mat under her glass.

'I'm sorry not to see your mother, Veronica, because I'm interested in some development she mentioned in her letter.'

'You mean, between you and my father?'

'On that subject.'

'You're immoral, aren't you?' she asked.

This was a shock, like some telling personal jibe from the mouth of a child. I recovered myself, and said quickly, 'I'm sorry if I should strike you as so.'

'It's a matter of fact, isn't it?' she asked simply.

'I can understand if my sharing a flat with your father is abhorrent to you,' I told her patiently. 'But I assure you that neither he nor I think of it as immoral. Can't you try and understand that we are very deeply in love with each other? It's no lighthearted, transient business.'

Veronica said nothing.

'Wouldn't it be better if we kept a sense of proportion over it?' I persisted. 'And preserved our moral strictures for the really bad things in the world? God knows, there's enough of them.'

She went on playing with the paper mat. 'But you're an immoral woman. You can't get away from that.'

I looked hard at her. To be lectured on my morals by a girl in her teens! Then I wondered if she were merely speaking from Myra's brief. That seemed the most likely.

'I suppose you think young people don't have morals?' Veronica continued in her thin voice. 'Or perhaps "morals" isn't the word I want. But your being with my father . . . that disgusts me. Yes, it disgusts me.'

I felt even more uncomfortable. Veronica, of all people, was getting under the cold armour I wore against the world. 'When you grow up, perhaps you'll see such things differently.'

'Are you being patronizing?'

I gave a shrug. Well, I supposed I was. 'But if you – or your mother – imagine that your delicacy of feeling can separate me from Kit, I'm afraid the pair of you are making a mistake.'

'I wouldn't have expected that. No, that wasn't my idea at all. I just wanted to let you know what I thought.'

'But surely, Veronica! The very fact that I want to marry your father, to enter into a proper and regular arrangement with him, must prove I'm not simply licentious?'

'Mother says it wouldn't make a jot of difference to anyone – to anyone but you – if you married him or not.'

'Very well. But that difference to me is enormous. Do you imagine I could tolerate all this fuss we're having otherwise?'

'I don't understand why you're insisting so much. You've got him with you.'

'I'm insisting for the simple reason that I want to be his wife.'

'Shall I tell you why you want to marry him?' She gave me an unexpectedly sly look. 'Because you want to possess him, don't you? All on your own.'

'That's a shameful remark,' I told her sharply.

But it was true, absolutely true, though it was something I hardly dared admit to myself. The way I kept Kit from my circle at Princess Victoria's, the way I hid him from my parents, the way I managed our life in the flat, above all the way I doled him out my money, I knew was all motivated by possessiveness. I suddenly couldn't bear talking to the girl any longer. I finished my drink and said quickly, 'It would seem that you despise me. So there's no point in our sitting here pretending to have a cosy chat.'

'I don't despise you. I don't believe I despise anything in the world. If you despise things it means you're arrogant, I think. And I couldn't be that.' She hesitated. 'But when I'm your age, I hope I shan't be anything like you.'

I called the waiter for the bill. 'Please tell your mother that I don't want to see either of you again. You not only waste my time, but you go out of your way to insult me.'

She seemed about to say something. But she changed her mind and looked at the carpet. 'Very well, I'll tell her.'

I got up, leaving her sitting there, and making through the crowded lobby strode out of the hotel, now in a temper. What a presumptuous little bitch! I thought. I caught a Tube, and sat biting my lip, my evening paper unread and clenched in my hand. I consoled myself that Veronica could know nothing of the complexity of my relationship with Kit. The young saw the world harshly in black and white, the subtleties of shade in between appeared only with maturity, until with age they filled nearly all the picture. But she was right. Of course she was right. I wanted Kit fiercely, and to myself. Or was I simply ashamed of him? But why? Was there anything particularly wrong, or at the most particularly inappropriate, in a woman of my profession living with another's husband? Surely not. Had I been a fashion model, like my successor with Henry, nobody would have thought twice about it. I hadn't even any patients to make me the target of their gratifying disapproval. Yet I did keep Kit a secret. I should have paraded him at the hospital, introduced him to Ma Saintsbury and to Tilly Dawes, brought him down to Longfield on that first visit. Then I might have got the job, I reflected bitterly.

I walked briskly from Fulham Broadway Tube station back to the flat. I found Kit in the living-room, on the sofa surrounded by pages of typescript. The novel, still unfinished.

'How did it go?' he asked at once. 'What's the "development"?'

'We shall never know. Myra didn't appear. She sent Veronica.'

'But why, in God's name?'

'Myra made some transparent excuse – a cold, of all things.'

'Veronica would seem to have nettled you?'

I threw down my bag crossly, flopped in an armchair, and kicked off my shoes. 'Your daughter's extremely stupid.'

Kit raised his eyebrows. 'The poor dear's not very bright, admittedly. But what's she done?'

173

'I don't want to talk about it. Yes, I do. She got all sancti-monious. She seemed to think I was a call-girl, or something. It was most irritating.'

'Perhaps a little strong,' said Kit dryly.

'It was humiliating.' I reached for a cigarette. 'She needs her arse smacking.'

'I suppose from her point of view our set-up here must seem rather shameless. The young can be surprisingly sensitive about such things, you know.'

'What right has she to hold views on it at all?' I demanded.

'Well, I'm her father.'

'But I come first, don't I?'

Kit looked uneasy. I could see he was torn between placating me and defending Veronica.

'Don't I?' I repeated, more savagely.

'Ann, my darling, we're starting to fight over some very complicated country. Can't we forget it? Anything Veronica says is bound to be pretty trivial.'

'It isn't trivial to me, being called a tart.'

'You're making too much of it, as usual.'

'Why this sudden burst of paternal affection? If you're so keen on Veronica, you'd better go back and live with Myra.'

'Myra can go to hell,' he said calmly. 'But surely you must understand my special feelings about Veronica? Can't we keep the kid out of the major row?'

'*I* didn't ask her to come and meet me this evening. If Myra sends Veronica, she must expect the child to take her share of my ill-feeling.'

Kit made no reply. I sat smoking, gradually simmering down. Of course Kit was fond of Veronica, it would have been highly unnatural otherwise. I mustn't blind myself to facts – that had done me damage enough at Longfield already. I was being unfair. Not on Veronica, who didn't matter, but on him. Sensing the right moment in my thoughts, Kit came across and kissed me.

'I'm sorry,' I said, much more amicably. 'It was a harrowing few minutes with the kid, that's all.'

'I'd never see Veronica again, Ann, if you really wanted me to.'

I knew he meant this. It seemed a reasonable triumph for me over her. 'Oh, no. I expect Veronica will get out of her high-flown ideas. She'll probably be shacking up with a boy of her own in a couple of months.'

'I fancy the desire is there, but so are the inhibitions. She's a terribly timid child. And like all timid people, once she forces herself into something bold she doesn't know when to stop. It's only the basically nervous who win the medals, you know.'

I noticed a slip of paper in the usual clip over the electric fire. 'Who phoned?'

There was only one telephone in the building, in our land-lady's flat on the ground floor. In deference to my qualifications, she let me leave her number with Princess Victoria's 'for emergencies'. I could easily have had our own instrument installed, but claimed it hardly worth the expense. Though I supposed, as Kit reached for the note, it was really just another way of hiding him from my everyday world.

'It was your pal McRobb. She wants you to ring her back.'

I went to the call-box on the corner and dialled the number of McRobb's flat in Kensington.

'Are you after me, Sandra?'

'Sheriff, I wonder if you could come round some time this evening? I've something you might be interested to see.'

'Why not come to us?' I suggested eagerly. I would change my policy, show off Kit, starting right away.

'You're sure it's convenient?'

A hidden meaning in her voice? Perhaps she imagined Kit and I rolling on the sofa, all day and all night long. Just as Veronica did.

'It's perfectly convenient. We're in this evening.'

'I'll be round about eight-thirty, then.'

'But what's it all about?'

'Nothing to do with the placenta,' said McRobb.

26

I HAD SOMEHOW expected McRobb to appear in a white coat. But she wore a dark-blue dress with white cuffs, which hung from her shoulders as if nailed to some rectangular wooden frame. It was an expensive garment – on her professor's salary she could of course afford to dress well – but she would never have allowed herself such finery in the hospital. As she came into the flat I noticed that she had put on lipstick and even powdered her greasy skin. McRobb had been doing herself up to meet the boy-friend. I found this immensely flattering and reassuring. It almost offset the effects of Veronica.

'This is Kit,' I said.

'I expect you're cussing me for disturbing your peace and quiet?' she greeted him. She accepted him as a matter of course, with the same affected surliness to which she treated all strangers.

'Quite the contrary. I bet you don't know what those lamps illuminate, on the pylons outside,' he said immediately and inconsequentially. 'Drama most intense, more subtle sometimes, than anything imagined by Sophocles or Shakespeare. Bloody, too.'

She gazed through the window. 'Some outdoor *avant-garde* theatre, I suppose?'

'It's Chelsea Football Club, "The Blues", idols of the noisy inarticulate.'

McRobb gave a thin smile. 'I've always wanted to watch a match. Such enthusiasm can't be dissipated into thin air for nothing.'

'What can I get you to drink?'

'Whisky.'

'With soda?'

'God, no. I'm a Scot, however attenuated by life in the lush south.'

To my relief, they seemed to hit it off. Perhaps Kit saw through her, that she was timid and sensitive underneath. Or perhaps he felt that no woman, however formidable, could fail to melt under the influence of his charm.

McRobb sat next to me on the sofa, Kit in the armchair. When he had brought our drinks, she felt in her large handbag and produced what I took to be a magazine.

'Now, Sheriff, just take a little look at this.'

I saw it was one of the advertising handbooks put out by General Drugs, folded open. I looked at a large photograph, obviously taken during one of the parties to which Lloyd had half-invited me before our row. Lloyd himself was smiling in the middle, with some satisfied-looking gentleman of foreign appearance, clearly the visiting medical dignitary. On the guest of honour's other side stood Sir Robert Boatwright.

'The Boatwright man!' I exclaimed.

'It says as much in the caption. When you talked about him in the lab. this afternoon, Sheriff, I knew I'd heard of the fellow somewhere before. Usually I toss these drug things straight in the wastie. But I suppose I must have glanced through this particular one for some reason or other.'

I passed it across to Kit. 'Well, darling – have you ever met him?'

Kit studied the photograph. 'No, and it's hardly a face I'd be likely to forget. How do some men manage to grow such aggressive moustaches?'

'Well, now?' McRobb folded her arms expectantly.

I took the shiny publication again. 'Do you suppose he might be one of their directors? I can soon find out.'

My file on cyclova was on the top of the bookshelf. I got up, and searched for Lloyd's letter acknowledging my report, remembering that the names of company directors were always given on the firm's writing paper. But there was only Lloyd and five people I had never heard of.

177

'No connexion,' I said.

'But he certainly seems a friend of the family,' observed McRobb.

'I expect they invite all sorts of business people to these affairs,' I told her, feeling dampened.

'It's strange,' said Kit. 'There's your two tormenting demons, sharing the same drinks.'

'Very strange,' said McRobb decisively.

I sat down again on the sofa. 'Let's try and look at this with detachment – like a clinical problem. Why on earth should we imagine that Boatwright was more than a casual acquaintance of Lloyd's?'

'Why *shouldn't* we imagine he had a stake in General Drugs?' Kit insisted. 'It would be something difficult to pin-point, admittedly. He must surround himself with a maze of companies to achieve his ends, whatever his ends happen to be.'

'Let us discount that.' I was taking charge. 'We'll assume he's a friend of Lloyd's. We'll even assume Lloyd knew that Boatwright was connected with the appointments' committee at Longfield. It's tempting to make the next assumption, but – do you *really* think Lloyd would tell him in so many words to stop my getting the job?'

'Not in so many words,' suggested Kit. 'Some people develop wonderfully sensitive antennae if there's money in it somewhere.'

'But why?' I demanded. 'Why should Lloyd even hint at such a thing? For revenge? I didn't do anything to him, except cause him a lot of trouble. Out of spite?'

'They certainly do get remarkably sensitive over their bloody drugs,' complained McRobb.

'No, we're misleading ourselves,' I objected. 'Can you imagine a perfectly intelligent businessman like Lloyd sinking so low? Or even putting himself to such bother? He'd be bound to see the risk of something coming out.'

'Something *has* come out,' said McRobb with satisfaction.

'I'm afraid Ann's right.' Kit lay back in his chair. 'However much they hated her dear guts, it would hardly be a risk worth running just to slap her down.'

'Unless, Sheriff —' McRobb blew smoke through her nostrils,

already starting to show red under the unaccustomed powder. 'Unless they wanted to silence you. Or at least to muffle you.'

'About cyclova?'

She nodded. 'You could have made a much more important noise from Longfield. They're afraid of you.'

'Isn't that rather hypothetical?' I had deliberately been fighting off their arguments, trying hard to convince myself that the immediate conclusion we drew from the photograph was illogical, emotional, and wrong. But now excitement began to seep warmly through me. 'If that *were* the case,' I admitted, 'if General Drugs really were afraid of me, it would mean they've got some doubts about cyclova after all.'

'Exactly.' McRobb took a gulp of whisky.

'And that would mean,' I said deliberately, enjoying every word, 'I hadn't made a mistake over the blood-samples.'

'Which I knew you did not, myself, all along,' said McRobb.

But I was travelling too fast on her enthusiasm. 'Supposing Lloyd told Boatwright that I was an unsuitable candidate for the job. He might have put it more strongly, for all I know. But a man like Boatwright certainly had no need to take orders from Lloyd, or anyone else.'

'Lloyd isn't a doctor, of course?' asked Kit. I shook my head. 'Then if a layman like Lloyd simply said you were no good, I should imagine Boatwright would at least test his opinion on someone in the profession itself.'

'That seems likely enough,' I agreed. 'Surely Boatwright would in the end make up his own mind on such an important item as an appointment to a university? Unless he were an out-and-out crook, or Lloyd's lickspittle, and obviously he isn't either. He'd try to discover if I really was so terrible, and in exactly what way. The question is, who would he have asked?'

'Who knows you and your work well enough?' asked Kit.

'Ma Saintsbury,' I said promptly. 'It could hardly be her.'

McRobb grinned. 'It wasn't me.'

'Perhaps Liz Kilson?' I frowned. 'Her husband might well have been friendly with Boatwright in the City.'

'But at the moment Kilson isn't at all friendly with her husband,' McRobb pointed out.

179

'Oh, you know Liz, Sandra. She'd babble away about anything. She's no sense of discretion. It's a wonder she hasn't been hauled before the G.M.C.'

I felt discouraged again. Perhaps we're only imagining things. Boatwright simply hadn't liked the look of me across the committee-table. Then I remembered Boatwright's knowledge of Kit.

'But he must have been talking to someone about me, quite apart from Lloyd,' I remarked. 'I can't think of any other way for him to find the juicy little personal details.'

'I think we should put all this to Ma Saintsbury,' decided McRobb.

'That's by far our best course,' I agreed. 'She's sensible, and if we're chasing a wild hare she'll make no bones about telling us.'

'But if the hare's a fox?' suggested Kit.

'That opens several intriguing possibilities,' said McRobb. 'Doubtless, in their collective mind, General Drugs think cyclova is safe. But if they've been gunning for Ann, I fancy that in their collective mind she has indeed sown a doubt. Now may be the time to water and fertilize that doubt with particular enthusiasm. It could be interesting seeing what it flowers into.'

I felt less aggressive than she. Too much fight had been knocked out of me recently. 'Do you suppose it would be worth resuming the battle?'

'With redoubled bloodiness,' said McRobb firmly. Kit saw her glass was empty. 'Yes, thank you, Kit, I'd like another whisky.'

It was strange to hear her use a Christian name. Then it occurred to me that she'd no idea what Kit's surname was.

We decided at some length how best to seek Ma Saintsbury's advice, relieved at the prospect of sharing responsibility. Shortly afterwards McRobb departed. She left me with the notion of Lloyd's indirectly losing me the job – which I could now do nothing about – lying less heavily on my mind than the identity of Boatwright's adviser about my professional abilities. If indeed one existed at all. When I lay in bed, my brain buzzing as usual, I began to tell myself again there could really be no conspiracy.

The sanest of us can develop so easily the delusions of persecution suffered by the paranoiac. At last I dropped off to sleep, dreaming confusedly. Sometime in the night I half-woke, gripped the bedclothes, and sat up with a cry.

'What's the matter, darling?' asked Kit sleepily.

'I've got it,' I said. 'I know who was behind my getting kicked out at Longfield.'

27

'MR TAMBLING IS still in the theatre, madam,' said the porter on the door of the Aldersgate Hospital in the Barbican. He consulted a complicated glass affair on the wall of his lodge, a constellation of small bulbs against the consultants' names giving their whereabouts. 'He's due in out-patients' in half an hour.'

'Then I'll go up to his theatre. Would you ring through to say I'm coming?'

'It's theatre B, madam.' The porter picked up a telephone. 'What name shall I say?'

'Dr Sheriff. He's expecting me.'

I remembered the Aldersgate fairly well. It stood amid the concrete money-making hives of the City of London, this geographical position possibly accounting for a stuffy, self-satisfied demeanour among its medical staff. Some of its assorted buildings were ancient, some merely old-fashioned. The cliff-like surgical block was new, its foundations being the bombed ruins of the old one (Ma Saintsbury was liable to give vivid descriptions of that particular night). Theatre B, I recalled, was on the fourth floor. I took the staff lift, and put my head through the frosted glass door of the anaesthetic-room, which was empty except for a young green-gowned nurse. 'Has the list finished?'

'Yes, we're just clearing up.'

'I'll find Mr Tambling in the surgeons' room, I expect.'

I remembered you reached the small surgeons' room down a narrow passage like a train corridor, skirting the theatre suite. I knocked.

'Come in.'

Henry's voice.

'Oh, there you are, Ann.'

He was in his singlet and white operating trousers, tied round his skinny waist with a strip of bandage. He still wore his green sterile cap, pushed back on his fair hair, and his mask dangled below his long chin. He was dictating something to his houseman, who stood in his white coat with two or three files of patients' notes clipped to boards.

'Just a second, Ann.' The same thin, cold voice. Once I decided that he actually *whined*. 'An end-to-end anastomosis of the proximal and distal sections of the aorta was completed, an arterial graft not being found necessary,' he ended to the houseman. 'Right-ho, you go and grab some lunch. I'll finish the other notes during out-patients' this afternoon.'

As the young man closed the door behind him, Henry said, 'Well, this is a surprise.'

'It's a surprise to me, too, needing to see you.'

Henry pulled forward a hard white chair. The room was furnished only with a table bearing a tray of dirty coffee-cups, some tall green metal lockers, and a folded white hospital screen on wheels. 'Won't you sit down?'

'I'm afraid I'm keeping you from your lunch.'

'I assure you, I don't mind about that in the least.'

Or was he ravenously hungry? You could never tell what Henry really felt about anything. I sat down and crossed my legs. 'How are you?'

'Very well. How are *you*?'

'I'm all right.' He took off his cap and mask. 'You're certainly looking very well.'

'Thank you. And so are you.'

We fell silent. We seemed to have come to the end of our conversation.

'I must get changed,' Henry announced. 'Do you imagine it quite proper in our present circumstances if I took off my trousers in your presence?'

Even his jokes were solemn. That was perhaps the most unforgivable thing about him.

'That's a rather delicate point of etiquette, isn't it?'

'Perhaps I'd better go behind this screen?'

'Do, if it makes you feel more comfortable. But don't forget, though I may no longer be your wife, I'm still a doctor.'

'True. But I don't feel inclined in such matters to set precedents.'

He pulled out the screen, took his suit and shirt from a locker, and modestly disappeared. 'Am I right,' came his voice, 'in thinking this is the first time we've met since the ... dichotomy?'

'You are.'

'How are you getting along? Are you happy?'

'Very happy. I'm not alone.'

'No, I heard you weren't.'

'Are *you* happy?'

'Yes, I'm extremely happy.'

'Good.' I lit a cigarette. There was no ash-tray. Chest surgeons don't smoke. 'Everything was for the best, then?'

'Yes. I suppose you could say that everything was for the best.'

Silence. We had come to the end of our conversation again.

Henry and I had married in the month of June, but the clergyman had still contrived to have a bad cold. As the stark sentences uniting us came in funereally hoarse tones, I had watched with fascination the clear drop repeatedly gathering on the tip of the man's nose, to be snatched away with increasing fury. I wore a long white dress, train, orange-blossom – the lot. Henry had a hired morning suit, and Charles Crawless as best man looked sleeker than ever. I don't know what a girl is supposed to think as she stands at the altar. I only found myself reflecting that the clergyman's catarrhal words were regulating the mainspring of mankind, harnessing a force which drove herds and tribes across continents, which occasioned both murder and the tenderest compassion, and inspired the varied genius of Michelangelo, Genghis Khan, and Karl Marx. More wonderful than antibiotics or atomic fission, was surely a Town Hall official's signature at the foot of a marriage certificate? Perhaps this was a bad start to our own marriage.

The wedding wasn't in Barnet, but in the chapel of Aldersgate Hospital, which was built after the Great Fire and as big as a church. The reception afterwards was in the hospital hall, a splendid apartment with lurid frescoes, usually reserved for sitting examinations. There was a little embarrassment about the cost, in the end mainly shouldered by Henry's father, who was well-off. Henry made some amiable lie to save my own father's feelings. It was the only tactful thing I remember him doing in his life.

It was an appropriate site for the ceremony because Aldersgate Hospital was delighted that we married. Perhaps that was the main reason we did it at all. I was working at the Cannonbury as a house-surgeon, following my first job at Princess Victoria's. My scheme, conceived as a student, was to win higher qualifications in not only gynaecology but surgery, then I could chase after the highest jobs – I had no doubt about getting them – and at forty be one of the top gynaecologists in the country. So far, the plan was unfolding with gratifying precision.

I met Henry after my affair with Liz's brother Trevor had already petered out. Henry was four years older than me, a registrar in thoracic surgery at the Aldersgate, in line for the next consultant job going. He worked partly at the Cannonbury, and it seemed only natural that he should pick upon 'the bright girl from Princess Vikki's'.

But there was a little more to it than that. Henry was clever, with a splendid future, perfectly presentable, and said to have a bit in the bank. He was the 'catch of the year'. Almost automatically, I decided that it would be I who caught him – or at least, prevented any of the other girls at the Cannonbury from doing so. I set out to interest him, which was easy enough with our common ground of surgery. Romance burgeoned.

After a month he formally proposed. He lived at the time in a small flat near Regent's Park, where we indulged in what is widely known as premarital intercourse.

Our first home was another flat, near Primrose Hill. Then Henry's father, impelled less by generosity than by his accountant, gave Henry a fair amount of money. We moved promptly to a larger and smarter flat in the Marylebone Road. We took on a Spanish maid, started to entertain more, to go out more, sometimes to places like the Crécy. I was working at Princess Victoria's again as Ma Saintsbury's surgical registrar, and I had examinations ahead.

'What are you so scared about?' Henry demanded. We had been married a year or so, and were dining together in some restaurant. 'You'll get through those exams without any trouble.'

'I'm frightened I'll fail.'

'What of it? All the best people fail their higher degrees a time or two. The first attempts are looked upon as practice shots, even by the examiners. They're glad enough to gather the candidates' fees.'

'I don't like failing exams,' I told him peevishly.

'God, Ann! There's no moral shame attached. Even I failed my Fellowship twice.'

'I hate failing at anything.'

'But failing an examination is a purely technical matter,' he persisted.

'That's taking the easy view.'

'I do wish you wouldn't accept all my opinions as personal affronts,' he complained.

'I'm sorry,' I apologized. 'But you can't expect me to abandon every previous idea in my head just because I got married.'

'Nor you me,' said Henry.

I looked at him crossly, and he said urgently, 'For God's sake don't get in one of your tempers here.'

'Well, I can either work for exams or act the society hostess,' I told him. 'I can't do both.'

'With your brain you can.'

'And it frightens me, spending all this money.'

'Why shouldn't we spread ourselves a little? Plenty of people our age do themselves as well, or better. In medicine, you're so long a student you enter the race a rather mature rat.'

'I suppose it's because I never had any before to spend,' I admitted.

'The faculty for spending money properly,' Henry declared

earnestly, 'is as important as the faculty for earning money properly.'

'That's only what Charles Crawless says.'

'He seems to do pretty well on his philosophy.'

Henry summoned the waiter to pour more wine. Charles Crawless was a constant visitor to our flat. He was still unmarried, and I think he was Henry's only real friend. The two were wholly different in temperament, which doubtless accounted for it. Charles admired Henry's natural carefulness, attention to detail, and austerity of thought. Henry admired the easygoing man-of-the-world way in which Charles spent a few hundred pounds or reached some impossibly difficult diagnosis. But I had already become very tired of hearing the things which Charles Crawless had said.

'Charles is older than you,' I pointed out. Henry picked up his newly filled glass. 'He's a consultant already.'

'I'll be a consultant next year. With the new cardiac unit at the Aldersgate, there'll be another job created. It's all cut and dried, right up to Ministry level. And I shouldn't lack for private practice. Charles will see to that. I'll get all his surgical opinions.'

'Is that why you keep in with him?'

'I never keep in with anyone,' said Henry firmly.

We had plenty of other squabbles, but we jogged along, perhaps because we had our work to stop our becoming obsessed with each other's shortcomings. Our temperaments fitted in many of the minor ways so important in cohabitation – we were a marriage of tidy minds. Henry could be cold and emotionless, but he could also be witty and dryly amusing. He often complained, or at least plainly hinted, that I wanted to dominate the partnership. And I didn't see why I should surrender to him my individuality along with my sexual freedom. He was a satisfactory, if decorous lover. I had wilder ideas about this, but he made me somehow too shamefaced to utter them. A watertight situation for the breakdown of any marriage.

Though we could probably with time have found a workable relationship, had it not been for another complication. Shortly after our quarrel in the restaurant we were lying in bed one night reading, myself in one of the brightly coloured, very frilly nylon nighties I fancied at the time. I was reading a textbook, and we had been talking of my career again.

'What if we start a family?' he said. We had been into this often enough.

'I told you, it'll be an interruption. An interruption I'd welcome and love.'

'You sound pretty casual about it, I must say.'

'I don't know why you should get that impression.'

'I imagined childbirth was the crowning achievement of any woman's existence.'

'That's true. But unlike most women I have other achievements in prospect. I must try to take a balanced view of my life.'

'You couldn't go on working at Princess Victoria's while you were pregnant.'

'Why not? Until I was too fat to get near the operating-table.'

'What about afterwards? The responsibility doesn't end with parturition, you know.'

'We can afford a nannie. Lots of medical women successfully mix a family with a career, and I don't see why I should be the exception. Jane down in Somerset runs a busy general practice, and has babies so often I don't think she even takes nine months over it.'

'We don't seem to be making much of a start with ours,' he observed glumly.

'You're just impatient.'

'We've been married over a year.' He considered for a moment. 'Perhaps you ought to consult that awful female McRobb?'

'Why? I know exactly what she'd say. You shouldn't worry until you've had eighteen months of regular intercourse.'

'A year's the correct figure, isn't it?'

'Eighteen months.'

'I'm certain it's twelve.'

'You never did a gynae. job.'

'I don't see why that should make me completely ignorant about anything that happens below the level of a woman's umbilicus.'

'Well, you're wrong.'

'I *know* I'm right.'

A stupid little argument. But we didn't have any of the regular intercourse *that* night.

To please Henry, a little later I did see McRobb. She was still an assistant, and referred me to her professor. The professor ended up by injecting radio-opaque solution through the neck of my uterus, into the womb itself, and through the twin Fallopian tubes leading from it to my ovaries. The professor told me that both tubes were blocked near their entry to the uterus. She added that it was possibly a congenital defect.

This was shattering news, but I tried to face it as calmly as I could. McRobb and I discussed my plight. The Professor had suggested she opened me up, cut the end of each tube beyond the obstruction, and replanted them into the womb. But McRobb was doubtful, and I agreed with her. The transplant operation was so seldom successful, from the practical view I was probably barren. I decided to shelve the idea, to make up my mind when I had passed my examinations. I was not so distressed as I might have expected. Perhaps I saw my disability as a lucky stroke to free my mind and my energies for my bookwork. Perhaps I saw the traditional crowning achievement of a woman's body as commonplace compared with the infrequent ones of her brain. Or perhaps I already knew that I didn't love Henry.

But I told myself that I *did* love Henry. Or at least, I loved our marriage. The notion of it breaking up was so abhorrent that I never considered it. It would mean that I had failed at something, and that was unthinkable. Henry had meanwhile, at the time of my first consultation, agreed to a sperm test, and the report came back, 'Highly fertile'. With Henry, it would.

The end was as swift as our courtship. Foolishly, I didn't believe that my being condemned as sterile would make any immediate difference to Henry. But he was desperate for a child, if only as a symptom of his own egotism. He won his expected thoracic consultant's job. He started his private practice, with rooms in Wimpole Street. He had everything he wanted, except for the elusive prizes awarded by Nature. Over a single week in summer, during my second year as Ma Saintsbury's registrar, he revealed that he had a girl-friend and that he was leaving me.

It was like stepping on a familiar stair, finding it wasn't there, and tumbling headlong to the bottom of the staircase. I had never suspected this woman. When he was seeing her, and I supposed sleeping with her, I had assumed he was busy with his work – doctors are favoured adulterers, as long as they don't pick on their patients. Henry solemnly packed his clothes and left, after telling me there was some money in the bank and that the flat was paid for a further quarter. He even sat down and wrote out the name of his solicitors, in a clear and careful hand.

I didn't know what to do. I went to McRobb, drawing comfort from her strange unemotional sympathy. It was cruel, horrible, and quite despicable of Henry, I told her, to leave me as soon as he discovered that I was unable to bear him children. I was already convinced that this alone had drawn him to the other woman. A simple failure to hold him was impossible to confess even to myself. There was a birdsong of gossip at Princess Victoria's. McRobb suggested I take a holiday, but I decided my work made a soothing activity. Then I began to feel unwell.

The month after Henry left, I found myself increasingly tired as I came home each evening to the empty flat. I would flop into a chair, wanting Henry back. Had he walked through the door I would have forgiven him. It would have shown that I hadn't failed after all. I had no urge to feed myself, nor to do anything. I often fell asleep in the chair, awaking stiff and cold with the curtains undrawn in the darkness. In the mornings, as I got in the papers and made myself some tea, I noticed my fingers seemed stiff. It wore away with the day, but it always came back, until my first few minutes of activity filled me with dread.

One morning, I had an appointment with some lawyers whom McRobb had suggested. On an impulse, sitting at my dressing-table, I decided to pull off my wedding-ring for good. I tugged. It wouldn't come. I looked more carefully at the small joints of my fingers. They were swollen, all of them. I stared at myself in the mirror. I was pale, as though on the point of fainting. I pulled myself together. Instead of the lawyer, I went to McRobb.

'I'm afraid it *does* look like rheumatoid, Sheriff.' She was only agreeing with my thoughts. 'You'd better see a physician.'

I had sat there, opening and closing my stiff hands as best I could. With rheumatoid arthritis you couldn't operate. When I was forty, the country would lack one of its top gynaecologists.

28

'I SAW A photograph of you both in the evening paper,' I now told Henry, smoking my cigarette while he finished changing behind the screen. 'You and – what's her name?'

'Brenda.'

It was an affectation. I knew my successor's name perfectly well. 'The day you got married. I remember the caption – "Surgeon Weds Model". It looked most romantic.'

He gave his short laugh, and appeared from shelter. I noticed how much better he dressed these days. 'Aren't the newspapers awful?' He agreed. 'No respect for the feelings of anyone.'

'I admit it shook me a little at the time. I'd grown used to thinking that Mr and Mrs Tambling were us. But the pain was fleeting. I've noticed there's a picture like that almost every day, some couple grinning outside a registry office. I suppose somewhere there's always two former spouses looking at it with varying degrees of ire.'

'Go on with you, Ann,' he said amicably. 'You were glad to get rid of me by then.'

'Yes, I was,' I told him. 'By then.'

He started gathering up his notebook, pens, and such things, sticking them methodically into his pockets.

'Well —?' he asked in a businesslike tone. 'And what can I do for you?'

'As you can imagine, Henry, I certainly shouldn't have embarrassed you by appearing here had it not been for something important.'

'I assure you it's no embarrassment. We're both past the embarrassment stage by now, aren't we?'

'Should I have said – I wouldn't put myself under any obligation to you, except for something important?'

He nodded silently.

'I want some information.'

'Professional information? About a patient of mine?'

'No, personal information. Only you can give it to me.'

He looked faintly worried. He must have feared I'd raked up something from the cremated ashes of our marriage. 'I'll certainly tell you anything I'm able. What's it about?'

'Charles Crawless.'

'Oh, Clueless Crawless.' He smiled. It was an old and misleading nickname. 'He's still jaunting about the United States.'

'Is there any connexion between Charles and General Drugs?'

Henry stood still, pausing in slipping his throat-torch into his breast pocket. 'Why on earth do you ask that?'

'I won't answer your question until you've answered mine.'

'There's no connexion that I know of.'

'Are you sure?'

'Ann! What is this, an inquisition?' He smiled, but I knew from experience that he was irritated. 'Won't you take my word?'

'Yes, of course I'll take your word.' I stubbed out my cigarette in the saucer of a coffee-cup. 'I just wondered if there might be some tie-up, that's all.'

There was another pause. 'That's that, then,' said Henry. 'A simple question, and a simple answer.'

I stood up. 'I'm sorry I bothered you.'

'No bother at all. Quite worth it to have a chat with you again, Ann.' Perhaps he really meant it. He looked at his watch. 'I see that I have precisely five minutes for my lunch. Would you care to step across the road and join me in a pub sandwich?'

'Would that be quite proper?'

'Oh, the students expect to see the senior staff there from time to time. Class barriers are down, even in places like London teaching hospitals.'

'I mean, wouldn't Brenda feel annoyed if she knew you'd been hobnobbing with me in a pub?'

'Ann, I never discovered if you were sometimes deliberately trying to be stupid, or if sometimes you really were.'

We both laughed. We went through the hospital to the pub, Henry talking about his latest work in cardiac surgery.

The pub was modern, in the base of one of the newly-raised office blocks of the area, and crowded with dark-suited business-men. I had a gin and tonic with a ham roll, Henry a plain tonic-water and a sandwich. As he paid for them, I asked, 'Do you still go to the Crécy?'

'Seldom. These days I've hardly time to go anywhere.'

'I was there a few weeks ago with Liz. You remember, my old girl-friend, Liz Kilson.'

'The one with the big tits and tendency to exhibitionism?'

I nodded. 'I must say, I rather missed the luxury living after we split up.'

'I'm sorry about that.' He hesitated. 'You know, I was perfectly aware how unhappy I'd made you at the time.'

'There are worse disasters.' The crowd had wedged us into a corner by the bar. I was sensitive to Henry's being so close to me, and wondered if he felt the same. 'Everyone seems to imagine that marriage, and marriage alone, equals happiness. It's the effect of the films and television, I suppose. But happiness is the crystallization of everything you value in life, which only occurs under the most delicate conditions.'

'If I didn't know you, Ann, I'd have thought you were putting a brave face on it.'

'Is that remark more flattering to me or to you?'

'Perhaps we'd both be more comfortable not discussing such things,' he decided.

'I hope you had a good time last summer in St Tropez?'

Henry looked at me sideways. 'How did you know about that?'

'I saw the photograph when I had dinner with Charles.'

'Yes, of course,' he recalled. 'He said you'd been out to his place.'

'And doubtless he said I didn't come alone?'

'Oh, I've heard all about Kit from him.' Henry swallowed his tonic-water. 'I hope he's looking after you, this fellow?'

'You needn't lie awake worrying on that score.' Henry gave a smile. I added, sounding kinder than I intended, 'And I hope you're being well looked after, too?'

'Brenda and I really seem a very good match.'

'Is she still modelling?'

'No, she gave it up because of the children. We've two now, you know. Two and a third, to be obstetrically exact.'

'I'm so pleased.' Now I didn't sound kind at all.

'That's a nice suit you're wearing.'

'Thank you. Personally, I'm getting a bit tired of it.' It was the mustard one again.

Henry looked at his watch. 'I'm sorry, Ann, but this is to be a fleeting pleasure. I really must get across to out-patients'.'

'Are you absolutely sure Charles has no connexion with General Drugs?'

'You *are* remarkably persistent.'

'I'm already aware he's pals with one of their top brass, you know. A man called George Lloyd. I suppose you heard I had a row with them over this oral contraceptive they're about to market?'

'Yes, Charles told me something about it.'

'I produced some adverse findings which must have shattered this Lloyd fellow. Because he took pains to seek out Charles that very night for his advice. Charles told me they'd met casually, but I don't believe it. I remember now, Lloyd said he'd planned to hurry home after seeing me, because he had some people coming to dinner.'

'I shouldn't read too much into that.'

'And Charles seemed remarkably well-informed about this contraceptive, cyclova. *And* about General Drugs. It was only Charles who successfully persuaded me to drop my objections. To admit that I'd made a mistake.'

'We all make mistakes, don't we?'

'Possibly. But I hate it.'

'I know that from personal experience,' said Henry ruefully.

'I should have thought it a fairly simple reaction to understand in anyone.'

'Nylon's a simple-looking substance, but it's the product of some highly complicated chemistry. That reaction of yours is exactly the same.' He fell silent for a second. 'Charles *is* connected with General Drugs,' he said unexpectedly.

'Ah!'

'There's no reason you shouldn't know. He advises them – mainly on their cardiological products, but on other drugs they put out as well. He has a flair for that sort of thing, for getting technical views across to businessmen, understanding the problem of making doctors prescribe their stuff rather than anyone else's – or, let's face it, in many cases rather than the cheaper non-proprietary alternative. They pay him handsomely, of course.'

'But why does he keep it so dark?' I exclaimed. 'Why didn't he come out with it to me? Then I'd have known where I stood. We could have had a proper and reasonable discussion about this cyclova.'

'You know old Charles. He took the job – oh, ages ago, when you and I got married. He needed the extra cash. Or at least, he wanted it. Now that he's trying to build up a fashionable private practice, he's even more touchy about people knowing he's in the pay of an enormous American drug firm. He's a bit of a snob. To me, one patient's exactly the same as another. But I suppose he's right, the news wouldn't do him any good with his blue-blooded customers, or what's more to the point, with some of his political ones.'

I tightened my lips. 'So that's the bastard's motive for talking me out of it.'

'You're putting it too starkly, Ann.' He came expectedly to Charles's defence. 'His motives were for the best. He really believes that cyclova is useful and safe. He felt it his duty to stop you hindering its advent – which, incidentally, is imminent.'

'His duty to who? To General Drugs?' Henry said nothing. 'I suppose Charles told you all this in detail?'

Henry gave a shrug. 'Well, yes. We met the day after you had dinner with him. We run into each other frequently, you know.

196

He gives a physician's opinion on my cardiac cases, I give a surgical one on his. Taking in each other's clinical washing, which keeps Harley Street going. That and the oil sheikhs from the Persian Gulf. Surgery's one of the country's most thriving invisible exports.'

'I suppose he told you all about my fiasco at Longfield, too?' My temper was starting to rise.

'He said you were up for a job there.'

'Which I didn't get. Do you know why? Because I ran into organized obstruction. Organized by a member of the selection committee, Sir Robert Boatwright. I happen to know that he's an acquaintance, to say the least, of Lloyd's —'

'Aren't you being fanciful? Why on earth should Lloyd ever have discussed you with him?'

'I should imagine everyone at General Drugs was discussing me after I sent in that report. But that's only the half of it. Boatwright knew about Kit, information which he could have got only from Charles.'

'These things get about in the most devious ways. Surely we all know that? You're not suggesting a conspiracy between Charles, Lloyd and Boatwright to keep you out of Longfield?'

'Yes.'

'That's too ridiculous to discuss.' He looked at his watch again. 'I must be going. There's a tremendously long list of appointments this afternoon.'

'Tell me honestly, Henry – was there a conspiracy or not?'

'How could I know?' He sounded irritable. 'But if you sit down and think calmly, I'm sure you'll realize those sort of things don't happen. Well, it was nice meeting you, Ann,' he said with finality. 'To see you looking so well – and so young. You'll keep quiet about Charles and General Drugs, won't you?' he remembered hastily. 'I really shouldn't have mentioned it. After all, Charles is the best friend I have.'

I made no reply. I had hoped for some confirmation from Henry about my suspicions over Longfield, and there was certainly no one else I could turn to. Now I would be left in a state of tormenting uncertainty for the rest of my days.

We left the pub in silence. Outside, I said in a more friendly way, 'Thank you for taking such trouble, Henry. I'm sorry I've disturbed your morning.'

'Good-bye, Ann. And better luck with the next job.'

He turned to go one way, I another. After I'd taken a few steps I heard him calling after me, 'Ann!'

I spun round.

'Ann —' said Henry. 'I'm sure I know exactly what happened. Lloyd decided you mustn't get that Longfield job. It would have made you too important, too dangerous. They couldn't have dismissed your findings so easily about cyclova. Besides, General Drugs had it in for you. They didn't want you sniping at them in future, from a vantage-point where the shots might count. They were out to squash you before you grew too big. And they'd do it again, if they had the opportunity – you're not the only victim, it's going on all the time. Charles had a meeting with Boatwright in his consulting-rooms in Wimpole Street. I know this for a certain fact. I've got the rooms above and came down immediately afterwards, when Charles told me. What went on exactly, of course we shall never know. But Charles said he'd discussed you with Boatwright, told him all he knew about you, and . . . well, agreed that you should be blocked from the job. I will only emphasize – and it's the truth, I swear it – that Charles co-operated with Boatwright over this only with the greatest reluctance.'

'Why did you tell me this, Henry?'

'I owe you something, don't I?'

I kissed him lightly on the cheek and hurried away.

29

WHEN I REACHED my laboratory at Princess Victoria's the following morning a telegram was waiting for me. It said:

HEARD FROM DAME CHRISTINA RE CYCLOVA
   FIGHT ON
                              TILLY DAWES

There would be no doubt about that. Cyclova had burst upon the world that very morning, in a wonderfully managed operation.

When Kit brought the papers up to the flat, I found that our 'serious' one carried a long front-page story about the new 'monthly pill'. The reporter had no trouble explaining to his readers its advantage over existing 'pills', because these were so striking and clear-cut. Cyclova needed taking but once every four weeks. A forgotten dose gave a whole month's grace. Each pill cost hardly more than the established ones, but only thirteen were needed a year instead of nearly three hundred. The newspaper ventured slickly into biochemistry, explaining how cyclova contained the same drugs as the more familiar oral contraceptives, but these were chemically treated to settle in the tissues of the pituitary gland itself. Because such a small quantity of the drug was needed in the body as a whole, the paper pointed out, its users were spared even the minor upsets – the nausea, retention of water, increase in weight, and depression – experienced by women on regular pills. More serious effects, like thrombosis of the veins, were even less likely. Above all, cyclova was absolutely safe. It had been widely tested on thousands of volunteers in the United States and many other parts of the world. No ill-effects had been found, none whatever.

I hurled the newspaper across the room, startling Kit. I'm afraid I had been in poor temper since leaving Henry the afternoon before.

Our frivolous paper had a front-page picture of a news conference held the previous evening in the Piccadilly offices of General Drugs. Lloyd was in the middle, looking pleased with himself. I bent over the page, searching for a glimpse of Boatwright, but the smudged faces were all strangers. Release of the drug was apparently occurring simultaneously in New York, and an interview with the firm's head research chemist would later be transmitted to British homes 'by satellite' – which seemed automatically to heighten the importance of his views. 'An everywoman's pill', Lloyd described it, jubilantly. General Drugs aimed at a world-wide campaign, he explained, and were generously offering it to poor governments with population problems at a price well below cost. A representative of such a bedevilled government was at the conference, and expressed his gratitude.

To me, all this was old hat. New was a 'spokesman' of the Ministry of Health describing cyclova as 'a breakthrough of enormous significance' – though adding that he much regretted it couldn't be supplied free of charge by the National Health Service. Lloyd even produced a Nobel Prize winner to pronounce his scientific benediction. The newspaper itself welcomed the new pill with a short dashed-off leader, and the cartoonist used it for a laboured political joke. Cyclova had clearly become part of the man-in-the-street's speech, like penicillin or heart transplants.

McRobb and I were seeing Ma Saintsbury in her office at lunchtime. I was glad that I had put off the meeting until approaching Henry, because now everything fell into place with deadly neatness. McRobb, in her white coat, perched as usual on the table. I leant against the tall narrow bookcase, hands clasped tightly before me. I had to control myself, to pretend almost that I was speaking of some other person, as I gave Ma

Saintsbury the story of General Drugs, Charles Crawless, Sir Robert Boatwright, and Longfield.

'Why, it's monstrous!' she exclaimed. 'Utterly monstrous! You must have a very good case indeed against them for slander, defamation of character, or something like that.'

'I don't think I want to swim in those sort of waters,' I objected.

'Why ever not, Ann?' She felt so strongly that she thumped the desk. 'You stick up for your rights. Don't let them treat you scurvily just because you're a woman. You musn't be feeble, you know.'

'But wouldn't it be awfully difficult to prove anything?' I pointed out, trying to be sensible. 'Charles Crawless and Boatwright got together in a room, without witnesses. Lloyd would certainly take care to see there was no record, no letters, about me at all.'

'But you've got your star witness,' she protested. 'Your former husband.'

'That's out of the question. I should never let anyone, anyone at all apart from you two, know that Henry gave me the inside story.'

McRobb snorted. 'There speaks a woman.'

'Anyway, all Charles's malevolence is in the past,' I continued, perhaps consoling myself. 'Certainly nothing can be undone now. And whatever amount of compensation some jury awarded me, it could never mend my feelings.'

'The way he turned on you!' Ma Saintsbury showed unaccustomed ferocity. 'And you always imagined Crawless as your ally. Why, we all did, the three of us. I remember feeling exactly the same in 1940, when Leopold gave in to the Huns.'

'Or as Hitler felt about Mussolini,' murmured McRobb.

'I *knew* who Crawless reminded me of!' declared Ma Saintsbury. 'Musso! Musso with a moustache. He's got the same taste for finery and Empire building, too. I might tell you, *that* Sawdust Caesar has had his last private patient from *me*.'

'The personal side of all this is really of minor importance,' I asserted. 'Of minor importance to anyone except myself, and I'm learning to put up with it. When I try and think calmly about the whole horrible business, there's only one really important aspect. And that's cyclova, now dumped on the unsuspecting population of the world. The fact that Charles Crawless went to such pains to talk me out of my lab. findings, that General Drugs went to such pains to gag me, that they wanted to punish me with such vengeance, points to only one thing —'

'They're afraid of you,' cut in McRobb.

'They're afraid of what I've found.'

'How can they be such fools?' demanded Ma Saintsbury.

'I should imagine they'd be scared stiff.' McRobb blew smoke down her pink-edged nostrils. 'A little interview with Sheriff wouldn't have looked so good in the papers, alongside the stuff they've put out this morning. The public are as sensitive as scalded cats. After all, nowadays they swallow drugs like fruit drops.'

'I'm more convinced now I was right over those immature blood cells,' I told her, 'than at any time since I first saw them.'

'If *I* had been one of their directors in America,' said Ma Saintsbury crossly, 'I should have sat up and taken a great deal of notice indeed of any report coming out of Princess Victoria's.'

'That's the trouble,' said McRobb. 'Who's heard of us in the big wide world? As far as the Americans are concerned we're fry too small to count.'

'Utterly disgraceful!' Ma Saintsbury seemed to swell. 'We must put these cyclova people in their place *at once*!'

It was good to warm my raw feelings in the glow of Ma Saintsbury's enthusiasm. But our difficulty was again not objectives, only means. The problem was far too mature, and far too urgent, to apply our original solution of interesting a few professional dignitaries and writing a polite letter to the medical press – through the good offices of Charles Crawless, of all people.

'Cyclova is on the market,' I said. 'For all I know, women are already taking it. We have to get it off the market. How?'

'We must start playing politics,' decided Ma Saintsbury.

'You mean, write to my Member of Parliament? I don't even know his name.'

'No, I don't think that would be *quite* the right course. With politics, even more than with anything else, it's not so much a question of what you know, but who. Your local man might think us merely a bunch of crackpots – they're much exposed to those, at all levels of society and of intelligence. You want to be sure of some politician who would be interested in our cause, as distinct from simply making something out of it.'

'Surely you must know some M.P.s, Dame Christina?' I suggested hopefully. 'Even members of the Government?'

She doodled with her ball-point on the blotter.

'The situation's a little more tricky than at our last council of war. According to my morning paper, the Ministry of Health have made approving noises about the stuff. All these Government departments tend to fight very shy of one another, you know. It would be like complaining in a hotel to the head porter that you've been poisoned in the dining-room. He'd swiftly refer you to the chef. And *this* particular kitchen suffers from strong feelings of infallibility. We could send for the manager, of course, but alas! the manager would remain inaccessible.'

McRobb sat with her hands on her knees, her legs spread as widely as a man's, a certain sign that she was worried. 'The nearest I can get is a boy-friend who fought an election as an independent,' she announced. 'He lost his deposit. And I had lent it to him.'

This was surprising news to spring from our conversation. I wondered who this dark independent gentleman could have been.

'Couldn't we take it up with the Parliamentary Commissioner – the Ombudsman, whatever he is?' I suggested.

Ma Saintsbury gave a loud grunt. 'My dear girl, even if you did get any action out of him, the drug might have slaughtered thousands by then.'

'What about Iris Quiply?' suggested McRobb.

'Ah!' Ma Saintsbury leant back in her chair. 'That's a really constructive idea, Sandra. You were a friend of hers, weren't you, Ann?'

'When we were both residents here. But that was about eight years ago. I've hardly set eyes on her since.'

'She was certainly quite a firebrand,' observed Ma Saintsbury fondly. 'Though I fancy the fire is blazing a little less fiercely today, as is so often the case. In many ways I rather liked Iris.'

'I'm quite prepared to remind her of my existence.'

But Ma Saintsbury didn't hear me. She started doodling again. 'Iris had such estimable confidence in her views and in herself. Which is essential if you want to get anything done, even if it's the wrong thing. I so remember when I came back after the war, when our world seemed to be run by Iris Quiplys. Some people were terrified by that Socialist Government, you know, you could almost hear the clang of the guillotine in their voices. But, of course, Mr Attlee hadn't then startled the country with the full fury of his naked moderation.'

She fell silent, and I imagined she was mentally assessing the qualities of Iris. But she went on with a sigh. 'Those were strange times, indeed. When I came home on demob. leave, my family got out the best silver and the Sèvres china in my honour, but all we ate off them was dried egg and meatless rissoles. I suppose one didn't notice the incongruity, in days when one bought one's whole month's sweet-ration in secret and munched the lot, completely unshared, alone in one's bedroom. I can still recall that particular ecstasy. We were so much better off in the Forces. When I was stationed in Brussels, the men could have any girl they fancied for a bar of soap, and for a carton of American cigarettes her sister and her mother as well. From such emerged our post-war world, with these ball-point pens, our ability to hurtle through space, nylon underthings and instant coffee.'

'Do you really want me to get in touch with Iris?' I cut in impatiently.

'What's that, Ann? Do speak up.'

I repeated the question more loudly.

'Yes, I think you should,' Ma Saintsbury told me firmly. 'Just put the facts to her, exactly as you put them to me. She's never been afraid to make a nuisance of herself in the Commons, you know. Perhaps that's why she hasn't held Government office.

I was rather puzzled at that. I always thought her one of my ablest girls, though I suppose intelligence doesn't count overmuch in these appointments. What was her last shindy about? Free milk for schoolchildren, I believe. She wanted to abolish it, absolutely right in these days of proper diets, it just makes the little beasts fat. *That* didn't make her popular with the powers-that-be in her party, I'm afraid. It's remarkable how milk and schoolchildren have such a peculiarly emotional connexion in politics.'

'A doctor-M.P. would give us a bit of extra leverage,' remarked McRobb. 'If she takes it on.'

'I can only ask,' I said. 'I'll telephone her.'

'She'll be delighted to hear from you, I'm sure,' Ma Saintsbury told me comfortingly. 'Successful people always are delighted to hear from their friends in obscurity, as long as they're certain they're not going to be asked for a loan. Please tell Iris that *I* am personally interested in this cyclova battle, that I regard it as a Princess Victoria's affair, and furthermore that I expect her, as one of my girls, to do her stuff.'

'I'll certainly put that to her, Dame Christina.'

McRobb exhaled smoke. 'Sure you don't mind seeking out Quiply, Sheriff?'

'No, of course not. I don't mind at all.'

I suspected that McRobb knew I wasn't enthusiastic to meet Iris again, and I suspected that she also knew why.

30

IRIS'S FLAT WASN'T far from the one where I lived with Kit. The address was a huge, newly built block in Pimlico, convenient for the House of Commons. I knew nothing about Parliamentary procedure, but I gathered the M.P.s hung about until summoned by the division-bell, to vote for their party without the tedium of sitting through the arguments deployed for the motion, nor even the need of finding exactly what the motion was. Though I suspected that Iris's sharp brain would needle out the essence of any issue set before her. She had been a clever young woman. If not so clever as myself, I decided half-smugly and half-judicially as I walked on to the springy, lawn-like carpet of the foyer, nor at the time so bossy. Iris had simply believed that she knew what was best for people, which was more dangerous.

A porter in gold braid informed me that she lived on the top floor. I had telephoned immediately after leaving Ma Saintsbury, and Iris had confessed herself delighted to see me at six the following evening – adding that she might have to dash away in the middle to vote, which impressed me enormously. Going up, I inspected myself in the long mirror forming one side of the lift. The same old mustard suit, the same expensive shoes. I wondered if *she* would think that I had aged. I smiled. I hoped not. It would never do, painfully shattering her youthful dreams.

I found that most disturbing phenomenon, a glass eye set suspiciously in her door. I rang the bell. Light footsteps. A pause. She was inspecting me.

'Ann, darling!' The door flew open. 'How lovely to see you.'

'Hello, Iris.' Just for a second, from a brief failure to control her expression, I could see that she was genuinely touched.

'But you look absolutely wonderful!' She assumed her usual bright look, kissing my cheek. 'How on earth do you manage it?'

'I'm an old hag compared with you.'

'Nonsense. Come in.'

The flat was bright, clean, and neat. The small hall had bare polished boards with a Persian rug of complicated design and bookshelves to the ceiling. The sitting-room beyond had lively gold-patterned wallpaper and an apricot fitted carpet. There were more bookshelves along one wall, all the volumes looking new, many in their dust-jackets, and I supposed on political subjects. Overflowing into neat piles on the floor were copies of *Hansard*, Blue Books and White Papers, and there was a low table in the middle of the room with carefully arranged copies of the *New Statesman*, the *Spectator*, *Tribune*, and the *Economist*. A pile of daily papers, folded with equal care, lay on the sideboard. Iris has been sitting in an easy-chair, snipping from a newspaper, scissors, paste, and scrapbook scattered on the floor. The furniture was expensive. There was a fireplace with an electric fire emitting a red, cold glow from a pair of plastic logs. Before it was spread a tigerskin rug, complete with head and frozen snarl. It wasn't an object seen often in homes these days. I wondered what Iris did on it.

'I hear you've been ill, you poor darling.'

'Yes, I developed rheumatoid arthritis.'

She gave a sympathetic shudder.

'My physician seems to have it fairly under control at the moment, thank God.'

'What's he giving you?'

'Smallish doses of corticosteroids. It started playing me up a bit this summer.'

'You poor lamb! What would you like to drink?'

'Gin and something.'

'How splendid. All the women I seem to meet drink sherry. The very smell of it makes me sick.'

She fetched bottles from the sideboard. 'You've a lovely flat, Iris.'

'It's home. We don't see why we shouldn't be snug. I share with another girl.'

I glanced round. There was no evidence of another's presence. No clashing belongings in that bookish room. Iris, as expected, ruled the roost. Or perhaps the other girl was a reader too.

'I hope I haven't scared your flatmate away?'

'No, she's out for the evening, that's all.'

I took my drink and sat down. Iris flopped again amid the press-cuttings, her arms drooping languidly over the sides of the chair. The gesture focused an impression in my mind since coming through the door. At Princess Victoria's she had always sat stiffly, sometimes bolt upright. The austere edge of her had blunted. I was certain that her surroundings, the loose green dress she wore, the stylish costume-jewellery clip, were more luxurious than she would have permitted herself in those days, even had she the money. As a young doctor she wore her fairish hair severely clipped, now it swung as free as a girl's. She had always been pretty in an athletic country-girl way, now she made up too heavily. Her very breath when she kissed me had an unaccustomed sickliness. Yes, Iris had gone voluptuous.

'I know you think I've changed, Ann.' She had noticed my glance. 'But have I changed out of all recognition?'

'You're very smart.'

'I have to be. They're continually photographing me for the dailies, though to tell the truth precious few of them get printed. It's not flattery. My colleagues are mostly pretty dreary to look at, male or female.'

I took out a cigarette. 'It's terribly grand, becoming an M.P.'

She didn't smoke herself, but leant across with a match. 'It's grand becoming a doctor, but you soon get used to the idea. Particularly when you find yourself surrounded exclusively by other doctors.'

'Your getting in wasn't a surprise for me.'

She smiled. 'It was rather too much of one for me.'

She had been returned with a wafer-thin majority by a northern constituency in the general election of 1964, riding becomingly on the technological coat-tails of Mr Wilson. In the 1966 vote she had trounced her Tory opponent, but by that summer, when the white-hot scientific revolution had failed to ignite, the opinion polls must have made uneasy reading for her.

'You always said you'd do it, and I'm sure your sense of purpose in those days was quite as steely as mine.'

'Did I really say so? I've forgotten so much that happened during my time at Princess Victoria's.'

That was nice of her.

'I expect you're wondering exactly why I've stepped out of the past?'

'That was rather bothering me.' She smiled again. 'Or have you been carefully avoiding me these whole eight years?'

Not so nice of her.

'Of course not! Old friendships simply drop, once your year starts to split up and go its separate ways. It was exactly the same with Liz. I met her the other week for the first time in ages.'

Iris sipped her gin without comment. I suspected I'd been too defensive. 'It's something really important which brings me here,' I continued.

'Connected with the hospital?'

'In a way. I don't suppose you know the sort of work I'm doing at Princess Victoria's. I got a readership in physiology —'

'Weren't you going in for gynae.?'

I opened and closed my fingers, and she understood. 'I've recently been engaged in research on contraception and population problems.'

'My God, the world needs it!' she exclaimed. 'I was out in India last February, with a Commonwealth delegation. I was horrified. Absolutely horrified. There were people everywhere, not only sleeping in the streets but living – actually living their lives – on the pavements. Bombay's the tidiest city in the world. Do you know why? There's no litter, because nobody's got anything to throw away. I used to look out of my window at the Taj Mahal hotel, to watch them grubbing in the mud of the shore with their toes for anything they could find. Hundreds of them. It affected me far more poignantly than the most eloquent speech from the United Nations.'

'That's our danger. Worse than the H-bomb.'

'Oh, the world is loving itself to death.' Her remark had a soft edge of gaiety, which certainly wouldn't have been there eight years ago. 'St Paul was absolutely wrong. Love isn't man's deepest well of joy and nobility. It's a drain, which syphons off his dignity, before he jumps in head-first and drowns himself.'

I gave a smile. 'I'm afraid it's an enduring fashion – accepting sexual love as the force dragging us irresistibly to happiness.'

'Rodin's *Kiss* and advertisements of young couples drooling over their new sports-cars,' she agreed. 'They're the same thing.'

Iris got up to fetch her half-emptied tonic-water from the sideboard. There was only a trace of her old determination in her walk. I noticed again her strong bony hands holding the small bottle. I wished that she didn't make up her eyes so heavily. They were always her best point. They could flash with anger, or if you were lucky sometimes take on a nun-like tenderness.

'Think of the energy expended in love!' She sat again in the same pose. 'Why, every night it could illuminate several cities.'

'One of the contraceptives I've been studying is this new one, cyclova,' I told her, deciding to come to business.

'I saw it in the papers yesterday. The wonder pill.'

'It's not so wonderful. Will you suffer my talking for five minutes?'

Iris had a gift rare among the articulate, of being able to listen. When I finished my story – though saying nothing about Longfield – she gave a low whistle. 'These bloody drug companies! Did you know, darling, they run a profit of fifteen per cent? That's compared with thirteen point eight in other industries. I got as much from the Socialist Medical Association.' We shared a failing for ready statistics. 'And some American companies over here, they average *seventy-three* per cent profit! Hair-raising, isn't it? On some drugs they even make up to *five thousand* per cent. An absolute scandal.' I wondered how much of her anger was personal, and how much political. 'A lot of this came out in the drug committee's report. Did you read it?'

'I glanced through it.'

'I must get it out to brush up my facts. Mind, we're not

letting this sort of racket go on much longer. Did you know, we can use any patent we like "for the services of the Crown" without paying through the nose, or even paying at all? And the National Health Service is a service of the Crown plainly enough, isn't it? It's wonderful what you can do with a few well-thought-out regulations.'

Iris had always believed that you could make people good, industrious, orderly, rich (or poor), selfless, and patriotic with a handful of Government edicts. Although I have no politics, I felt this a mirage from which so many Socialists had gone to drink and died of thirst.

'What exactly do you want me to do about this cyclova, darling?'

'Stop them selling it,' I told her briefly. 'Unless *someone* does, one fine day the world will tumble to it that the leukaemia figures are creeping up faster than they should.'

She gave me a look I had often seen before, but seldom directed at myself. 'You're sure of yourself about this, darling, are you? About what you found in those original blood-smears?'

'Everyone asks me that.' I didn't sound angry now, only weary. 'Of course, even Pasteur or Florey must have made their mistakes. But have you ever known me to be sure, really sure in my own mind, about some fact in the wards or in the lab., and then to discover I was wrong?'

'Very well, darling, you have my faith.'

This was exciting. I had gained my first objective, as Ma Saintsbury might have put it. 'Surely it's a crucial matter of public importance?'

'After all that you've told me, I agree. Though I shall have to think a little, darling, before definitely making up my mind. We may be fools in politics, but we don't often rush in where the newspapers fear to tread.'

I stubbed out my cigarette. 'Naturally, I understand that.'

'Perhaps I might put down a question for the Minister of Health,' she speculated. She spoke of operating even one of the minor levers of power with impressive nonchalance.

'The very fact that you can air doubts about cyclova without fear of libel proceeding is a wonderful advantage.'

'Oh, I'd word the question nastily enough, leave it to me. Perhaps I'll have a chat tonight with someone in the Ministry. How urgent is it?'

'Obviously, a day or two can't make much difference.'

She reached for a large, red, leather-covered desk diary on the table with the periodicals. 'Tomorrow afternoon I've a speaking date in the country – it's Friday, and not much happens in the House. I'm going straight on for the week-end. I've bought a little cottage in Dorset.'

'I expect you need a bolt-hole.'

'It's not for me, really, but Nina. She's the girl I share with. I'm taking her down for a rest. She's been tired recently, out of sorts. Nothing organic, that I can make out.'

'Early next week, then?' I didn't want to risk her losing enthusiasm.

'Why not see me here on Tuesday, about eleven in the morning?'

'I can't tell you how grateful I am, Iris.'

'We Princess Vikki's girls must stick together,' she said with mock-boisterousness. 'At least, that's what Ma Saintsbury kept telling us. Does she like being a Dame?'

'You know she's fond of rank. Though I fancy she'd have preferred being made an honorary general.'

Iris laughed. 'I wonder what the weedy little husband thinks? What a pity a Dame's consort doesn't have some sort of title – a "Gallant" would sound quite nice.'

I rose to go. We carried on an inconsequential conversation crossing the hall, but as I paused to tell Iris again and more formally of my gratitude we heard the key scrape in the lock. The door opened, and a small, pale, dark young girl in a brown jersey dress stood gaping at me. Nina had obviously come home earlier than she had been instructed.

'Nina, this is Dr Sheriff,' Iris introduced me blandly. 'You remember, she was coming to see me.'

'Pleased to meet you,' said Nina in a crushed voice.

'I've been admiring your lovely flat,' I told her politely.

She stood looking at Iris and myself alternately. Both of us seemed to worry her deeply.

'Nina, go and get yourself a drink,' Iris dismissed her. I advanced to the open doorway, saying good-bye. Iris held the door ajar, hesitated, then smiled. 'I met her last Christmas, working in the local supermarket. It was like an electric flash. Wonderful! When I was in India she wrote to me every day, and nearly died.'

That was the second case I knew of Iris and love at first sight, I reflected.

31

THAT IRIS QUIPLY and I had, eight years before, occupied a pair of residents' rooms away from the others at Princess Victoria's was a matter of pure chance. The accommodation of the newly-qualified doctors was settled by someone in the hospital secretary's office, with no fuss about trying to keep the men and women apart. I hadn't been a particular friend of Iris's during our student years. Nobody had. She was then a tight-lipped, hard-working, rather spotty girl, who made no particular mark apart from editing *The Victorian*, our hospital magazine which no one ever seemed to read. She was the first woman editor since the medical school became mixed, and I fancy she went after the job for that reason. But it was useful for her. The editors were always given a resident appointment for their pains, so she became house-surgeon to the throat department. Later, the training with galley-proofs and deadlines helped her on to the editorial staff of one of the lesser London medical journals. This was her base. She studied economics and took an external degree in her spare time, she forayed with her pen into the partisan weeklies, she started speaking at meetings and generally gained confidence while making something of a name for herself as yet another political doctor.

'Did you go to boarding school, Ann?' she asked me in my room at the hospital one evening.

I shook my head.

'I did. Lady Clare's in Gloucestershire – not particularly fashionable, but I suppose academically adequate.'

'I often wish I'd had the chance.'

214

'Oh, I hated it,' she said offhandedly.

She moved her legs, tucking them under her on my bed. She still had her white coat on. Isolation at the end of a long corridor had thrown us on each other's company, and she came into my room most evenings, after supper and before our night-rounds in the wards. Like all the residents, we chatted mostly about our cases.

'Being at home, were you brought up strictly?' she inquired.

I was sitting on the only chair, a hard one, my elbow resting on the dressing-table with its cracked mirror. 'I wasn't brought up at all. Long before I went to secondary school – I imagine when I was nine or ten – I started running my own life. I made up my mind what I wanted to do, and I did it.'

'That's starting female independence rather early, isn't it? How did your parents feel about it?'

'Frightened. I was something of a cuckoo in the nest. I'm much more intelligent than they are.'

'Aren't you being a little hard?'

'No. It's a fact, so why not face it?'

She took a sip from her glass. I generally had a bottle of gin in my wardrobe, which we drank with tap-water out of our toothglasses. Iris never had more than one drink, sometimes leaving that unfinished. Tippling with me was for her an act of politeness rather than of pleasure.

'We're neither of us particularly well off, are we?' she asked.

'I thought your father was a g.p. in Wiltshire?'

'He drinks,' she announced laconically. Perhaps this explained her abstemiousness. 'Yes, it's really quite a problem. He ends up in court now and then, because of the car. Though God knows, our local police fall over backwards to let him get away with it. We live in a small town, and he's popular among the locals. He's very hail-fellow-well-met, let-me-buy-you-a-double-scotch-old-boy. But it doesn't add up to a profitable practice.'

Those few sentences disclosed more of herself than our entire six years together in the medical school.

'What's your mother think?'

'She's dead.'

'Oh, I'm sorry.'

Neither had she revealed this.

'My mother was awfully strict. I'm an only child, which didn't help. She was deeply religious, a member of some odd sect – I forget which, exactly, now. I don't know how my father chose her, but I think the religion more and more took over her life. It's often the case in an unhappy marriage, isn't it? Perhaps his drinking was the same thing. And she was a vegetarian, which was worse. She was quite cranky, she even wore rope soles on her shoes. When I was fourteen she killed herself with an overdose of aspirin.'

I was horrified by this casual revelation. 'That must have been awful for you.'

'Particularly as the local hospital, her being a doctor's wife, did their damnedest to save her. In the end, she just suffered five days of lingering death. I'm sorry, Ann,' Iris broke off, 'I'm sure you don't want to listen to all this sordid family history.'

'That's what your friends are for.'

'Friends?' She made a wry face. 'I never make any. Not in this place. Have I a cold personality, do you suppose? Do I lack "affect"? Is there any possibility that I'm a schizoid?'

'Now you're being silly.'

'Do you know that I've always envied you, Ann?'

'But I don't make friends all that simply.'

'Not only over human relationships. You've got a style about you. You stand out from the rest of us. Everything seems to come so easily to you.'

'Yet nothing does,' I told her feelingly. 'I have to struggle, whether it's to pass examinations or to make myself presentable.'

'You succeed in both, don't you?'

'There's no guarantee I shall in the future.'

'Haven't you sufficient confidence in yourself? I have. In many ways we're much the same, Ann. We're pushers. And we despise people who look unlikely to push anywhere in particular.'

'Perhaps you're right.' She was flattering me, and I found it pleasant enough.

'Do you get a lot of men chasing after you?'

I laughed. 'I've just lost one, and that's an unbelievably dull story.' I had no intention of matching her frankness with the story of Trevor. 'Anyway, I haven't time. McRobb blows up on every occasion that I snatch an evening off.'

'That surly bitch,' said Iris, wrinkling her nose. 'Don't you even get time to study politics?'

'I'm not in the slightest interested in politics.'

'That's mistaken of you, Ann,' she rebuked me. 'It's like the brain declaring it's not interested in digestion or excretion or locomotion. They're all part of the same body, the same process of living. Without a political structure we should cease to exist, for all practical purposes. Can't I lend you a book to spark off some ideas? It's a shame, someone of your ability having no political awareness.'

'But when should I find time to read it?' I protested.

'Please, Ann. I'd very much like you to.'

She sounded so imploring, I agreed. She fetched from her room an ancient second-hand copy of Bernard Shaw's *Intelligent Woman's Guide to Capitalism and Socialism*. I thought the title pleasantly ingratiating.

I read half the book, taking it very seriously. Later, I came to agree with Kit that Shaw wrote a good deal of knowing froth, even about music. During the evenings, Iris now involved me in political arguments, which I always lost. Like the politics of most young people, hers were rooted in emotion rather than intellect. She was a surprisingly old-fashioned Socialist, obsessed with such pensionable bogies as international bankers, shareholders, and the owners of anything more extravagant than her own meagre personal possessions. Only when she penetrated the outworks of the citadels of power did she become more sophisticated and politically more her natural self.

'But you frighten me,' I told her after one argument, 'the way you want to bring the individual under the same rigid collective control as everything material in the country.'

'Well, perhaps you can put it down to a vegetarian mother and a drunken father,' she agreed graciously. She hesitated. 'Can I tell you a secret? My father once tried to have intercourse with me.'

217

'That's not an unknown situation, is it?' I commented calmly. I was determined to be no further staggered by her personal revelations.

'It was just after my mother had died. I was home for the holidays, and we were alone in the house.' Afterwards, I suspected that Iris had made up the story, as a somewhat unimaginative lead into what happened next. 'He was drunk. He had his penis out, a great pink thing. I was scared. He got his fingers up my skirt, but I managed to talk him out of it.'

'A good thing you kept your head.'

She seemed to have become jumpy, and she was drumming her fingers against her leg. I put the agitation down to her memories.

'I'm afraid the effect of the episode was to make me frigid.'

'How do you know you are?' I demanded promptly.

'I've never had a man, if that's what you're after. But I feel numb down there sometimes. Perhaps I'm anatomically abnormal. Would you have a look?'

She was sitting as usual with her legs tucked underneath her on my bed. She stretched them apart and pulled up her skirt. It was a premeditated conversation, because she had no pants on. Justifiably, I felt uneasy.

'My clitoris feels numb.'

'Well, it looks all right.'

'What's the nerve supply of the clitoris, Ann?'

'I can't remember,' I confessed. 'And I'm staring at the damn things all day. It's got a dorsal nerve, hasn't it? Coming off the pudendal – sacral two, three, and four.'

Any doubts, or rather pretences, that ours was a clinical conversation were swept aside by her adding, 'Touch me, Ann.'

I looked hard at her, and found her eyes at their tenderest.

'Touch me, Ann,' she repeated.

What complicated psychological machinery extended my fingers I shall never understand. Perhaps I had become subconsciously attached to her. I knew a lot of intimate things about her, more than of any other girl in the hospital. I liked her. I had grown to admire her – and admiration is the most deadly of

218

weaknesses in a woman. It was largely admiration which later led me to accept Henry.

I touched her and suddenly she gave a gasp, as I triggered off her orgasm. Immediately I felt disgusted with myself.

I tore away, saying angrily, 'Why did you make me do that?'

'Didn't you enjoy it?'

I made no reply.

Iris stayed on the bed, pulling down her skirt. 'Haven't you done it before?'

'No, of course not. Only with myself. Not with another woman.'

'Don't be cross with me, Ann. I don't deserve that, do I?'

'You're a pervert,' I snapped at her.

'That's rather a sledgehammer word, isn't it? It raises visions of whips and shackles and button-boots.'

I hastily lit a cigarette. 'I wish you'd never started coming in here.'

She patted the bed. 'Sit down, Ann,' she said gently. 'You're upset, but was that really something to make yourself unhappy about?'

I made a hopeless gesture. A display of outraged temper would get me nowhere. Iris seemed firmly in charge of the situation.

As I sat beside her, she said, without touching me, 'I'm quite a bit in love with you, Ann.'

'Love? How can you use that word?'

'You sound contemptuous, but I think the term's correct,' she replied thoughtfully. 'I've never loved a man. I couldn't, it's just impossible. But I should imagine it's exactly the same emotion. You'd know surely? You must have been in love with one or two.'

'Not really,' I admitted. 'Not in the wide-eyed sense.'

'Then perhaps there's hope for me yet with you?' she suggested slyly. She reached out her hand and laid it on the top of my thigh, outside my dress. I made no move to reject her. 'I always want to be with you, Ann. I love talking to you. I'm thrilled, sometimes, when I catch you glancing at me, in the dining-room, in the corridors, anywhere public in the hospital.

I want to be close to you and to feel you.' Her hand slipped down to press between my legs. 'That's love, isn't it? I want to spend my life with you, darling. To eat with you, sleep with you, talk to you whenever I feel like it. To share my worries and excitements with you. To draw pleasure from your body, to give you pleasure with mine. That's love, surely?'

'But those ideas are fantasies, Iris.' I now spoke sympathetically. I was beginning to see into her mind. 'How long have you been entertaining them?'

'Entertaining them seriously, since I found you'd the room beside mine. Entertaining them in general . . . well, for years. I think I fell for you almost when I saw you.'

I asked out of interest, 'Have you been in love with a lot of girls?'

'I used to sleep with a girl in my digs now and then. She was a student – history. But it wasn't satisfactory. She had nothing of your sensitivity. I couldn't possibly have lived with her, but I could live with you, Ann. I'd love to. And why not? Two professional women sharing the same house. No one would think it particularly unusual.'

I smiled, and shook my head slowly. She took her hand away and went on more prosaically, 'I'm sorry for what happened just now, Ann. I must have been feeling pretty sure of myself. You've made me quite ashamed that I'm a Lesbian.'

'I certainly wouldn't care to burden you with obsessions of guilt.'

'But I *am* ashamed of it. Deep down. You're right, it's abnormal. Any unprocreative sex is abnormal.'

'That's throwing the net pretty wide, isn't it?'

'I felt terribly guilty about it at school. It was the boarding-school which turned me queer, you know.' She said this defiantly, though I suspected it more a fault of present personality than of past environment. 'That's why I hated the place. God, the mental torment! I used to make myself swear, out loud on a Bible, when I was alone, that I'd never do it again. I always did, though.'

'Wasn't that part of the upset of puberty? You shouldn't suffer so much now.'

'No, I don't. But sometimes when I wake in the morning, with the sun shining into my bedroom, I've a moment of happiness shot to bits by the thought, "You're a Lesbian". It must be the same if you've been diagnosed as having some serious disease, a carcinoma for instance. Think of the horror – you wake, a second of contentment, perhaps a feeling of unease, then the memory floods in. It's how a man wakes the morning they're going to hang him. No, I have to hide it, but I don't think I have to be ashamed of it any more. This is my own body. And my own mind, which is more important.' She fell silent then looked up. 'Won't you kiss me, Ann? Please kiss me.'

I leant over and kissed her lips, feeling her tongue, knowing that I was taking too long over it.

Afterwards, Iris came into my room frequently enough, but always gave the appearance of being in a hurry, never sitting down, often leaving the door open. She had left me with the hungrily gnawing anxiety that perhaps I too was really a Lesbian. I felt sure that I *wasn't* a homosexual, though I knew there was something of one in all of us. I remembered reading in psychiatry books that very few escaped some similar sort of experience in a lifetime. Then my affairs with Cliff and Trevor – they had both been heartless, in their different ways. I might find that no man could arouse my feelings, as distinct from my passions. Any stimulus would do. Had I, after all, enjoyed masturbating Iris? I daren't give myself the answer. I had dreamt about it, once, but dismissed that as of no significance. Was I 'in love' with her, as she would have put it? I repeatedly checked myself, as I found that I was looking for her in the crowded residents' mess or round the hospital, somehow always seeming to catch her eye, to invoke her quick smile. I became nervous that Liz or one of the others might notice, but I don't think they even began to suspect me. Then one afternoon, as I walked downstairs from the gynaecological department with McRobb, Iris hurried past us going up.

'That girl's soft on you, Sheriff,' said McRobb.

I was much disconcerted. 'Why should you say a thing like that, Miss McRobb?' I exclaimed.

'You don't give me much credit as a diagnostician, do you?

Particularly in a place like this, where it's as endemic as yellow fever in Brazil.'

I knew my face was flushed. I supposed McRobb was enjoying herself. 'I haven't noticed anything.'

'No, I don't suppose you would. You're penis-orientated.'

It was one of the most heartening things she ever said to me.

The next week Iris stopped coming into my room at all, having fallen flat for one of the sisters.

32

SO IRIS QUIPLY, my seducer, now a Member of Parliament, was to make common cause with me against cyclova. It was my first real encouragement since that afternoon, almost three months before, when I had sent my letter about the blood-samples to Lloyd's office. After leaving her flat, I tried to dissect her motives in helping me. They were probably mixed – a political dislike of profits, a real concern for public health, a feeling of duty, and undoubtedly an eagerness for publicity. Our old friendship may have helped. But that incident in my room at Princess Victoria's was surely a fossil in our lives, buried under so many layers of events. An odd-looking one to dig up, perhaps, but stony and dead.

I speculated on Iris's line of attack. She might put down a Parliamentary question, as she had suggested – 'Is the Minister aware of the existence of an adverse report on the oral contraceptive cyclova, prepared by Dr Ann Sheriff, Reader in Experimental Physiology at Princess Victoria's Hospital . . .' What glory! Or perhaps she might go more stealthily, dropping a word in the right ear, with Lloyd finally carpeted before some thunderous politician. Though I didn't care much what happened to him, only what happened to his dangerous wares. I read another snippet about cyclova, in my paper on the Tube to Princess Victoria's that Saturday morning, and told myself smugly, 'Just you wait!' I wondered how Iris was enjoying her week-end in Dorset with Nina. I reflected with amusement that her taste seemed to have deteriorated with age. But attraction between the social poles was always an epiphenomenon of homosexuality.

In the Gothic doorway of the hospital I found McRobb, in her white coat, looking glum.

'They gave Mrs Ramsay four years,' she announced at once. 'The fools. God knows who'll be poking about inside the local girls now.'

'I suppose the law must be obeyed,' I told her, almost consolingly. She had heard about Iris from me the morning before.

'The law!' McRobb sounded contemptuous as we walked together into the hospital. 'The law shouldn't meddle with professional matters.'

'The doctor knows best?' I suggested unsolemnly.

'The law deals only with facts. We deal with people. Do you know, Sheriff, if I were a judge I wouldn't sentence anyone, not for any crime at all, until I'd been to his home, talked to his family, tried to understand what made him go wrong.'

'That wouldn't leave you a lot of time for sitting in court, would it?'

'I've had policemen nosing round *me*, you know,' she disclosed. 'About the abortions I'd been doing. That was before they changed the rules. Though they never got very far. I've my own standards, and I always obey them. So why should I have any compunction about taking the law into my own hands? Do you know that I've committed murder?'

This sounded alarming, but I said nothing. I was in a lighthearted mood that morning, and McRobb was grimly serious.

'Haven't most of us in medicine?' she asked. 'Not as a sin of commission, but of omission. When I've delivered a hopelessly malformed baby, do you imagine I haven't switched off the incubator? Or withheld its feeds? It probably wouldn't have survived long, anyway, but if it had, just think of the tragedy.'

I had heard rumours of this practice when I had worked as her house-surgeon. 'Doesn't it ever lie on your conscience, Sandra?'

'Of course it does.' She stuck her hands deep into the pockets of her coat. 'Whenever you stop human life it lies on your conscience, even when you've made an unavoidable mistake or hastened an inevitable end. I suffer more than the kid's mother. But I put up with it, because I know that I'm doing right.' We

224

reached the door leading up to my laboratory. 'Do you know, Sheriff,' she said seriously, 'sometimes I tell myself that I could do a good job as God.'

You were always finding surprising new things about Mc-Robb.

I had not only the morning but half the afternoon to work alone in the lab., because I had arranged to visit north London that Saturday for tea with my brother. I hadn't been back to my parents' house since the row, and I was feeling troubled that my irritation during one particular half-hour might have come between them and the bungalow of their dreams. Ronnie had reluctantly agreed over the telephone to receive me at last in his own home at Cricklewood. He gave me directions from the nearest Underground station, but I found his address to be in Hendon, a nearby but superior district, in a quiet, tree-lined road of well-built houses standing in largish gardens. If he was existing on crime, he was at least making a success of it.

The American car was parked outside. He opened the door himself, looking embarrassed. I found the darkish interior furnished with depressing suburban solidity. I don't know what I was expecting – a cellar, packing-cases for furniture, candles in bottles, and firearms drawn against all visitors. Paula sat in a formal woollen suit with gold fringes, amid silver teapot, silver kettle on a silver spirit-lamp, silver tray, neatly-cut sandwiches, and two sorts of cake. Ronnie was in week-end slacks and sweater, and I noticed that he had a large new gold wrist-watch.

I greeted his wife. 'This is all very grand, Ron,' I told him appreciatively.

'We like to be comfortable,' he said grudgingly.

'I'm afraid I behaved rather badly, last time at the old folks',' I confessed, as Paula handed me a cup of tea in her customary silence.

'I shouldn't worry. We all know our Ann by now, don't we? You stoke the fires, have a good boil-up, and it comes out through the safety-valve.'

'Were they very upset?' As usual, we had started to ignore Paula.

Ronnie bit the corner of a sandwich. 'Mum got a bit weepy.'

'Yes, it really was awful of me,' I decided. 'I should have been more considerate. It's so easy to forget they're growing old.'

'Mum's getting a bit bonkers, if you ask me. She gives me the creeps sometimes. All this psychic stuff of hers.'

'That's all nonsense,' I told him firmly.

'I dare say.' He finished his sandwich. 'She's got it in for *you*, you know.'

'In what way?'

'On the – what would you call it, the "spiritual" level. She's been looking in her crystal ball, or whatever she's got there upstairs. She keeps on about you and a bed of sickness.'

'There's nothing magic about that. She knows perfectly well that I've had rheumatism for years.'

'A bed of sickness and death.' Ronnie cut himself a slice of chocolate cake. 'Cheerful, isn't it?'

'We needn't think twice about that rubbish. Saying such things simply restores her pride. There's no harm in that. And it's reasonable enough, after the way I behaved to her. How did Dad react after I'd stormed out?'

'You know how Dad reacts to everything. If you'd have cut his throat, he'd have made a joke with his dying breath. I don't know why he doesn't write for the telly. He'd make a fortune. His gags aren't more horrible than the ones we have to put up with every night.'

'How's business?' I looked round the room, searching for some clue to his occupation but finding none.

'All right,' said Ronnie.

'You must realize why I've come? About this damn seaside bungalow. Can't you scrape up the money for them?'

Ronnie looked gloomier. 'It's not all that easy, these days of the squeeze.'

'Can't they get a mortgage, or something?'

'What, at their age?'

'But it isn't an enormous sum for you to find, surely? It's not as if they were after a villa in the South of France.'

'Ron and I have been looking at some lovely villas out there,' said Paula. 'Only the photos, mind.'

I looked inquiringly at her, and then at my brother. 'We thought we might buy one some day,' he said uncomfortably. 'When our ship comes in.'

'One day!' exclaimed Paula shrilly. 'You said next year, that's what you said.'

'Conditions are very difficult,' he told her quickly. 'The currency restrictions, and so on.'

'Since when have you worried about all that lot?' she demanded. 'You told me next year, only yesterday you did.'

'I hope you'll invite me to stay?' I asked.

Ronnie now looked deeply distressed. He had left half his chocolate cake, a profound sign of inner agitation. 'I shouldn't have asked you out here,' he grumbled.

'Well? What comes first? St Tropez for you, or St Leonard's for our aged parents?'

'All right, all right! I'll see what I can do. I might be able to raise the wind.'

'You promise?'

He had no alternative. 'I've got a friend in the estate agent line who might help. Those dead beats in Dad's office wouldn't make a proper living if they dealt in gold mines.'

'Thank you, Ron,' I told him, with relief. 'I knew you'd cough up in the end.'

'Oh, don't mention it,' he said sarcastically. He added after a moment, 'It'll be nice, getting them a bit farther away. Those suppers every month! They get more diabolical every time.'

'I suppose it's a terrible thing to say, but I agree. I'd like them out of sight, too. After all, we're only seeing them off to the seaside, not to the crematorium.'

To my surprise, this provoked from Paula her loud, high-pitched laugh.

Ronnie looked at me sideways. 'Why did you say that, Ann?'

'About the crematorium? No particular reason. It was a figure of speech, that's all.'

'No one's been telling you things?'

I felt lost. 'What sort of things?'

'It doesn't matter. Forget it.'

'Go on, Ron, let her into the secret,' urged Paula. 'She's bound to find out one day.'

Ronnie sat with his hands on his knees, thinking. I was silent, in delightful expectancy. Then he slowly got up, and made towards a side-table against the wall. 'I've done plenty of things already in my short life,' he observed. 'Property, though there aren't the pickings there were. Licensed victualling, though now I've sold most of the shops. Bricks and booze. It was a good start. People need both. I'm in a different line now. And I suppose I'm getting a bit bored with the mystery.'

He brought back from the table a plain, mauve, silk-covered album, a foot and a half long, with tassels on the spine.

'Have a look inside,' he invited.

I took it. 'Betting shops?'

'No. But almost as profitable.'

The book was full of photographs, huge, formal, glossy, expertly taken photographs. Hearses, coffins, flowers, cemetery gates, men in black with top-hats. Underneath each funeral was neatly typed the name of its sadly unaware leading actor. There were aldermen, colonels, doctors, a Q.C., even a knight.

'But they're beautiful photographs, Ron,' I exclaimed admiringly.

'Do you think so?' He sounded relieved. 'If you like, I've got some newer ones upstairs, in colour.'

'They're most impressive. I suppose a bit grim, but even photographs of wars can be impressive.'

He stood looking at me awkwardly. Paula silently gathered my teacup.

'But how long have you been an undertaker?'

'I'm not one, strictly speaking. I couldn't handle the practical end of it.' He shivered. 'I thought it a business which needed rationalization, that's all. I took over a couple of small firms, just to see what I could make of them. They grew. I've taken over more. I've injected some efficiency. Do you know, they hadn't changed their methods for a generation?'

'So you're a chain undertaker? A Pickford of the grave?'

'Don't make jokes.' He took the album away, almost snatching it. 'I'm sensitive about it.'

'But why? It's no occupation to be ashamed of.'

'You have to be born into undertaking,' he observed seriously. 'I'm just scared of people thinking I'm a bogyman. If I see a funeral in the street, I dodge down a side-turning. Honest. They upset me. I was in a traffic-jam once, I looked in my mirror, and there was a hearse right behind me. God! We seemed stuck together for ages. I could hardly start the car afterwards.'

'I hope it was one of yours?'

'I told you, no jokes.'

'Anyway, all that explains Mum's nonsense,' I smiled at him. 'It's a matter of occupations. The bed of sickness is my job. The other thing is yours.'

'I hope you're right,' said Ronnie sombrely.

I hoped so myself. My mother's magic had always scared me. Sometimes as a child I had lain awake for hours in the darkness, too terrified to take away the tightly-grasped fists pressed into my eyes. And the supernatural makes children of us all, even the most stridently level-headed scientist.

33

'IT WAS QUITE delightful,' said Iris Quiply. 'The coast down
there is wonderful, you know. Huge broken-up masses of chalk,
a giant's toothpaste smile. And of course the weather made all
the difference. I always regard bathing in this country as a spot
test of national resolution, but we were in and out of the water
all the time. I hope you got away somewhere yourself?'

I shook my head. 'I haven't even a car.'

'Ah! So *you're* the one in London without one? Of course,
you're right, darling. Driving has become such a strain. That's
why I'm teaching Nina, to take some of the workload.'

'Them gears!' said Nina feelingly.

It was about eleven on the following Tuesday morning, and
this time Nina had been allowed to stay in the flat. On my
previous visit Iris must have been unsure of my attitude – that
I might have grown prudish, or perhaps, I thought with alarm,
that I might have taken too much interest in the girl.

'Nonsense, you've got a natural talent for cars, my pet,' Iris
told her firmly. 'You'll pick it up in no time.'

Nina lay sprawled in an armchair, her legs stuck out, a
cigarette drooping from her thin lips. She was much more
uppity this time, I supposed through Iris's own reassurance
about me. 'The old cow I ran into didn't think much of my
talent.' She had a nasal voice, likely to benefit from the atten-
tions of a throat surgeon. 'The language she used! Positively
vulgar.'

'Remember what I said, darling, be a good girl, work at it,
and you can drive me across the Continent during the recess.

That was a promise. Now Ann and I want to be alone for a few minutes,' Iris added firmly.

'I'll shut my ears.'

'You do as you're told.' Iris's voice became sharp. As Nina didn't move, she warned, 'Go along! You don't want me to punish you for disobedience, do you?'

Punish her? I asked myself. I wondered if the tigerskin rug somehow came into it.

'Oh, all right. The kitchen's good enough for me, I suppose?' She rose surlily from her chair and stamped out.

'She's sweet, isn't she?' said Iris fondly.

I said nothing, Nina's charms having escaped me.

'She gets wildly jealous, you know. Quite insanely. I've only to talk to another woman, and she sulks for a week.'

'I hope I'm not disturbing the nest?'

'Oh, you know what I mean,' said Iris significantly. 'She wouldn't worry about *you*.' That was reassuring. 'She's quite a temper,' she imparted. 'Sometimes she actually becomes violent.'

'But aren't you worried?'

'About what?'

'That there might be some sort of scandal.'

'I don't think anyone cares about a bit of wholesome Lesbianism these days. Nina and I live an active social life together, in London anyway. And people have rather abandoned the sweet idea that single women made close friends for the sake of companionship.' I had taken out a cigarette, and Iris rose from her chair to lean over me with a match. 'The sort of people *we* mix with understand, which is all that matters. And I personally don't give a damn. I've got past that stage. I wouldn't give her up, you know. Whoever made a fuss, I'd never do that.'

'But what about the people who vote for you? Would they understand?'

Iris delicately dropped the spent match into a large, clean glass ash-tray. 'Does a doctor run his private life to please his patients? Or an actor to please his audiences? All the actors I know heartily despise the people who pay good money to see them. Authors despise their readers, company directors their

231

shareholders, trade union secretaries their members. And we our constituents. There's nothing malevolent or even vain about it. It's the natural attitude of the gifted few who rely ultimately for their bread and butter on the many dimwitted.'

'An attitude which strikes me as concealing a trap,' I said guardedly, remembering Longfield.

Iris resumed her seat. 'I prefer the comfort of my indifference to the pains of conformity.'

'I suppose being quite blatant about your relationship must at least save you a lot of unnecessary worry.'

'Blatant? That's severe, isn't it, darling? Do you talk of a man and woman being "blatant" about their marriage? I assure you, with Nina and myself it's exactly the same thing.'

'That's a view you once put to me before,' I remarked.

'Did I?' asked Iris absently. She didn't want to remember. The fossil must be left unearthed.

'I didn't mean to sound severe,' I apologized. 'On the contrary, I'm glad you've found happiness. There's precious little of it about.'

'You speak feelingly, Ann. I heard you'd got married and divorced, of course. I hope you've managed to stitch the tatters together, to make yourself something to keep out the cold.'

'In many ways, I've been extremely fortunate.' I had no intention of telling her about Kit, and anyway was anxious to reach our subject. 'About this cyclova, Iris. What's the next move?'

'I've been busying myself *wildly* on your behalf, darling. Don't you ever say that Parliament's a clogged-up old machine, which never gets anything done. Parliament's a play, really – a peculiar one, with all the real action going on backstage.' Her long forefinger traced a pattern on the arm of her chair. 'The very night you came to see me, last Thursday, I had a word with someone at the House. Not someone in the Ministry of Health, but high up. You'll forgive me for not naming him? It was informal and confidential, much the best way of tackling these things.'

'Of course, I don't mind,' I assured her readily. 'I'm simply and truly grateful. I still haven't read in the papers a single word of criticism, or even of reservation, about cyclova. Quite apart from its contraceptive effect, it seems to have induced a nationwide state of euphoria.'

'I think the population feels secure enough with our existing safeguards for new drugs,' she asserted. 'And we're tightening up the regulations, you know. Under the new Medicines Bill the Dunlop Committee will disappear. The Ministry itself will decide in its wisdom whether or not to issue licences for new products.'

'Of course, I'm aware of all that Parliament has done, and is doing. But I've always had the fear that some suspicious ones were bound to slip through. One *has* slipped through, in fact.'

'Ann, darling, I know that's exactly what you believe, and most sincerely so.' At her tone, I felt a sickening sensation. 'You've put yourself to enormous personal trouble over this cyclova business. Even to tackling me. It's all an effort, and you must be an incredibly busy woman. But I don't know if I can be quite as much help to you, darling, as I should like.'

'Why not?' I asked sharply.

She sat wondering how to put it. 'Parliament is a far more complicated affair than even the most knowledgeable outsiders can imagine. The same goes for hospitals, for medicine itself. Surely you appreciate that? What may seem simple to the un-initiated can in reality be terribly complicated.'

'The reason I'm sitting here is simple enough.' I was becoming annoyed. 'Cyclova is a self-obvious matter of public importance.'

'Yes, darling, I know that's how you see it. That's how a lot of people would see it. But I have to handle the technical side. Like the surgeon who has to perform the operation. And in Parliament it's fatal to start hares running. There's no knowing which burrows they might end up in.'

'But this *isn't* some wild complaint,' I protested. 'I'll bring you my report, if you like, and you can see my results with your own eyes. I'll bring you the blood-slides, if that's what you need to convince you.'

233

'It's sweet of you, darling, but in fact I've read your report.'

'How?' I demanded. 'There's only one copy, and that's in my flat.'

'I got it from General Drugs.'

'But why General Drugs, for God's sake? You only needed to ask.'

'Naturally, I had to have a word with General Drugs. I had to hear their side of the story.'

'Did you? I suppose if I'd complained there was a homicidal maniac at large, you'd have taken him to one side and asked politely if he really meant to wield his axe on anybody?'

'As I told you, darling, I know precisely how you feel about this,' Iris responded calmly. She must have experienced countless wrathful petitioners, over everything from microbiological warfare to the siting of electricity pylons.

'Who did you speak to at General Drugs?' I asked angrily, 'Lloyd, I suppose?'

'I honestly forget the name.'

'And you agreed with him that I'd made a mistake interpreting the blood-smears?'

'I certainly did not. But really, darling, does the question of your making an error or not come into it, for practical purposes? Cyclova's been tested in the States and elsewhere with enormous care, on a comparatively huge selection of women. And let's be brutal, and face exactly what you have to stand against it. One solitary suspect case.'

'Isn't that a straw in the wind?'

'A straw in a whirlwind.' She was becoming impatient. 'I know how you see that single case, darling. It's stuck in your mind like the Rock of Gibraltar. But it's only one case. You can't expect me to move the British Government with it.'

'Oh, God,' I said. I suddenly felt tired. Too tired to fight, too tired even to get angry.

'Don't take it to heart, Ann.' Iris sounded genuinely kind. 'Can't you see it from my point of view? You were always so reasonable.'

'But there's a doubt,' I insisted. 'Isn't that enough to make General Drugs think again? To forgo a little of their profits, to

234

investigate it, to clear it up? You told me last time how acquisitive the drug companies were. Surely you've the courage of your convictions.'

'I think we learn as we grow older to temper both our passions and our convictions.'

'You mean, you've just become cynical,' I accused her.

'No, I've just had to become more sophisticated, politically speaking. Though I can understand your saying that. The two aren't readily distinguishable. Perhaps they're the same thing. A certain hard-headedness is necessary for the efficient running of anything, particularly when the raw material is human beings. Equal rights for women, equal education for women, equal pay for women – they're all issues close to my heart. But I can't do more than make pretty speeches about them. The Government wouldn't thank me for trying to wreck our incomes policy. The stupid thing is, darling, that I could sally into battle for you tomorrow, if I were in opposition. But you must see that a certain amount of discipline is necessary in the party. Government of the country would be impossible otherwise.'

I said sarcastically, 'You would hardly have brought the Government tumbling down by asking one Parliamentary question.'

'A question isn't something you embark upon lightly, you know. Not even a trivial one. Supposing that I made a nuisance of myself over cyclova? Supposing it turned out to be a red herring? Ministers have long memories. Ministry officials have inexhaustible ones. It would lessen my chances of making a bigger nuisance of myself about other things of more obvious importance. It would lessen my chances of getting a Government job.'

'*That's* cynical! You can't get away from that.'

'I still don't think so, not entirely.' She clasped her big hands together. The joints gave a crack which startled me. 'We all think about number one a bit, whatever our occupation. Unless we're saints, and they're by definition abnormal. Have you ever heard of a surgeon who never looked at his bank statements? And this career of mine hasn't the comfortable security

235

of medicine, you know, darling. In many ways it's like the stage. Up or out. I've my future to think of.' She nodded towards the closed door. 'I've Nina's future to think of. She hasn't a penny, of course.'

'And you put her before your duty?'

'What is my duty? My duty is to the Government. The Government has had ample opportunity to object to the new pill, and it has not seen fit to,' she ended decisively.

'But the Government hadn't all the facts,' I persisted. 'The facts in my own report.'

'You're wrong there, darling. The person I mentioned actually read your report. It was a tremendous concession on his part. Maybe you can't realize that. And he decided that there was no need for official action. So that's that.'

There was a silence. I stood up. 'Thank you, Iris, for taking such trouble.'

She stood up too, quickly, anxious to be rid of me. 'I can appreciate you're disappointed, darling. I'm satisfied I've done what I can. I hope I've satisfied you that I couldn't have done more.'

We were standing close together in the middle of the room. She was taller than me, and I looked up at her. 'I'd hoped you might have done more, Iris. After all, when we were residents together at Princess Victoria's there was a real affection between us.'

As soon as the words had gone I knew it was stupid of me to say them. She gave an artful smile. 'Times change.'

The door opened. The girl, bored with kicking her heels outside, or more likely eavesdropping, stuck her head inside the room. Iris nodded in her direction, and added, 'Or are you putting yourself in competition with Nina?'

That was an awful thing to hear. But I had asked for it. I could only shake my head, unable to say anything, even some reflex anger failing me. It was humiliating, much more horribly so than Kit calling me a tart. I made for the door, saying to Nina, 'I hope you have an enjoyable holiday abroad.'

'Oh, thanks. It'll be lovely, getting away from dirty old London.'

'I'm sure you're right. Though doubtless this flat is somewhat less so than wherever you happened to live last.'

Iris permitted me this. She smiled at the front door as sweetly as ever, 'Good-bye, Ann. It was delightful seeing you again. I'm only sorry you found it all so frustrating.'

I made no reply, but walked out.

'Oh, Ann —'

I turned.

'Ann, darling, if you ever wanted a seat in the public gallery to hear a debate, you'd be sure to let me know, wouldn't you?'

34

THERE WAS A telephone box on the pavement outside the Gothic gate of Princess Victoria's. I strode straight into it from my taxi, dialled the number of our landlady, and asked her to fetch Kit. She sounded surly, but obliged me.

'Hello, my darling,' his voice greeted me cheerfully. 'How did it go with that woman?'

'Kit, I want you to take me out to lunch.'

'Oh.' He paused. 'Was it bad?'

'I'll tell you about it later.'

'Where would you like to go?'

'The *Principe e Savoia*.'

This was an Italian restaurant in Soho, where the food was good and the wine cheap, which fitted into our habit of life by opening on Sunday evenings. We had enjoyed some of our happiest times there, and it would give me reassurance.

'Are you sure you're all right, Ann? You sound dreadful.'

'I can't even think at the moment. I'm in pieces. I must see you, darling, to glue me together again somehow.'

'I'll be there sharp at one,' he promised. 'Try not to brood too much, darling, won't you?'

I went out of the telephone box and through the gate, which led to a strip of tarmac wriggling among the jumble of hospital buildings and lined in white paint for the consultants' cars. Briefcase in hand, in the action of entering his Mercedes, was Charles Crawless.

'Hello, there, Ann!' he greeted me genially. 'I'm only just back from the Wild West.' As I stood staring at him, he noticed my expression. 'What's the matter?' he asked seriously.

238

'I've been crying.'

'Oh, dear.' He regarded me with the mixture of concern, embarrassment, and fright with which men face weeping women. 'Is there anything I can do?'

I shook my head. I seldom broke down and cried. After Longfield, I had reason enough. Now I wasn't weeping because of Iris, nor even because I saw it so hopeless to continue fighting, to take on not only General Drugs but the British Government. I wept from a sense of frustration, from persistently being let down, from repeatedly being told that I was wrong – a silly little woman, in fact.

'Yes, there is one thing you can do, Charles. Never speak to me, never come near to me, ever again.'

He jumped as I said this, but asked blandly enough, 'That's a very strange thing to hear from you, Ann. Have I offended you in some way? I'm sure it wasn't intentional.'

'Everyone's offending me,' I told him bitterly. 'Nobody will lift a finger to help me, because nobody will believe me.'

'Not this old cyclova?' He looked relieved, I suspected through finding such a familiar cause for my distress. 'I should have thought an eminently sensible woman like you, Ann, would have stabled that hobby-horse long ago.'

'*You* never believed me,' I accused him.

'That's true enough,' he admitted mildly. 'Though, of course, I gave you my opinion that evening exactly as I give my opinion on some other physician's diagnosis. When I disagree – and quite often I do – well, there it is, and the patient benefits by a little extra thought from both of us. There's never anything personal in it. There couldn't be. So don't be too hard on me please.'

I checked myself a second from going further. It would inevitably bring Henry into the argument, and I didn't want that. But I burst out, 'You heard I didn't get that job at Longfield?'

'Ma Saintsbury told me this morning. That was bad luck.'

'Luck? There wasn't much luck about it. It was what you wanted, wasn't it?'

'I'm afraid I don't follow you,' he replied innocently.

'You follow me bloody well. You took care to see that one of the selection committee chucked me out.'

There were by now a couple of ambulance men and the gate-porter staring at us with curiosity. Charles looked uncomfortable, and suggested, 'Hadn't we better sit in my car?'

'No. I won't sit anywhere near you. I don't even want to talk to you.'

'Get in the car,' he said, with surprising sternness. 'You've just made a somewhat damaging accusation. I'm entitled to ask your attention for my explanation, even if not your acceptance of it.'

He opened the car door, and I sat in the passenger seat, staring fixedly through the windscreen. He went round and entered the other side, tossing his briefcase in the back.

'I suppose it was Henry who spilt the beans?' he asked.

'That was a bloody thing to do behind my back,' I told him furiously.

He pressed a button, raising his side-window for privacy. The metal capsule was already unbearably hot.

'I was aware at the time, and very unhappily aware, that would be your reaction if you found out.'

'I did find out, which is too damn bad for you, isn't it?'

'Ann, may I ask you to look at my action calmly?'

'Calmly! My God, why does everyone keep asking me to take my calamities calmly? What do you all think I am? A machine, something without feelings? Just because I've made a career for myself, do you imagine I'm desiccated, hard – totally insensitive to pain, like the human brain itself? Of course I'm not. I'm like every other woman, water inside.'

'Of course, you've every right to be deeply upset and very angry,' Charles went on steadily. 'That is precisely why I hoped my role in the Longfield affair wouldn't come to your ears. A perfectly selfish attitude, but a perfectly human one. None of us cares to be confronted with the unpleasant sequelae of our actions. It's unbearable when they are embodied in an old friend.'

'That's cool. You mean, you didn't care to face the consequences of your little bit of treachery.'

'I am quite prepared to face any consequences. I acted as I thought correct. And however much you may rant and rage at me, Ann, I can assure you it will change my opinion not a jot.'

'But *why*, Charles?' I implored him. 'Why did you do it?'

'Listen quietly to me for a moment, will you? Please.' I clasped my fingers tight on my knees, still staring straight ahead. 'I met Sir Robert Boatwright in connexion with General Drugs, of course. I'm not even troubling to assume that Henry kept secret my appointment there. In any case, one of these fine days I shall be bringing it to an end, as my practice gets busier. I had hardly more than a social acquaintance with Sir Robert. His side of affairs is conducting the firm's finance, as doubtless you know, too.'

I did not, but I made no change of expression.

'Sir Robert asked to see me one day, and it was convenient to meet in my consulting-rooms. He explained that he was on the selection committee at Longfield —'

'Which you knew.'

'Perhaps I did,' Charles admitted. 'I certainly knew he was involved in Longfield affairs. Successful financiers so often interest themselves in academic matters – generally with much benefit all round.'

'It wasn't much benefit to me.'

Charles slowly stroked his moustache. 'Quite so. But please hear me out. General Drugs were naturally glad to have someone who was so closely associated with them also closely associated with a university like Longfield, with all its scientific emphasis. They may even have eased his way there – I don't know, I should imagine such assistance would have been unnecessary. But all was above board. Why, quite often industrial firms who donate heavily to research institutions claim, and are seldom denied, at least a small say in how their money is spent. Though I know that to you, Ann, it would appear otherwise – that Sir Robert Boatwright was specifically planted on that committee for the purpose of excluding you from the job.'

'And that is exactly how it *does* appear to me.'

'But Ann, you're out of this world! You certainly don't understand Bob Boatwright. He takes his duties most seriously, on every committee he attends. He's an independent cuss. He assuredly wouldn't let himself be unduly influenced by George Lloyd, by Professor Dawes, by Lord Wrotham, or for that matter by me. He wanted to make up his own mind about you. For that reason he asked my confidential opinion of you as a candidate. Naturally, I should have liked to have praised you to the skies. That would have been my easy way out. But I had a duty to speak my mind.' He set his jaw. 'Which is precisely what I did. To be perfectly candid, Ann, I didn't think you were up to the job. Not at this stage in your career.'

'Why didn't you tell *me* that he'd asked you?' I demanded. 'Why didn't you give *me* that opinion yourself, face to face?'

'I'm afraid, Ann, that if we all followed such a practice, the selection of candidates for any job whatever would come to a halt. It was an awfully hard thing for me to say. But in our profession one has to say a lot of hard and tragic things. Of course, I know how disappointed you are – Ma Saintsbury told me as much. Perhaps you're disproportionately cast down, being such a perfectionist, so anxious for success with everything you turn your hand to. But you wouldn't have been happy at Longfield. It was a tremendous job they were offering, very taxing even for a man. Building up a new department! I know from experience that means an extended running fight with everybody already installed in the place. With no holds barred. It would have worn you out, completely worn you out. You're much better off staying in Princess Victoria's, for a year or two more at any rate. And then, perhaps, when you've wider experience —'

'You smooth lying bastard!'

Charles shrugged his shoulders. 'I'm only telling you the truth.'

'I don't believe a word of it.'

He gave a little cough. 'Quite frankly, Ann, it is a matter of supreme indifference to me whether you do or not.'

I got out of the car, and shut the door. I strode away, hearing him start up the engine and drive off with great rapidity.

I reached the restaurant to meet Kit with my mind made up. I was fed up with Charles, Lloyd and General Drugs. I would throw up the cyclova business for good. If anything went wrong, the manufacturers could face the music. If nothing went wrong, if I had in fact made that mistake with my blood-slides – then no one should be more delighted than I. I was going to forget the drug had ever existed. It was backsliding, but it was a solution to my troubles so simple, and a relief so profound, that I was even gay when I sat down with Kit, deliberately not mentioning Charles. He seemed relieved. I must have been trying to live with, the past few turbulent months.

'I went back to the fight by seeing Iris, and did even worse,' I told him across the table. 'The net result is simply to make myself bloody miserable. Let's forget about the past and make plans for the future,' I went on eagerly. 'Plans for you and I. I've been so obsessed with cyclova I'd almost forgotten a future existed. Let's get back our sense of proportion. I've still got a month's leave to come. Where shall we go? How about Switzerland?'

'Cherry-jam, cuckoo-clocks, awful cigars, and mountains forever looking over your shoulder.'

'Oh, you're fastidious even about your geography,' I laughed at him. 'I've always wanted to go to Switzerland. Even looking at the coloured photographs makes me feel cleaner. And what about Christmas? What shall we do at Christmas?'

'We'll go to a big seaside hotel with open coal fires and play bridge all day.'

'That would be wonderfully comforting. Do you suppose they'd find out we weren't married? Perhaps we might be, by then?'

'I'm sure Myra's caving in,' he said confidently. 'She's got nothing to gain, nothing except indulging her obstinacy, and even she gets bored with that.'

'Can't we move to a house, Kit?' I implored him. 'Do say we can move to a house. A house with a garden and a dog.'

'Your eyes are shining.'

'Couldn't we at least start looking for one?'

'Why not, my darling?' agreed Kit expansively. 'You choose the house, I'll choose the dog.'

I laughed again. Making plans however shaky, concentrating

my thoughts on personal matters however overworked with argument, was wonderful therapy for my mind. We were interrupted by a voice declaring, 'Ann, this really does look a super little eating place.'

I looked up in annoyance, to find Liz standing over our table. I remembered recommending the restaurant to her, and cursed myself. She had broken my mood.

'Hello, Liz. This is Kit,' I introduced him.

'Do you mind if I join you?' I was even more annoyed to find she hardly noticed him. I suppose I had expected some outburst of appreciative rapture. She was preoccupied with herself, as usual. I didn't want her company, but she sat down, remarking, 'I've had a simply *terrible* morning in Trevor's office. You can't imagine the things that Derek is getting up to.'

The waiter hurried up to lay her place, and she ordered a meal, extremely fussily, asking our advice on every item. Then she arranged her forearms comfortably on the table and started again about Derek. I suddenly heard her say, 'Ann, you're not listening.'

'Yes, I am.' My mind had strayed back to Charles Crawless, to Iris, and to cyclova. 'It must be awfully harrowing for you.'

'I was only asking you about dividing the cars.' She looked offended. 'Should I take the Jag and make Derek take the Mini? But of course, the Mini's so useful for shopping and things.' She broke off, looking doubtful as she was served a plate of spaghetti. 'Do I have to eat this stuff by twirling it round in a spoon?'

'Eating spaghetti and making love are essentially matters of personal style,' Kit told her gravely.

'I suppose that's why the Italians are so fond of it,' observed Liz glumly. 'How far did you get with Iris, Ann?'

'Nowhere.'

Liz raised her eyebrows. 'I thought she was such an eager crusader?'

'I think there comes a time when even the eagerest crusader feels inclined to hang up his sword and think more about home comforts.'

'Gone soft, has she? I'm sorry she let you down. But I'm not surprised. She always was so unreliable, and I never liked her. Between you and me, I think she went in for other girls.' Liz performed complicated and largely unsuccessful manipulations with her food. 'I can't understand why you don't get the law on them, Ann. On these cyclova people.'

'I've lost all interest in these cyclova people,' I told her briefly.

'You should have invoked the law in the first place,' she persisted. 'It would have saved you no end of trouble.'

'I don't feel inclined to march into General Drugs' office at the head of a squad of police, if that's what you mean.'

'I mean the civil law. Surely you must have a case?'

'Ann's really very tired of the whole messy business,' said Kit.

Liz took no notice. 'Why don't you go and ask Trevor? He'd tell you if you had a case soon enough. He's terribly good at his job, you know. Makes absolute thousands.'

'I'm sure Trevor doesn't want to be bothered with me.' And I was far from anxious to meet Trevor.

'But he'd *love* to see you again. He's always asking after you. I'll ring him up, and make an appointment.'

The struggle had been too long and too bitter to prevent my hesitating, wondering if it were worth searching the armoury for one last overlooked weapon. Then I decided to abide by my surrender. But before I could say anything, Liz pushed her plate aside and got up abruptly, complaining, 'This stuff's like trying to eat animated knitting. I'll ring Trevor now. He eats in his office, and I'll catch him before his afternoon appointments.'

I said something to dissuade her, but she was already off to the telephone, demanding the waiter to bring her next course. In such an improbable way began the last round of my fight with General Drugs.

35

IT HAD ALL happened during my first month as a resident at Princess Victoria's, eight years before. I hadn't found my feet in the place. I was still dead scared of McRobb. Iris Quiply in the room next door was still sizing me up, and doubtless calculating her chances. Then I had my affair with Trevor, which might have been brief – that was sadly inescapable – but at least it was dramatic.

I had more or less unthinkingly agreed that summer at Monkhood Hall, amid the excitement of our jobs and the fuss of my row with Liz, to meet Trevor again in London. Only my second or third day working in the hospital he telephoned and invited me out to dinner. I enjoyed the evening, and it was a thrilling experience for me then to visit even a modest London restaurant. Trevor himself, away from his family, struck me as less guarded and more amusing and considerate, if somewhat neurotic. In the taxi returning to the hospital I braced myself for an onslaught like that on the bridge, but instead he kissed me goodnight like a bird picking at a split coconut.

The next morning a box arrived from Harrods. It contained a dress, a wonderful dress, lime-green silk with a flared skirt, better than any I could possibly have possessed in my life. A note inside said simply, 'From Trevor'. I held the garment against myself, twirling delightedly in my room in front of the cracked mirror. Well, I reflected, it's pleasant to know that he thinks so much of me.

I naturally wore it when he took me to a theatre the following week, and he kept telling me enthusiastically how lovely I looked.

'You're spoiling me,' I chided him humorously. 'It must have been outrageously expensive.'

'Nothing could be expensive, compared with my pleasure in seeing you wearing it.'

The next day he sent me another dress, white and gold this time. This was a shade embarrassing, but I consoled myself that his generosity was only to get me in bed with him. And that would be all right with me, I decided. Trevor was delicate, quite tender, and clean. I had experienced no other since Cliff, and was ready to enjoy anyone. My view was strengthened the following day by a further offering of stockings, bra, suspender-belt, and pants. The undies were black, in nylon lace, the sort of thing I supposed tarts wore, and extremely impractical. The next evening that Trevor took me out I had them under the new dress, though they were a size too small and uncomfortable. It seemed only polite, if he stripped me down to them, to show I appreciated his open-handedness.

But afterwards he took me back to Princess Victoria's in a taxi, holding my hand. His mood on the bridge seemed to have evaporated, leaving no residue. To give him some encouragement, I said, 'I've got the lot on, you know. Tonight you've dressed me right down to bedrock.'

Only then did he seem moved, saying eagerly, 'I can get you plenty more, if you like, Ann. Any amount of underwear. Did you like black? I was so hoping you'd put them on tonight.' He added coyly, 'Even the suspenders?'

I pulled up my skirt, displaying them. He delicately reached out his fingers, and twanged one against the skin of my thigh several times. That seemed to satisfy him for the night.

My failure to stir him was puzzling. His behaviour was beyond my personal or professional experience. I should have liked to discuss it with Liz, but that seemed hardly the thing. But the next time Trevor took me out, to a smart hotel off Grosvenor Square, I sensed that something was up. He was even more nervous than usual, sitting in the bar, fiddling with the mat under his drink, picking at the crisps and nuts in their glass

247

dishes, clasping and unclasping his hands, speaking vaguely and disjointedly.

'What's the matter with you?' I complained, less sweetly than I might. 'You're like a stretched elastic band. If you're not careful, you'll fly to bits.'

'I'm sorry.'

He paused. I was wearing the first dress, and to bring his mind to something definite, I remarked, 'You haven't told me how I look.'

'Even lovelier than ever tonight.'

'I'm afraid I had to abandon the underthings,' I confessed. 'They caught me too much.'

He seemed crestfallen at this.

'It doesn't make any obvious difference,' I consoled him.

'No, but I find it rather nice looking at a girl I've dressed from top to toe. Even to the things you can't see.'

'That's a bit involved, isn't it, Trevor?'

'I *am* involved. Haven't you noticed?'

'No, I think you're just shy,' I reassured him. 'You told me that day at Monkhood House you had never had much luck with girls.'

'I'm not obsessed with sex, if that's what you mean.'

'Wouldn't you like to sleep with me?' His indecision was getting on my nerves.

'I should, Ann, very much,' he said soberly.

'Well!' I exclaimed. 'You needn't sound as though you were making an appointment with your dentist.'

'I'm sorry,' he apologized. 'But I take these matters seriously.'

'You mean, I don't?'

He looked flustered, and said quickly, 'Of course not. That would be a terrible thing to tell a girl. I meant that I wasn't the easygoing sort of man, the type who gets along with women apparently without giving it much thought. You're the first woman I've ever felt really comfortable with, to tell the truth.'

'I'm complimented, Trevor.'

'Except for my mother,' he added miserably, spoiling the effect.

He had a flat near by in Mount Street, and without referring

248

to the matter again he took my arm after our dinner and walked me there. He had been fiddling with the cutlery all the meal, which had been most irritating. As I expected, the flat was large and expensively furnished. There were so many flowers about the place I wondered if he had been planning my arrival. Or perhaps he filled the vases each time he took me out, in the hope that he could wind up his courage during the evening to invite me.

Trevor limped about the flat, fussing with cigarettes and drinks. It was heartening to find myself with a man of such timidity. I had nothing of the sexual experience of Liz, who had let three or four of the boys in the medical school amuse themselves with her. But my natural self-confidence, my awareness that I never made a failure of anything I set myself to, put me calmly in charge of the situation. As I watched him moving nervously about, it struck me this might possibly be the first time for Trevor. It hadn't crossed my mind before. I had better make a success of it, or God knows what neuroses and complexes I should leave him with.

He came to rest beside me on the sofa. I immediately grasped him and kissed him, and said, 'Haven't we somewhere more comfortable to go?'

'The place where I sleep is through there.'

We went to the bedroom, and I started to strip. He took off his jacket and tie. He seemed breathless before he had even started. I put my bare arms round him. 'Darling, why are you so nervous?' I asked gently.

'I just want to do everything properly.'

'Now you sound as if you're drawing up your will.'

He didn't seem to hear this. 'I suppose there's no risk? Babies, and things?'

'Well, I work in exactly the right place if there is, don't I?' I helped him pull off his shirt. He might have been a patient. 'There won't be a risk if you take precautions.'

'Yes, I've got some . . . precautions.' From a bedside table he produced a packet of three condoms. He looked at me inquiringly. 'Do you think I ought to wear two?'

'That might be a little overcautious.'

249

He finally got off his clothes. There was his osteomyelitis scar, burning redder than ever. Perhaps it, too, I thought, was inflamed with passion. The poor man was awfully skinny. And the organ on which the continuance of our evening's enjoyment depended was woefully uninterested.

I was hurt that anticipation had not flattered me better. I stroked him, but the normal erectile reflex remained unfired. Trevor lay back submissively on his elbows, not trying to fondle me at all, looking down on the operation with an expression of pained interest. Then suddenly he said savagely, 'It's no use.'

'We've only just started,' I said encouragingly. 'Just relax, let me try harder.'

A cold prawn.

'It's never any use!' He tore himself away and stood with his skinny back to me, his head in his hands. 'You're laughing at me,' he said accusingly.

'No, I'm not.' I sounded sharp. 'I'd never do a thing like that.'

'Yes, you are. You're laughing at me.' He abruptly dropped his hands and turned round.

'You see?'

'I'm sorry, Ann,' he muttered. 'I thought you might laugh at me, that's all.'

'Quite the opposite. I'm very sympathetic.'

'I'm sorry about this. I'm sorry about the whole stupid idea of getting you up here. I've only upset myself. I must have upset you much more.'

'Honestly, Trevor, you mustn't add to your state by worrying about me.' I really felt filled with pity for him.

'Aren't you supposed to feel unsatisfied, or something?' he asked distractedly.

'It doesn't worry me.'

'You're awfully kind, Ann.'

He stood there, penis dangling in the most infuriating of all immobility. 'Don't you ever get an erection at all?' I asked.

'Yes.' His voice sounded cracked. 'It's all right, usually. On my own, you know. But not when I'm with a girl. I've tried, God knows. I've had some horrible times trying. I've even gone picking up girls, girls you pay. I'm not a queer, you see, nothing like that,' he added defiantly.

'I'm sure you're not.'

'I'm just impotent.'

'But you're *not*. You just said as much. Complete impotence is very rare.'

'But nothing ever happens with a girl,' he said angrily. 'What to God's the matter with me, then?'

'I expect it's bound up with an anxiety neurosis.'

He sat on the bed. Lying there, both of us without a stitch, I was giving a consultation.

'I *do* get anxious about things,' he admitted. 'About everything.'

'So there you are. Perhaps you were too anxious the first time you tried to make a girl.'

He nodded. 'I was very anxious.'

'You found you couldn't manage it, so the next time you were twice as worried. It all builds up.'

'But what can I do about it?' he asked desperately.

'Nothing succeeds like success.'

'But if I couldn't manage it with you, Ann, I know I couldn't manage it with anyone.'

'Shall we have another try?' I suggested half-heartedly.

He shook his head. 'No, no, the farce is over. You really do excite me, Ann, even though I'm not able to show it very satisfactorily.' He stared into my eyes. 'You're the first I've tried it with for a long time. I'd grown far too scared about making a fool of myself. But you see,' he ended simply, 'as you were a doctor, I thought it would be all right.'

I thought that another touching example of the public's blind faith in the medical profession.

'I'll tell you the real villain.' He pointed to his misshapen leg. '*That.*'

This was too much for my scientific mind, even when lying naked on his bed. 'That's not right at all, Trevor,' I protested. 'They're two completely unrelated things.'

'No, they're not,' he contradicted me. 'They're all of one piece. If it weren't for my leg, I'd be a normal man.'

'But you are a normal man.'

'How can you say that after tonight's fiasco?' he demanded savagely.

'Physically you're normal,' I told him patiently. 'You're determined to make a minor disability into a major one, that's all. Your limp's not bad. After a few minutes' acquaintance you hardly notice it.'

'I'm *not* normal. If I were normal, I'd be able to have all the girls I wanted. But I'm a cripple, an impotent cripple. It's the fault of this leg. You leg, you leg, you bloody leg!' He suddenly started beating the scar fiercely with his fist. 'God! I wish somebody would cut it off. Can't you get somebody to cut it off?'

'Trevor —!' I grabbed his hand. 'Listen, Trevor, forget everything that happened tonight. But remember this. Never persuade any surgeon to cut your leg off, even if you could find one to think of it. Never! You've transferred all your disappointments and frustrations to that scar, haven't you? It isn't so uncommon, though the culprit's usually less tangible – lack of education, lack of a chance in life, sometimes parents, sometimes a wife, sometimes a whole nation. If you lost your leg, you'd only find something else to blame. I can assure you of that. Something in your body, or what would be worse, in your mind.'

He made no reply, but must have known well enough in his heart that I was right. As he reached for his shirt he asked, 'Well then? What must I do? Do you imagine that I should consult a psychiatrist?'

'That's an idea. He might help you to overcome your anxiety.'

'I'm not particularly keen on it. I'd hate disclosing my failing to a stranger, to anyone at all.' He added nervously, 'You won't say a word to Liz?'

'Of course I wouldn't.'

'Liz looks down on me already. What would she think if she knew the whole story?'

'You know, people are much more sympathetic than you imagine, Trevor. Or perhaps more than you care to imagine.'

He put his arms in his shirt. 'I suppose sex isn't everything,' he said resignedly. 'I've still got my work, and thank God I'm interested in it. It's a good firm I'm with – plenty of variety and satisfied clients. Do you know, Ann, they're making me a full partner at the end of the year?'

For the first time since I had entered the flat he looked cheerful.

My taxi stopped. The address Liz had given me in the Italian restaurant was in South Audley Street, and I saw that the Trevor who now made absolute thousands practised from one of the former Mayfair houses of country gentlemen, long ago converted into offices. It was less than an hour after Liz's telephone call, and I had gone on the errand alone, with neither hope nor enthusiasm. I rang the bell, and a demure girl showed me into a downstairs waiting-room, furnished in the chilling Regency style favoured by Harley Street consultants.

'Mr Monkhood won't be long, Dr Sheriff,' she apologized. 'While he was lunching an unexpected client appeared.'

For the sake of conversation, I said, 'An important one, I hope.'

'All Mr Monkhood's clients are important, madam,' she said primly, shutting the door.

36

'DR ANN! BUT how splendid. It's wonderful to see you. And I must congratulate you on such a brilliantly successful career. Liz has, of course, been giving me an account of it *in extentio*.'

Upstairs in the lofty-ceilinged Mayfair house was Trevor's office, a large room with a moss-green fitted carpet, its walls covered with teak shelves filled with books in leather bindings which appeared to be polished daily. There was a silver bowl with red roses on his tidy leather-covered desk, and three crystal vases of blooms spaced round the room. Perhaps he had simply been fond of flowers, after all.

'It was so kind of you to fix up Liz with that job.' Trevor had come to the door of his room, and led me to an upright chair by the desk. I was looking for his limp, but it was much better, hardly noticeable at all. 'A job was exactly what Liz wanted to take her mind off her worries. Though possibly that's not quite the way to look at an appointment carrying responsibility for the health and happiness of our fellow humans.'

'It's not really a very demanding post, I'm afraid.'

Trevor sat down, smiling at me across the desk, his fingers playing with an ivory paper-knife. He looked pinker and healthier, his fair hair was thinning, two furrows now joined the sides of his nose and mouth, and he gave in general the appearance of a well-scrubbed elf. He was so much more at ease than I remembered. Maybe he had been to a psychiatrist in the end.

'You've only just left Liz, haven't you?' he asked. I nodded. 'Naturally, she likes practising medicine of some sort, because it makes her feel again she's doing some good in the world.'

'That always was one of your sister's little failings.'

He laughed, and I noticed the same cracked note in it.

'I was sorry to hear about her domestic troubles,' I told him. 'I've been through the divorce court myself since we last met, you know.'

'So Liz said.' He offered me a silver cigarette-box. 'I hope it wasn't too harrowing an experience?'

'I should have much preferred achieving the result through a surgical operation. Without anaesthesia.'

'These things can never be pleasant. I see so many matrimonial squabbles, I'm relieved that I'm not married myself. But whether my dear sister's petition will ever reach a court, I shouldn't like to risk an opinion.'

'You mean, she's not in earnest?' I had suspected this all along.

'You know Liz, Ann. All fuss and no action. Champagne with no body. Though admittedly, Derek's treated her pretty badly. I wouldn't have expected it, really. He always seemed rather a dull fellow. Doubtless, like a lot of dull middle-aged fellows he embarked on his final fling – without realizing he was flinging something of a boomerang. Liz will make him pay for it once he goes back to her, which I have not the slightest doubt that he shortly will.'

'Perhaps he misses the Jaguar?' I suggested.

Trevor laughed again, and hitching up the trousers of his smart grey suit sat back and asked, 'What can I do for you?'

A new confidence flourished in him, I noticed. I much hoped that it extended to the distal end of his penis.

'I feel rather stupid being here at all, Trevor. I only came because Liz insisted.'

'I'm glad she did,' he said politely.

'Of course, I'm after legal advice.'

'Haven't you a solicitor of your own? I only ask because we can't tread on toes in my profession, any more than in yours.'

'A friend put me on to her own solicitors for my divorce. I've never been back to them.'

255

'I should think that's fair enough. What's the problem? Liz has been telling me on and off that you're having some trouble with a drug company.'

'You've heard about this new contraceptive, cyclova? It's in all the newspapers.' He nodded. 'Well, it's unsafe.'

'That sounds somewhat alarming. You mean, it doesn't work?'

'It works all right. But it's liable to give rise to a blood disorder. Which could be serious and very possibly fatal.'

He raised his fair eyebrows. 'And who found this out?'

'I did.'

'I see.'

'I ran a trial of cyclova at Princess Victoria's, starting last November. The number of volunteers was rather restricted because I didn't have much of the drug. But my results were quite conclusive – to my mind at any rate.'

'But surely, Ann, you brought your opinion to the eyes of the drug company concerned?'

'Yes. They didn't take any notice.'

'That sounds extraordinarily reckless of them.'

'It wasn't recklessness, only disbelief. They thought I'd made a mistake.'

He jotted a note. 'They told you as much?'

I nodded. 'Any recklessness lay in their not checking my results properly, to be absolutely certain that I *had* made a mistake.'

'And had you?'

'No.'

'Well, that's a good start,' he said.

I sat up in the chair, crossing my legs.

'Before we go into details, what exactly are you aiming to do with these drug people?'

'Stop them selling the drug,' I said simply.

He tapped his lips with his gold pencil. 'I should have thought that a case for political rather than legal action.'

'I've tried political action, and got nowhere.'

'As is so often the case.'

He faced me squarely. 'Do you feel very strongly about this?'

256

'Extremely. No, that's wrong. I did feel strongly about it, terribly strongly. I could see the disaster ahead if they marketed cyclova. At that early stage I didn't appreciate the strength of my opposition – anyway the ruthlessness. And my own feelings were involved. I don't like being repeatedly told I'm in error when I'm absolutely certain that I'm not.'

'Don't we all feel that?'

'Few as strongly as me, I suspect. It's really a weakness, isn't it? Obstinacy, pig-headedness. Though it's one I share with a good many women in medicine. However hard we try to put our work and our emotions in watertight compartments, there's always some seepage. Men are more successful.' Trevor pursed his lips at this. I wondered if he himself might suffer from such a feminine admixture. 'This cyclova business has become so personal to me, it's tangled in my mind with all my other troubles, even with my trivial domestic worries. It's taken possession of me these last two or three months. And it's led to nothing. Nothing but disappointment and humiliation. It's been heartbreaking, really.'

'You must have been remarkably resolute,' he said admiringly.

'I wasn't. I was only stupid. Anyway, today I decided to have no more of cyclova. I came to see you to please Liz more than anything else, I think. If you feel nothing can be done, Trevor, please tell me straight out, and I'll go home and forget about it.'

'I think something *can* be done.' He frowned. 'But as to *what*, exactly, I'm afraid you've floored me, Ann.'

'Liz seemed to imagine you could stop the drug company acting against the public interest.'

'That's undoubtedly what needs to be done. But I'm afraid that under the law as constituted it's impossible. It just wouldn't wash at all. Of course, if anyone actually suffered an illness from the unwonted effects of this drug, that would be different. Then they, or their relatives if they were deceased, could start a thumping action for damages.'

'But *that* situation is precisely what I have been battling these past months to prevent.'

'Quite so.' He tapped his pencil several times on his desk. 'We

257

might get them on a public nuisance,' he hazarded. 'That could raise some interesting points in a judge's mind, public nuisances being mostly concerned with cesspools, pig-sties, lime-kilns, dangerous ditches, that sort of thing. No, I fear it would be stretching the law beyond the limits of its elasticity.' He pressed a bell on his desk. 'But we can't get anywhere at all without the facts before us, can we?'

'Trevor, I think we should abandon the idea,' I decided. 'If it's started something which is likely to fail, I'd rather not risk it. I don't think I could stand another rebuff.'

'I see that well enough, Ann. But when a patient comes to you, you at least take off his shirt and listen properly to his chest, don't you?'

The secretary who had shown me in appeared at the door.

'Miss Griggs, take down a statement of facts from Dr Sheriff, please.' Trevor sounded disconcertingly commanding. 'Let's start at the beginning, Ann. What was the name of this drug again?'

'Cyclova.' I wished that I'd never heard of it.

It was a familiar recitation. I said nothing about Charles Crawless and Longfield – I could prove no conspiracy and perhaps there never had been, it was so easy to build self-elaborating fantasies of persecution. But I told Trevor of Charles's trying to dissuade me from attacking General Drugs, and of my discovering his connexion with the company.

'I suppose this information was reliable?' Trevor asked.

'Extremely so. I heard it from Crawless's oldest friend. My ex-husband.'

'Not a common source of confidences,' Trevor murmured.

'But once my former husband makes up his mind to say or do anything, personal considerations never temper his decision. Otherwise, we should still be married, I fancy. Anyway, Crawless admitted his job with General Drugs this morning, and I'm sure it could be easily confirmed.'

'I agree, Dr Crawless and General Drugs might be an important point,' Trevor remarked, as the girl left to type out her shorthand. 'Though exactly how we can make use of the information, I'm still at a loss to say.' He sat in silence for a moment. 'It might just be worth getting counsel's opinion,' he decided. 'Would you agree to that?'

I turned this over in my mind. I was the patient, Trevor the g.p., counsel the specialist. I had been through the formula with my divorce. 'If you really think it a step worth taking.'

'I do, even in a negative way. Counsel will probably tell us that we've no hope, but it's worth a few guineas to hear that from the voice of authority, surely?' He smiled. 'I hope you can afford his fee? My own advice, of course, comes *gratis*.'

'Advice isn't the first thing you've given me, Trevor. I had some lovely presents from you.'

That was unfair of me. I had determined not to hint at the past, but a love unremembered is a love lost, even one so inconclusive as ours. I wondered if he would become flustered, or alternatively sentimental, but he nodded briskly and remarked, 'Yes, I gave you a dress once, didn't I? I expect I chose quite the wrong style.'

'It was delightful. I remember it distinctly.'

'We used to have some fun together in those days,' he observed. 'You and me and Liz.'

The neatness of this plea for amnesia filled me with confidence over his legal abilities.

'I must have been more in touch then,' he went on. 'I wouldn't even know where to go for a dress today. It's all boutiques, isn't it, in the King's Road? To tell the truth, I'm far too busy to find time for squiring ladies at all.'

We were interrupted by another girl bringing a tray of tea. The china was delicate and feminine-looking, and with some pains Trevor explained how he had chosen it. The office, he added proudly, was entirely to his own plan, he had recently discovered in himself a talent and fondness for interior decoration. I supposed it was a better outlet than buying girls black nylon underwear.

Though I was obstructing his afternoon's appointments, Trevor insisted I waited until his secretary returned with my brief statement. He read it through and announced, 'Yes, we'll have a go. Who shall we try? Romhead, I think. He's a very competent junior at the Chancery Bar who specializes in injunctions, that sort of thing. Miss Griggs,' he directed, 'ring Mr Wilfred Romhead's chambers and ask his clerk for a consultation some time tomorrow. That would be convenient for you, Ann? We'd better not let any grass grow, if this stuff's as dangerous as you say.'

The girl came back with an appointment fixed for eleven the next morning. As Trevor saw me to the door of his room, I said, 'I warn you – unless your Mr Romhead is sparkling with enthusiasm, I'm going to drop the case.'

'Members of the Chancery Bar do not sparkle with enthusiasm,' said Trevor.

I turned in the doorway. 'There were two dresses, you know. Both lovely.'

'I hope you found a suitable occasion to wear them,' he told me firmly. 'It was so delightful meeting you, Ann. I'm afraid tomorrow morning at Romhead's chambers we'll be too rushed to chat about anything but business.'

37

TREVOR WAS DETERMINED not to give me any chance for idle conversation. I had arranged to meet him the following morning at eleven outside Mr Wilfred Romhead's chambers in Lincoln's Inn, an area I remembered from the time of my divorce. Its many clocks were striking the hour as Trevor bustled up, wearing a bowler hat, umbrella and briefcase in his hands. He hurried me with hardly a word up the bare wooden staircase to the top floor, where a plain white-painted name over the door announced that Mr Romhead practised within. Before even seeing the barrister I regretted the expedition. When I had told Kit about it the previous afternoon he had simply said I was mad. That I kept the appointment at all was mainly because Trevor had taken such trouble, and it would have been discourteous not to.

In a small, untidy outer office sat a girl at an old-fashioned typewriter, who almost immediately took us through to Mr Romhead himself. His room had the self-conscious Dickensian air so favoured by the bar. His desk, the side-table, some of the chairs, the deep sills of the mullioned windows, even parts of the floor, were covered with heavy books marked by slips of paper, and piles of neatly-tied documents. I noticed at once that a few were coated quite thickly with dust, the burial of somebody's once lively hopes. There was an empty cup on the desk, three pipes, a sprinkling of tobacco ash, and a fragment or two of biscuit. It was a room which proclaimed smugly that its occupant must be absolutely top-class to get away with it.

Mr Romhead rose to greet us affably. I knew that a 'junior'

at the bar could be of any age, and I was not surprised to find him a little fat man in his sixties. He had half-moon glasses, and a ring of fluffy grey hair round his bald head. He wore the usual black jacket and striped trousers, with bands below his wing collar. His wig and gown lay across more documents in a leather armchair beside the gas-fire, and he apologized that such a hastily-called consultation had been squeezed into his timetable, and that he was obliged to leave for court in twenty minutes. Trevor handed him my typed statement, and I my report on cyclova, which I had brought in a large envelope.

'My client and I are both aware that you may not be able to offer us much encouragement,' Trevor started, as we took two chairs facing the desk.

'I suspect I'm only making a nuisance of myself,' I apologized.

Mr Romhead beamed at me. 'I'm always delighted to advise members of the medical profession. I always seem to get so much unpleasant advice from *them*.'

I smiled politely. The barrister who handled my divorce had said exactly the same.

We sat in silence as Mr Romhead read through my statement.

'Well, yes, Mr Monkhood,' he announced. 'And what exactly are you after? An injunction to stop them selling cyclova?'

Trevor nodded.

The barrister turned to me. I noticed that he had the habit of clasping his hands together under his chin and bouncing slightly on his chair while he thought. I suspected that the judges must have found it very irritating. 'Dr Sheriff, *why* are you proposing to start this action?'

'To put it quite simply, to prevent women being killed by taking the drug.'

'My client has a commendably acute sense of public duty,' said Trevor.

'Yes, indeed,' agreed Mr Romhead. 'But I'm afraid that won't get her very far in the courts.'

He sat, hands clasped, bouncing gently. Mainly to justify my wasting his time, I added, 'I had imagined, in my innocence,

262

that cyclova being a public danger, some judge might order General Drugs to stop marketing it.'

'But how do we know that it *is* a public danger?' he objected.

I nodded towards my report on his desk. 'I felt I'd spelt that out plainly enough.'

'I'm sure this is a most damning document,' he said amicably. 'But unfortunately it wouldn't cut any ice in this particular connexion. You want an injunction against General Drugs,' he reiterated. 'So the question is, how do we obtain one? Let's see, now. Have you suffered any wrong in the hands of the General Drug Company, Dr Sheriff?'

'I've suffered an injustice.'

'I'm afraid that's not quite the same thing.'

'If we could claim damages for our injustices,' said Trevor with a smile, 'we should all be rich.'

'You haven't been damaged at all by these people?' the barrister persisted. 'Have they, for instance, exploited your work in any way? Or stolen any of your ideas?'

'None whatever.' I looked at Trevor. 'Isn't this just prolonging the agony?'

'No, we won't give up quite so easily,' Mr Romhead declared. 'Had you any interest in the manufacture or the development of this drug?'

'None at all.'

'Then why did you ask the company for samples to test in the first place?'

'Out of curiosity, mainly. I learned of its existence quite by chance through a paper in an American journal. I thought it would be worth-while trying out.'

'I see. I know you're interested in this particular branch of medical science, Dr Sheriff, but had you any special reason for doing so?'

I thought for a second. 'Yes, I had. You must have read in the newspapers, Mr Romhead, that cyclova is unique among oral contraceptives because it's long-acting. The woman takes only one pill a month, not one a day.' He nodded. 'I had already done some rather inconclusive work myself on a similar long-acting oral contraceptive.'

He looked at me over his half-moon glasses. 'And how long ago was that?'

'Three years ago.'

'You say this research was inconclusive, Dr Sheriff —'

'Quite frankly, my pill didn't always work. I tested it on rabbits, but the breakthrough ovulation rate – the number of times the animal produced eggs, and therefore became fertile when it shouldn't have been – was twenty-eight per cent. That was far too high. The very fact there was breakthrough ovulation at all ruled my pill out. These oral contraceptives are expected to be one hundred per cent reliable. As I couldn't see any way of improving the drug, I abandoned the project.'

'But even inconclusive work is sometimes published in the relevant professional journals, isn't it? Was this the case with your drug, Dr Sheriff?'

'On the contrary, I kept it rather dark. I think I was rather ashamed of myself, or at least annoyed with myself, for indulging in such a biochemical wild-goose chase.'

'Had you published your findings we might have gone after them on that score,' Mr Romhead reflected. 'Though it would have been only for breach of copyright. And we shouldn't have got an injunction on *that*.'

There was a silence. I sat fidgeting with my skirt, starting to feel impatient. I had work waiting for me at Princess Victoria's.

'There was no similar drug – similar in its long-acting qualities – being developed elsewhere?' asked the barrister.

'I certainly heard of none.'

'And of course you would follow closely any developments in this field.'

'I read all the relevant journals, naturally. Though some other research worker might have got as far as me, quite independently, and refrained from making his results public for exactly the same reasons.'

Mr Romhead smiled. 'Others might not be so conscientious as you over their comparative failures, Dr Sheriff. But doubtless the work you did on this drug is all written down somewhere, like your report here?'

I nodded. 'I've got all the experimental data and conclusions in a file at home.'

'When you did this research, three years ago, the drug cyclova had not of course been invented, and might well not even have been thought of in its present form?'

'That could be the case,' I agreed.

'Now, supposing that General Drugs used your basic research with your rabbits to develop cyclova? Without, of course, paying you a penny, or even asking by-your-leave. Do you imagine that could have occurred?'

'I should be horrified if anything I had done contributed in the slightest way to the development of cyclova.'

'Of course, Dr Sheriff, I appreciate your feelings. But might I ask you to accept two views of this drug, cyclova? To adopt a "split personality", you might call it.' He seemed pleased at this mild joke. 'Cyclova is dangerous, you say, through its effect on the blood. But apart from that, would you not also say that it is perfectly satisfactory in performing the job it is advertised to do?'

'That is correct,' I admitted.

'So your basic research might have led to the development of cyclova. Your further research might have led to the discovery of this one ill-starred property. Indeed, it did.' He looked at Trevor. 'It occurs to me that there might possibly be an action for breach of confidence.'

'That was in my mind too,' Trevor agreed.

'Dr Sheriff certainly had an exploitable asset – her own pill. Possibly General Drugs exploited it. Hence lies an action for damages.'

I began to feel lost. The two men were facing each other, ignoring me. 'Perhaps you would amplify that?' I asked.

'Let me explain, Ann,' said Trevor considerately. 'Supposing you invented a new sort of mousetrap. You went along to a mousetrap manufacturer and told him all about it —'

'In confidence,' put in Mr Romhead sharply.

'Naturally, in confidence. Three years later, the manufacturer produces a mousetrap identical or very much like the one you thought up yourself. He may deny that you imparted to him

265

any information about your own marvellous mousetrap. He may claim to have performed himself all the research necessary to produce his own mousetrap. But if you can prove that you told him about your mousetrap, and in confidence, then you've got a case against him for damages.'

'The only snag,' Mr Romhead pointed out, 'is establishing that General Drugs heard from you in confidence about your drug.'

'That's another dead end,' I told him flatly. 'There was no possibility whatever.'

'Let's give it a moment's thought,' he insisted. 'Just take your mind back if you can, to three years ago, when you were working on this drug of yours. Did you talk to anyone at the General Drug company about it?'

I shook my head. 'Most definitely not. I never had anything to do with General Drugs until I wrote asking for samples of cyclova at the end of last year. I've done routine investigations on their ordinary oral contraceptives, but it was never necessary for me to communicate with them.'

'You didn't speak to any of their employees at that time? Perhaps to one of their research scientists? You might have met such a person at some conference or other, or perhaps even socially.'

'I can't remember doing so.'

'Had you done, I would have imagined it possible you mentioned your drug as a matter of common interest. And if you felt such strong dissatisfaction with your work, you would as likely have asked him to respect your confidence.'

'I could see that *might* have happened, Mr Romhead. But the plain fact is that it didn't. I am absolutely positive that I never spoke to anyone at all in General Drugs.'

'Well, that's that,' said Mr Romhead.

Trevor and I stood up. The barrister smilingly handed back our documents. 'Thank you very much for giving up your time,' I said.

'Not at all, Dr Sheriff. It's a rather interesting little problem, as a matter of fact. And as I have four married daughters, I shall certainly advise them not to touch this cyclova stuff with a barge-pole.'

We shook hands affably. Mr Romhead reached for his gown and wig. I was already in the doorway when I gave a gasp. I saw both men looking at me anxiously. Perhaps they imagined that I was going to faint. 'I *did* speak to someone at General Drugs,' I remembered.

Mr Romhead paused, arms half through his gown. 'About your own pill?'

'Yes. Three years ago. In strict confidence.'

'Ah,' said Mr Romhead.

'I know I insisted on secrecy, for exactly the reason you suggested. Personal dissatisfaction with my work.'

'Have you any proof of your imparting this information?'

'Yes, I think so. I'm sure of it, in fact. There'll be a letter in my files. I recall it now, it just thanked me for my kindness in passing on the details. I always keep every letter I'm sent.'

'A very wise woman,' murmured Trevor.

'And who was the recipient of your confidences?' asked Mr Romhead. 'One of their employees?'

'Yes, in a way. Though at the time I didn't know he was.'

'That's immaterial. You're sure now?'

'Absolutely.'

'What was he? A chemist, someone on the business side?'

'He's a doctor. A consultant physician, who for some years has been advising General Drugs on their products. His name's Dr Charles Crawless.'

'The same man who tried to put you off,' exclaimed Trevor.

'C-r-a-w-l-e-s-s.' As I spelt it out Mr Romhead pencilled the name down, gown drooping over his shoulders. He looked up at Trevor and said, 'Things seem to have fallen into place. Yes, I think we might try for an injunction.'

'It certainly sounds good grounds,' Trevor agreed.

'Our client has been damaged. She is entitled to compensation. She is entitled to stop them marketing a drug in which she has a financial interest.'

I exclaimed, 'I *haven't* a financial interest in cyclova. None whatever.'

'But you have, Dr Sheriff,' Mr Romhead pointed out blandly. 'Cyclova might well be based on your original drug.'

This was a startling thought. 'Compensation is the last thing I want. I only want to stop cyclova being marketed, for the sake of common humanity.'

Mr Romhead pulled up his gown, and glanced at a clock on his marble mantelpiece. 'I much regret that common humanity isn't a good argument in law. Your possible damage is.'

'But I couldn't go to court on that count,' I protested. 'I myself know perfectly well that I haven't been damaged at all.'

'You *don't* know that, Dr Sheriff. How can you? This Dr Crawless could easily have passed the information you gave him to his employers. Indeed, he might have considered it his duty to. Your work three years ago might very well be the basis of cyclova. Might very well indeed.'

'But this is a Gilbert and Sullivan situation. Can I only stop General Drugs from selling cyclova by claiming to be its inventor?'

'Exactly. I'm afraid the law may sometimes seem a little devious, but there it is, and we have to make what use of its convolutions we can.'

I shook my head. 'I couldn't possibly go ahead with an action – not on that basis. I'd feel a hypocrite. A perjurer, almost.'

Mr Romhead glanced at his clock again. 'Of course, that is for you to decide, Dr Sheriff. Though I assure you there's no question of perjury, if all you have told me is correct. You are perfectly within your rights.'

'I just couldn't do it.'

'Ann, are you perfectly sure?' asked Trevor. 'Have you ever failed to do your best, even in the most unpromising of situations?'

I was so confused by the argument, only afterwards I wondered if he was referring to the night in his flat. But I hesitated. His remark incited me to say, almost impulsively, 'All right. We'll have one last fling at them.'

'Will you settle a writ now, Mr Romhead?' asked Trevor at once.

'Yes, I fancy I have the time.'

Neither seemed affected by the pain of my decision. I found

myself ignored, the patient, his case being discussed over his head. It is remarkable, the callousness of people who try to do you good.

'We'll need a notice of motion asking for an injunction,' Mr Romhead continued briskly. 'Your client will of course have to swear an affidavit.'

'Yes, I can look after that. If she swears it before me this morning, I can have it engrossed by tonight.'

'Good. That should be soon enough.'

'Do you consider we ought to go *ex parte*?'

'No, I don't think this motion could be seen as quite so urgent. It's not like premises emitting smoke, the pollution of streams, and suchlike.'

'Quite so,' said Trevor.

'Let me see, today's Wednesday. We could serve the writ before four o'clock on Thursday – I take it these people have a registered office in London? – for hearing on the first motion day next week, which is Tuesday.'

'So quickly?' I exclaimed in astonishment. 'I thought it would take months to reach court.'

Trevor smiled. 'When really necessary, Ann, the wheels of the law can spin like a turbine.'

'I think we've a fair chance,' said Mr Romhead. 'A lot depends on which judge we get, but I'd say a fair chance.'

For the first time it occurred to me that, however mysteriously it had been accomplished, I had at last an opportunity to stop General Drugs in their tracks.

38

I PUT ON the mustard suit again. It was getting more wear than I had anticipated when I bought it.

It was the following Tuesday, 'motion day' in the courts, when applications such as mine for court orders came before one or two of the sitting judges. I hurried from the bus along the crowded Strand at ten in the morning. Trevor in his bowler was waiting at the overpowering main entrance of the Law Courts. On this more portentous occasion he could hardly avoid meeting me with some time to spare. He looked at his watch, and said, 'We can discuss coming events over coffee. The witching hour for the law is ten-thirty.'

'I know. My divorce provided me with a crash course in legal procedure.'

'Nervous?'

'Not especially.'

'I don't think anything makes you really nervous, Ann.'

'Plenty of things do. But nothing more so than myself.'

We went through the arched entrance into the huge, vaulted, Victorian, cathedral-like hall, designed to impress miserable supplicants with the lofty majesty or divine infallibility of English law. It was busy with robed and wigged barristers, attendants with gold crowns on their collars, and dark-suited men with stuffed briefcases, hurrying everywhere wearing the intensely purposeful expression seen on the medical staff moving about hospitals. Then there were people like me, the patients, appearing suitably cowed. In the middle of the hall stood long printed notices in glass and wooden frames, like station timetables. Trevor paused, and pointed.

'There you are, Ann.'

On the top of the column was CHANCERY DIVISION, in Gothic characters. Underneath, I read,

NEW COURT No. 1
Mr Justice Millhaven
Motions List 'A'
Sheriff *v*. General Drugs (Great Britain) Ltd.

'At least I've seen my name in print,' I observed dryly.

'Not for the last time in this affair, I fancy.' As I looked at him inquiringly, he added, 'The newspapers, you know.'

'Surely they won't be interested?' This complication had never occurred to me. 'It seems such a private row. "Breach of confidence" – the very expression suggests an argument in whispers.'

'The Press, Ann, has a nasty suspicious mind.'

'I hope they don't make too much of it,' I said doubtfully. 'The profession doesn't take kindly to publicity. Even though nowadays we're used to photographs of surgical transplant teams looking as if they'd just won the world football cup.'

There was a crypt-like room at the far end of the hall, where Trevor left me at a formica-topped table while he fetched two cups of coffee from the cafeteria. As he put them down, he complimented me, 'I think you're one of the coolest litigants I've come across.'

'I find it genuinely stimulating. Is that rather indecent? I've been thinking over the week-end, and I admit the reasons I'm bringing General Drugs to court aren't ones I'd have chosen myself, in fact I'm downright ashamed of them. But had our positions been reversed, they'd have done exactly the same to me.'

'I'm sure they would.'

'And at least I've come to grips with them. It's my only possible ground to fight. Our beloved lady Dean at Princess Victoria's explained at some length it was for exactly the same reason we sent out soldiers to Italy during the war.'

'I hope we shall be equally victorious.'

'She's in love with the war. An affair of remarkably lingering tenderness. She was a medical officer.'

'I never did national service, even in peacetime. I've this leg of mine to thank for that.'

'Your leg's much better, isn't it?' I was surprised at his mentioning it. 'I can hardly see a limp at all.'

'The thing's still short, of course, one can't do anything about that. Should we say, I'm adapting myself to it?'

'I think that's the best treatment.'

Trevor drank some coffee. 'When Liz telephoned, and I knew that I'd have to see you again, I told myself firmly that it had never happened. That I'd dreamt it. You know, that awful evening.'

'Very well, Trevor, I'll tell myself the same. As we're the only two in the secret, it didn't happen, did it?'

'That's a pleasant piece of feminine reasoning. But it doesn't matter one way or another, because I can see the funny side now. Though at the time, thank God, you didn't think it funny. You never laughed at me, you know.'

'You seem to have remembered the details.'

'How could I forget them? But the fact that you didn't laugh, Ann, that you were so sympathetic, made a tremendous difference. I won't say it changed my life. That would be too flattering altogether.' He smiled. 'A lot of things happened about that time. I got my partnership, I was given work which I managed to do well. I grew in confidence. But it all started in my flat. You were so sensible, I suppose that even *I* could see I was being somewhat hysterical.'

'That's flattery enough for me,' I told him.

'I didn't take your advice about seeing a psychiatrist, though. Now I have professional dealings with several of them, I'm glad that I didn't.'

'Do you still get anxious?'

'Much less. You mean about things in general?' he corrected himself. 'Or in particular?'

'That particular thing.'

'To tell the truth, I began to bother less and less about the

272

sex business. It isn't the be-all and end-all, though you'd imagine so from the papers and so on. I'm happy enough.'

'Have you had a girl yet, Trevor?' That was mischievous of me, but I couldn't resist it.

'Yes, I have,' he said with emphasis. 'But it was rather complicated.'

'Perhaps you'd prefer to talk to me about our case?'

'In that you are perfectly correct.' I took out a cigarette, and struck a match. 'You will have nothing to say in court, of course. You sit there while Romhead does his stuff. I'm glad we're up before old Millhaven. He's civilized. Some of the Chancery judges are tartars, I suppose because they live on a diet of dry facts without an occasional taste of human blood at the assizes. Millhaven regards the whole process of the law as something of a joke. He's right, I think. Unfortunately, it's a practical joke, so the bucket of water has to descend on one side or the other.'

'How long will we take?'

'Today, not long. The other side will appear and ask for an adjournment.'

I made a wry face. 'Which will add to my costs.'

'I'm afraid so. Though I hope they'll not be an embarrassment to you.'

'My brother has lent me a few hundred pounds – he's a successful businessman. Or rather, his wife has, my brother being somewhat tight-fisted. When I went to his house yesterday, the little woman raged at him with devastating effect. I'd always imagined he sat on her, but that was only the impression she gave in public. An intelligent woman, I admire her enormously.'

'Ann, there's one financial aspect of this case which I've not made as clear as I should. It's the same with all cases of this nature. Let's say we get your injunction, next week, after an adjournment. There may even be a further week's adjournment, but now we're in July, the Trinity term ends with the month, and they'll be as anxious as us to have a decision before the courts rise for the vacation. We get our injunction, and we can stop General Drugs marketing cyclova from that very moment.'

I nodded.

'But that, of course, isn't the end of the road. We should only be granted an injunction pending trial, not a permanent one. There'd be a full-dress trial of the action later – Sheriff v. General Drugs, for breach of confidence. Perhaps as long as a year later. You understand that?'

'Yes, I knew as much. But the trial in a year's time would be something of a formality, surely?'

'I don't know if I would put it as a formality, exactly.'

'But if we get our injunction now, we'll be certain to win our action later?'

Trevor slowly rubbed his chin. 'We'd have a good chance. But all sorts of things might happen. A different judge. Different facts brought to light. I'd like to guarantee results, but I honestly can't.'

'Naturally, I understand that.' I was disappointed, imagining the whole affair would in effect be over and done with in a couple of weeks. 'And if we *did* lose the action in a year's time,' I added glumly, 'I suppose I should be liable for the costs of the entire case?'

'I'm afraid your liabilities might be more extensive than that.'

I stared at him. 'The costs would be crippling enough.'

'I want you to be quite clear in your mind about this, Ann. I should really have put it to you before we issued the writ, but everything ended with a rush in old Romhead's chambers. The fact is, apart from any costs, if the eventual action went against you, you would then find yourself liable to pay damages to General Drugs.'

'But I don't understand, Trevor. Surely I'm trying to get damages out of *them*?'

'Let me explain. Your injunction would stop General Drugs from distributing cyclova until the trial takes place. Right? Obviously, they would lose a good deal of money in the meantime. After all this advertising and ballyhoo, a *great* deal of money. Or at least, they could easily claim so. If – and I repeat, if – the action next year ended in their favour, you would be liable for their loss.'

I gasped. 'But my God, Trevor, how could I find anything like that amount? I'd be ruined for my life.'

He patted my arm. 'Let's take one thing at a time. We'd better be making for court, at least to set the ball rolling.'

Trevor went on talking, but I didn't hear him. I followed him through some arches on the left of the main hall, dazed with the news of this horrifying liability. And the more I thought of it, the more bitterly I saw it as a perfectly logical arrangement. I should clearly have to win all along the line, or simply give up now. A demoralizing start to my case.

We went along a low, brightly-lit corridor crowded with barristers and their clients, confidence conversing with uneasiness. I had expected to find myself amid the light oak and jet ironwork so disastrously beloved by Victorian church restorers, but the court was smallish and modern, lit from a translucent ceiling, the floor plastic tiles, the walls of chocolate-coloured woodwork and bright blue paint, the empty judge's chair in scarlet with the Queen's initials in gold, above it the lion and unicorn of a Royal Arms which struck me as stylish, indeed raffish. The clerk of the court below the judge's dais was a woman, resembling McRobb in a wig. On the benches facing her sat some twenty people, including half a dozen wigged barristers. I took a seat on the rearmost bench, next to Trevor. Mr Romhead, my champion, turned and smiled from three or four rows in front. I looked round, half-expecting to see Lloyd or Charles Crawless, but there was nobody.

An usher shouted. We all stood up. The judge appeared, large, square, and grey-faced, in a short wig and a black gown with a scarlet sash. The barristers bowed to him. He bowed back. He took his seat, assumed a pair of heavy glasses, rubbed his hands, and said, 'Now, then,' just like any other man starting his day's business.

'Mr Huntingdon, do you move?' the judge asked in a conversational tone.

Directly in front of me rose a tall, stooping barrister, his hair whiter than the wig perched on top, who bowed solemnly and sat down again.

Trevor whispered, 'The most senior counsel present are

275

invited to put motions first, even though they haven't one to put.'

'I see,' I murmured absently. I was still thinking of the damages I might owe General Drugs.

'Mr Bright,' the judge continued in the same voice, 'do you move?'

Another elderly barrister rose. 'My Lord, may I mention the action Abernethy v. Pott?'

Inspecting some papers, the judge frowned. 'But, Mr Bright, isn't that *in re* an infant? I should be sitting *in camera.*'

'No, my Lord. It concerns the exposure for sale of seed potatoes.'

'I was mistaken,' said the judge affably. 'Errors so early in the day are forgivable. Please proceed, Mr Bright.'

I listened to a short and highly technical speech about potatoes. I found the judge's reply equally incomprehensible. But the barrister seemed pleased enough, said 'I thank your Lordship' very gravely, and sat down. The ritual dance of the law proceeded.

'Mr Romhead, do you move?'

I suddenly did feel nervous. I wished that I had brought Kit. But he had decided to stay at home, feeling that his appearance at my side might necessitate stupid explanations, and perhaps embarrassments – perfectly rightly, as it turned out some half-hour later.

'My Lord —' Mr Romhead was on his feet. 'I would mention the action of Sheriff *versus* General Drugs (Great Britain) Limited. I am instructed by my client, Dr Ann Sheriff, a doctor of medicine, to move for an injunction. It may take a little under half an hour. Perhaps your Lordship would care to dispose first of any non-effective motions?'

'Are there any?' The judge looked round. No reply. 'Very well, Mr Romhead.'

I sat listening to my story in the affidavit sworn before Trevor. It sounded hearteningly convincing in Mr Romhead's mouth, though it was strange meeting such familiar memories in that atmosphere of muted pomp. Mr Romhead explained how three years ago I had performed basic research on a long-acting

276

female contraceptive drug, how I had imparted the details in confidence to Dr Charles Crawless – at that time a consultant retained by the General Drug Company – how I had heard of cyclova the previous autumn only by mere chance, how I recognized it as fundamentally the same drug as my own, how I had been offered by the drug company neither money nor acknowledgement. There was no word of my blood-stain, my findings in the suspect case, my report, or its rejection. I supposed they knew what they were doing.

'On the evidence of this affidavit, my Lord,' Mr Romhead ended, 'I submit that my client has been damaged through a breach of her confidence to Dr Crawless. I further submit that there can be no doubt that her communication with Dr Crawless three years ago was, in fact, in confidence. That is plain from the letter in my client's possession, which she mentions in the affidavit. I therefore move for an injunction, until trial of action or further order, to restrain General Drugs (Great Britain) Ltd. from selling cyclova.'

He sat down. Immediately beside him rose a young barrister, fiery red hair protruding strangely under his grey wig.

'Mr Wilson-Ball?' invited the judge.

'My Lord, I am instructed by the General Drugs Company (Great Britain) Limited, whose registered office is at number 484 Piccadilly, W.1. My clients deny most strongly the allegations contained in the affidavit read to your Lordship by my learned friend. Furthermore, my clients welcome the opportunity to establish in open court that the plaintiff had no interest whatever in the research and development of the drug cyclova, which was the product of scientific work conducted exclusively in their own laboratories. I ask your Lordship for an adjournment, in the first instance, of one week.'

He sat down.

'You heard that, Mr Romhead,' said the judge amicably. 'What have you got to say?'

Mr Romhead rose again. 'I would make no objection, my Lord.'

'I grant an adjournment for one week,' said the judge.

Trevor nudged me. 'Come along. That's all.'

277

Mr Romhead smiled in the doorway of the court, and hurried away on other business. As I walked down the long hall, I said to Trevor, 'That was short and sweet.'

'It'll be somewhat longer when we thrash things out.'

'I might have found it more fun, if you hadn't told me first about compensating General Drugs.'

'There's a perfectly good chance you'll never be in that position, Ann.'

'It's pretty scaring.'

Trevor smiled. 'You said earlier that you were scared most of yourself.'

'I am. Only my temperament got me in this particular position.' We reached the entrance of the Law Courts. 'I must get back to Princess Victoria's. Thanks for the moral support, Trevor.'

'Shall I get you a taxi?'

'No, I'll walk. It's not far, and I want some fresh air.'

I stepped on to the pavement. In an instant I was surrounded. Cameras were staring at me, men and women with open notebooks seemed everywhere, one had the microphone of a taperecorder pushed under my nose. Everyone was talking at once. 'Dr Sheriff, which is your hospital? Dr Sheriff, how old are you? Are you married, Dr Sheriff? Why are you bringing this action, Dr Sheriff? What is your frank opinion of the new birth pill, Dr Sheriff? Do you think there are any unrevealed snags about it, Dr Sheriff? Would you say that it was perfectly safe to take, Dr Sheriff? Was Dr Crawless a personal friend of yours, Dr Sheriff? Do you think women make better doctors than men, Dr Sheriff . . . ?'

Trevor pulled me into a taxi. As I fell backwards on to the seat someone took another photograph through the open window. I was aware of showing an enormous amount of leg.

39

THE PRESS HAD a nasty suspicious mind, sure enough.

I spread that evening's papers across the table in our flat. In the first, a black headline said,

BIRTH PILL: ARE THERE DOUBTS?

As Kit had pointed out, the story underneath was cleverly done. They had used my action against General Drugs merely as a peg, revealing that I had tested cyclova at Princess Victoria's and was in disagreement with General Drugs over it. I wondered who they had got the information from. Perhaps they had cornered Ma Saintsbury, who would certainly have made no bones about it. The newspaper continued that my report on cyclova had never been published, though keeping a prudent silence over its hostility. I found myself described personally most flatteringly. A woman doctor, particularly a presentable one, who single-handed fought a huge and powerful drug company, was something the papers could take to their stony hearts. They had printed a photograph of me, the one with all the leg.

'But I've made my point, I've made my point already!' I told Kit. I was elated, my worry over Trevor's warning had temporarily evaporated. The sudden publicity, seeing my long-suppressed thoughts in bold black and white, I found exhilarating. 'Any woman taking cyclova who reads this – what would she think? She'd certainly hesitate before swallowing her next month's dose.'

'It'll get their backs up good and proper at General Drugs,' observed Kit.

'I don't give a damn about that.'

'They'll fight tooth and nail now, to stop you getting this injunction. Two can play the innuendo game. They've got to rout you completely to justify their bloody poison.'

'They don't need any excuse for ruthlessness. Look at that Longfield business.'

'Anyway, you'll win, my darling. You're in the right.'

I laughed. 'I'd have believed that meant something, before I started talking to lawyers. The law's a game, you know. Played to elaborate rules which no one outside can understand, and all very stately. Like real tennis, with its peculiar sagging net and the unexpected traps in the walls.'

I turned to the other evening paper, which treated the story more warily, under the headline, COURT RULING SOUGHT ON 'PILL'.

'You must feel like a film-star or a pop singer,' said Kit.

'It's heartening, really. This publicity takes away the awful feeling I had until this morning, that I was battling alone. Anyone who reads it must take some sort of interest in my case. Though it's strange, isn't it? At breakfast-time, nobody had heard of me. Now all the men going home in the commuter trains are looking at my legs.'

'I'm jealous.'

I inspected the photograph again. 'Next time, I'd better wear tights.'

'Next time they may not be so interested,' Kit warned me. 'You were lucky today. The news is thin. No wars, strikes, or economic crises – at least, none that everyone isn't thoroughly bored with. Not even any particularly enterprising crime. Even the Test Match at Birmingham sunk as a draw in the rain.'

'Maybe. I remember, they took my photograph on the pavement after I divorced Henry, but they never printed it. I looked a mess, anyway.'

'I hope to God they take one of Myra when she finally gets round to unloading me. She'd love that, you know. Getting in the papers would for her be compensation enough.'

'By then she'll be too senile to care.'

'I live in hopes,' said Kit lightly. 'She always had a great talent for frustration.'

I kissed him. 'To hell with Myra. I'm glad of her, really. She's something to blame all our little disappointments and failures and rows on. Every couple needs a Myra. Usually it's mother-in-law or the neighbours or the mortgage.'

'You *are* in a good mood,' said Kit appreciatively.

I left him to start in the kitchen. Even the ephemeral heroines of the Press have to cook.

I was scraping the new potatoes and dropping them into the pan when our doorbell rang.

'I'll go,' Kit shouted from the sitting-room.

'If it's a newspaper after my life-story, charge them the earth,' I called back.

'It's more likely Andrew, cadging a gin on the strength of this sudden fame.'

When he reappeared up the four flights of stairs, puffing a little, he had a bulging foolscap envelope in his fingers. 'It's for you, delivered by a young man in a Lotus Elan.'

I dried my hands on the dishcloth. The envelope was hand-written, and I frowned at it, fancying that I had seen the writing before. 'It's probably something about the case from Trevor Monkhood,' I decided. I tore it open. 'Why, it's from Charles Crawless.'

The letter, too, was in handwriting, closely covering several sheets of familiar white paper headed 'Princess Victoria's, Hospital'. It said:

Dear Ann,

I am sending this letter across London by my houseman, and I hope you will be at home to receive it because I want to address myself to you as soon as possible. My legal advisers have, of course, warned me in no circumstances to communicate with you. I observed this prohibition over the week-end, after your writ had been issued. But from what I have learned of your remarks about me this morning in court, I feel justified in taking whatever risk there may be. There has

281

become a personal element involved. With you, Ann, if you will forgive my saying so, there always is.

You swore in your affidavit that you imparted to me in confidence, three years ago, information about your own long-acting contraceptive. Which was anyway, as you admit, in a primitive state of development. You could not yourself have thought highly of it. Had you done so, you would have gone ahead to perfect it with your usual energy and determination, or taken it to some pharmaceutical company for them to do so.

I honestly believe that you mentioned your drug to me as a matter of passing gossip. I asked you to send me details because I was interested in all drugs, in my capacity as consultant to the General Drugs Co. – a connexion which you did not at the time know, and which even your former husband did not know for some years.

You kindly supplied me with this information, asking me not to disclose it because you wished no rumours flying about of something which you regarded as a failure. To one who knows you as well as I, this was somewhat typical. Out of courtesy, I sent you a note saying that I should respect your confidence. From these ingredients you have concocted the stew in which we now all find ourselves.

But I shortly put your own drug out of mind. I thought that it was impracticable. I had quite genuinely forgotten it when I heard from George Lloyd about eighteen months ago of cyclova. It is now a shock to find the trivial exchange between us, three years in the past, your basis for putting General Drugs to great inconvenience and expense. And, incidentally, yourself to both.

Moreoever, it is I who find myself plainly, if innocently, the bull's-eye of your target. This is a great embarrassment to me, and as you can imagine it is not viewed particularly kindly by my friends at General Drugs. I am the more upset because I believe that I know your motives. Perhaps I know them better than you do yourself.

When we first had your writ, George Lloyd decided that you were simply after money. We didn't think you had a particularly good case, but you had one of sorts, and in the hands of enterprising lawyers you might profit from it. George in fact suggested buying you off, nominating a fairly substantial sum for the purpose. But I could tell him at once that would be a useless and possibly damaging gesture.

You have three reasons for bringing this action, I consider. The first is simple. You wish to stop us marketing cyclova. Well, that is fair enough. You think it is dangerous. We do not. We are all entitled to our opinions, even if our opinion in this matter is backed by an immensely heavier weight of evidence than yours.

Secondly, I do not believe that you would have persisted in trying to push cyclova off the market had you not felt so personally involved. A medical man or woman should sit and view such a clash of opinion as this in an impartial and detached way. But you felt hurt and slighted. I agree, you were justified to display certain bruises on your feelings. George Lloyd made no softening of the blow with which our board of directors poleaxed your report. I think he sees this now. He really is extremely bad at handling people, and if it is any gratification his head may well roll, whichever way the lawsuit goes. But his own lack of sensitivity was, I feel, no excuse for your own excess of it.

Your third reason is myself.

I'm afraid I was not very polite to you when we met by chance at Princess Victoria's the other morning. I apologize for this, and assure you that the lapse was painful in afterthought. You are against me not, as you officially claim in court, because I betrayed your confidence. You are against me because I advised Sir Robert Boatwright that you would not be a suitable candidate for the post at Longfield University.

I told you at our chance meeting why I gave this advice to Sir Robert. Will you permit me to amplify it?

You are a clever woman, Ann, none of us would deny that. You have many qualities valuable to a research worker or the head of a scientific department – your enthusiasm, your determination, even your obstinacy in the face of sometimes half-imagined adversity. But you have one weakness which destroys your strength. You must let me be frank here. Your weakness is the other sex.

Please don't imagine that I am attacking your morals or anything stupid like that. We are all far from saints, and I have often noticed in my professional life how intelligent women as well as intelligent men partake of an active and varied love-life. But your temperament always seems to run into such trouble with men. Henry was happy with you, until you made his life impossible by continually trying to overmaster him. When he left you, you reacted quite hysterically, giving up your promising career as a gynaecologist and burying yourself in a laboratory. I admit, you had the misfortune to be diagnosed as having rheumatoid arthritis. But as you know, with modern corticosteroid therapy this need be no bar to an active life. And it was patently clear to my eyes, at least, that you did not have the disease as badly as you were anxious for the world to assume.

What if another emotional crisis had occurred after your appointment to Longfield? You might have reacted the same way, let your department go hang, your research go unfinished, your students go untaught. This surely was not a hypothetical possibility? I like Kit well, and I am sure that the pair of you are pleasingly matched. But Kit is not your husband. He is freer than Henry was to leave you. What might have happened then?

And, of course, there is your temper! When you are good, Ann, you are very, very good indeed. When you are angry, you are quite impossible for everyone.

There it is, then. I have made a clean breast. You may now have added reason to hate me. But you have less to misunderstand me.

I am not asking you to withdraw your action against General Drugs, however well you may be advised to do so. I am giving you the facts on the personal side of our quarrel as I see them, and as I so wish you could bring yourself to see them.

You may come to view cyclova in a similarly dispassionate light, when I am sure you would decide of your own free will the action should be halted. If so, I shall certainly do all I can to get you adequate compensation for your indignities in the hands of the company. Despite my having forfeited your friendship – which saddens me.

I know that you will treat this letter with strict confidence –
if I may, under our present circumstances, use the word!

Yours sincerely,
Charles.

I handed the letter without speaking to Kit. I sat in silence on
the kitchen chair while he read it through. I noticed that I still
had the dishcloth in my hand.

Kit turned the last page. 'All in longhand, too,' he murmured. 'It must have taken him hours to write.'

'My God!' I snapped, 'The man's a bastard.'

'There are two ways to look at his somewhat pneumatic
prose,' Kit decided. 'One, it's a straight try-on. All inspired by
General Drugs, an attempt to make you back down fairly
painlessly. This allusion to compensation – it gives body to the
idea. And of Lloyd getting the sack.'

'If that's the case,' I told him sharply, 'it's an encouragement
for me to press on. It shows they're scared. If they thought they
were going to win, they wouldn't have put Charles up to it,
surely?'

'It's a manoeuvre which might be a little crude for General
Drugs,' Kit admitted. 'So our alternative is to take these
pompous outpourings at their face-value.'

'But how can we? Those things he said, those terrible things,
my God, he makes me sound like a . . . sex maniac, or something, a man-eater. And about my rheumatism. How could he
be so stupid, so callous? Of course I had to give up my career,
lose myself in a laboratory. Of course I had to stop operating. I
couldn't move my hands, could I? I couldn't tie a stitch. I
couldn't handle scissors or forceps or any kind of instrument.
I was crippled, I just couldn't go on, that must be obvious to
him, he's a clinician, he knows the disease.'

Kit threw the letter down in disgust. 'It's a pack of lies. A
pack of sadistic lies.'

Still holding the dishcloth, I buried my face in my hands.
'It isn't,' I managed to say. 'It isn't. I know that every word of
it is true.'

285

40

IT HAPPENED JUST before five o'clock on a Sunday afternoon, almost a fortnight later. The previous Tuesday I had been to court again. There was Trevor. There was Mr Romhead. There was the ginger-haired counsel. The judge's pantomime was repeated, the ginger barrister asked for a further week's adjournment, Mr Romhead rose to accede. We all split up again. This time there was only one newspaperman outside, and he wanted my views on the ethics of heart transplants.

My introspection over Charles's letter had toppled me from elation into a mood of utter misery. I could see only the gloomy side of the case, that I should lose, or worse still lose in a year's time. I wanted to give up, but Trevor insisted I persevered at least until the injunction was settled one way or another. If I won it, he explained, I should have the means in my hand to negotiate with General Drugs some sort of settlement. If I lost, that would be the end of it, and not too much harm done.

I had scores of letters redirected by the newspapers, from worried women who had started on cyclova and implored my advice. Two weeks before I should have been delighted, but now they didn't move me. And my rheumatism was troublesome. It was real, *of course it was real*, I told myself. I could see it. I tried tugging at my wedding-ring, and found it fixed tight. My temper became jagged, and I seemed always short with poor Kit.

Then came that Sunday afternoon. We were in the living-room, Kit on the sofa, myself in the chair, idly turning over the coloured supplements to the Sunday papers when, stimulated by some item in the pages before me, I complained, 'The whole bloody world seems to be getting divorced except you.'

'Patience, my darling, patience,' he murmured. 'They took time to split the atom. My bond is fortunately not quite so indissoluble.'

'Why does everyone keep telling me to have patience?' I demanded. 'To be calm. To disembody myself, to look at things dispassionately, to pretend they're all someone else's troubles. You're all the same, you, Charles Crawless, the legal people, even McRobb and Ma Saintsbury.'

'Don't I respect your feelings, Ann darling? I try.' He was very patient with me those bad days.

'Then why don't you bloody well put a bomb under Myra?'

'I've done my best.'

'I can't remember you doing anything at all. The only arguing has been entirely between Myra and myself. You haven't so much as lifted a finger.'

'It was your idea tackling Myra, not mine.'

'All right, it was my idea. Because I didn't think you could start matching up to her.'

'There you are, then.' He became less submissive. 'You believe anything I might do in the matter would be ineffective. So what was the point of my bothering?'

'Oh, words!' I said impatiently. 'It's a pity you can't make some money out of them, instead of hiding behind them.'

Kit turned back to his paper. There was a silence, as I wondered whether his obvious pains to avoid fighting me came through concern for my torn feelings, or because I was more unreasonable than usual.

'I'm fed up with my situation,' I persisted. 'It's all right for you, you've got all the amenities of married life handed you on a plate.'

'But, Ann, what difference would it make if we married tomorrow? I've done all I can to straighten things out for you. I've already suggested you take my name. Though nobody we know cares, one way or another.'

'People *I* know care.'

287

'Crawless? We shouldn't lose sleep over what he thinks.'

'They used it against me down at Longfield.'

'Don't you think you might start trying to forget about Longfield?'

'How could I?'

'You seem rather to enjoy making yourself miserable over it.'

'That's a bloody lie. It was the most humiliating experience of my life.'

'Perhaps that's what I mean. You like inviting a bit of pain, don't you?' I made no reply to this. 'But returning to our domestic condition. There aren't many real snags. If we were going to have a child, of course that would be different.'

'Why do you want to bring that up?' I snapped at him angrily.

'I'm sorry, I'd forgotten it was one of your sensitive areas. It's difficult to remember them all.'

'That's something else people imagine I don't care about. "Look at it calmly, Ann, you're sterile, your tubes are blocked and the failure rate with the corrective operation is eighty-five per cent. It's a very interesting case, Ann, your salpingograms were fascinating." Christ, I'm fed up with that attitude.'

'Now *you're* being callous by assuming it's an attitude of mine. I know how a woman must feel, realizing that she can't have a baby. Anyway, you could have tried the operation. You still can. But I don't think you want to.'

'That's rubbish,' I said quickly. 'It's all right for you to talk. You've got a child. Even if she is a silly and lazy little bitch.'

'Veronica isn't all that bad,' he said defensively.

'She is, every bit of it. She's malicious. The way she spoke to me about us. God knows how she lets herself go behind our backs. She's a mixture of spite and stupidity, which is dangerous and pitiable.'

'You're jealous of her.'

This infuriated me. 'Jealous of a brainless child? You're ridiculous.'

'You're jealous of my feelings towards her. Of course, I love Veronica, that's only normal. And you resent it. That isn't

288

normal at all. You resent it, because any love going you want for your own sweet self.'

'That's pure fantasy.'

'It may be, but most of you *is* fantasy. You want to possess me, exclusively – no Myra, no Veronica, no pocket-money even, to give me a shred of independence. You've got to be boss.'

'How can you say that?'

'I didn't say it. Charles Crawless did.'

He stopped abruptly. At first I didn't understand what was happening. He had been sitting forward on the sofa as our exchanges became hotter. Now he gave a gasp and sat staring at me, his hand at this throat, his mouth falling loose.

'Kit—'

He had gone white, I saw sweat on his forehead, and his eye as he looked at me was frightened.

I screamed. 'Kit!'

I jumped up, cradling his head in my arms. 'Kit, darling Kit!'

'Oh, Ann,' he muttered. 'This is a sad end to it all.'

I automatically felt for the pulse at his wrist, finding it soft, thready, and quick. I laid him down on the sofa, ripping off his tie, opening his shirt, noticing with strange intentness how I pulled off a button and it rolled on to the floor. 'The pain?' I asked urgently. 'Where is it?'

'Just here – at the top of my sternum.'

'Any in your left arm?'

'Yes, a bit.'

I got some books and propped them under one end of the sofa, raising his feet. I hurried into the bedroom, came back with my stethoscope, and listened to his heart. A low-pitched extra heart-sound at the apex. Triple rhythm.

I took the stethoscope out of my ears. 'Have you had any symptoms?' I said distractedly. 'Any pain in your chest?'

'I have, yes,' he told me weakly. 'Since we were in France. I thought it was indigestion, something like that.'

If only he'd told me, if only he'd *told* me.

'It's a coronary, isn't it?' he asked.

'I don't know,' I lied. 'No one can tell until we've taken proper tracings with an electrocardiogram.'

I looked round the flat. I had no morphine, no drugs at all, not even apparatus to measure his plummeting blood-pressure. I should have to leave him. I kissed his forehead and ran downstairs, hammering on the landlady's door. I dialled Princess Victoria's and demanded Charles Crawless's house physician.

'This is Dr Sheriff here.' I was lucky, the young man came quickly to the telephone. 'Perhaps you remember, you delivered a letter at my flat the other evening?'

'Yes, of course, Dr Sheriff.'

'Listen. A friend of mine has just had a coronary. Have you a bed free in the intensive care unit?'

'I'm sure that can be fixed,' he said sympathetically. 'I'm sorry she's a friend of yours.'

'The patient's a man. And I want you to get Dr Crawless. I suppose he's available?'

'He's at his home this week-end.'

'Please say that I particularly wish him to come in.'

'I'll certainly do that. What's the patient's name?'

'Mr Christopher Stewart. Aged forty-four.'

'We do seem to see so many young coronaries these days, Dr Sheriff.' he said sombrely. 'I'll fix up an ambulance straight away.'

I hurried upstairs again. There was a little vomit on Kit's shirt and his colour was dusky, he needed oxygen. I waited impatiently until I heard the weird notes of the ambulance horn, and remembered they would be carrying a cylinder. Two uniformed men appeared with a stretcher, the practised custodians of disaster. In the ambulance I held Kit's hand, and he said with the same frightened look, 'Myra. You'll have to tell Myra.'

'Don't worry, darling. Don't worry, leave it to me. Leave everything to me.'

The houseman was waiting in the Gothic hospital doorway. They wheeled Kit to the intensive care unit and put him to bed, surrounded by a gallery of electronic equipment to monitor his heart and circulation. A nurse adjusted the oxygen mask, and as I saw the houseman with a syringe I cried out, 'What's that?'

He looked startled. 'Twenty milligrams of morphine, Dr Sheriff.'

'Of course, of course . . .'

I should have known. But my clinical abilities had flown.

The houseman took me to one side, in his hand a blank form for hospital notes clipped to a board. He wanted a history of the attack.

'Mr Stewart and I live together,' I told him. He didn't seem impressed one way or another. 'Apparently, he started having chest pain about a month ago, while we were abroad. We both ascribed it to dyspepsia. About an hour ago he had this infarct, suddenly.'

'Was he undergoing any particular effort at the time?'

'No. Yes,' I corrected myself. 'We were having an argument – a row.'

'I think it would have happened sooner or later, even without any particular emotional strain,' he said comfortingly.

I looked round. Charles had entered the ward, wearing a smart tweed suit. We met at Kit's bed.

'I'm so sorry, Ann.'

I looked at him, said nothing, and hurried away, leaving him with his patient.

I sat on a wooden bench outside. I had no cigarettes. Neither had the ward sister. I could only wait until Charles Crawless had finished. I sat telling myself it was my fault, all my fault. All the fault of my temper. I don't know how long I sat there, it might have been ten minutes or an hour. Then Charles appeared, holding some long strips of pinkish graph paper. 'It is a coronary, I'm afraid, Ann.'

'I knew that.' I sat on the bench with my legs stuck out, not troubling with an attempt at elegance. I was in slacks and an old blouse, my hair was a mess, my face was suffering from its Sunday neglect. 'Is it a bad one?'

'Fairly severe. It's an anterior infarct. I've brought the E.C.G. tracings.'

Still standing, he handed me the strips of paper with their

continuous line of regularly-repeated purple squiggles. Kit's death-warrant. If not now, one day. I struggled to interpret the exact significance of the tracings, but I couldn't see them, because I had started to cry.

'What's to be done?' I asked, feeling helpless.

'We'll certainly give Kit the best possible in the way of treatment. He'll be monitored twenty-four hours a day, of course. We've some excellent new equipment for that – Japanese. We've also close-circuit television, so that sister can watch him continually from her desk.' I saw how Charles's enthusiasm for electrical gadgets had spilt on to his work, and it gave me a sickening feeling. 'Meanwhile, as you know, there is not a great deal we can do in the way of active treatment. It's largely a matter of waiting patiently until the infarct heals, the clot becomes fibrous scar tissue, and the coronary circulation re-establishes itself.'

I nodded dully. 'What's the prognosis?'

'I won't minimize the immediate dangers, which of course you're also aware of. There's always the possibility of a second infarct soon after the first. On the other hand, Kit's got no signs of heart-failure and isn't particularly severely shocked. So I would be inclined to look on the hopeful side, by and large.'

'Thank you.' He was really being very kind.

'As for the ultimate prognosis, Ann – well, there are plenty of important and active men in the world with healed coronaries, aren't there? Presidents of nations, captains of industry, teachers, writers, countless doctors. A little care will be needed, but I don't see why you shouldn't enjoy many happy years together. I constantly admire the way a woman adapts herself after her man has a thrombosis.'

I noticed he didn't use the word 'wife', and wondered if it were deliberate. 'How long will you keep him in hospital?'

'He'll need four weeks' complete bed-rest for a start. Then we shall see.'

'Are you putting him on anticoagulants?'

'Not immediately. They're still somewhat debatable, you know.'

I nodded again, slowly. The clinical discussion was over. 'May I go back and see him?'

'I'd rather you didn't, Ann. Not just at the moment.'

'Of course, I understand.'

'But do stay in the hospital, if you wish. We can easily fix you somewhere to sleep.'

'I'll go home. I'm within reach of a telephone.'

'I'll ring you tonight, anyway.'

He hesitated. 'Why did you particularly send for me?'

'You're an expert cardiologist.'

'There are others.'

'It comes naturally to me, putting my trust in you.'

He started slowly rolling up his strips of cardiac tracings. 'I hope that letter didn't upset you too much, Ann?'

'It upset me, but not in the way you imagine.'

He nodded, not understanding me. 'I'm glad you did send for me, Ann. I feel I can look after Kit as well as anyone possibly could.'

He went back to the ward. I knew there was a telephone box at the end of the corridor, and hurried to ring Myra. Having no idea of her number, I had to search through all the Stewarts in the book to find her address. She answered herself.

'Myra, this is Ann Sheriff. I'm afraid I've bad news. Kit's been taken ill. He's had a coronary thrombosis – a heart attack.'

There was a silence. 'Oh.'

'He's been admitted to Princess Victoria's Hospital.'

'Is he very ill?' Her voice had its inflexible vagueness.

'It's a serious condition, but the physician in charge expects him to pull through all right.'

'Had I better come and see him?'

'Yes. I'll tell the ward to expect you and Veronica. Though the doctors may not let you in right away.'

'I see. Yes. Well, then I'll come. We'll both come. Will you give Kit our love, Dr Sheriff?'

'I'll make sure he has your message.'

I put down the telephone. 'Oh, God!' I said suddenly, out loud. 'Oh God, please God, let him live.'

There was a God. The force which drew the sperm into the egg. Without which, the universe was pointless. That was God.

As I came out of the telephone box the brightly-lit corridor shimmered in front of my eyes. I had migraine, and that evening I was half-blind with it.

41

I FIXED MY eyes on the rakish Royal Arms as the judge started speaking.

It was the following Tuesday morning, and I was much more cheerful. Kit was alive, even starting to get better. The previous two nights I had spent mostly in the hospital, even hanging about outside his ward when I wasn't allowed in. I felt happier separated from him only by swinging glass doors, rather than bricks and mortar. I remembered all the crushed-looking figures I had seen round the entrances of wards when I was a houseman, and of the unthinking heartlessness with which I had generally treated them. Perhaps I should control myself more over Kit – I should be the professional woman and rein in my emotions. Then I imagined life without him, and I knew such restraint was impossible.

I saw Myra twice in the hospital. She still spoke in her distant way, and still looked over my shoulder. We were both too concerned about Kit to provoke one another, we even struck a peculiar relationship like the parents of a sick child. I wondered what to God the ward staff made of the pair of us, visiting him in turn. But hospitals become used to all manner of surprising social arrangements.

When Trevor had telephoned me at the hospital on the Monday evening, for the first time I told him of Kit's illness and for that matter of Kit, though I expected Liz had gossiped joyfully about my domestic affairs. Trevor was sympathetic, but thought I should be in court. This time the ginger barrister spoke at length, to my own ears pulverizing my case. But

Trevor beside me whispered, 'Don't worry – that letter three years ago from Crawless will be decisive. They can't get out of that.'

'I wish I'd destroyed it,' I told him in an undertone. 'I wish I could destroy it now, erase it somehow from the case.'

Trevor gave a faint smile, not comprehending. I wondered what Charles had thought when his house physician had telephoned on Sunday with my plea to attend Kit. The ethics under which we both worked gave him no chance to refuse, and I doubted if the notion even crossed his mind. It was a singular profession which automatically imparted nobility on its members.

'Well, now,' said Mr Justice Millhaven. He adjusted his glasses, and began in his conversational tone, 'The plaintiff is moving for an injunction, pending trial of an action for breach of confidence. Her case is that three years ago, she was conducting scientific research on a drug – which has not, it seems, been christened with any name – of possible use in the control of female conception. The plaintiff's drug was unlike all others then, and until recently, prescribed for this purpose. The female concerned would be obliged to take her dose of this drug at intervals of one month, rather than one more or less every day. This was achieved by chemical treatment of the drug, so that it exerted its effect by settling in the pituitary gland, instead of being dispersed uniformly throughout the body.'

It was strange to hear scientific jargon rolling so easily from his lips. I supposed judges grew adept at it. A fortnight before he had been pronouncing equally glibly on seed potatoes.

'The plaintiff complains that she imparted at that time certain information about her drug to Dr Charles Crawless, a consultant physician and a colleague of hers on the senior staff of Princess Victoria's Hospital in London. She further claims that at the request of Dr Crawless she sent him a written account of her scientific work on this drug, accompanied by details of experiments she performed with it on ferrets.' The judge paused, and looked at his papers. 'I beg your pardon, the experiments were performed on rabbits.'

The ginger barrister in front of me nodded, as though this were of deep significance.

'As evidence of this transference of information to Dr Crawless, the plaintiff cites a letter from him. This acknowledged the receipt of her documents, and also indicated his full knowledge of the plaintiff's wishes for them to be kept confidential. As I understand it, these documents are still in the possession of Dr Crawless, or may well be. At the time when Dr Crawless received them, and when he wrote the letter, he was retained by the General Drug Company of Great Britain on a part-time basis as a consultant. His duties were to advise the company on its various pharmaceutical products, to indicate fields in which the company might profitably embark on new research, to keep them abreast of medical problems at the patient's bedside as distinct from those in the laboratory, and similar activities. At that time the plaintiff was unaware of Dr Crawless's position in the company, or even that he had any connexion with it.'

Mr Romhead clasped his hands under his chin and bounced slightly.

'None of these facts are denied by the defendants. It is therefore common ground that the plaintiff invented this unnamed contraceptive drug and gave Dr Crawless a full account of its properties, its chemical composition, the experiments on the rabbits, and suchlike. All in confidence. The plaintiff now claims that the long-lasting female contraceptive known as cyclova, which is marketed by the General Drug Company, is the same or very similar to her own. That they have, in fact, pirated her work, selling her drug under the name of cyclova without making, or even attempting to make, any payment in the form of royalties or otherwise.'

I was wondering how Kit was, and how soon I should be able to see him again.

'The defendant company, on the other hand, claim that they had no knowledge of the plaintiff's drug. They say that such exchanges as occurred between her and Dr Crawless were wholly personal, and the confidence in which they were entrusted was never broken. They deny – they deny with some force – that they would have expected him to break such an obligation simply because he was in their employment. Moreover, they hold that knowledge of the plaintiff's drug would have been no assistance to them whatever in the development of their own drug, cyclova. The plaintiff's "pill" was not in fact commercially viable. Alternatively, they claim that had they known of it, no resemblance could now be seen between that unnamed drug and cyclova. The defendants would have been obliged to change it so radically as to have produced, in effect, a different drug.'

Trevor whispered again, 'That's where we don't agree.'

The judge rested his square chin on his clasped hands, and continued affably, 'I refuse to let myself be blinded by science. I am not wholly convinced that the affidavit sworn by the head research chemist in the United States, put in by the defendants, establishes that point beyond doubt. The chemical formulae of the two drugs may differ, but the effect, and the site of the effect in the pituitary gland are both similar. The plaintiff's drug is less effective, that is all. Indeed, it did not even reach a reasonable level of efficiency when tested on those rabbits. And this leads me to what, I think, is the first of two decisive points in this case.'

'Now we're getting down to business,' muttered Trevor.

'Nobody has enlightened me as to *why* the plaintiff should have bound Dr Crawless to secrecy. The obvious reason is that she wished to develop her drug, to perfect it, eventually to market it, and to receive some sort of reward or recognition for her pains. But she did not take any steps in this profitable direction. She went no further than the rabbits. She would seem to have forgotten all about the drug, until her memory was stimulated by the appearance on the market of cyclova. This does not suggest that the plaintiff had great faith in her drug as a commercial or clinical possibility. And the plaintiff is hardly an innocent in such matters. As a member of the research staff of a leading London hospital, she would be competent to decide whether it would, with further research and development, turn out usefully or not. I cannot distinguish in this respect between the plaintiff and the scientific staff pursuing similar research in the laboratories of the defendants.'

The judge looked directly at me, and gave a smile. 'If the plaintiff wishes her reasons for demanding confidence to remain a mystery, then I shall not unravel it. But I find it difficult to believe that Dr Crawless would lightly betray that confidence. He was at the time, he tells us in his affidavit, a close personal friend of the plaintiff and of her late husband.' He hesitated. 'I beg the plaintiff's pardon, I should have said her former husband. Moreover, the medical world is accustomed to maintaining discretion in all professional matters, among which I should be inclined to place those now under our attention.

'The second point is simply *why* the defendants should stoop to exploit the plaintiff's "pill". As they say in evidence, they have a very large organization for research, they have teams of chemists running to several hundreds, the best medical opinions in the world are theirs for the asking, the whole programme is supplied with able administration and funds on a scale of some magnificence. In my view, General Drugs had no need for the plaintiff's pill, and it is not established that they learned of it. They developed cyclova entirely on their own initiative. The court therefore does not grant the plaintiff an injunction.'

We picked our way along the benches and out of the court, as some other voice rose to plead some other cause. In the corridor, Mr Romhead said, 'Too bad we went down. I warned you it might be touch-and-go.'

'Thank you for your help, Mr Romhead.' He gave a little bow. 'I'm glad we lost, in a way. I wouldn't have slept for a year, worrying about the eventual outcome.'

'Millhaven's remarks give some idea of how the trial might have gone,' said Trevor sombrely.

'Well, it all looked very nice in the newspapers,' observed Mr Romhead.

There was no more to be said. Trevor had some documents in his briefcase for me to sign, and suggested that I needed a drink. There was a bar in the Law Courts, in another crypt opposite the cafeteria – a discovery which shocked me, like finding one in a cathedral. I had two drinks while Trevor chatted pointedly about nothing in particular. But it was impossible to escape from the morning's defeat.

'However rocky our case, you must be very disappointed you lost, Ann,' he said consolingly.

'I am. I hate losing even an argument. But far less bitterly so than had it been tried a fortnight ago. Even cyclova is reduced in importance compared with Kit's illness.' I looked at my watch. I must get to Princess Victoria's and see him. 'Over the last three months people have been repeatedly trying to convince me I'd made a mistake over that damn blood. Now I don't really care any longer one way or another.'

'Things do become inflated if you dwell on them,' said Trevor with sympathy. 'I see that so much in legal practice.'

'I think I allowed my emotions to infect my judgement over cyclova,' I admitted. 'Like a colony of bacteria infecting the body, they grew until they disabled and nearly killed their host. Though perhaps part of the blame was on the people who had to tackle me for one reason or another over the affair.'

McRobb and Ma Saintsbury had done nothing to lower the fever, I reflected. Others had only thrust me into varying depths of frustration and disappointment – Lloyd, Charles Crawless, Henry, Iris Quiply, even Trevor. And Sir Robert Boatwright. Or was I being unjust? Had there been a conspiracy? Henry had certainly assumed so, that morning I'd confronted him. Charles had naturally denied it, taking refuge in my own frailties. I should never know. And that didn't matter now, either.

'I'm afraid you'll get a fairly stiff bill from old Romhead,' remarked Trevor.

'Yes, I expect I shall. Well, my brother will have to pay it,' I told him. With luck, the country would be in for a hard and mortal winter.

I had wasted almost half an hour, and outside the Law Courts Trevor hailed a taxi to drop me at Princess Victoria's on the way to his office. We parted, both making vague promises of meeting again. As he drove off and I started through the hospital gateway I heard my name. I turned, to discover Myra.

'How is he?' I asked at once. I hadn't been in the hospital that morning.

'He seems rather more cheerful, Dr Sheriff.' Myra was still looking over my shoulder, at the traffic passing in Holborn.

'Oh, I'm so glad.'

'That Dr Crawless is wonderful, isn't he?'

'He's one of the ablest physicians in the country.'

'Yes, he's very able,' she repeated vaguely. 'He had a long talk with me last night. He thinks Kit's going to recover, you know. Though he'll always be an invalid.'

'He'll be able to do almost all he wants.'

'He'll be an invalid,' she insisted. 'And he was always so active. I suppose it's retribution?'

I suspected an ill-intentioned reference to myself. 'Disease isn't sent as a retribution. That would be witchcraft.'

'I mean a retribution for the life Kit led. The drink, you know.' I couldn't trouble to contradict her, and perhaps she was partly right. 'It was such a pity about the drink. It ruined Kit. He's a very clever man, you understand. You're a clever woman, Dr Sheriff. You must see what a clever man Kit is.'

'I've always seen that.'

'He could have been a politician, a great writer, or an editor. Don't you think Kit would have made a good editor for a newspaper? He has a racy way of putting things. But it was the drink which spoiled his chances.'

'He doesn't drink so much now,' I said defensively. 'He's far from an alcoholic.'

'Doesn't he? Of course I wouldn't know. I haven't been out with him socially for some time. Or perhaps he isn't so clever after all,' she decided abruptly. 'He has all the affectations of a writer, and none of the abilities.'

'He's written a novel.'

Myra ignored this. 'Veronica is clever, like him, Dr Sheriff. Perhaps she will make a doctor or a lawyer one day.' In exactly the same tone, she continued, 'You will be pleased to know that I have decided it best to divorce my husband. It was a very difficult decision, the more so since he became ill. Yet that is the reason for it. Dr Crawless tells me he will need looking after. I cannot do it. Not properly. Not with a headstrong man like Kit. You can, Dr Sheriff. You are trained to do such things.

Yes, I shall divorce him. You shall be free to marry him, and to look after him. I'm doing so entirely for Kit's sake.'

I said nothing. I just stared, unable to believe her.

'I really mean it, Dr Sheriff.' Now she looked me in the eyes. 'In a week or two, when he is out of danger, I shall speak to my solicitors. Of course, I don't love Kit as much as I once did. That's only to be expected, don't you think? But Veronica loves him, and I didn't see why I should exert myself to weaken the link between them. And I hate you, Dr Sheriff. You are an evil and grasping woman. Though I think you will look after Kit.'

She turned and walked away, disappearing quickly among the lunchtime crowds in Holborn.

Her insults stung. But I told myself quickly she was only intending to give me in Kit what was already mine. And for once she really sounded decisive. Not only might Kit and I at last be free to marry, but I suddenly realized how life without Myra overshadowing it would be a delight in itself. Particularly as Kit, with a healed coronary, would need escape from as much mental stress as possible. They were confused half-formed reflections, anyway interrupted by the gate-porter, who had been viewing the scene from his cubby-hole.

'Dr Sheriff, there was a visitor for you a minute ago. I directed him up to your lab.'

I pulled myself back to the world. 'Do you know who it was?'

'No one I'm acquainted with, Dr Sheriff.'

'Very well, I'll go up.'

I supposed it was a reporter. I should have told the porters to let nobody into my laboratory without permission. I wanted to see Kit, but I decided that I had better dispose of the intruder first. I made my way upstairs, slowly, because my arthritis was troubling the joints of my feet, and could make me stumble. I found in the laboratory, alone and sitting awkwardly on the high swivel chair, George Lloyd from General Drugs.

He got up. 'Ah – Dr Sheriff.'

I shut the door behind me.

'Will you excuse my coming unannounced?'

'You're the last caller to be expected, I must admit.'

He nodded, politely indicating the chair. I shook my head, and we stood looking at one another.

'I hoped you would allow me a few minutes, Doctor. Though I knew it would be unpleasant setting eyes on me so soon after that most unfortunate wrangle in open court. Once I was telephoned the result, I decided, as I had planned, to waste no time before seeing you personally.'

I shrugged my shoulders. 'I really don't see your point.'

'I'm afraid in our former dealings, Doctor, I was not as considerate towards you as I might have been. I certainly don't want to lay myself open to that charge on a second occasion.'

'It doesn't matter a damn any longer, does it?'

'I don't think you need allow yourself too painful regrets over the decision of the court, Doctor. You rather forced us to stand our ground, you know. After the newspaper publicity, we were fighting not some rarefied dispute about a breach of confidence, but for our reputation. You appreciate that, no doubt, Doctor.'

I nodded. '"Humanity is our Business"? Yes, you are quite right, Mr Lloyd. That was my intention in bringing the action.'

'So we had to win. We did win. But you have achieved your aims, Doctor. Leukaemia has been diagnosed in five women in the United States taking cyclova since the start of the original trial. One has died. General Drugs have therefore already withdrawn the product from sale.' He nodded towards my microscope on the stained laboratory bench. 'You were right, Dr Sheriff. You made no mistake over the blood at all.'

I looked at him without speaking. So it was I who had won. My fight was justified. I had been *proved right*. But I found I was hardly interested. These things didn't matter so much now, not compared with Kit.

42

THE NEXT DAYS were better days, because Kit was starting to get better. He had avoided any complications and Charles Crawless, who came to inspect the flickering gadgets attached to him twice a day, assured me that the immediate danger was past and his chances of complete recovery from the attack stood high. When General Drugs officially announced, in another masterly exercise of public relations, that cyclova was to be withdrawn from the market, I felt that I really ought to give some small celebration for my supporters. Kit's steady improvement anyway put me in the mood for it.

McRobb had just left on holiday, so it was some weeks before we got round to the party. I booked a table for lunch one Saturday in the little Italian restaurant. That was to be a wonderful day, anyway. Kit was so much better, the same afternoon he was coming home from hospital.

I had naturally invited Ma Saintsbury as well, but at the last moment she had to cry off. Some crisis in international medicine – which I gathered were as frequent and as painful as those of international diplomacy – had sent her hurrying to Longfield to confer with Tilly Dawes.

'Ma Saintsbury seems to be getting rather heavily engaged on the world medicine front,' smiled McRobb. We were sitting at a corner table and she was drinking whisky with osso buco – a weird combination, I supposed another of her obscure affectations.

'It'll give her an occupation when she retires from Princess

Vikki's,' I suggested. 'And she enjoys administration, ordering people about. It's just like the Army.'

'God knows how she hears what those foreigners are saying. The woman really ought to wear a hearing-aid. It's pure vanity! It strikes me as quite disgusting, at her age.'

'At her age, it strikes me as quite heartening.'

'Maybe you're right, Sheriff.' McRobb finished her whisky and turned to order another from the waiter. She wore an expensive blue linen suit and had made herself up for the occasion, though her hair was as messy as ever and I noticed she still had wrinkled stockings. 'So Kit's being discharged today?'

My face lit up. 'I can hardly believe it. Now I can start looking on him as a man again, rather than an invalid. I'm collecting him from the ward after lunch. I've got his clothes out there, in a case in the cloakroom.'

'He's come through it pretty well, hasn't he?'

'He could have died,' I said simply. 'It's so much sadder, a man dying like that in his forties than one of your infants dying at birth. Yet Lamb wrote a poem called "On an infant Dying as Soon as Born". And nobody spills elaborate tears over the collapse of a middle-aged stockbroker.'

'How are you going to manage at the flat?' asked McRobb, who had a more severely practical turn of mind even than myself.

'We'll carry Kit upstairs somehow. He'll have to live on one floor for a while, which will be a terrible bore for the poor darling. But once he's fit enough we're going on holiday – we're borrowing a flat in Antibes from a friend of his. We were there earlier in the summer, and we loved it. Kit says autumn's the best time in the South of France, the heat's less trying, the tourists have gone, and the prices are down. Then this winter we're moving,' I went on excitedly. 'I've already found the house. It's just a little one, a villa in a row, out at Bromley. But it's got a garden with a Japanese cherry, a lawn to mow, and even a little pond for goldfish. We're going to become sub-urban.'

'We're all suburbanites now,' asserted McRobb. 'Once you

get out of the suburbs of one town you're in the suburbs of the next. But I thought you told me Kit was rather anti?'

'That was last June. Now he's thought again. He says that if the knowledge a man is to be hanged in a fortnight concentrates his mind wonderfully, the awareness that he might have perished one Sunday afternoon six weeks ago is even more effective.'

McRobb's whisky appeared, and she raised her glass. 'To you and Kit. Much happiness.'

'That's sweet of you, Sandra. It's significant, too. At last the way's clear for us to get married.'

'That wife's divorced him?'

'No, but the process has started. I didn't really believe her at first. But now we're deep in correspondence with solicitors. We hope it'll be heard before the end of the year.'

'I trust the judge will have more sense than the one in your last case.'

I laughed. 'But I won in the end. You know, it gives me no feeling of elation. Of course I was excited that morning Lloyd suddenly appeared in the lab. Now I can think only of the poor women who were ill, or had died, or are going to.'

'So you were in the right, Sheriff, all the time,' said McRobb grimly. 'And only you knew it.'

'I always know I'm in the right. That's the saddest failing in my life. The most dangerous one, anyway.'

She gave a sniff. 'General Drugs were decent enough to you afterwards, I suppose?'

'Well, they paid my legal costs and offered a fairly large sum as a sweetener.'

'Which you had paid to the unfortunate victims.'

'I could hardly have done otherwise.'

'Nonsense!' she said forthrightly. 'General Drugs had to pay them compensation, anyway. The whole operation must have cost them a packet.'

'That's their worry.'

'So we end up lacking a revolutionary new contraceptive?'

'Perhaps we're best off with the old methods.'

'Yes,' said McRobb. 'Free love with a capital F.L. Not that

I've had much of it.' She hesitated a moment. 'Sheriff, do you think that I should go to a beauty parlour?'

I took a second to realize that she was serious. 'Why not?'

'It would shake them at Princess Vikki's.'

'Only momentarily. They'd soon get used to the new-look professor.'

'I fancy it would be too much fuss and bother,' she decided. 'If you're going to finish nowhere in a race, what's the point of entering? Nothing looks more stupid than competing out of your class.'

'That's a defeatist attitude.'

'Possibly. But that's often the only realistic one.'

'Hadn't you a boy-friend once? The man who stood for Parliament?'

'Oh, him.' McRobb made a wry face. 'It didn't work very well. Mechanically, I mean. And me a gynaecologist, too.'

'I wish I had your ability to split the sexual side of life from the professional side.'

'It's a masculine ability,' she told me dourly.

'Yes, a man can tidy away his sex notions like his golf clubs and his gardening tools when not actually in use. He only starts thinking about it when he goes to bed. A woman starts thinking about it every morning when she wakes up.'

'Exactly,' agreed McRobb. 'And that's why we are comparatively such bloody failures in medicine.'

After the meal I paid the bill and collected the case with Kit's clothes. McRobb went back to her flat. I took the Underground to the hospital. It had been a tempestuous summer for me, but this was its most exciting moment. I knew that life would be difficult with Kit for weeks, perhaps months. It would be horribly tedious for him confined to the flat, unable to visit the pub, missing his friends. I should have to be firm, but from now on I would be careful about over-asserting myself. I would be so much more considerate, over every detail of our life. I'd make some new arrangement about our money, as soon as he was well enough to get out and about. Though everything would be all right in the end. His heart was healed, he was getting his divorce, we should marry and next summer sit on the lawn in the sun, under the shade of the cherry tree watching the gold-fish. He was mine, he would soon be entirely mine, and when he was stronger we should make love, and I should hold him and bite him, and get him to twist my arm, and feel his sperms spurting into me once again.

I walked through the Gothic gate of the hospital with my suitcase. I was of course wearing the mustard suit again. I went briskly past the old buildings and into the medical block. Kit had for some weeks been out of the intensive care unit, transferred to Charles Crawless's ordinary ward on the fourth floor. I saw Charles himself, standing outside the swinging glass doors.

'Ann, we were trying to get you,' he said. 'Kit had another infarct just before lunch. I'm afraid it was instantaneously fatal.'

43

I HAD SLIPPED on the Quai du Mont-Blanc near where the jet d'eau would bound into the air during better weather. It was December, and the snow had started to fall again. A grave, grey-uniformed Swiss policeman helped me up, and I thanked him in as good French as I could manage. He handed back my rubber-tipped stick, and even held my arm for a few paces, before saluting smartly and leaving me to totter along the slippery pavement towards my hotel.

The hotel was one of the best in Geneva, superbly well run and luxurious, though I still found its rooms unbearably hot. I would have a week or two more there, until the people in my bureau found a reasonable flat for me – probably after Christmas. A commissionaire opened the double doors, and I was glad enough in those first few moments for the warmth. I made for the desk, asking the head porter, 'May I have my key? Number two-four-four.'

'Certainly, madam.'

'Are there any letters for me?'

He scanned his lines of pigeon-holes. 'The midday mail is just being sorted, madam. I'll see.'

I wondered if he was as attentive to all the guests, or only to those who looked as helpless as me.

As I waited I heard English being spoken, too common an experience in Geneva to turn a head. I noticed a fair-haired, blue-suited youngish man sitting on a low sofa near the desk, talking animatedly to a smartly-dressed girl, a pair of pre-lunch Martinis amid the cigarette packets and book matches on a table in front of them. From her admiring little interjections I told myself she was English, too. I listened, overhearing some story which seemed amusing, scandalous and clearly based on inside knowledge, about some dignitaries in the United Nations headquarters at New York.

The porter reappeared. 'Two letters, madam.'

'Thank you.'

The first was addressed in Liz's bold childish handwriting. I stuck it in my overcoat pocket. I knew exactly what would be in *that* – scrawled pages about dear Derek, the child, the nanny, the dog, and possibly the Mini and the Jaguar. The secretary had been accepted as a passing madness, and I hoped the episode had done both of them good. The second envelope was typed, with the address in the corner of the Fleet Street literary agency run by Kit's friend, Jim.

'Have you a letter-opener?' I asked the porter.

'Yes, madam.'

I slit it open, though my fingers had been getting much better at envelopes over the past month. It said:

Dear Ann,

I know how anxiously you have been waiting to hear of poor Kit's novel, and I'd like the news to be good. But I am afraid that cannot be so. The manuscript has now been to six of the leading London publishers, always with a personal note from myself, but without success. They all say the same thing – that it simply is not a novel.

I must admit that I agree with them. Some parts of the book are most readable, others are amusing, and here and there it is outstandingly witty. But it is too diffuse, and in some sections almost incoherent. I think the fault lies in Kit's rewriting it so many times over such a long period. It is far from the first work with this fault to come my way.

If Kit had managed to get it published in its original form some years ago, his later work might have grown more expert and he might have made a name for himself as a novelist. But of course that is something we simply cannot tell.

I will certainly try again if you wish, but quite honestly if I sent the manuscript to every publishing firm in London I doubt if I would make a sale. I am prepared to take that trouble, but I feel it would simply be delaying the inevitable final disappointment.

So unless I hear from you, I shall send the manuscript next week to Switzerland. I do hope that you are finding Geneva agreeable, and your new appointment some distraction from the last sad months.

Please let me know if there is anything whatever I can do for you in London.

Yours,

Jim.

Well, that was that. I stuffed the letter into my pocket, and taking my key made carefully across the marble hall towards the lifts. It might have been dangerous without my stick, though I hated the thing. It made me look so old. The stiffness, the faltering gait, were bad enough, but a stick put me down as a cripple. I had lost a lot of weight, my eyes were sunken, and I hadn't bothered to tint my hair since Kit's death. I looked a mess and I didn't care. I stood waiting for a lift, moving my fingers. They were getting easier, which was encouraging. This time, I had got a man to cut my wedding-ring off for good.

'I say, it's Dr Ann Sheriff, isn't it?'

I turned slowly, to find the blue-suited Englishman from the sofa.

'That's so.'

'Do please forgive me, but my companion thought she recognized you. I'm not often in London, but last summer I gather you were something of a national heroine.'

'It's flattering of you to say so. And flattering of your friend to recognize me. I've been rather ill with arthritis since them.'

'I am sorry,' he said sympathetically. 'My name's Crawford. I'm diplomatic correspondent of *The*—'

'Yes, of course, I read your article in yesterday's paper.'

He inclined his head graciously. 'I'm really here to cover the

311

conference, but I'd love a few words from you for our diary column.'

'I hope I can find something interesting.'

'Splendid,' he said cheerfully. 'What exactly is your work in Geneva, Dr Sheriff?'

'I'm head of the new international bureau for population control.'

'Marie Stopes, that sort of thing?'

'Not exactly. As I have said so often before—and shall now have to say louder and louder – contraception has become more than a personal matter between couples. We are concerned about checking the enormous growth of world population before we simply overrun our planet.'

'That sounds highly alarming.'

'It *is* alarming. To continue reproducing even at our present rate is a course set fair for disaster. Within two hundred years there'll be fifty times the world population of today. We shall simply start starving to death. I'm not trying to make your flesh creep,' I smiled. 'My office can produce the exact facts and figures.'

'I assure you, I take your word for it,' he said hastily.

'I only wish more people did. Influential people – I mean Government officials, social workers, doctors, heads of churches, heads of states. My job here is essentially bringing those personages round to my way of thinking.'

'Do you think you'll succeed?'

'I don't know. But I'm a very determined woman.'

He gave a smile, and made some notes in a small leather-bound book. The lifts were coming and going, but I was enjoying the interview. My loneliness in Geneva was horrible.

'What decided you to accept this rather daunting task, Dr Sheriff?'

'I've been interested for some time in the subject of population control. I had no hesitation when I was offered it by Dame Christina Saintsbury in London. I expect you've heard of her?'

'I'm afraid not,' he said politely.

'She's become very active in international medicine recently. And quite frankly, an office job is more suitable with this disability of mine.' I added after a moment, 'Perhaps my publicity over that drug company encouraged the powers-that-be to accept me.'

'You lightly call it "an office job", but it's obviously one of enormous importance in this day and age. The responsibility would scare me stiff.' He paused, thinking of another question. 'Do you imagine it might eventually lead to a Nobel Prize?'

'Well, Mr Crawford, I've only been here a month, but they haven't offered me one yet.'

He laughed. 'Has any woman ever won the Nobel Award, Dr Sheriff?'

'Marie Curie won two,' I told him. I was the informative professional woman. 'Her first was for physics in 1903, her second for chemistry in 1911. You may remember that in 1964 the chemistry Prize went to Dr Dorothy Hodgkin, from Oxford. And perhaps that in 1938 the Award for literature went to Pearl Buck.'

'No, I didn't know that. Thank you, Dr Sheriff. I can only give you my best wishes for your new job, and my hopes that one of those awards will some day come your way.'

As he went back to his girl, I stood leaning on my stick waiting for a lift to appear. I glanced at my room key. The man at the desk had given me number four-two-two by mistake. I shuffled my way back across the hall. The journalist was checking through his notes of our conversation, and neither of the couple noticed me. I heard the girl ask, 'What was she like?'

'A dedicated woman.'

'That sounds chilling.'

'Not so much chilling as rather sad. She's quite good-looking, or she must have been once. She's got a sense of humour. She's tremendously intelligent, of course. But the poor thing's dried up, quite sexless. She could never have had a man in her life.'

And he went on telling his funny story about the United Nations.

Richard Gordon

THE FACEMAKER

'Should firmly establish his reputation as a serious novelist, for it is highly enjoyable and amusing without benefit of slapstick. . . . There is a generous sprinkling of Gordon aphorisms.'

Robert Baldick, DAILY TELEGRAPH

'Mr Gordon publicly outgrows his hospital farces and becomes the novelist his fans have always seen in him . . . the novel has a sparkling surface and is full of sardonic entertainment. Mr Gordon's fertility of comic metaphor is unimpaired by the seriousness of his aims.'

PUNCH

'*The Facemaker* is of a category of novel that will endure for many years. For Richard Gordon it represents the point of no-return to the laughter-chain that began with *Doctor in the House.* It is, nevertheless, a human comedy, and if—for this reader—there is a touchstone to it in terms of characterisation, it is in the works of H. G. Wells.'

THE BOOKMAN

SURGEON AT ARMS

'The background of interconsultant jealousies carried over into a world of doctors in uniform and wartime hospital services is etched with best acid. Although this is a deeply serious study of goodness in leaky vessels, it is secondarily a gay and sardonic survey of a transitional period of medical history. Unlike some successful farce-writers who raise their ambitions, Mr Gordon retains his original skills. He is still funny; but he is relevantly funny. . . . He can also keep a story-line alive.'

R. G. G. Price, PUNCH

'Richard Gordon is able to write from the inside. He has a nice sardonic approach to human happiness.'

EVENING STANDARD

'Richard Gordon has produced here a character of great force and great humour and is certainly well on the way to establishing himself as a novelist who must be taken into account in any consideration of the literary scene.'

WESTERN MAIL